SON of NEVERLAND

CAL R. BARNES

FIRST EDITION, OCTOBER 27th, 2021.

Copyright © 2021 by Cal R. Barnes
Los Angeles, CA
CalBarnes.com

Published by *Magic Hour Press.* Publishers since 2017. All rights reserved under International and Pan-American Copyright Conventions. Including right of reproduction in whole or in part in any form.

This book is a work of fiction based on several characters originally created by J.M. Barrie in his work, *The Little White Bird,* first published in 1902, and his work, *Peter and Wendy,* first published in 1911. Those works have since entered the public domain. Names, characters, and incidents (both original and adapted), are either products of the author's imagination or are used fictitiously. Any resemblance to actual events or locales or persons, living or dead, is entirely coincidental.

No part of this publication may be reproduced, stored in a retrieval system, or transmitted in any form or by any means, electronic, mechanical, photocopying, recording, or otherwise, without written permission of the author and/or publisher. For information regarding permissions, contact the author through his website at CalBarnes.com.

CHARITABLE FUND

True to the spirit of J.M. Barrie's legacy, his pure love of the imagination, and his unyielding support of children's charities, 10% of the net proceeds from this book will go directly towards supporting children's hospitals, charities, organizations, institutions, and causes worldwide that are designed to keep children safe, healthy, creative, imaginative, and ultimately make their lives better. By purchasing this book, you are literally helping to make the world a better place.

Author and publisher reserve the right to distribute the fund as they deem appropriate.

Cover Art by Adrian Doan Kim
Adriandkc.com

ISBN 978-0-9991610-7-4

1 3 5 7 9 10 8 6 4 2

Created, manufactured, and printed in the United States of America.

TABLE OF CONTENTS

TO ALL THOSE WHO HAVE PERSEVERED… AND TO ALL THOSE WHO STILL BELIEVE…

"*It is a blessing that he did not know, for otherwise he would have lost faith in his power to fly, and the moment you doubt whether you can fly, you cease for ever to be able to do it. The reason birds can fly and we can't is simply that they have perfect faith, for to have faith is to have wings.*"
— J. M. Barrie, *Peter Pan in Kensington Gardens*

"*Genius is nothing more nor less than childhood recovered at will.*"
— Charles Baudelaire, *The Painter of Modern Life*

"*The kingdom of God does not come with observation, nor will they say, 'See here!' or 'See there!' For indeed, the kingdom of God is within you.*"
— Jesus Christ, The Gospel of Luke 17:20-21

"*You have unlimited power. You must cultivate that unlimited power, that is all.*"
— Paramahansa Yogananda, *Journey to Self-Realization*

"*The difference between him and the other boys at such a time was that they knew it was make-believe, while to him make-believe and true were exactly the same thing.*"
— J.M. Barrie, *Peter and Wendy*

"*You belong to the stars, just make it a point to remember continuously that this is your destiny.*"
— Osho

"*Let go your earthly tether. Enter the void. Empty, and become wind.*"
— Guru Laghima, *Avatar*

"*Most assuredly, I say to you, unless one is born of water and the Spirit, he cannot enter the kingdom of God... the wind blows where it wishes, and you hear the sound of it, but cannot tell where it comes from and where it goes. So is everyone who is born of the Spirit.*"
— Jesus Christ, The Gospel of John 3:5-7

"*You just think lovely wonderful thoughts... and they lift you up in the air.*"
— Peter Pan, *Peter and Wendy*

FOR A HIGH-DEFINITION, COMPANION MAP TO READ ALONGSIDE THE STORY, VISIT —

SonOfNeverland.com/Map-of-Neverland

SON *of* NEVERLAND

* PROLOGUE *

— The Fall of Captain Hook —

The waters of Cannibal Cove raged below as the defiant boy stood on the blood-soaked deck of the ship, staring down the large tyrant before him. He wore a garment made of skeleton leaves and was armed with only a magical dagger that glowed hot in his hand. At first glance, he appeared to be a youth, sinewy and ruddy, with bright eyes and straw-colored hair — indeed, he was beautiful to behold — but upon looking deeper, there was something ancient about him that escaped his physicality, as if he had already lived a million years and his body was none the wiser. This boy… was Peter Pan.

Across from him, towering over him by two full feet, was the boy's great and worthy opponent. He wore a crimson-red coat that hung down to the top of his buccaneer boots, and a mane of black locks flowed from beneath his large, feathered hat like a dark river of death. Pure blood-lust and hatred filled his eyes, for the boy and his squadron of pesky children had laid waste to his entire crew, but combined they would still be no match for him, for he was the Great Captain James 'Jas' Hook, the terror of the seven seas and the master of this world, and tonight he would put an end to the flying menace once and for all.

The last remaining pirates, seven boys dressed as warriors, and a single teenage girl in a nightgown gathered around them in a circle. Their swords hung loosely at their sides and blood dripped down their exhausted faces, soaking into their battle-worn clothes as they stared at their two fearless captains that were destined to duel. The fate of either side rested solely in the hands of their individual commanders… this was the battle that all of Neverland had long been waiting for…

At first glance to the foreigner, this may have looked absurd, like a good bit of acting or perhaps a person's best make-believe, but when the boy lifted off the ground so that he could look the large pirate in the eye, it is this storyteller's promise that nothing could have been more real…

"So, Peter," Hook shuddered with resentment as the boy flew before him like a young deity. "This is all your doing. Plotting against me, killing my men… are you enjoying yourself?"

"Ay, Jas," came Peter's stern answer. "Considering you tried to poison me in my sleep like a codfish... I haven't had this much fun in a while."

Hook's eyes narrowed at the boy's answer — his arrogance, his cockiness — it had always driven him mad with rage.

"How did you survive?" Hook jeered, for indeed he had tried to poison him — a final solution that he was sure would take care of the pest for good — but the boy had come out of it alive, and he couldn't help his curiosity as to how…

"You could say I have an angel on my shoulder," Peter answered, referring to Tinker Bell who had just saved his life by drinking the poison in his stead, nearly dying in the process — but Hook did not yet know that, and he didn't need to — "or maybe I'm just immortal."

Hook's eyes narrowed further. He was sure the poison would have done away with the menace, but here he was all the same. Clearly, by some trick of the fairies he had survived. Still, no man in all of the worlds would dare stand or speak against him in such a way, yet here the boy did it without any fear of consequence whatsoever. It was the childlikeness of this boy's entire demeanor that drove him to the edge, and today he would finally quench his torment with the steel of his blade.

"Proud and insolent child," Hook jeered as he pointed his longsword right at Peter. "Prepare to meet your doom."

A peculiar smile spread across Peter's countenance as he looked down the sword at its wielder. Here was a man that had rained down hell upon his reality for so long. The pirate captain had hunted him and had tried to vanquish him more times than he could remember. He had also threatened and attempted to kill the three women he loved more than life itself, and the three which he could not live without. First, Hook tried to drown Tiger Lily at Skull Rock far out in the Eastern Sea, to which Peter had narrowly saved her. Next, Hook poisoned Tinker Bell when she drank the assassin's poison intended for him in his stead, to which she narrowly survived, and lastly and just recently, Hook tried to make Wendy walk the plank! Indeed, this man was a menace to Peter's entire life and everything he held dear, and yet, Peter could hardly imagine a Neverland without him, for in a twisted way his existence made life so much more exciting. Still, if it was freedom that was calling upon him this day to avenge what was good and bright, then he would answer the call, and he would win…

"Dark and sinister man," Peter answered with a mischievous sparkle in his eye. "Let's go."

BANG! — Dagger clashed against sword as the Great Pan and the Great Pirate Captain transversed the space between them in a split second! Hook was the first to strike, aiming a deadly slash at Peter that would have cleaved a tree in two.

Peter expertly parried, deflecting the energy from the powerful attack away from himself, and countered with a series of lightning quick stabs that narrowly missed Hook's body. Peter was the superior in speed, but still being a small youth, he did not yet possess the reach to drive the blade home. He would have to get in even closer if he was to strike true, putting him in dangerous proximity to the captain's deadly hook.

The captain came down with two more deadly swings that Peter narrowly dodged. Hook was an expert fighter, and the reach of his longsword was doing an excellent job at keeping Peter at bay.

CLING! CLING! — CLING! CLING! Peter expertly parried Hook's attacks as he continued his onslaught. To Hook, every moment the boy continued to draw breath was a miracle, for each time he thought he saw victory at hand, the boy found a way to slip his attack at the very last second. Indeed, the boy was the fastest fighter he had ever fought, and in most cases it would not have mattered, but on this occasion it was to the boy's advantage that he was such a small target, for it was the very reason that he still had both his arms.

The captain came down with all his wrath, and Peter slipped to the side, barely dodging the edge of the blade as it literally shaved the hairs off his skin. With a mighty shout, Peter rose up underneath the attack using an uppercut with his dagger that was aimed to kill. The captain barely pulled his chin back in time to avoid being impaled through his neck!

Hook was on the defensive now as he fell back. He barely dodged the speed of the dagger as the boy came at him in all his wrath. How was it possible that this mindless child was giving him such hell? He had once conquered a whole pirate squadron by himself, and now this arrogant youth was pushing him back on his own ship?! It was impossible, but the boy was doing it anyway. Suddenly, Hook felt a great swell of pride for the sake of his name and lineage emerge from deep within him — he would not fall to this boy, not like this — he let the rage of that thought fuel his being…

"ARGH!" The captain screamed and slashed down at Peter with his hooked hand, sending a deathly swoop through the air that Peter narrowly dodged. He continued to scream as he regained the offensive, trudging up the deck and slashing down at the boy with everything he had.

Peter fell back, being sure to keep his breathing steady and his eye on the blade that was slicing through the air with deadly force. He dared not parry, for the captain's superior strength coupled with his current wrath would surely blast through his block and cut him in half. In the past, it would have done Peter well to fly away and let the captain's anger cool, then return to do battle when the odds were more in his favor, but today the captain held his friends captive in order to keep his feet glued to the ship, and if he was to fly away now it would surely mean the death of them all — no, it was all up to feeling now, and intuition, and only one of them would be leaving the ship alive.

SWOOSH! SWOOSH! — Hook continued to rain down death, but each time his strike hit nothing but air. It was astonishing to him, a foreign feeling, for when he'd typically strike, it would be steel or flesh that his blade tasted, but not air — never air — and his frustration continued to build with each empty slash he took.

Hook screamed in exhaustion and desperation as he slashed down a final blow with his clawed hand, but once again he connected with nothing but sky as Peter doubled under, and —

seeing the momentary lapse in the Hook's defenses — lunged fiercely and pierced the captain in the ribs.

"ARGHHH!" Hook screamed as he fell back. He knew that what was happening to him was impractical, but it was happening all the same. Then, seeing the peculiar color of his own blood — which he always took offense to — his sword fell from his hand, and he was at the flying boy's mercy.

Peter looked down at his enemy cowering before him. Here was the Great Captain Hook, the terror of the seven seas, and the great and worthy opponent of himself, the Great Peter Pan — here was the sworn enemy that had haunted his dreams for so long, finally on his knees in defeat — was this it? Had the day finally come that he had defeated the Great Captain Hook? Was this to be the final moment of their eternal quarrel?

Peter was perplexed as he stood over the defeated captain, and for a moment he found himself frozen with indecision, for he could not imagine a Neverland in which this rivalry did not exist.

"Run him through!" Screamed the lost boys that had encircled him, for they had been dreaming of this victory for centuries, and now was the time.

Then, Peter did something that was unimaginable — something that was completely counterintuitive to victory and all common sense, but all too like him — he gestured to the pirate captain to pick up his sword.

Hook did so without hesitation, but under the sickening feeling that the boy was showing better form than himself, and although the youth may not have finished him with his dagger, he had finished him by slaying his pride.

"What are you, Peter Pan?" Hook asked as he stared in bewilderment at the smiling boy looking back at him. "Who and what are you?"

"I am youth. I am joy," Peter answered with total joy and defiance, and he felt all the life-force in Neverland surge into his being upon the words. "I am the little bird that has broken out of the egg."

Hook stared at the boy in absolute awe and confusion — it was all gibberish, all nonsense — but it was proof that the Pan did not know who or what he was anymore than Hook did himself, and it was in this moment that he knew he had met his master. The child's unlimited open-mindedness was the pinnacle of good form, for he lived without limitation, and his skill could not be restrained.

Then, Hook felt one last dose of pride rise up from within him, and with his final surge of energy he attacked the boy in absolute wrath. All form was out the window now, and he slashed and clawed at the air in desperation, trying to land one hopeful blow on the tyrannical, infinite child that danced all around him as if he was composed of the very wind itself, and it was impossible.

Once again seeing an opening in Hook's crumbling defense, Peter lunged with his dagger… and struck true.

"ARGH!" Hook fought without hope now as the boy picked him apart. The battle was over, but if he was to die, then the boy would die with him. He retreated and rushed into the cabin where the black powder keg was stored, and fired it.

"It's over, Pan!" Hook cried as he staggered out, holding his wounded side. "In thirty seconds, this ship and all those you love will be blown to pieces!"

Quick as lightning, Peter flew into the cabin, retrieved the powder keg, and flung it overboard, rendering Hook's final, desperate play as completely useless.

Hook stared at Peter at a complete loss as his mind began to collapse and his reality began to close in all around him. What kind of form was he now showing himself? Reducing himself to cheap tricks? Was this how he was going to go out? Pawing and slashing at the ground like some kind of helpless, whipped dog?! He didn't even mind that the lost boys were now dancing around him and jeering in victory, for the honor of his name was at stake.

The captain's mind then took him back to his childhood, when he was just a young boy playing in the fields — what would that young boy think of him now? — Then he was a youth again, dressed in his evening's best, and everything was right. He had a debonair attitude at his disposal, a doting lady on his arm, and a whole universe to explore and discover. Indeed, the possibilities of life were infinite.

Then, his mind was pulled into the near past. He had all but conquered Neverland, and its inhabitants regarded him with fear. He saw himself raiding the Indian villages, and ordering his men to kill countless innocents. He saw himself stealing the Princess

Tiger Lily out of her tent in her sleep. She was terrified, but he didn't care. He tied her up and left her to drown on Skull Rock, and if it wasn't for the boy that flew in and saved her a the last second, she would be dead. He then witnessed himself sneak into the Pan's discovered hideout under Hangman's Tree and poison his medicine in his sleep. When he awoke, Miss Bell snatched the vial out of his hand and drank the poison before he could, saving his life, and nearly dying in the process. Yes, the captain had grown from an innocent youth with unlimited potential for good, into a truly evil and dark shadow of his former self, and it was only now, here, in a far corner of this strange, eternal world, at the edge of his very life, that he saw how the choices he had made had put him at the mercy of a vengeful child with near limitless power… and it was over.

Then, Hook's consciousness was pulled back to the present, and he saw the flying boy advancing through the air, shining like the sun, prepared to deal the final death blow. Hook then sprung upon the bulwarks, ready to cast himself into the sea, for he would rather sink into the deep abyss of Cannibal Cove then die by Pan's hand — his body would not live to see another day, but he would see to it that his name became immortal, no matter the cost.

"It's over, old man," Peter said as he dropped down before him, his dagger at the ready. "Surrender, and leave Neverland, or you leave me no choice."

It was then that Hook broke out into a fit of hysterical laughter. Not just any laughter, but a joy that came in the face of death — total exclamations of pure ecstasy — and it was terrifying.

"Over!" Hook exclaimed between heaving breaths. "It's never over, boy! For there is a darkness in this world that you cannot comprehend, and you shall never defeat it!"

Peter and the others watched in horror as the captain steadied himself on the edge of the ship, and it wasn't his treacherous position that made their eyes go wide, but rather, they had never seen the captain laugh before, and this was a very extreme circumstance in which to experience it.

"You may have the allegiance of the Light, Pan," the captain crowed from his perch, "but you shall never be rid of me. You can stab me, drown me, burn my body. You can send me to the deepest, darkest recesses of the abyss, and throw away the key, but I shall return — even if I have to partner with the dark one himself, I shall return — I swear it this day. As God is my witness, I will return and put an end to you and all you hold dear."

There was a moment, and all was silent, and the captain's foul words hung like a stench upon the air, corrupting all who had heard it. Then…

TICK… TICK… TICK…

"No…" Terror took the captain, and a shudder coursed through his body as his evil and wrathful smile fell into one of total and absolute fear. Hook turned to look below, and saw the sinister, greedy eyes of the crocodile moving towards him through the sea

— the one that had an appetite for him ever since the boy had cut off his hand and cast it to him — it was his greatest bane… even greater than the Pan himself.

It was then that Peter seized his chance, for the captain's words of terror did enough damage to their hearts and minds already, and he could not be allowed to speak again. He rose into the air, and attacked the captain head-on — Hook would die by his dagger, or be sent to Davy Jones.

In his final moment, the captain turned to look at Peter. Time seemed to slow as he was faced with one final choice — to die by the hand of his great and worthy opponent, or to be a feast for the crocodile? — How was it that he wanted to be remembered?

Then, in the final moments of his life, standing on the edge of his very own ship, the captain felt as if he had never seen with more clarity, for if he was to die by the boy's blade the child would boast forevermore about his victory, but if he went the way of the crocodile — although gruesome — it would haunt the boy everlasting, and he would eternally wonder if he had ever won clean.

As Peter flew through air, descending upon him with his dagger, the captain took a final and fearless slash at him with his hook, which Peter was forced to slip underneath, and deliver a kick to his chest instead.

"Bad form," the captain said, locking his gaze with Peter as he cascaded over the edge. Time seemed to slow as his eyes narrowed accompanied by a knowing smile. "We'll meet again…" Were the captain's last words, then he went into the jaws of the crocodile.

The others ran over, and watched silently from the deck as the crocodile consumed its prize below. Their eyes did not waver, for Hook had tormented them for so long, they were not completely convinced that this wasn't another one of his traps — as if he might spring up from the sea at any moment and lay waste to them all if they believed that he was truly gone, and so they continued to stare at the waves, uncertain…

From the air, Peter looked down, expressionless, for he was not as naïve as the others, and he knew that this was the end…

Thus passed Captain James Hook… and a new age for Neverland was born…

* CHAPTER 1 *

— The Age of Peace —

The sun was just breaking over the windy mountains above Crocodile Crack, illuminating the edges of the Neverland Forest. In its center rested Lake Mirror, a quiet, mystical body of water that reflected the eternal sky above. For the human being, it would indeed appear to be infinity, that is, a place where everything and nothing could happen at the same time, and it wouldn't so much matter, for in a million more years it would still be there, and that's a very long time to try and remember something.

On this particular morning, it was cool, and crisp, and silent, until…

"COCK-A-DOODLE-DO!"

Peter's reflection appeared over the face of the deep. He smiled widely as he peered down onto the mirror surface of the water, for each time he saw himself it was a completely new experience to him, as if contemplating himself for the first time, a peculiar trait that had arisen from the infinite riddle of his existence. He was more substantial now, and had grown from a small and budding youth into a completely physical and capable young being. Through many centuries of living in Neverland, his body had finally been optimized for eternity, and it was in this final form that he would stay as long as he existed.

He laughed with child-like joy and began running across the surface of the water, his footprints sending ripples that resounded across the glass, creating what looked like the beginning of new worlds altogether, but despite some of the fairies speculation, Peter did not yet know this power — although he did hope to find it someday.

With a final shout, Peter launched off the lake like a springboard, and sent himself rocketing up into the sky at lightning speed. Within a matter of moments, Lake Mirror and the Neverland Forest shrank below him, becoming like play things in his mind as he zoomed past the clouds, and in a shorter while more he was well up into the atmosphere, all of Neverland spread out before him and shimmering in the breaking sunlight.

As he did nearly every day after his morning flight, Peter observed his world. Tucked under the long arm of the Great Eastern Peninsula was Mermaid Lagoon with all of its new sub-developments that offered every imaginable luxury life could bring. Paradise Beach had always been one of his favorite places to play — long before the private contractors moved in and developed the land, turning it into a trove for pleasure seekers — the fairies liked to vacation there on the weekends to get away from the hustle and bustle of the Fairy Quarters. They'd bask in the warm sunshine and cool waters of Infinity Pools during the day, and celebrate by drinking at the bars located around the various beach cities deep into the night. It would sometimes annoy Peter by how quickly the population was increasing, as many of his favorite places around Neverland were not so private anymore, but in truth, he wasn't surprised by its growth. He always knew that the choice piece of land that spanned across the southern side of the Great Eastern Peninsula, from Paradise Beach and Infinity Pools, down to Moonstruck Beach and Lover's Cove, all the way down to Nirvana Point would not stay hidden for long, especially during an age of peace. It was a place that existed to be enjoyed, and enjoyed by many.

Peter then smiled when he thought of chatting up the mermaids across the various islands scattered throughout The Enchanted Isles. The largest island in the lagoon — Marooner's Rock, where they used to meet — was now overrun with tourists hoping to grab a snapshot of a mermaid, but many of the islands were still uncharted and undiscovered by human and fairy folk, mainly because they didn't like to stray too far away from the beaches in fear of getting swept out of Serenity's Gate into the unpredictable waters of the South East Inlet, and all the unsolved mysteries that existed down there.

To his knowledge, Peter was the only being in Neverland that didn't fear venturing into its south eastern corner, but he rarely went for sport, for it was a dark place, full of mystery and high tales. It was said that in the years before Hook died, he buried Blackbeard's body and all his treasure on the Island of the

Forgotten at the far reaches of the South East Inlet. Peter had since searched the island for the body and treasure multiple times, but could never seem to find it. After several unsuccessful attempts, he had since given up.

The Island of the Forgotten was a disorienting place at the far edge of the world. He could never think straight there, and didn't feel like himself when adventuring upon it. The whole South East Inlet for that matter from the south side of Kingdom's Point at the tip of the Isthmus of Mysteries, down and across Swindler's Bay to Marauder's Rock at the edge of the Unspoken Lands, was full of myths, riddles, and incalculable tales. The sparse population made it an ideal hideaway for pirate hideouts, buried treasure, and general devious behavior. Blackbeard's Landing off Swindler's Bay was said to be where Blackbeard first entered Neverland when he discovered its shores… that age was long before Hook took over…

Peter shook the strange place from his thoughts, and got his mind back on the mermaids that liked to bask in the sunshine of the Enchanted Isles of Mermaid Lagoon. Indeed, they all loved him, but it was hopeless for most of them because Peter preferred girls, and it was not just because of why one may think — that it was because Peter was shaped like a boy — yes, although that did help in the conventional sense, Peter was fascinated by all sorts of creatures, but of all the female beings under the sun, it was girls he loved most, because collectively their love for him was the strongest, and it was one of the essential components of his existence that made him who he was.

Thinking of girls, Peter turned his attention towards the Indian camps at the far end of the Western Cape, where his favorite girl in all of Neverland, Tiger Lily, resided, for today was their one-hundred-year anniversary. He had loved her since he first laid eyes on her centuries ago, and not an ounce of his feeling had changed. In truth, he never loved her more.

He did love spending days with her when they had the chance. Tiger Lily's tepee was located right against the shimmering waters of the Princess Isles that were named in her honor, a majestic string of islands that were some of the most beautiful in all of Neverland, and more importantly, off limits to non-native developers. Because of their control and ownership of the entire Cape, Tiger Lily's father — Chief Great Big Little Panther — and the Piccaninny Tribe had become quite wealthy and powerful, and had done very well for themselves in business. They were still traditional by all means, and stuck to the old ways, staying clear of much of the new technologies that had entered Neverland, but profiting greatly off their land and resources was their way of life. Peter, for the most part, stayed out of tribal dealings, but he was happy that they had found so much success since Hook's downfall — what was good for Tiger Lily, was good for him.

With their now busy schedules, it was a rare occurrence, but how Peter relished those days when he got to wake up with

Tiger Lily next to him when they had nothing to do. They'd sleep in and start the morning late, then walk right out Tiger Lily's back entrance and swim across the Princess Isles to Tiger Island — Tiger Lily's private getaway that she owned in the northern tip of the isles that was also named after her — they'd bask in the sun all day completely sheltered from the wild antics of the fairy paparazzi, most of whom would do anything to get a shot of Tiger Lily in her bathing suit during her morning swim. Tiger Lily was old blood royalty in Neverland, and had long been the favorite subject of neverwood tabloid fodder, even more so now since Tinker Bell's new found fame for her breakthroughs in synthesizing fairy dust in a way that allowed fairies to become human size for short periods, made her Neverland's hottest new it-fairy. The fairy press loved to pit them against each other. The fact that they were both involved in Peter's life exasperated this even more, and they loved to make it look like they were in constant competition with each other for Peter's heart — Neverland's legendary Indian Princess, and Neverland's iconic new-money fairy, both vying for the affections of Neverland's favorite Son — it was pure gossip, and a whole industry had been built on it, an industry that was very profitable. The tabloids focused on the ladies even more than Peter himself. They were both very fashionable, cinematic creatures, and the camera loved them both. Peter didn't care much… he basically wore the same thing every day.

For the most part, the neverwood paparazzi's efforts to get a shot of Tiger Lily during her luxurious private getaways with Peter were all for not, however, for the closest the Tribesman would allow the pesky photographers to get was on the northside beaches of the nearby Island of Eden, to which they'd charge them ruthlessly for passage to the very expensive, and very exclusive piece of land. Even with their most powerful cameras the distance was far enough that they could barely make out Tiger Lily's voluptuous form if she happened to walk down the southern side of her private beach that day, which she'd only do if she was very, very bored and wanted to entertain herself by watching the flashes from across the isles. More times than not, however, the lottery ticket seekers went home empty handed, and much poorer for it. Exploiting the celebrity of their princess had become a very profitable venture for the Piccaninny Tribe.

Tiger Lily's fame didn't bother Peter, and vice versa — at least so he thought — Peter was much more interested in adventuring than being extravagant like the rest of Neverland's celebrities. The fairy stars loved the camera, and the camera loved Tiger Lily too, but she didn't much care, she had been famous ever since she had been born. Peter had been offered many starring roles in big budget fairy tales over the years. It seemed to be the mission of all the big-wig, neverwood producers to get Peter into a superhero role — especially with Tiger Lily playing his love interest, that apparently was their box office dream — many of neverwood's best screenwriters had already written up hundreds of stories for Peter to star in, but not one of them could compete with even a normal day in his life. Every day for him was a blockbuster, and he didn't have the patience to deal with a film crew.

He once starred in a few independent features a few decades back to try it out — both of which were ridiculously successful — make-believe was in his blood, so he was a naturally good actor, but even those few months on set were agonizing for him. At one point, things got so slow that he would have to leave set and fly around to keep his sanity. The production assistants would then have to signal him when it was time for a take, then he'd fly back down and always nail it in one go. From that experience, he just couldn't imagine spending six months living in slow-motion on set making a blockbuster, when his typical day involved flying around Neverland going on high-speed adventures. The thought of it alone just didn't make an ounce of sense for him. He liked the filming part, but there wasn't enough filming to justify the waiting around part, so to the dismay of all of neverwood's investors, he decided it wasn't for him, and publicly announced his retirement from the neverwood film industry after just two pictures.

Peter wasn't in the habit of saying things he didn't mean, but even after several decades, there were still a handful of neverwood's top big-ham producers that thought they were going to be the one to get Peter Pan back in the pictures, and for some of them this idea seemed to be a full-time job. Sadly, they were all full of hot air, and their efforts were futile, for Peter had made up his mind. Tiger Lily also opted to stay out of the pictures. She valued her sanity even more than Peter did.

Next, the entertainment industry went after Tinker Bell — especially since she got famous for her fairy dust breakthroughs — but she made it very clear to them all that she was an inventor only by trade. Tink had a ton of star quality, and Peter knew that she could have been a fairy star from the day cameras ever entered Neverland if she really wanted too, but Tink was a private fairy, and she let very few people get close to her. In fact, she was likely tucked away in her lab at that very moment, working on her latest and greatest fairy dust concoction that was primed to blow the most creative fairy minds in all of Neverland once again. That was Tink. She took no half measures in life. It was always all or nothing. That's probably why she and Peter got along so well.

On the topic of fairy dust, in the south west Eternity Island shone in all its glory on the fringes of the Southern Sea. It was the home of the mining camps, where the miner fairies worked day and night to harvest the precious substance. They'd send it by shipload out of Eternity Bay, up through the Gulf of Creation, through the Princess Isles, and around the Western Point of the Cape into the Great Western Ocean, where they'd drop back in through the Gulf of Neverland and dock at Port Royal for distribution to Pixie's Landing.

Fairy dust mining was one of the core industries for the fairies over the centuries, and Eternity Island their greatest source, supplying roughly eighty percent of all the mined fairy dust in Neverland. The roots of the island went deep into the core Neverland, which was said to go on for eternity — hence the name — for the fairies had been mining the island since their beginning, and nobody had ever reached the bottom. Whether this was true or false, Peter knew not, for Neverland was not round in the way that humans liked to think of their world, but it was rather formless on the whole, and would not fit into any of the human shapes. Neverland was really more in the shape of a star than a planet, but what was the shape of a star? Peter didn't quite know himself, and he didn't have a word to describe it.

In the southern mainland — just north east of Eternity Island — there was the gaping mouth of Cannibal Cove, the place where he defeated Captain James Hook and his pirates one hundred years ago to the day, freeing Neverland, and although he'd used his best make-believe to forget those days — even fooling Tinker Bell, Tiger Lily, the lost boys, and the other inhabitants of Neverland — the memory for him had never been more present, for the terror that man unleashed upon their world was unrivaled by any since the beginning of the age of the fairies, since the Dark Father himself mythically ruled its shores, until he was finally vanquished by the Light. Of this legend Peter had only heard whispers, for during the dark one's reign he was only an infant, and fairies were not keen to discuss the past, in fact, they made it a point to live only in the future, and because they were so small the attempt at doing so kept them conveniently forever in the present.

Peter shuddered and shook the unpleasant memories from his mind, and brought himself back to the pleasant thought of his and Tiger Lily's one-hundred-year anniversary. He stared longingly at the end of the Western Cape. How Peter did love spending time with his true love there, hidden away, on their own private island on the edge of the world. Together, they satisfied each other's every need, every desire, and their passion for each other increased ten-fold every year that their relationship rolled into eternity. Tiger Lily had a way with Peter that no other girl had ever had, and the pleasures she bestowed upon him were unlike anything he had ever experienced before. To put it lightly, she knew how to lock a demigod down — at least so much as any woman ever could — and for the last hundred years Peter had been quite satisfied because of it. Now, when he went looking for adventure, it rarely involved other girls anymore... he knew as much as she, that he had the best in all of creation…

The thought of it was almost too much for him, and he wanted to be there with her now, but he still had a full day ahead of him before their anniversary dinner that night — including cooking his signature yams, which he only did once a year on this very day — Peter didn't care much for food in comparison to humans and most other beings, not because he didn't like it, but because he rarely had time to think about it with all his adventuring. It was lower on his priority list than most people, but he enjoyed it when he got around to it, and, like the fairies, he only ate foods that grew directly from the ground. He found that anything else affected his flying, and slowed him down in the air. whenever he flew to earth — which was rare these days, for it had been a few decades — Peter reasoned that other than lack of faith, it was the human's obsession with food that kept them tethered to the ground. If they could learn to eat properly, possibly some of them could learn to fly, but then again, it appeared the majority preferred gorging themselves on strange animal flesh and its derivatives over evolving — a poor trade off, in Peter's opinion.

Tiger Lily really liked food, and she talked about it way too much for Peter's liking, but he noticed this was true for most girls, and it gave them something to talk about so that was fine by him. Nine times out of ten, Peter was happy if Tiger Lily was happy. He really only ever learned to cook for her — and it was only once a year, and always the same dish.

Peter smiled at the thought of Tiger Lily enjoying their anniversary dinner, and then he smiled even more when he thought of how much she'd probably reward him after, if he did a good job. With that, he took in a breath of fresh air, then rocketed north towards the Fairy Quarters, flying as fast as the winds would carry him.

* CHAPTER 2 *

— Pixie's Landing —

A band of wild horses raced down the shoreline of the Western Cape. They had spent their entire day basking in the cool waters of the Gulf of Creation to escape the heat, and were now headed up north to feast on abundant grasses of the Great Plains. As they neared the end of the cape, they veered north and started up the Western Trail, which would take them all the way from Southern Neverland to their meal-time destination.

Behind them, riding on the wind, Princess Tiger Lily was hot on their trail. She rode upon Fleur, a beautiful black and white speckled mare, who was the swiftest horse in all of Neverland, and her animal companion since she was a young maiden just old enough to ride.

Tiger Lily laughed and Fleur whinnied as they easily caught up with the group. Even though the other horses were running as fast as they could, it was nothing more than a light gallop for Fleur.

They kept pace with the group for a while as they continued up north. It was a big day for Tiger Lily — it was her one hundred year anniversary since her engagement to Peter — in truth, she was supposed to be already getting ready for him, for Peter liked her when she was at her most feminine, and feminine she was. She was the belle of the Piccaninny Tribe, and the most beautiful of the mythical Dusky Dianas, a group of fair maiden spirits throughout Neverland who the locals believed to be the ancient goddesses of the woods. Like Peter, she also had many titles…

Although she was grateful for all the advantages her beauty brought her, Tiger Lily was, at her core, a born free spirit, and what she really longed for most was absolute freedom — freedom from the pressures of royalty, freedom from the press, freedom from having to be perfect for everyone, and all the time — she had grown up famous, and knew no other world, but she also saw it for what it could be — a cage — she felt most herself when she was by herself, racing across Neverland on Fleur, with the warm sun on her copper skin and the cool wind in her long, black hair. It was in these moments that she felt the closest to what she believed true freedom really could be.

That is what attracted her most to Peter — his infinite and unbound spirit — in fact, she found herself envying him sometimes, not in a malicious way, but because of the freedom that she believed his ability to fly gave him. He was beyond her in adventures — she just couldn't keep up — even Tinker Bell as a second-class being had the ability to fly, and because of that she was the only one Peter ever really wanted to go on adventures with, even if he wouldn't admit it. Tiger Lily was still grateful she wasn't born a fairy, but it never sat quite right with her that her species could rarely fly.

Peter was the exception.

Through some sort of exertion and dominance of will, he had evolved into something greater — something higher — and it was so effortless for him that he didn't even know how he did it. To Tiger Lily this was frustrating, aggravating, and impossibly attractive, and she couldn't get enough. Peter had a whole other dimension to his existence that she herself had never known, and she longed to be as close to that freedom as she could possibly get… that is why she knew they were destined to be together ever since he first saved her life. She loved him.

Although she longed for true freedom in her soul, she also believed in duty — to her position, to her tribe — and marriage to Peter would fulfill that responsibility. Peter was highly regarded by the tribe as the deity of Neverland, and nothing would please her father more than their official union. If she could step up and finally commit to a formal marriage, then so could he, and tonight was the night she was going to make that happen.

Thinking of Peter, she had lost track of daylight, for she had stretched her time alone on her special day as far as she could, and she really did need to get back to get dolled up for the big night.

"Ready, girl?" Tiger Lily asked Fleur, and she whinnied strongly in agreement, for she had been bored for some time from slowing herself to the pace of the other horses.

"Yah!" Tiger Lily yanked lightly on Fleur's reins, and with that, Fleur whinnied joyously and rocketed up with Western Trail towards the Fairy Quarters, leaving the rest of the wild horses in the dust behind her…

***

Peter zoomed north over the Neverland Forest, following the beaten path of the Western Trail from overhead, which was the broad passage that connected the Cape to the Fairy Quarters of Northern Neverland. It was the fastest route from northern to southern Neverland by foot that was publicly known, and for that the one most widely used by land-bound travelers. Closely rivaling it in popularity was the Eastern Trail, which ran all the way from the Fairy Quarters in Northern Neverland, along the Northern Strait, all the way to the mouth of the Great Eastern Peninsula. There were other passages that Peter knew of, but those two were the most popular by far. Then, still, there were passages that he himself knew he did not know — for Neverland was ancient, and it would take one an eternity to fully discover its passages — also, Peter, conducting most of his travel by air, had very little use for secret passages, although he did not deny their inherent usefulness should a day ever come. Still, the lack of immediacy during times of peace and the current impracticality of these hidden paths during his journeys kept him from taking action towards their further discovery — there was simply too much to do that demanded more of his attention.

He also took great care to avoid flying directly over the Windy Mountains above Crocodile Crack during casual adventures, for a tribal legend said that there were evil spirits there, and on his flights he sometimes would catch a glimpse of one ducking in and out of the mists. Ghouls, they were. Fairies that gave into the dark side of their nature during the reign of the dark one, and were hence trapped in Neverland until restitution was made. They guarded the enchantress, a mountain witch that was said to live up near the top of the mountains of Crocodile Crack, and although Peter had adventured there many times over the decades, he had still never laid eyes on her. Indeed, it was probably a legend, but if so, it was always curious to him where the story came from…

Peter cleared the edge of the forest, and flew over the Great Plains, past Sunshine Beach, and Starlight Beach, all the way up towards Pixie's Landing at the mouth of Port Royal, which connected the shimmering waters of the Fairy Quarters to the greater Gulf of Neverland that stretched all the way out into the endlessness of the Great Western Ocean.

As Peter neared Pixie's Landing, sounds of life began to reach his ear. As he did every morning, he smiled as the familiar shapes of the Fairy Quarters began to come into view. Attractive fairies and Indian maidens walked the streets, mingling with lost boys of all types, who, by their faith, found Neverland, seeking refuge from their earthly bonds, for there was always room in Neverland for the faithful, and the faithful would always find it — it was this very freedom that Peter represented, and what he lived to uphold.

"It's Peter Pan!" A fresh faced, lost boy shouted as Peter flew down towards the Fairy Quarters.

"What's a matter, kid? Haven't you seen Peter Pan before?" Another boy shouted.

"I haven't," the fresh-faced boy answered. "It's my first day in Neverland!"

"Good morning, Peter." The fairies called out to him as he flew low through Pixie's Landing, hovering just a few feet above the ground, as if resting in the air. Peter answered them only by smiling, and by playing his pan-pipes, which maidens and fairies always loved, and in truth, the melodies from his own pipes calmed him, for music was one of the ways that he communicated directly with his soul.

"Solomon must be getting hungry," Peter remembered suddenly.

Solomon was Peter's mountain goat and companion that he rode all the way to Neverland from Kensington Gardens when he was just a week old. He was given to him by one of his first friends, Maime Mannering, who he met in the gardens. Solomon was imaginary at first, but then became fully real once Peter got to Neverland, and they had been good friends ever since. He didn't have a name when he first got him, so he named him after the crow,

Solomon Caw, another creature he also knew from the gardens when he was first learning to fly, mostly because Peter liked the name and he thought it was very fitting for a mountain goat.

Peter hovered over to a cart of fresh produce and grabbed a nice, juicy carrot for Solomon's breakfast, for he knew how much he liked them. He then tossed a large clothes button — which served as a physical form of Neverland's currency for basic bartering — to a youthful lad behind the cart.

"Thanks, Peter! Have a great day!" The lad shouted after him.

With a grunt, Peter flew on through Pixie's Landing into the quarters, for he didn't like to break the silence of the morning, and tried to refrain from speaking for as long as possible. He always did his best thinking when it was quiet, and he would have the whole rest of the day to speak when it was necessary.

For a few more minutes, Peter floated through the Fairy Quarters, playing his pipes, and soaking in the atmosphere, for nothing brought him back to the present moment like going into his senses. The sights, sounds, and smells of the quarters were all around him, and he breathed in the cool, moist air, filled with the scents of evergreen trees mixed with fresh produce, cinnamon, coffee, and nutmeg from the bakeries, and the subtle smell of rich perfume from the fairies. Ah yes, the fairies, there could never be enough said about them, for all the beings from all the worlds knew that the fairies in Neverland were beautiful, and now, thanks to one of Tink's neverbrew concoctions, they had found a way to become human size. Lost boys and adventurers from all across the universe attempted great journeys to Neverland just to gaze upon them, taking them to be angels, and only a trained eye could tell the difference. Peter knew, however, and they loved him for it, for like them Peter was caught between the physical and spiritual ethers, and it was through this bond that they were eternally connected. "Lord of the Fairies", some explorers called him… one of Peter's many titles he was not entirely comfortable with.

Solomon saw Peter floating in the distance, and began to stomp his hooves and buck his head in anticipation as Peter approached his stable.

"Hey Solomon, hey boy… I brought you something." Peter revealed the carrot, to which Solomon strained even harder to reach. After a bit more teasing, Solomon bleated loudly in annoyance.

"You sure do love carrots." Peter laughed as he fed it to him. "Probably more than anything alive."

Peter rubbed his ears in just the way he liked as he ate, and marveled at how much Solomon had grown over the centuries, from a tiny, imaginary creature that once existed only in his mind, to a fully grown mountain goat in his own right. He was about the size of a young stallion, and ten times as strong, with majestic, formidable horns that sprang up from the top of his skull, and regal, pointy ears that shot up two feet on either side. His coat was silvery-grey, and his beard as white as snow. Indeed, Solomon was a site to behold, and a national treasure in Neverland. He was one of Peter's oldest friends, and since their arrival to this timeless world they had been on many adventures together, and escaped death many times. Peter's love for him was rivaled only by few.

"I'll see you later, all right," Peter said as Solomon finished his carrot. "Take it easy on those jennys…" Solomon shook his head up and down in agreement.

Peter continued his morning float through the quarters until he reached its center, and approached the base of a giant tree. It was surrounded by about twenty neverwood paparazzi that lounged around, clearly waiting for someone famous inside. One fairy photographer saw Peter coming and jumped up, and then the herd was awake… and the flashes began…

"Peter, how about a smile?!" The first photographer said, running his direction and taking dozens of photos as he did.

FLASH. FLASH. FLASH — FLASH. FLASH. FLASH.

"Peter, today is your one-hundred-year anniversary?! How does it feel to be engaged to a Princess?!"

FLASH. FLASH. FLASH — FLASH. FLASH. FLASH.

"Peter! When's the wedding?!"

"Peter, how about that Tinker Bell?! She's pretty cute too, huh?!"

Peter never talked to them or said anything — whatever he said would be taken out of context anyways — he'd just typically force a cool smile through the blinding flashes and nod.

FLASH. FLASH. FLASH — FLASH. FLASH. FLASH.

"Peter, I'm with the *Fairy Journal!*" a reporter screamed, making his way to the front of the hoard. "We'd love to discuss your engagement! Can I get an exclusive?!"

"Peter, what do you think of Aster Starbright's new film?! Word around town is that she fancies you?!"

FLASH. FLASH. FLASH. — FLASH. FLASH. FLASH.

Peter floated through the hoard of photographers until he neared the tree, and then flew up above them leaving the flashes far below. A majestic door was carved in its trunk about twenty feet from the ground. For Peter, this was not a problem, but for the common man it would appear that the builders had allowed for no point of entry. It was accessible only by flight for Peter and the fairies, and for the select lost boys and tribal braves that were allowed access, ropes were dropped down from the branches above. This was *Tink's Lounge* — known to the locals as simply *Tink's* — where Neverland's elite came to see and be seen. It was owned and operated by none other than Tinker Bell herself, and the location of Peter's true home and stomping grounds.

Peter leapt up, and flew up to the door…

***

The door swung open automatically upon Peter's approach, for there were few that were granted unprecedented access to all the favors in Neverland, and Peter was one of them. Inside an entire floor had been carved out of the giant tree, and it was filled with Neverland's beautiful elite. Neverwood fairy stars and a handful of Neverland's top celebrities mingled with high-end fairies in cocktail dresses and dapper lost boys in their finest garb. Dolled-up Indian maidens lounged around polished oak-stump tables, waiting for the wealthiest braves of the tribe to find their courage and come buy them a drink. Indeed, a lot had happened in one hundred years… Neverland had officially become… a society.

Peter entered and glided through the crowd, and all eyes revered him as he passed, for even his humblest attempts at walking held a certain ethereal quality to them, which marked his presence as something greater, something eternal and untouchable — the great flying boy that killed Captain Hook — there was nothing like him in all the world.

Despite his childlike disposition, over the decades, slowly, Peter had become aware of his growing celebrity. Never mind all the movie offers, it didn't much affect him, because Peter had always thought of himself as great in his own mind, and to him that was all that mattered. His indifferent attitude about it all only seemed to make girls like him even more than they did before — if that was possible — and it subtly added to the compounding feeling of greatness within himself, and a boy could never have enough of that…

"Hello, Peter. Great day of flying I imagine."

Peter looked over at the bar, and spotted a sweet, humble lost boy with a round body and a baby face mixing a drink for a human-sized fairy. Peter smiled at the sight of one of his oldest friends, and flew over.

"Tootles, you seen Tink?" Peter asked.

"She's around here somewhere," Tootles answered, then turned to the fairy. "There you go, miss, one neverbrew martini… that should keep you up to size for a while."

The fairy smiled flirtatiously at Peter as she grabbed her drink, then floated away.

"What I'd give to be you for a day," Tootles said as he watched the fairy go in total amazement, his jaw nearly touching the ground.

"Take it easy, Tootles," Peter consoled.

"I'll tell ya', in all the years we've had this stuff… I don't think I'll ever get used to it — human sized fairies — Tink's a genius."

"That she is," Peter agreed.

"Not to mention she's making a financial killing." Tootles followed his remark as a drunk lost boy stumbled up to the bar. Peter recognized his face from some of the billboards around Pixie's landing. He was one of neverwood's newest "picture kids" as Tootles liked to call them. They were part of the usual crowd at *Tink's*. One could usually catch them stumbling around drunk trying to get with one of the newest fairy starlets, to which success was usually negligible.

"One neverbeer," the boy mumbled impolitely.

"Fifteen buttons," Tootles answered.

"You serious?" The boy exclaimed. "You're actually going to make me pay? — *Me?*"

Tootles just stared at him indifferently, waiting for payment. He also didn't mind throwing it back on these picture kids now and again, maybe because he remembered how much he and his friends had to go through to get to where they now were, and what they had to do to make Neverland what it now was.

"Say, barkeep," the boy sassed back. "Don't you know who I am—"

"Don't start with that neverwood crap on me, laddo," Tootles said sternly. "In this room you're *nobody*… it be good for your head to remember that."

Embarrassed, the boy took his gaze from Tootles and glanced at Peter, then glanced at the ground — his attempt to look cool just backfired savagely into his face.

"Now you give me fifteen buttons — like a nice, normal person — and I'll get you a neverbeer."

Beaten, the lost boy reached into his pocket, pulled out a silvery ten-button piece and five single bronze buttons, and reluctantly set them on the bar as Tootles poured him a neverbeer. Tootles added up the buttons, and, satisfied, handed the boy the beer.

"There you go, sir," Tootles said. "One neverbeer as ordered. Pleasure doing business."

Without thanks, the boy took it and began to leave.

"No tip?" Tootles said flatly.

Guilty, the boy reached back into his pocket, and dropped another button on the counter. Then he left in a hurry.

"Harsh," Peter whistled as the boy scuttled away.

"These neverwood kids," Tootles said, "they want it all for free."

"We all started as kids, Tootles," Peter replied. "In a way, we sort of still are."

"That may be true," Tootles admitted, "but we ain't cheap kids. Eh! Eh!" Tootles threw a few friendly slaps in Peter's direction, to which he avoided without effort. "How about a neverbeer?" Tootles asked.

"I'm good, thanks," Peter answered, for he didn't care much for the psychological effects of neverbeer — it slowed him down, dulled his senses — and he was quite happy with how he normally was. "Where are the others?"

Tootles nodded to a corner table at the back of the lounge and Peter spotted his friend Nibs, a thin, bright lost boy, whose natural charm and style had made him a neverwood film star, and Slightly, a lean, cocky lost boy who was the lead singer of the popular rock band, *The Neverbirds*. Despite Peter and Tink's disinterest in the entertainment industry, Nibs and Slightly had jumped at the chance, and had landed themselves two very petite, very attractive fairy starlet girlfriends in the process. Their names were Violet Prettyflower and Aster Starbright, and they sat on either side of them sipping at drinks.

"Look who it is," Nibs exclaimed as Peter approached, "Pan the man." Peter and Nibs slapped hands, for they had always been the best of mates.

"Hello, Peter," Violet and Aster said in unison as they both turned red, for no matter the charm of Nibs and the other lost boys, Peter was still the most desired, the most accomplished, and the most unattainable. The fact that he was with Tiger Lily made them burn with jealousy.

"Ladies," Peter said, acknowledging them, and they both looked down, for they found it overwhelming to look him in the eye. "Nibs, you seen Tink?" Peter then asked.

"You mean that little number over there." From his slouch in the corner, Slightly nodded coolly across the room towards a bottle service table and a familiar face.

Tinker Bell, the traditionally lovely, petite, blonde, and passionate fairy, had become human size. She wore a tight, dark green cocktail dress under her wings that showed off her figure to its best advantage, and she had a certain glow about her that separated her from the other fairies. In this physical state, she was as voluptuous as the most desired of maidens in Neverland, and she had suiters from throughout the worlds, for rumors of her beauty and fame had spread through the galaxy. She owned and operated *Tink's Lounge* — that's how it got its name — for the many years before she became a famous inventor, and although she no longer needed the money, she needed a proper adjustment period to the fact that she was literally rich. She still liked to work the floor from time to time to quote unquote "retain her social sanity." Her fame was great for business, and she liked to serve her friends in this private, nostalgic space. She felt safe there, and keeping *some* things the way they once were gave her the needed feeling of having some measure of control over her life.

Peter watched in admiration as Tink brought a bottle of neverbrew over to a group of three formidable looking tribal braves surrounded by beautiful tribal maidens in their evening's finest — a motley group of ruffians that looked anything but welcoming to anyone that was not their own — Pax was on the end keeping watch, a large brave made out of pure, lean muscle, who spoke very little. His arms were like tree trunks, and his chest looked as solid as iron.

Sulking in the middle there was Marco, the meanest of the bunch, and Peter could say nothing good about him. Indeed, this brave appeared to be rotten to the core, and his intentions seemed to be always evil. He was what any normal person would consider to be born bad, picking up a knack for inflicting cruelty on other kids and animals at a young age. When the other braves got old enough to realize the harm they were causing others through their actions and stopped, Marco only wanted to discover ways to cause more and more pain. Since so many of the young braves looked up to Peter, the chief asked him to talk to Marco once when he was a boy to try to help him, but the child only seemed to be terrified of him, and ran away. Since that day, Peter had always kept his distance, but he always felt sorry for the strange creature… and a creature he had become…

Marco had no natural physical deformities, and actually used to be quite handsome in his early youth, but because of his twisted mind, his physicality was now quite horrendous. His beady black eyes sunk into his long, ghoulish face, and his paper thin, pigment-less skin was pulled leathery over his skeleton-like frame. He was a being that had no love left in him, and never allowed himself to receive love from others. He was pitiful, really — a true disgrace — and the darkness that surrounded him was palpable. The only reason he was allowed into the lounge was because of his association with his leader, Charlie, who smiled boldly at Tinker Bell as she brought them drinks.

Charlie was the most charming and strapping of all the braves, and the most handsome and desired by the maidens. He was both fierce and swift in battle, and was the only brave in Neverland that could present a challenge to Peter, should the day ever come. Charlie had no plans to challenge Peter willingly, however, for to challenge the Great White Father in open field, one-on-one combat would be to accept the certainness of his own fate, and despite his expert skill, Charlie was intelligent enough to know any chance of survival against such a powerful being was improbable, even for him. Still, it had never been done before, and Charlie would be lying if he said he didn't enjoy the idea of being the first.

Off Charlie's right shoulder, dark, and elegant in the corner, sat Tiger Lily, now all dressed and done up for the evening. Through the swiftness of her mare, Fleur, she had made it back in time to get ready, and even early enough to hit the bar first. She was sitting with "her people" — even though she didn't care for their behavior much, for many of them were full of spite and ego — but in a social warzone like *Tink's,* a girl could use all the social support she could get, and Charlie was cool — he was egotistical — but cool, insomuch as the other maidens liked him. He really only put up with Marco because their bond from many battles ran deep, and Charlie was loyal in that way.

In truth, Tiger Lily would really rather hang out with the lost boys, but her beauty and status were too much for most of them in general situations. Really the only person that could handle her outside her tribe was Peter, that's why when they spent time together, it was usually alone. And she loved it… she loved that he treated her like a normal person.

Peter's eyes flared from across the bar at her presence… even after countless years, Tiger Lily's extreme beauty never ceased to take his breath away. It was going to be a great night.

"Nice dress, Tink," Charlie said as Tinker Bell poured their drinks. "Now that you're our size… I'd love to see what you look like out of it."

Marco and Pax snickered at the whit of their clever leader.

"I'm glad you like it, Charlie," Tinker Bell answered easily, for she was used to fielding compliments, and knew the power her beauty held over men. She didn't fear men, however, for she was as powerful as she was beautiful when it came to skill in battle, and she knew they knew it.

"Why do you still serve here?" Marco jeered. "Aren't you a neverwood star now?"

"Yeah," Charlie chimed in. "I heard she got a posh place over in the Royal Hills with all that money — a real nice place, too."

"Don't act like you're complaining," Tink teased back.

"Who are you saving it for anyway?" Marco jeered with a flash of lust in his beady eyes.

"Wouldn't you *love* to know," Tink teased again. They didn't stand a chance — she was an expert at keeping up this facade while working her lounge.

"Don't be a fool, Marco," Charlie followed. "Everybody knows she's got it out for Peter Pan." Charlie then turned directly towards Tink and stared coldly into her big, blue eyes. "I mean, that's why you did it, right? That's why you became our size… to get closer to your *dream boy*?"

Tink's eyes narrowed as she stared right back, and it took everything in her being to control her extremely hot temper which often got the best of her. Back when she was smaller, she would have lashed out and bashed their brains in right then and there while screaming all sorts of profanities, for she was so tiny back then she only had room for one feeling at a time, and she did not possess the capacity to control herself. Now that she was in a human sized body, however, she had much more space inside to juggle her emotions, which gave her the power of choice, a new phenomenon that she was still getting used to aside from her fame. She found it to be overwhelming much of the time, for now she understood why human children were so difficult, because they had too much space in their newborn bodies in which to store emotions, and they got more and more room every year as they grew up to the point that — unless they escaped to Neverland like Peter and the other lost boys — it eventually killed them.

Yes, it wasn't easy for Tinker Bell having so much choice now, especially with her predisposition towards temperament, but she figured this was as good a time as any to try and exercise it. Although it came with extreme difficulty, she consciously chose to let it go, and took a breath instead…

"Why don't you have this bottle on me — on the house," Tink said with a forced pleasantness that had come with years of running her lounge and dealing with vagrants.

"Speaking of the boy wonder," Marco interrupted. "There he is right over there."

Impulsively, Tinker Bell spun around in anticipation, for even the slightest thought of Peter triggered a physical response within her body, as her love and desire for him was that strong — a desire that she could rarely control.

As she wasn't looking, Marco slapped her on her shapely backside, letting his hand rest there a little too long. Tink knocked the hand away, but before she could, Peter and Nibs saw it all. This aggravated her even more. Embarrassed, she waved at Peter, and he smiled and waved back, then she turned to face the culprit.

"Are you gonna step in?" Nibs asked Peter as they watched from across the room.

"Please," Peter chuckled.

"All right, who did it?" Tink asked the group of braves, and her tone was anything but light. From the corner, Tiger Lily watched unemotionally. She saw what happened, and although she didn't condone it, she didn't try to stop it either. She'd be lying to herself if she said that she cared at all for Tinker Bell, for she found her arrogant and rambunctious, and her new found fame and genius posed a real threat to her own established grace. The fact that Tinker Bell was now the size of a human showed how beautiful she truly was, and although Tiger Lily didn't feel directly threatened by it, Tinker Bell's attractiveness combined with her work ethic made her a formidable bit of competition for the young princess. Tiger Lily never really thought she cared about being in the public eye since she was born into it, that was, until she wasn't the only girl people talked about anymore. Then the realization that fame was something that could be diminished became a part of her reality that she now had to come to grips with, all thanks to Tinker Bell. As if she didn't have enough on her plate already by having to be the poster girl for the Piccaninny Tribe, day in, and day out, year, after year, after year. In all truth, Tiger Lily tolerated Tinker Bell only because she was Peter's favorite fairy, and Peter's happiness carried much weight with her.

“Who did what?” Charlie said with a cocky smirk.

“I’m not gonna ask again,” Tink said sternly, and it was clear that she meant it.

“Hey, what are you accusing us of?” Marco stood up aggressively from the table and got into Tinker Bell’s face. “You might think you’re pretty clever, with your fairy dust and all… but our size or not, you’re still nothing without him.”

Marco tried to push Tink, but before he could land a blow, Tink grabbed his arm and slammed his face down on the table with lightning quick-reflexes developed from decades of going on adventures with Peter. Drinks flew everywhere from the force of the blow, and maidens screamed and ran for cover, all except Tiger Lily, who watched coolly from the corner, undisturbed by the quarrel.

Pax then stood up to come to his friend’s aid, but before he could react, Tink grabbed a glass off the table and threw a drink right in his eyes, sending the giant brave falling back in agony. Marco writhed in defeat and humiliation as Tink held his face against the table with a well-placed arm bar. Due to the leverage, he was helpless against her.

“Apologize,” Tink said as she had him pinned.

“Never,” Marco scowled through his smashed face, his big, haggard lips flapping uselessly on the table.

Tinker Bell applied more pressure and Marco howled in pain. “You sure?” Tinker Bell asked.

Then, from behind Tink, in her blind spot, Charlie raised a bottle over her head to strike. "I'll finish this little fairy once and for all," he thought. "The Great White Father will really love that — when he sees his favorite fairy with her skull cracked open on the ground."

Charlie's arm began to plummet towards Tinker Bell's head with deadly force, ready to render a killing blow, then —

His arm was suddenly stopped by some great power. Indeed, this power came down upon him so quickly it appeared to be invisible, but it was as strong — or stronger — than he was, and Charlie could do nothing against it.

"You wouldn't hit a lady would ya?"

Charlie looked up to see the bright countenance of The Great White Father smiling back at him. His eyes sparkled with fearless wonder, and his boyish face was as menacing as that of a tyrannical conqueror, for this boy represented everything that he feared, everything that he felt had been taken from his people — choice, freedom, power, and even Neverland itself — for when the boy rid the land of the great tyrant Captain Hook nearly one century ago to the day, his people worshiped him like a god, and crowned him the Savior of Neverland. They called him The Great White Father, and Chief Great Big Little Panther betrothed his daughter, Tiger Lily, to him as his prize. She was the most desired maiden in Neverland, and a beauty that Charlie had long fancied since he was a young boy, but she was royalty, and he had risen up from nothing, and now the Pan had taken her too.

Indeed, the boy now had everything, and Charlie could not control the resentment he felt against him, for he remembered right where he was when he watched the great pirate captain fall upon the blade of the boy's dagger before going to the crocodile. He was just off the starboard side of Hook's ship in Cannibal Cove, with a group of war hardened braves in a canoe, ready to board and conquer the enemy. They had come all the way down from the Western Cape, past the Eternity Isles in the South Channel, all the way around the Southern Point into the stormy waters of Cannibal Cove just to participate in this legendary battle.

If only it had been him who got to the ship before the Great White Father, he could have slayed the tyrannical pirate and been crowned Savior of Neverland, and he could have the world and everything in it like the boy now had, but he didn't. The cold, hard fact was that he could not fly, and Charlie reasoned this the main reason that gave the boy the win — an unfair advantage that cost him the victory — a loathing dread then shot through Charlie's body in this moment, for he was face to face with a being of unknown and potentially limitless power, and the fight was over.

Charlie didn't answer, he just stared at Peter with utter hatred. Peter shrugged and turned to Tink. "You all right?" Peter asked.

"I had 'em," Tink answered.

Marco and Pax got up from the table and joined Charlie by his side, squaring off on Peter and Tink, while Nibs ran over to get Peter's back. In Nibs' absence, Slightly yawned, and put his arms around Violet and Aster, who gave each other curios looks, but didn't seem to mind. At the bar, Tootles poured himself a drink, getting ready to savor the building scuffle.

"You think you're the king of this world, boy," Charlie started, "but I got news for you… you ain't."

"Nice one, Charlie," Tink teased. "Did they teach you that in basket weaving class?"

"Oy!" Marko shrieked. "You shut your mouth little missy, or I'll shut it for you."

"How about I cut your tongue out," Nibs countered. "You leather-faced arachnoid."

Slightly, Tootles, and Nibs all chuckled in unison at Nibs' comment from around the room, and Marco stewed with resentment.

Peter stood in the center, completely unaffected by the rising aggression. If there was fear to be felt, he felt none, for he had been in power for so long he couldn't even remember what fear was.

"All right," Peter said. "Everybody just calm down—"

"You think because he can fly, he is God?" Charlie directed towards Tink, then turned to face Peter with a spiteful expression that spread across his face like sea fog on a dark night. "No… something is going to come for you… something that you'll never expect… something that you can't possibly imagine…"

"Well…" Peter pondered. "It has been a while since I've had a good surprise."

"It will be a surprise all right," Marco jeered. "A surprise that will make you wish you'd never been born."

Nibs stepped in. "Say when fellas, me and any two of my best mates will take you on anytime, anywhere… with or without Peter, you're no match for us." Nibs stared Marco down. He always despised this Indian brave, for his twisted, evil soul was something that only wished harm upon others — indeed, there was not an ounce of good in him — Nibs saw him as a sick dog that needed to be put down. If it wasn't for Marco's protection from Charlie, and Peter's allegiance to Tiger Lily, he would have ended him decades ago.

"Soon," Charlie said, flashing a vengeful smile at Peter. "Soon." Then he and his braves turned to leave.

"By the way, you're banned!" Tink yelled after them. "And take your floozies with you!"

The maidens they left behind turned to look at Tink. "You heard me," she said to them forcefully.

They recognized her authority as the superior female, and followed the braves out of the lounge. Tiger Lily, however, was nowhere to be seen. She had disappeared during the scuffle.

"Peter, what do you think he meant by that?" Nibs asked, amused.

"It sounded like a challenge," Peter answered. "Can you remember the last time we were challenged, Nibs?"

"I'll say, it must be ages ago now… not since the ol' Hookie days I reckon," Nibs followed, then Peter fell silent. "Oh, right… we don't talk about that."

"It was one of Neverland's darkest times," Peter said as the memories came flooding back. "We should all be thankful to be alive."

Nibs looked down at the ground, ashamed, for he loved Peter dearly, and even the thought of hurting him was too much to bear. Of all the lost boys, Nibs was most like their leader, and Peter cherished his loyalty. In truth, they were like brothers. Peter sensed his regret, and smiled.

"Still," Peter continued. "He was a bit of a codfish wasn't he?"

"Not as much as you are, mate," Nibs teased.

Peter howled with laughter and flew directly at Nibs, tackling him to the ground. The boys started to wrestle, then Peter finally pinned Nibs down.

"Slightly, help!" Nibs called from the ground.

Slightly showed no signs of getting up with Violet Prettyflower and Aster Starbright cozied up against him. In fact, he was right where he preferred to be. Tink rolled her eyes at the two wrestling boys, then she flew over and bopped them both on the head with a bottle.

"Ouch, Tink! What did you do that for?" Peter yelled, rubbing his head.

"Yeah, Tink! What's that all about?" Nibs followed

"Not in my bar," Tink said sternly. "Now either behave yourselves like real gentlemen, or get out."

"All right, all right," Peter said, getting up from the ground. "We're just having a little fun."

"Yeah, we're just having a little fun, Tink, that's all," Nibs followed.

Tinker Bell held her ground. "You can have 'a little fun' outside. There's a whole world out there for you to terrorize."

Suddenly, Tiger Lily appeared out of the shadows behind Peter, and slipped a delicate hand around his waist while poking an arrowhead in his lower spine. Tink rolled her eyes.

"If you move, you're dead." Tiger Lily spoke in a light, controlled voice that was the epitome of femininity. Over the years of living with Peter and the fairies, her English had become perfect, and her native accent was all but gone. This is how she preferred it, and Peter didn't mind either way, for he loved her voice more than anything in the world… even back in the first days when he couldn't understand her…

"Understood," Peter said, careful not to move a muscle.

"Tell me," Tiger Lily continued. "What am I?"

"No human can sneak up on me," Peter said coyly. "Therefore, you must be a goddess."

"Look upon me, boy," Tiger Lily said seductively. "And see for yourself... if you dare."

Peter slowly turned and saw the lovely face of his betrothed staring back at him. He took a moment to take in her beauty, admiring her round, delicate features — that perfectly shaped chin, that button nose, and those big, brown eyes that were like pools of chocolate stardust that went on forever — indeed, she was the girl that had his heart, and the girl he had fallen in love with. He bent down, and they kissed each other deeply, and everything else faded away — all the cares of Neverland, all the pressures of life and of living forever — all of it was gone, and together, they were everything…

They finally pulled away and stared at each other deeply. "Don't mind Charlie and his gang," Tiger Lily said as she looked up into her lover's big, bright eyes, her body melting against his, for she had always found him attractive, but she truly fell in love with him the day he saved her from drowning on Skull Rock all those centuries ago, and they had been bonded together ever since. "They're just jealous."

"I wasn't minding," Peter said honestly, then he smiled and they kissed once more.

"See you tonight." With great effort, Tiger Lily forced herself to pull away, for she had some last minute tribal affairs to attend to before dinner. If she had it her way, she would stay by Peter's side forever, but life had a way of continuing regardless, and she would tend to her duties just so she could find her way back into his arms again. Peter watched her go dreamily.

"Bloody hell," Nibs said with big, huge eyes, completely blown away by the heroic display of passion. "You two only have one speed."

Tink could absolutely stand it no longer. “You silly ass,” she huffed, then flew off towards the back of the lounge.

Concerned, Peter flew to catch up with her…

* CHAPTER 3 *

— The Fairy Genius and the Prophecy —

Tink flew with all her might through the lounge, trying to clear her mind of Tiger Lily and all she had just witnessed, for it had been one hundred years to the day that Tiger Lily and Peter had been officially together — the same fateful day that Peter put an end to Captain Hook and liberated Neverland — and though it had been celebratory for many, in truth, it was bittersweet for her. Although she had gotten used to the idea of Peter and Tiger Lily being together over the last hundred years — she had to, really, in order for her heart to survive — it didn't make it any easier, and she had a difficult time accepting that this was the way it was supposed to be.

She didn't see what Peter saw in Tiger Lily. Sure, she was beautiful, but there were plenty of beautiful maidens about, and with much less attitude. Tink reasoned herself to be just as attractive as Tiger Lily, and, depending on the eye of the beholder, even more so. Additionally, there were plenty of other reasons. Peter, of course, could fly and Tiger Lily could not, he was more playful and adventurous than she was, and Tink even reasoned

Peter looked more like a fairy than a human — well, as far as she was concerned — yes, in Tink's mind Peter and her were destined to be together. It was only a matter of time, and they had an eternity to figure it out. Meanwhile, to cope, she had thrown herself headfirst into her work, in which she had become quite skilled, and she knew it. She had become famous throughout the land for her skills with fairy dust — another advantage she had that Tiger Lily couldn't touch.

Tink reached the back of the lounge where a thick, golden door encrusted with bright red rubies, deep green emeralds, fiery blue sapphires, and a host of other precious gems were lodged into the trunk of the tree. There was a glow to it, and it had the appearance of being infused with some kind of magical property.

"Thimble," Tink whispered as she bent down to the door, and from there it sprang open and she flew inside… before it closed… a shadow slipped in behind her…

***

Tink entered into a large, circular fairy dust lab carved into the backside of Hangman's Tree. Surrounding her on all sides, huge floor-to-ceiling beakers of golden fairy dust filled the room with golden light, and long tubes ran this way and that into beakers of all different shapes and sizes. In a familiar fashion, Tink threw on a pair of safety glasses and a white lab coat, and approached a beaker of golden liquid boiling over an open flame. She was skillfully checking the measurements when a shadow silently approached behind her…

“I know it’s you, Peter,” Tink said without looking.

Peter jumped out from the shadows of a giant beaker and finally chose to announce himself, for he was light on his feet, and swift, and could generally avoid being seen for as long as he wished, but with Tinker Bell, it was a different story. “You’re the only one I know that I can never sneak up on, Tink,” Peter said playfully. “I can’t get my head around it.”

“It’s because I feel where you are all the time,” Tink said with a sigh, and she meant it, for she had looked after Peter since he was a small boy, and the bond she had with him was not completely unlike a mother to a child. “But I wouldn’t expect you to understand it.”

“Well, that’s good,” Peter said with a laugh. “because I don’t.” He then took flight around the room, and weaved in and out of the golden light. Peter could come across as blunt sometimes, mostly because of his naivety to other’s feelings, but it was never malicious, for he was always on an adventure in his mind. Tink knew this was true of his nature by default, and never took it personally when he didn’t understand her. She knew as a matter of fact that deep down he loved her, and one day he would truly see it — she herself would make sure of it.

“What’s wrong, Tink?” Peter asked as he landed next to her. “You seem down.”

"I'm fine, Peter," Tink answered as she continued to check her measurements, but her hand faltered.

"You don't seem fine."

"I'm fine, Peter. Really," Tink continued, but underneath her pleasant exterior she had a hot temper, and Peter's natural insistence had a way of aggravating her and pushing her buttons like no one else could.

"I don't know," Peter followed. "The way you flew away from me, Nibs, and Tiger Lily without saying goodbye—"

"I don't know what you see in her! She can't even fly!" Tink erupted as she flew across the lab towards another beaker.

"See in who? Tiger Lily?" Peter said as he flew after her.

"Hmph," Tinker Bell huffed as she kept her back to him.

"She's just a girl, that's all," Peter explained. "Come on, Tink. What's wrong?"

"A whole eternity together and you still don't know," Tink said as she turned to face him, her big, oval shaped eyes completely open and vulnerable.

Peter stared blankly back at his best friend in the world, and he didn't know what she wanted from him. Tink had always been nice to look at — even when she was small — and now that she was human size, he could really appreciate her beauty and finer features. She had an exquisite face with a button nose and big, blue, oval shaped eyes that fluttered under long dazzling lashes. When her golden hair fell out of her pony-tail bun she liked to keep up on top of her head, it would cascade down and mix with her lashes, and Peter thought that she had to be as pretty as any girl he had ever seen — but Tinker Bell wasn't a girl in his eyes, she was a fairy — and his best friend, and the thought had never crossed his mind of it ever being more than that. He continued to stare at her, curious.

"Here I am, Peter!" Tink proclaimed. "See, me!" Tink wiggled her lovely, voluptuous, human sized body, whose curves were scarcely hidden beneath the lab coat, and presented herself to him — completely open, completely vulnerable.

Peter continued to stare at her, clueless. "It's a nice lab coat, Tink, really."

"UGH!" Tink huffed as she stomped her feet in frustration, then flew towards the back of the lab where a thin, funny looking alchemist fairy that donned a lab coat and glasses was bent over a beaker.

"Almost there…" Spark said in deep concentration as he took a precise measurement.

"Spark!" Tink exclaimed as she flew upon him.

"Ah!" Startled, Spark botched the measurement, and nearly spilt the beaker.

"What do you got for me?" Tink asked eagerly.

"Not so fast, Lady Tinker Bell, please…" Spark pleaded as he corrected the beaker measurements. "Spark requires a great deal of concentration to get this right."

"I know, sorry… how's it coming?"

"It is going well."

"Well? Well?!" Tink exclaimed. "What's that mean?!"

"Patience, Lady Tinker Bell, patience… good things come to those who wait."

Tinker Bell crossed her arms over her chest and huffed. "I hate waiting." She pouted as Spark gleefully returned to his task.

"*Fairy dust, fairy dust, boil and spout*," Spark began to sing. "*I've got a potion that will turn you inside out!*" His excitement was about to crescendo, when suddenly—

"What are you working on?!" Peter flew out of the shadows and down upon Spark with lighting speed, for he had been watching him work on his potion from above, and his curiosity could stand it no longer.

"AH!" Startled, Spark jumped and hit the beaker with his thermometer, which sent it falling off its burner where it shattered on the floor, totally obliterating it. He hardly noticed, however, for the flying boy was hovering right next to him. "Holy mother of fairies! Peter Pan!"

"Ugh! Peter! Look what you did!" Tink accused him.

"I didn't do anything," Peter said defensively. "Spark dropped it." Both Peter and Spark looked at Tink sheepishly.

"Ugh! I was so close," she groaned. "I've been working on that forever. Now I have to wait a whole other month to get it right…" Tinker Bell's head fell to her chest in disappointment.

Peter noticed this and was determined to make it right, for he loved Tinker Bell as if she was his own sister — as if she was blood — and he would never be happy unless she was. "What was it, Tink?" Peter asked, hopeful. "Maybe I can find you some more."

"You can't find this, Peter," Tink answered, defeated.

"I bet you I can," Peter said, defiant, for he didn't like to be told he couldn't do something, and would never stand to hear it from anybody, even his best friends. "I can find anything."

"No you can't," Tink said, stern, her agitation growing.

"Yes I can." Peter wasn't backing down.

"No you can't."

"Yes I can!"

"Peter!" Tink exclaimed with finality. "You just can't, okay." Tink walked over to a round, orb-like beaker full of golden, glowing fairy dust, and sat down upon it. "This is just… something I have to do on my own…"

Peter stopped and stared at Tinker Bell, concerned for his friend. He had definitely heard her, but he couldn't quite understand what all the fuss was about. Peter had known Tink for a long time, and knew that she could be quite prone to moods. She also had a temper so he figured it was one or the other. Before he could decide, Tink started glowing and flickering and dropping in size rapidly.

"Tink, you're shrinking…" Peter warned, for he knew she didn't like getting small.

"Oh…" Tink got up quickly and flew across the lab to a surplus of little vials filled with golden liquid. She grabbed the nearest one, popped the cork off, and rapidly drank its contents, quickly returning herself to human size, then she smoothed out her dress and composed herself. “There we go, all better.”

“Wow, Tink,” Peter followed, attempting to make light of it. “I haven’t seen you small for so long, I almost forgot you were a—”

“Fairy,” Tink answered.

There was silence as Tink stared into Peter’s eyes with deep longing, completely vulnerable. A moment passed between them, but only Tink knew what it really was.

“There’s nothing wrong with being a fairy, Tink,” Peter said, hopeful. “Fairies are some of the best creatures I know.”

“Creatures,” Tink murmured under her breath. “As long as I’m a fairy I’ll never be like you guys… but I can’t let that stop me… I won’t — Spark!”

Spark, who had been crying over his spilt creation on the floor that had taken him months to cook up, sprang to life once more. “Yes, Lady Tinker Bell,” he said as he ran over. “How can I be of service to thee.”

“Start another batch,” Tinker Bell commanded. “I want you on twenty-four seven lock down, understand? And no mistakes this time.”

“Yes, my lady, right away.” Spark obeyed Tinker Bell without question, for he worshipped her genius with fairy dust as if she was a goddess, and he had sworn himself into her service. His chief aim was to be by her side as she achieved the unachievable.

“What are you making, anyway?” Peter asked curiously.

“Nothing,” Tink smiled easily as she grabbed Peter’s arm. “Come on, I’ll buy you a neverbeer before your big date tonight with what’s her face.”

“Tiger Lily?” Peter inquired.

“Whatever,” Tink said as she rolled her eyes, for she had given up on the thought for the day, and was feeling quite excited about her new plan.

As Peter and Tinker Bell exited the lab, Spark watched them go in awe. “He’s so beautiful… I have seen Heaven on Neverland… and now I shall die a happy fairy.” In ecstasy, Spark began to sing — “*Fairy dust, fairy dust, boil and spout… I’ve got a potion that will turn you inside out!*”

***

Smoke rose over an open fire in the Indian Camp up towards a full moon where braves and great warriors crowded around the flames. Charlie, Marco, and Pax were among the faces, and sat close to the front of the fire. Tribal drums resounded, setting the tone for the important ritual.

Front and center, Chief Great Big Little Panther sat deep in introspection as he searched the very depths of his soul. Although he was both wise and ancient with experience, he couldn’t get his mind off his daughter, Tiger Lily, and what he feared may be ahead for her and her friends. He would have to drop the thought if he was going to become attune enough to gather information from the spirit world, for on this night, it had never been more urgent. He resolved himself to do so, and settled into his meditation.

As he did, the tribal drums kept going deeper and deeper, but in the chief's mind, they were getting louder and louder.

Deeper and deeper… louder and louder… deeper and deeper… louder and louder… DEEPER and DEEPER… LOUDER and LOUDER…

Suddenly, the drums stopped. The chief's eyes snapped open in the silence as he entered into an ethereal dream state, a place where he and his people had gone for many moons and many centuries to seek council from other places, whether above or below, it was not always clear. He looked into the peaceful, dancing flames while everything else dropped away.

After a moment, a calm, ethereal feminine voice pierced the quiet.

"*You've felt it... a reckoning... you know what is coming for Neverland... you've always known.*"

The chief's eyes narrowed at the unsettling words.

"*Darkness,*" the voice continued. "*Death.*"

Suddenly, quick flashes of fire and destruction assaulted the chief's vision — flashes of pain and suffering — then, as quickly as it came upon him, it dropped away and was peaceful again.

The chief leaned back and took a breath. He was not shaken by the vision, for he was not new to the play of the worlds, and aside from the good things — light, joy, and abundance — he knew what horrors the dark side of life could bring. Still, it had been some time since he had seen such things in his mind — indeed, it had been nearly one hundred years — and it could be possible that their age of peace was coming to an end. He sat back and pondered some more, looking at the flames…

His mind moved in deeper… there was a storm, lighting, and thunder…

***

The chief's mind fell through the ethers, through time and space, where it quickly came upon earth and hovered over its oceans… lightning raged over the Bermuda Triangle… his mind continued to fall…

***

Three ships braved the ferocious seas of a deadly storm, the crests of even the smallest ones large enough to swallow them whole. In the front on the lead ship, pirates shouted and screamed for dear life as they tried to keep her afloat among the vicious onslaught.

On the helm, a tall, dark figure looked into the building lighting storm in a state of infused serenity. His powerful presence was reminiscent of Blackbeard, and the devious look in his eye rivaled that of even the great and notorious Captain James Hook. He was lean and sinewy for his tall stature, and his dark red sailor's coat hung elegantly down to the top of his buccaneer boots. On his waist hung a gleaming, silver sword, and he had a curious way about him that made it clear he was searching deeply for something.

A group of pirates crawled up the deck against the hurricane rain and winds, finally reaching their leader.

"We must turn back, Captain!" one of them yelled. "The storm will swallow us whole—"

Before the coward could finish his sentence, Captain Brubaker pulled his sword from his waist with lightning quick reflexes and stabbed the man behind him, emptying the contents of his guts upon the deck. Horrified, the other two silenced themselves for dear life as the man dropped dead before their eyes. Brubaker doubled down on the helm, and never once did he take his eyes off the storm ahead… this was it… what he had been sailing the seven seas of earth searching relentlessly for… the moment he had been waiting for his whole life…

The lightning storm continued to rage, building and collecting into an orb of white light energy, creating a kind of portal where space and time converged…

The immense energy sent the pirates behind him cascading down the deck as the rest of the crew ran below for cover to avoid being swallowed up by the hungry sea... leaving only their captain above to face what appeared to be certain death.

With eyes alive and full of thrill, Captain Vincent Brubaker steadied his grip on the helm as the portal consumed them… taking them further, still, into the great unknown…

* CHAPTER 4 *

— The Anniversary Proposal —

Peter sat up at the very top of Hangman's tree, high above the bustling night life of the Pixie's Landing below him, for there was no place in Northern Neverland that he liked to come to more in order to think and manage his world. When he really needed to get away from everyone — even Tiger Lily from time to time — he'd fly to his most exclusive hideaway in the south western most corner of Neverland, deep out in the Gulf of Creation, on the westernmost tip of the Eternity Isles. Most tourists and explorers believed that Eternity Island was the last island of the isles, but it wasn't — Pan Island was — only he, Tiger Lily, Tink, the lost boys, and a handful of select fairies truly knew about it. Due to the unpredictable currents in that region, the island was, for the most part, accessible by flight only — keeping the majority of humans away — and few fairies dared stray too far from the mainland, for there was much fear among them about the sea as a general population, and they typically preferred the air — and keeping the ground below them in the process — due to all these factors, Pan Island was very private, and Peter stored many of his most prized treasures there. In fact, it was really due for a checkup, but it was a three hour flight from Pixie's Landing to Pan Island — only for him at his top speed — and he rarely made it down there anymore. He just couldn't find the time to get away, and spending time with Tiger Lily on her island was usually preferred for obvious reasons.

Peter looked out over the Fairy Quarters, closed his eyes, and felt the breeze on his face. The air was warm and balmy, and there was a certain kind of energy in it that came with a population living their days in joy and peace. He took a deep breath and looked up at the sky he loved so much, enjoying the serenity of his existence while he counted the shooting stars that flew through the sky… one… by one… by one…

Suddenly, Peter felt a shiver run through his body, something subtle, yet unexpected, for over the ages he had become very attune with his senses, and felt many things that he once thought were outside him, but now knew it wasn't so. His experiences and voyages in the spirit realms with Tiger Lily's father over the last century had taught him that he was a part of everything, and that all of the universes and all of the worlds moved and breathed together in harmony, to which he was but a part. Peter squinted his eyes and looked out on the horizon, and although he could not yet see anything, there was something unfamiliar in the ether…

"My yams!" Peter remembered, and all concern fell from his mind as he dove gracefully from the top of the tree and raced down the edge of the long trunk. As he neared the bottom, a stump at the base of the tree felt his presence coming and opened, revealing a secret shoot that went into the depths of the ground below it, for the tree was completely alive and filled with the very spirit of Neverland, and it knew its keeper…

Peter gracefully dove into the chute, and it closed behind him…

***

Underneath Hangman's Tree was Peter's residence. It had long been rebuilt since Captain Hook and his pirates blew it up over a century ago, hoping to kill Peter in his sleep, to which they were, of course, unsuccessful. Since those days, it had not only been rebuilt, but expanded, a testimony to the century of abundance Neverland had been experiencing under Peter's reign.

Peter gracefully popped out of a chute and landed at the base of his living room. He had a door as well higher up the trunk, with stairs dropping down for guests, but he always preferred the chute, for he felt — perhaps unnecessarily — that it kept him young at heart. It reminded him of old adventures, and of how his home had been good to him, and of how it kept him safe many times.

Peter quickly glided through what was basically an underground treehouse, the ultimate boys den. The furnishings — which were mainly composed of plunder that he and the lost boys had taken from conquered pirate ships — were beautiful and expensive. On the walls, hung trinkets of buried treasure that Peter had found by land and sea. Tiger Lily didn't much approve, but Peter didn't care, for it was his home and he was going to surround himself with items he loved and things that made him feel good about his life. If they ever got their own place together, she could be in charge of it, but for the foreseeable future, his place was his own.

Peter reached the kitchen just as the doorbell buzzed, then a moment later emerged carrying a tray of hot yams in oven mits.

"Coming!" Peter yelled, dropping the yams on the center of his polished stump dinner table, where the rest of the meal had already been set. He then quickly lit two candles, flew over to the door, and pushed the buzzer, letting the caller inside.

Peter stood up rigid and tried to compose himself, and got the feeling that he didn't quite know what he was doing. He felt out of sorts, and he didn't like feeling that way, for nine times out of ten, he was always very sure of himself, but this night was going to be a special night, and he'd be lying if he said that his nerves weren't getting the better of him.

After what felt like a lot longer than it actually was, Peter looked up the stairwell to see Tiger Lily standing there in a hooded coat.

"Sorry," she said. "I had to wear it to hide from the photographers."

She let the coat fall from her shoulders. She looked quite ravishing in her black evening gown that she wore underneath, and Peter thought, as he often did, that she might be an angel.

"Tiger Lily…" Peter said as he looked at her with big, wide eyes. "You look — what?"

Peter paused as Tiger Lily giggled in her signature, coquettish way that Peter, despite his better self, could not get enough of. He then looked down and noticed he was still wearing the oven mitts on his hands he used from taking the yams out of the stove. He laughed sheepishly as he quickly threw them across the room, then he moved in towards Tiger Lily and looked into her eyes. No matter the state of anything else in the universe, tonight was their night, and he was going to make her feel like the princess she was.

"Your coat," Peter said nobly with a bow, and he didn't feel at all awkward doing it, for he was the master of make believe and doing such things was second nature to him.

Tiger Lily spun around and let her coat fall into Peter's hands, and his eyes grew even bigger as he saw more of her blossoming figure revealed. Indeed, over the last century Tiger Lily had grown to become an intoxicating young woman, and although they were barely scraping their teenage years when they first met, the last century of life had been good to her in many ways. The wisdom of time had shaped her both physically, mentally, and spiritually — and not in the conventional sense, for time didn't exist in Neverland — but with experience that comes with days lived. She was at the height of her womanhood, and that's how she would stay… forever.

Peter led Tiger Lily over to the table, and continued his display of chivalry by pulling the chair out for her, in which she accepted and sat. She was impressed with the candlelight and Peter's attempts at cooking. They began dishing up.

"Do you like your yams, my lady?" Peter asked as they tucked into the feast, and Tiger Lily stifled another giggle. "What? I cooked them myself."

"No Peter, the yams are fine," Tiger Lily said as she gazed at him. "Why did you call me 'my lady'?"

"It's a nice thing to do," Peter answered, defending himself. "You're a lady… so I called you 'my lady'."

"Where did you hear that?" She asked, curious now.

"Oh, I just picked it up," Peter said off hand, but in truth he knew exactly where he heard it — it was earlier that day, when Tootles served the fairy at the bar — but he didn't feel like giving Tootles credit for what he liked to believe was his own wittiness, for tonight wasn't about Tootles, the lost boys, or even Tinker Bell for that matter — it was about them — and he wasn't going to let anything get in the way of that.

"More wine?" He asked.

Tiger Lily smiled with a little nod, and in a flash Peter leapt gracefully into the air, grabbed the wine jug, and began to fill her glass as he floated over the table. It was so smooth and effortless for him, and performed with so much finesse and skill, that all she could do — and all any girl could do for that matter — was smile and shake her head as she admired him, for indeed he was great — he was the greatest boy in all the worlds and all the galaxies in the universe, the Son of Neverland… and he was all hers.

"You are something else," she said as she gazed upon him in the air.

"Oh, right," Peter said as he dropped smoothly to the ground and set down the wine, for despite all he had learned in the last hundred years, he was still not completely aware of the full effect he had on women. "No flying at dinner." He then began to eat his yams ravenously.

"So, how was your day?" Tiger Lily inquired after a moment.

"It was great," Peter answered with a mouthful.

"Oh, yeah?" Tiger Lily responded spiritedly. "What did you do?"

"I just flew around Southern Neverland, per usual," he said coolly.

"And?" Tiger Lily inquired.

"And I had a great time, that's for sure," Peter said quickly. "How about you?"

"I laid out in the sun this morning, then I took Fleur riding for a few hours."

"That's nice. I love the sun." Peter responded vaguely, subconsciously avoiding the conversation he knew was coming by focusing his best efforts on his meal.

"Peter," Tiger Lily inquired after another moment of watching Peter attempt to stuff his face. He wasn't typically a big eater, so she saw through this act.

"Yes," Peter answered with a forced mouthful.

"How long have we been together?"

"I don't know, Tiger Lily," he said between breaths. "A long time."

Peter did in fact know, but through real effort his mind was now focused on his yams, and because he had so many thoughts in his head he often suffered from short-term memory loss, but in one way or another, the truth always circled back eventually.

"Yes, Peter, it's been a long time," she continued, staying patient with him. "Do you know how many years?"

"I don't know," he said with another mouthful. "Fifty?" Peter blurted out, then he stopped chewing and waited for Tiger Lily's response, hoping that he got the correct answer.

Tiger Lily smiled. "It's ninety-nine actually."

"Wow!" Peter exclaimed, hinting at shock. "Ninety-nine years. That's a long time, Tiger Lily. That's almost a hundred."

"Yes, it is," she confirmed in a matter-of-fact tone. "It will actually be a hundred…" she checked the clock on the wall. "Right now."

"A hundred years," Peter said with wide eyes. "Merlin's beard, I can't even keep track anymore — we're getting old." Finding himself hilarious, Peter then burst into a fit of outrageous laughter, which Tiger Lily didn't find funny.

“Peter,” she continued in patience. “Seeing as we are going to be together for… for-for…”

“Forever!” Peter exclaimed ecstatically.

“Yes, seeing as we are going to be together for… a *very long time*… I was wondering if for our hundred year anniversary… you might like to get—”

“— Sure, Tiger Lily, you can have any place you want,” Peter interrupted.

“What?”

“Name it,” Peter continued confidently. “Any place you want in Neverland, it’s yours. They’re building some new high-rises over in Paradise Beach that are supposed to be super exclusive. I’ve checked them out, I think you’ll really like them.”

“No, Peter,” Tiger Lily giggled, grateful for the chance to relieve her own tension. “I was wondering if you’d like to get married.”

“Married!” Peter instantly took to the air, the very word to him like a pirate ambush.

“Yes,” she confirmed. “It would please my father.”

“But Tiger, we can’t get married… getting married is what grown-ups do.”

“No, Peter, it’s what adults do.”

“But we’re not adults,” Peter argued.

“We are, actually,” Tiger Lily pushed back. “In the human world—”

“This isn’t the human world!” Peter exclaimed in absolution, then he turned and flew across the room. He took a moment to collect his thoughts and take a breath, for it was supposed to be a special night, and he knew there must be a way to get his point across without arguing.

“Back in the day, when we’d get bored,” Peter continued. “Tink and I used to fly to earth and laugh at all the people making themselves miserable with all their rules and titles. They are all so serious about everything, it’s the very reason they can’t see the Truth… is that what you want? To end up like them?”

“Ah, so that’s it…” Tiger Lily began in a knowing tone that cut through Peter’s argument, for he knew that tone, and although he wasn’t fully aware of the manipulations it had upon him, he always felt powerless against it. “It’s her isn’t it?”

“Who?” Peter said with a shake of his head.

“Your little pixie girl,” Tiger Lily hissed.

“Tinker Bell?” Peter was dumbfounded as Tiger Lily’s eyes narrowed more at the name.

“Hmph,” Tiger Lily pouted, tilting her head in indignation.

“Tink’s my friend,” Peter continued. “Besides, she’s just a fairy.”

“Not anymore,” Tiger Lily stated, and she had trouble hiding her resentment, for in truth she detested the fact that Tinker Bell had discovered and isolated the strand in fairy dust that gave her the power that she considered her to now have — that is, the power to be seen as human in Peter’s eyes — Tinker Bell had always been beautiful, but before any sort of romantic relationship was a physical impossibility, and Tiger Lily preferred it that way. No matter how beautiful or alluring Tinker Bell was, she was just a tiny little fairy — nothing more or less than a voice in Peter's head — but now, all that had changed drastically.

"Charlie's right," Tiger Lily continued, her resentment building. "She *did* do it all for you."

"Enough!" Peter exclaimed as he stared her down, angered that she had pushed their night into this territory. As far as he was concerned, the conversation was over — she would stop what she was doing, and she would stop it right now.

"If you won't even consider marriage as a possibility, then I don't see the point to any of this." Tiger Lily said, disobeying Peter's orders, for unlike everyone else in Neverland, he did not rule over her, and he would not rule her now.

Peter stared down his beloved in the eye, calling her bluff, for despite her being born into royalty and her elevated social status she knew not fully what she was up against — the things he'd seen, the battles he'd fought, the enemies he'd conquered — yes, he knew that he was greater than her, and he knew that she knew as well… she was just very great at hiding it.

"I'd choose your next words very carefully, little princess," Peter cautioned.

"And if I were you, I'd think twice about what you stand to lose if I walk out that door, fly boy." Tiger Lily stared right back, for she knew her value — especially her value to men — and she knew that he knew there wasn't a female in Neverland that could hold a candle to her.

The two lovers continued to stare at each other, neither backing down, and perhaps, if they looked deeper, they'd realize that this kind of savage passion was the cause and effect of their relentless and undying attraction to each other. They were each other's greatest challenge, and they were addicted to it.

After what seemed like a great long while, the intercom buzzed. Peter didn't move. Tiger Lily huffed and walked over to answer — "Pan residence."

"Tiger Lily," Charlie's voice broke over the line. "The Chief summons you immediately."

"I'm on a date," she stated coldly.

"It doesn't matter. You have to come with me now. He says to bring the Great White Father."

Tiger Lily sighed and rolled her eyes, then looked to Peter. "We've been summoned. I have to bring '*The Great White Father*.'"

Peter shook his head, his anger dissipating at the title. The Piccaninny Tribesman first called him that when he saved Tiger Lily from drowning by Hook's hand all those years ago on Skull Rock. In their eyes, he saved their princess' soul from a dreadful fate, for in their ancient texts there was no path by water to the happy hunting ground of the afterlife. Since that day, the elders of the tribe continued to revere him as a god, and pass the legendary story down to their children, and their children's children, and although many had been born after those days and the tribe had evolved immensely since, the archaic title stuck as a point of reference — a title that could be used in reverence, awe, spite, or in this case, absolute and unapologetic mockery.

Peter didn't mind the strange title at first — actually he even enjoyed it — probably because he associated the memory with Tiger Lily first falling in love with him. She started calling him that back when she couldn't speak English, but then he'd kindly correct her that it was Peter. Yes, it was a sweet memory that they both shared, but after a few centuries, outdated titles could get old.

"I don't think I'll ever fully get used to being called that," Peter said with a blank expression, and Tiger lily giggled coquettishly.

***

After Tiger Lily put her evening coat back on, Peter followed her up the once-secret passage to the base of the tree where Charlie was there waiting for them. The neverwood paparazzi were all there with their cameras, and the flashes began as Peter and Tiger Lily ascended. The boys shared glances of disdain.

"What does he want?" Tiger Lily stated coldly through her cloak, shielding herself from the flashes, for she had been enjoying her evening, and Charlie's sudden and unwanted presence and the summoning by her father was nothing more than annoyance to her.

"That is not your concern," Charlie stated harshly, for he could never stand Tiger Lily's entitlement. She had always been that way — ever since she was a small girl — and even though she was the princess, it didn't change his opinion about it. "He demands your presence immediately."

Tiger Lily just stared at Charlie, her anger building from within. Who was this brave to command her? Tiger Lily, the Great Princess of Neverland, and Belle of the Piccaninny Tribe. This brave was overstepping his position, and whether her father was involved or not, she would make him feel the insignificance of his endeavor.

"That means *now*," Charlie continued, unphased by Tiger Lily's attempt at pulling rank.

"No," Tiger Lily said, and she stuck her nose in the air.

"Don't make me drag you," Charlie threatened.

"I'm not his little girl anymore." Tiger Lily said, frustrated. "He knew this was a special night for me."

"He has his reasons — let's go." Charlie grabbed Tiger Lily forcefully by the arm, then Peter stepped in and pushed him off, shielding her.

"Hands off," Peter stated with authority, and he left no room in his voice for interpretation.

"You're coming to," Charlie stated in absolution, then he mocked — "*Great White Father.*"

Suddenly, Peter lifted off the ground as energy buzzed all around him. His bright eyes lit up with the thrill of a coming fight. "You'd be making a mistake."

Charlie was suddenly struck with the reality of how powerful Peter truly was, and although shaken by Peter's sudden display of vitality, his loathing for the Pan and all that he represented gave him a sudden burst of strength. He bared down into a fighting stance, his hand sliding towards his tomahawk. "On you," he said boldly.

FLASH. FLASH. FLASH. — Lights from the cameras exploded as the photographers ate the moment up — this was going to be one hot story!

The tension continued to build, both warriors about to strike, when…

"Enough!" Tiger Lily threw herself between them and pushed them apart. "I will go to see my Father — Peter, you're coming with me."

"No!" Peter exclaimed. "He can't just summon us whenever he wants. I'm sick of it."

"My father's been right about things before… he must have his reasons."

Tiger Lily pleaded with those big eyes of hers, the ones that Peter loved to gaze into for days, and he felt his heart soften. Then, the darkness took him — that sharp wit that he possessed that could cut through flesh and twist like a knife — he was not yet over the argument that they had at dinner, and he saw an opening in her vulnerability.

"All right, I'll go," Peter agreed, "but only if you ask me nicely."

"Get over yourself," Tiger Lily said, eyeing him vehemently. "This is more important than that, and you know it."

"I'm sure it is… that's why I'm simply requesting that you ask me nicely." Peter grinned at her wickedly, causing Tiger Lily to burn in resentment towards him.

"Enough of this," Charlie stated, appalled by the immature behavior. "What are you, children? Your world needs you… and you *will* answer the call."

Peter continued to stare Tiger Lily down, his sharp grin sinking into her like a blade. "Fine," he said after a moment, letting off, "but I'm bringing Tink."

"My orders were to bring Tiger Lily and you," Charlie stated. "Not the fairy."

Tiger Lily was now completely overwhelmed by the situation. It was supposed to be their special night. How did she let it get out of control? And so quickly? She touched Peter's arm, trying to console him as the flashes from the paparazzi cameras continued to explode, but it was too late.

"Not without Tink!" Peter pulled away from her and jetted off, disappearing into the night sky, and they were helpless to stop him.

“Are you two all right?” Charlie bumbled after a moment, giving his best attempt to console her — a skill he wasn’t necessarily versed in.

“Tiger Lily! Did you and Peter Pan just break up on your anniversary?!” A reporter screamed.

“Tiger Lily!” Another reporter screamed from the back of the horde. “Tell us about your relationship with Neverland’s Savior!”

Frustrated, Tiger Lily took a breath and looked up at the sky, for she had become quite accustom to drowning out the external noise of bright flashes and stupid questions. Her real concern was that the night had gone in the complete opposite direction of what she planned. She had pushed her beloved away, and there was nothing at all for her to do about it now then to move forward, deeper and onward, into the center of it, for she knew it was the only way to make it to the other side… she was then suddenly taken with the feeling that it would be a very long night.

“If only I could fly,” she thought. “Then he couldn’t just run away from me.” Tiger Lily took one last breath then went with Charlie, who took her down the Western Trail towards home…

***

Peter flew through the night with haste, the warm winds of the season resounding through his ear drums, helping to drown out and soothe his aching mind. Regardless, his blood still boiled hot.

How could Tiger Lily push him towards marriage like that? What was the great rush? Didn't she know that they would live forever? Besides, he had a world to look after. It was a burden of responsibility that she couldn't possibly understand, let alone carry if she had to. No, it was his burden to bear, and his alone… she couldn't understand… she wasn't meant to understand…

He ascended upon the twinkling lights of the northern quarters below him near Pixie Hollow, which was home to the majority of Neverland's upper class. Then, he veered west towards the Royal Hills, where a posh cluster of luxury treehouses were built, nestled across the great trees between Northern Point to the north, and Neverwood to the south, where all the fairy stars lived. The Royal Hills was where the who's-who of Neverland resided — the inventors, the geniuses, the top celebrities — and over the last century Tinker Bell had found herself amongst them. Residency was granted by invitation only, and although Peter had been invited to live there as Neverland's favorite son, he wouldn't have it.

In truth, he much preferred to mingle with the common boy, for as quickly as greatness was thrust upon him by the population, he never forgot where it was that he came from — that he was just a boy, that through faith found himself in this eternal world, free from the bondage of the material, and his infinite freedom was much more important than the subtle prisons of luxury, which he saw as another reason for man's downfall. Yes, he was the boy that could fly, and many worlds worshipped him because of it, but he never forgot that it was the Great Spirit inside him that gave him all things, to which he gave his full allegiance.

These thoughts raced in and out of Peter's mind as he came down upon Tinker Bell's treehouse. He was happy that she had found so much success that she was able to move out of her quaint apartment in Pixie Hollow, into her new luxury treehouse in the Royal Hills. Pixie Hollow had always been one of the safest neighborhoods in Neverland, but there was nowhere safer than the Royal Hills. It had all-hours security, and was unreachable from the ground, which was mainly why only rich and famous fairies bought places there. The neighborhood didn't discriminate against other species moving in, but wealthy humans typically found that the design didn't fit their lifestyle.

Peter smiled again, knowing she was so safe. He really couldn't wait to see her, for she was his best friend, and she always knew what to say to make things all right. If they were being summoned, he couldn't think of a better companion to go on an adventure with. Tink was his greatest ally and a powerful warrior in her own right, and he'd never think of doing anything important without her by his side. Yes, he did love her — he loved her like she was his own self — and the thought of her cooled his temper.

Maybe he'd surprise her. Yes, that was it, that would take his mind off things — off Tiger Lily, off the anniversary, off the marriage ultimatum, off Charlie, off that old chief's trigger-happy summonings — for Tink was always up for a good adventure, and he knew without a doubt that she'd join him now.

Peter landed on the porch and snuck up to the door…

***

Tinker Bell sat on her luxurious couch in front of her huge television screen watching reruns of *Lying Little Fairies*. She blew her nose into a handkerchief as she stabbed at a gallon of fairy cream.

"Stupid Tiger Lily," Tink sniffled to herself. "'*I'm just a pretty little princess… oh, take me on an adventure, Peter, won't you… if only I could fly like you and Tinker Bell!*'"

Tinker Bell stabbed down hard into her fairy cream just as there was a knock upon the door, sending her jumping into the air with a shout!

"What's up, Tink?" Peter said as he floated easily through the window.

"Please, just, come on in…" Tinker Bell answered. She was startled, but she was all too used to it by now, for Peter always did whatever he wanted, and when he was excited about something or wanted to do something, there was little use talking to him about the boundaries or feelings of others.

"Wait," Tinker Bell remembered, "aren't you supposed to be on a date?"

"We've been summoned," Peter said offhand as he floated over to the couch.

"Summoned? By who?" Tink found herself suddenly concerned as Peter sprawled out on the couch and began flipping through the channels on the television. "Hey, I was watching that."

"By Chief Great Big Little Panther, that's who," Peter said, quite seriously. "Now come on, it's a long flight to the Cape!" Quick as a flash, Peter forgot all about the television set and was up in the air. He grabbed Tink by the arm and started to pull her with him.

"Peter, no!" Tink exclaimed, pushing him off her.

"What?" Peter looked at her, confused.

Tink found herself overwhelmed with emotion at the sight of the clueless boy staring back at her. He was more youthful and gorgeous than the most handsome of young men, and he had a power surging through his veins that made his presence entirely magnetic, but he was still a boy at heart, and he had the impulses of a child. It was this combination of traits that allowed him to get away with just about anything, and despite completely knowing this she couldn't help but have the utmost patience with him.

Yes, she did love him, but she considered herself to be a mature young woman now, with natural needs and desires. She wanted Peter in a way that he refused to acknowledge, and despite his naivety she truly believed that deep down this place for her existed in him, and it was only a matter of time before he would come to his senses and see it. Until then, she never agreed to be his mother, but he often left her no choice and she found herself forced into the undesirable role nonetheless.

"You can't just come barging in here like this," she corrected. "Expecting me to drop whatever I'm doing and go flying with you in the middle of the night."

"Why?" Peter asked, innocently beaming back at her.

"Because you just can't, all right…" Tink continued, feeling as though it was pointless. "We're not… we're not kids anymore…" Peter looked confused by the statement, confirming her feelings. "Forget it," she finished.

Peter didn't like Tinker Bell's downtrodden attitude — not one bit — it was far from the Tinker Bell he preferred to go on adventures with, and he would get her back up to speed.

"What's gotten into you?" He said. "You're always up for a good adventure."

"Yeah, well, not tonight." Tink sulked and sat back down on the couch. Peter noticed her red cheeks, the used tissues, and the stabbed-at gallon of melting fairy cream.

"Wait…" Peter started. "Have you been… crying?"

"What?" Tink jumped, suddenly consciously aware of the sad and embarrassing state she was in. "No. No, of course not."

"Because it looks like you've been crying," Peter continued.

"I haven't been crying, Peter, all right," Tink lied. "I just haven't been feeling great, that's all."

Peter flew around the couch and faced his friend, and he knew just what to say — "A good adventure will cheer you up!"

"Peter, look at me," Tinker Bell said honestly. "Do I look like I can go on an adventure right now? I mean, seriously."

Peter looked long and hard at the cute little fairy on the couch with big watery eyes and puffy red cheeks. "You look good to me," he said.

"Ugh!" Tinker Bell huffed. She grabbed the melting gallon of fairy cream and flew over to the fridge. She was done with Peter's insensitive antics — if not forever, at least for the night.

"Please Tinker Bell, I need you," Peter pleaded. "Tiger Lily and I just got in this huge fight you see, and I think we just sort of broke up—"

"What?" Tink asked, her little, pointy ears suddenly pricking up.

"Yeah, I think Tiger and I just broke up," Peter admitted. "I don't know, I'm not sure yet."

"Oh, Peter, are you okay?" Despite her joy at the thought of them no longer being together, Tinker Bell was first and foremost overwhelmed with concern for Peter's heart, for his well being was of the utmost importance to her. Peter flew over to the window and looked out on the twinkling lights of the Fairy Quarters sprawling below him.

"Yeah, I'm fine," he said gruffly, for he didn't like being babied, least of all by Tinker Bell. "It's just… Tiger can be so intense sometimes… it's too much."

"Why? What happened?" Tink asked, her curiosity pushing her forward.

"She wants me to—" Peter still couldn't bring himself to say it, but Tink continued to stare at him, expecting a response, and he knew she was never going to let him off the hook now. She'd pry, and pry, and pry until she got an answer, so he decided to save himself the suffering and just come out with it. "She wants me to *marry* her."

Tink felt a stinging surge run through her body and her blood boil in hot fear at the word she thought she heard, for it threatened everything that she had been working so hard to achieve.

"What did you say?" Tink asked cautiously, thinking before she reiterated that she really desired the confirmation.

Peter looked back at his friend, and the seriousness upon her face, and decided against it. "I didn't *say* anything." Frustrated and disheartened, Peter looked up at the night sky. It was a mistake to tell Tinker Bell, and he would pursue it no further.

Tinker Bell thought critically for a moment. Even though he wouldn't confirm it, she knew the word he spoke — Tiger Lily was looking to marry him — of course, it all made sense. Peter was the most desired being in all the world, and she was the Indian Princess. They had been together now for a century, so of course she was going to push him towards marriage. Tinker Bell knew the day would come, she just didn't think it would be so soon, especially because time didn't exist in Neverland. A hundred-year engagement was nothing to the fairies, and in truth, marriage after such a short time was considered premature and unwise.

Nonetheless Tiger Lily was acting fast, and it must have been because she now saw Tinker Bell as a legitimate threat.

Of course! It made sense, their dislike towards each other had grown ever since Tinker Bell discovered and created the neverbrew that gave her the power to be the size of a human. As Tinker Bell's fame spread, Tiger Lily's resentment seemed to grow against her as well, and Tinker Bell's celebrity gave her a status that rivaled that of royalty. Yes, she was a threat — a real threat — and when Spark was finished with the new and improved batch of neverbrew potion that would allow her to stay human sized forever, she would be much more than a threat — she would win!

Yet Tinker Bell wasn't naïve about what she was up against. She knew that Tiger Lily was a cunning girl with unlimited resources and access, and although Spark's work on the eternal neverbrew was top secret knowledge reserved for only them two, Tinker Bell knew that Tiger Lily would have her ways of finding out about Tink's newest creation, for if she was in Tiger Lily's position, she knew she would do the exact same thing.

Whether it was all just speculation on Tinker Bell's part, or pure intuition, she reasoned Tiger Lily now knew the truth of what she was creating in the lab, and she knew that Tiger Lily wasn't going to be waiting around for her to be successful. If Tiger Lily wasn't waiting, Tink couldn't either, and she'd have to act fast if she was to get what she ultimately wanted.

"Let's round up the boys," Tink said, springing to her feet, suddenly filled with a new determination and energy.

“What? Really?” Peter said, invigorated by the new excitement.

“Yes,” Tink confirmed. “I suddenly feel like a good adventure is just what I need.”

“Wahoo!” Peter exclaimed, catapulting himself into the air. “It will be just like old times, Tink.” He then flew over to her and gave her a big hug.

Tink welcomed his strong arms around her, and melted into his touch, smiling decisively. “I’m counting on it,” she said, and fell into his chest.

* CHAPTER 5 *

— Enter the Void —

Filled with new life and energy, Peter and Tinker Bell flew through the Neverland sky like two flashes in the night. Although Tink was a born fairy and naturally gifted, Peter was the more skilled flyer, and more often than not it was her trying to keep up with him, as was the case that night. Tinker Bell admired him as she flew behind him — his finesse, his talent, his speed — she was one of the swiftest flyers out of all the fairies, and yet she couldn't hope to challenge him, for he believed so strongly in himself and his abilities that the only option available to him was to be the greatest at all things. He was confident, yes — borderline on cocky — but she could not help her attraction to his unlimited self-assuredness. Peter made her feel safe in a way that no other being could. She had known him since he was just seven days old, just a little tot of a boy in Kensington Gardens, with deep bright eyes, straw hair, and a smile that hoped in all things. He started as a beacon of unlimited innocence, possibility, and light… and now her boy had become something much greater.

Peter glanced behind him and saw Tinker Bell right on his tail. He was impressed, for no other being in Neverland could keep up with him in the air except her. He loved that she had the ability to fly with him, for it wasn't always fun being superior at absolutely everything. He longed for a companion of comparable ability — someone that could challenge him from time to time — and Tink was first in line. He came upon a ridge in the hills, and decided to turn on the gas a little to see if she could keep up. He plunged over the ridge and dove past a few very extravagant treehouses, then shot up into the air in stealth mode. He had a way of positioning his body by angling all his muscles and joints into perfect alignment that allowed him to cut through the air in such a way as to be undetectable and untraceable to other beings, whether by land or by air — or even by sea if he was trying to hide from Mermaids who otherwise always seemed to know he was coming — in fact, he was so silent at times that he was undetectable even to himself, so he could be very quiet indeed when he wanted to be.

Using his technique, Peter skyrocketed into the air silently, then waited in the pitch blackness of the sky, the twinkling lights of the Fairy Quarters sparkling below him. He waited, then smiled, believing he lost her for a moment — and of course he did, for he could avoid being seen if he wished, and not even Tinker Bell was skilled enough to keep up with him. He was about to fly back down to a lower altitude, when…

"Are we done playing hide and seek?"

Peter turned around and saw Tink coolly floating up behind him. He could always spot Tink by her natural glow, for small specs of golden, glowing fairy dust always drifted off her aura, and whenever they went on adventures where she had to be truly invisible, she would have to cover up with her cloak or use an invisibility potion, but she hadn't been able to come up with a recipe yet that worked for more than a few minutes at a time, so it usually ended up being a cloak.

"Ahh, Tink," Peter said as he came up behind her. "It's been a while since we've been on an adventure. I just wanted to make sure your senses were sharp… I figured you might be a bit rusty," he teased.

"Sharp enough to keep up with you," she teased back. That was all it took to trigger Peter, and he flew towards her.

"No!" Tinker Bell shrieked in delight as she began to fly away from him as fast as she could.

Peter chased her through the air, gaining on her as she darted this way and that. He was going to tackle her into submission like he did to all the lost boys whenever they challenged him. It was always playful and came from a place of love, but it was important to always remind them who was boss at the end of the day, and the same always went for Tinker Bell if she became too sassy.

Tink flew as fast as she could, and despite her best efforts, Peter was gaining on her. She knew it was only a matter of time before he caught her with his superior speed, but it didn't mean she had to make it easy on him. As he approached, she let off a volley of fairy dust that blasted Peter in the eyes and mouth.

"Settle down, Tink!" Peter yelled as he spat and sputtered the fairy dust out of his mouth and eyes. "You can fly, but you can't hide!"

Peter dodged another volley of fairy dust and tackled Tinker Bell in the air. They began wrestling and Tink showed off a surprising display of strength, for her ingenious neverbrew potion gave her other magical powers that went far beyond size. She continued to push him and put up a fight, but she knew that no matter how hard she fought back she'd naturally be overwhelmed by his superior strength.

"Do you yield?!" Peter said as he pulled her arms up above her head, accentuating her curvy frame.

"Never!" Tinker Bell yelled, enjoying the challenge, but Peter pulled harder, and she could take it no longer. "All right, all right," she said. "I yield."

Peter smiled as he held her in submission. He let go of her arms and watched as they gracefully fell from the top of her golden head. With her body pressed up against his, he felt strange. He didn't have that feeling of boyish dominance he felt when he defeated one of the lost boys — no, this was different — his blood began to boil hot as he looked down on the beautiful being below him, blonde and golden, and as fascinating as the morning sun, and he felt himself overcome with passion… not too unlike when Tiger Lily touched him in their moments together…

"Tink… I—"

"Yes?" Tinker Bell said, looking up at him with her big, blue eyes that were like pools of eternity, reflecting and lighting up the night sky. She was completely open to him, and wanted him to move forward with her — to do what she knew he really wanted to do — what she'd been longing for him to do for so long…

Suddenly and in a flash, Peter's mind returned to him. What was he doing? He was with Tiger Lily, besides, Tink was a fairy and his best friend. He must banish this thought from his mind as if he was banishing a pirate — it simply wasn't a possibility, good, or right — and he would never let it happen, not ever, not so long as he ruled in Neverland.

He pulled away from her without a word, and let the thought breathe upon the air no longer. It was important that Tinker Bell didn't know what he was feeling, and it was important to him that he used his best make-believe to forget it entirely, for of all Peter's gifts, that's what he valued the most — his ability to will and believe anything into being — and it was this very gift that allowed him to shape his reality into what he wished.

"Come on, Tink!" Peter yelled joyfully. "The lost boys are waiting!"

Tink smiled as she watched Peter fly away. Although she was disappointed he didn't go further with her, she knew that was as close as she'd ever gotten with him, and her intuition told her everything she needed to know, for she reasoned she knew Peter even better than he knew himself — at least as far as his emotions when it came to women were concerned — she knew that whatever she was feeling inside, he was feeling as well, for they were mirrors of each other and she had existed long enough to have a basic grasp on the concept. Ultimately, her plan was working. Whether or not Peter was aware of it, becoming his size had helped him see her as a real object of substance and affection. It was only a matter of time now… then they'd be bonded together forever…

"I'll race you there!" Tink yelled, then flew off after him into the night.

***

At the very top of Hangman's Tree, right below where Peter liked to perch, there nestled a large, luxurious playhouse. This place was for the cream of the crop, and reserved for the world's best, and only Neverland's favorite bachelors could occupy it...

The lost boys were treated like gods of Neverland, to which Peter was their crowned and fearless leader. Like him, they stayed young forever, and were instrumental in the battle of Cannibal Cove that took down Captain James Hook over a century ago and gave freedom to their world. Because of their favor with both Peter and the country, they had their heart's desire, and as much of it as they wanted. Being as close to Peter as they were, and having additional friends in high places — such as Tinker Bell — they naturally instigated jealousy from those on the outside, but they were skilled warriors in their own right, and would die for Peter should he ever require it… he had given them everything, and he would forever have their allegiance.

Inside, the treehouse was the ultimate bachelor pad, filled with every fantasy a young man could ever want. Slightly lounged on a big, spacious couch playing video games, and the famous Aster Starbright leaned against him. Nibs sat with one arm wrapped around the beautiful starlet from the lounge, Violet Prettyflower, in which she welcomed his touch. From the ceiling of the treehouse hung a series of large, spacious hammocks. Tootles lay passed out in one, holding a jug of neverbeer tightly to his belly which looked to be full of the delicious potion already.

Curly, a thin, reckless lost boy with strawberry blonde, curly hair — to which he garnered his name — sat at a long, polished oak table playing cards with the Twins, two identical boys clothed in racoon skin garments that acted and reacted as if they were one person. They didn't say much, but when they did, one could be sure that they'd be hearing from them both.

"There it is, boys. Full house!" Curly yelled as he threw down his cards on the table — aces over tens.

"Nothing to say for yourselves?" Curly continued as he started pulling in the large pot of golden buttons towards him from the middle of the table. "I just took all your buttons."

The Twins didn't respond, they both just stared at him with big, Cheshire cat smiles on their faces.

"That's what I thought," Curly reiterated as he continued to rake in the loot, pleased with himself, but something about their demeanor made him uneasy…

Then, the Twins threw a heart flush over the pile, beating his hand.

"Oy!" Curly howled, feeling the sting of defeat.

"Ay, keep it down over there, Curly!" Nibs yelled from the couch.

"These little buggers cheated me!"

"You cheated yourself, mate," Nibs continued. "Everybody knows you don't play the Twins in cards… you'd have better luck pulling a feather from a neverbird."

Curly chanced a glance at the Twins, where they continued to stare at him with big, bright, Cheshire grinning faces. "I'll be telling Peter about this, you best believe it," Curly shivered, but the Twins didn't react, they didn't even take the pot, they just continued to grin at him, relishing the joy of their simple victory.

Curly shook his head. "You two are an odd lot…"

"COCK-A-DOODLE-DO!"

The room was suddenly full of Peter's crow as he and Tinker Bell came flying in, shattering the serenity of the boy's quiet evening.

"Tootles! Nibs! Slightly! Curly! Twins!" Tinker Bell flew around the room at lighting speed, filling the space with fairy dust as she bopped all of the boys on the head, one by one by one.

"Let's go boys!" Peter commanded. "Chief summons us." Peter flew up and flipped Tootles out of his hammock, sending him sprawling onto one of the big couches in a neverbrew induced stupor.

"Ay! Ay! Captain." Nibs was the first on his feet at Peter's command, and all the boys jumped up in unison after, ready to serve when called by their great and fearless leader.

"Say, whatzz the biig idear?" Tootles groaned from the couch, holding his head. "Put a cork in that racketz wouldcha!"

Violet Prettyflower was disgruntled at the sudden call to action, for she didn't like surprises and hated it when the call to adventure took her boy away from her, but she knew where Nibs loyalties were aligned. She was known for being difficult in the press, but in this case she knew better than to bite the hand that feeds. As far as she was concerned, Peter Pan was the Lord of all things in Neverland, and although she didn't understand him and didn't like how he ignored her or the other fairy starlets, she found herself undeniably fascinated by him. He seemed to have eyes for only one fairy — Tinker Bell — and even then she knew it was only friendship, for all knew that it was Tiger Lily that truly had Peter's heart, but what was it that he saw in Tinker Bell that kept her so close by his side? Besides her practically being his mother.

Sure, Tinker Bell was an exceptional beauty, but Violet reasoned herself to be just as attractive, perhaps even more so, depending on the eye of the beholder. She was one of the most famous fairy stars in all of Neverland, and while the other boys stared at her, often with their tongues hanging out of their heads, salivating like dogs, he appeared to hardly notice her at all, even when she was standing right next to him. Indeed, he was practically untouchable in this regard, and she reasoned Nibs was the closest thing she'd ever get to truly being with him, and she had come to accept that. Nibs, after all, was the greatest of all the lost boys, and Peter's favorite, and to have his affection — at least while it lasted — put her into the upper, upper class of Neverland's elite that she had long craved to be a part of. She had no plans of ever letting her status go, and she would hold onto it for as long as she was able.

"I'll see you later, babe," Nibs said as he coolly pecked her on the cheek. "Duty calls."

Violet shrugged Nibs off and looked over at her friend, Aster Starbright, to which Slightly was doing the same song and dance, only with much less effort. Violet tried to play it cool, for she didn't want Nibs to know how much she cared for him, or how worried she was. She knew he could have just about any fairy he wanted, and she didn't want to come off as easy. Even in the most uncertain of times, she always had to appear to be a challenge — that was the only thing that would keep boys like him coming back for more.

"Just try not to hurt yourself, Curly," Violet said indirectly from across the room, but she was really aiming the statement at Nibs. "I'll be sad if you come back too tired to play."

"Me? Tired?!" Curly exclaimed. "Baby, I could outrun three cheetahs and still take you on a ride in the hammock that you'd never forget."

"Spoken like a true boy," Aster yelled from the couch. "What Violet is lookin' for is a man."

"Ay! I'm man enough," Curly yelled at Aster. "Slightly, reign in your woman before she starts strutting around the treehouse in pirate boots."

At that, Slightly burst into a fit of hysterical laughter — which he rarely ever did.

"Shut up," Aster commanded, hitting Slightly's arm. "Or I'll stick my spurs into your gut." She then made a hard kicking motion towards his groin.

"Ay, watch where you're aiming there, pixie stick." Slightly tackled Aster to the couch and kissed her passionately. He then lifted his head and looked into her eyes. "Be good, baby. I'll see you soon."

Aster couldn't help blushing as Slightly lifted his lean body off of her. After Peter, there was no one more mysterious than Slightly, and he had really taken her on a passion-fueled ride over the last year. She considered herself to be the luckiest fairy in Neverland to be with him. She was just a lowly merchant fairy in the southern quarters before the entertainment scouts swept her up for her beauty and put her in the pictures. Indeed, it had truly changed her life, and fast. She went from selling bartered goods from sunup to sundown, to now being friends with Violet

Prettyflower and dating a rock star lost boy who was best friends with Peter Pan. It was more than a dream come true. Mind blowing, really. A previous impossibility before the camera came to Neverland… she really owed so much of what she now had in life to that one device.

Curly let out a war cry, preparing himself and the boys for the coming adventure, then he looked back at the Twins, who had still not moved from their position at the table. They just sat there, grinning like Cheshire cats with what seemed to be all the energy in the world.

"This isn't over," Curly said as he leaned in and tapped the poker table, then he and the other boys disappeared down out of the treehouse into the night, ready to embark with Peter Pan and Tinker Bell on their next adventure.

***

Peter flew up ahead of the others, for it was a several hour journey by horse from Pixie's Landing to the Western Cape, and even though the lost boys were fast riders and could do it twice as fast as the general population, he knew he had some time. He wanted to reach Tiger Lily beforehand and make things right, as he couldn't stand the thought of going into an important tribal meeting leaving things as they were. He flew so fast he even left Tink behind… or so he thought…

From the air, the tribal drums reached his ear, and he could see the great bonfire burning as he descended upon the camps. As he got closer, he saw Chief Great Big Little Panther preparing for the ritual as the rest of the camp gathered around him. Charlie, Marco, and Pax were there with him, and Peter's eyes narrowed in distaste… but he didn't see Tiger Lily.

Peter flew down low through the camps, silent, like a spectre in the night. All the teepees were deserted as the villagers had gone to join the ritual. At the very west end of the camp, with the melodic sound of the Princess Isles behind it, was Tiger Lily's glorious teepee, fashioned and designed in her essence by the greatest tradesman in the tribe. It was well protected, and because the guards were at their post, Peter knew Tiger Lily must still be inside. As the Great White Father, he could easily approach, announce himself, and enter, but on this particular occasion he didn't want anyone to know he was there, for on the whole, the night had been rather embarrassing for him. He had lost his temper and ruined the evening, and it was best if that information stayed between them — at least until it came out in the press tomorrow.

Peter landed nearby and whistled from the shadows.

"Who goes there?" One of the guards yelled, pulling out his tomahawk.

"It's just a bird," the other guard said. "Don't fret… the princess will come out when she comes out."

Peter whistled again, and the other guard perked up.

"You still say that's a bird?" Said the first guard.

"It's one of those damn lost boys," said the second guard maliciously. "They are messing with us again."

"Shh, pretend as if you don't hear them," the first guard reasoned. "Then they'll be forced to be louder and give away their position."

Being raised by fairies, Peter had evolved to develop a slight point to his ears, and along with it an extremely acute sense of hearing that was the equivalent to superhuman. He, of course, heard the whole conversation. He grinned and whistled louder.

"There," the second guard said. "On my mark… three… two… one…"

The guards silently charged to the position behind the teepee where Peter was. As they left their post and neared, Peter leapt up over them into the air and landed at the entrance of the now unguarded teepee. He slipped inside like a shadow into the cracks of a wall. Little did he know he wasn't the only one…

***

Inside the teepee was lavish and spacious like only a princesses' could be, with Neverland's best serving as its décor. Large silk rugs from her father's pirate trades, and great furs from the best of brave's hunts vying for her affection lined the floors. In her closet hung dresses from Neverland's top designers, all given to her for free in hopes that she might wear one out so that they could capitalize on her celebrity. At the back of the room, a large bed rested with white linens draping down from above, and a crystal chandelier hung from the ceiling that was said to be made in England, a far-off continent from the planet Earth that was known for their fine items.

In front of a large mirror, Tiger Lily sat brushing her hair. She was wearing her standard tribal garments — adjusted for the warmer months — with black leg-ins, a brown leather skirt, and a leather halter top adjusted to hold her in place. Although she was quite slim and graceful, she inherited the voluptuous curves of her mother, and had been given the body of a goddess. She knew her beauty had its advantages, but she found her curves to be quite cumbersome in battle, and always had to go to extra effort to tighten everything down for maximum balance. Despite the additional time it took, it worked marvelously, for she was swifter than any brave, and was the best shot with a bow and arrow in all of Neverland, winning the annual competitions every year by a landslide, in which she remained unchallenged.

"Those were my best guards," Tiger Lily spoke into the mirror as she gave another stroke to her silky, black hair.

For a moment, it appeared as if she was addressing only silence, then a shadow appeared upon the lamplight, and Peter Pan walked into view. Tiger Lily wasn't surprised, and although she could never hear him or see him when he was being sneaky, she could *feel* him, and this made Peter's powers useless upon her. Indeed, if there was one being Peter could not sneak up on in all of Neverland, it was Tiger Lily, for she was his lover, and as far as she was concerned he might as well have entered using a blow horn.

Peter didn't speak, but rather came up behind her and stood over her in the mirror, his face barely illuminated by the dim, hanging light. He then dug his strong hands into her shoulders, in which she gave into his touch and put her cheek on his hand, and for a moment, everything was all right.

He continued to caress her neck, then she began to lift off the chair involuntarily. She stood, and kissed him passionately, and their bodies began to lose control, both of them overcome with the power of each other's energy.

"Let's get out of here," Peter said between heavy breaths. "Let's swim to Tiger Island… disappear…"

"Peter, not now…" Tiger Lily murmured between passionate breaths, for she had just gone through all the trouble getting dressed, and she didn't want to be put out of sorts only to have to do it again, but Peter didn't stop, it only pushed him forward. It was all right, for in truth she really didn't want him to stop. She needed him not to stop…

"Peter, no!" She finally exclaimed, and although she didn't want to, she found strength to push him off her. "There are more pressing matters at hand. We can't afford to lose ourselves now."

Peter grinned an understanding smile, honoring her wishes, then floated back, disappearing into the shadows, back into the night.

Tiger Lily looked into the mirror and centered herself as she fixed her make-up. She loved how much her young god wanted her, and there would be plenty of time to do all of that fun stuff later, but her father would only summon the guardians of Neverland at such short notice if matters were extremely pressing, and she could not allow herself — and least of all Peter — to get lost in themselves. Anniversary or no anniversary, the safety of Neverland was more important, and she would do her duty as one of its primary keepers.

She took one last look in the mirror, composed herself, got up, and exited, leaving what appeared to be her silent bedroom behind her, but in the shadows a cloaked figure was hidden, and when she emerged a golden glow illuminated the space when the cloak dropped from her shoulders.

Tinker Bell's big, blue eyes shone bright and pondering in the lamplight. She had used a basic invisibility potion to follow Peter inside and get passed the guards. She wouldn't normally use magic to invade others' privacy — she respected magic greatly, and felt a great sense of responsibility for wielding it — but these were extenuating circumstances.

She had seen and heard everything that passed between Peter and Tiger Lily, and she did not yet know what to make of it. It was hard to see them so physical like that, but after all, they had been together for a hundred years now, and she was much too intelligent not to know that intimacies on that level and greater were happening between them.

Then, suddenly, a great jealousy shot through Tink's body against Tiger Lily at the reality of her getting to be physical with Peter, and her cheeks glowed red hot as she felt herself hating her — she hated her, she truly hated her — why was it that Tiger Lily got to be physical with Peter and have all the fun, and she didn't? It wasn't fair.

Then, as quickly as it came on, Tink felt her anger subside when she remembered how Tiger Lily pushed Peter away. Whatever it was, she was clearly concerned enough to deny Peter his passions, and Tink reasoned that nothing in all the worlds could make her push Peter away if he was kissing her like that.

Tink sighed as she threw her cloak back over her shoulders, shielding her glow once more, and plunged back into the night…

***

Tribal drums beat brazenly against the roaring fire as Peter, Tiger Lily, Tinker Bell, Tootles, Nibs, Curly, and the Twins joined Chief Great Big Little Panther and the rest of Neverland's guardians at the sacred ceremony. It had been many moons since they had all been together like this, and the tension of a dire importance filled the air.

In the center, Peter sat next to the chief, with Tinker Bell and the other lost boys directly to his right. Tiger Lily sat directly on the other side of her father to the left, with Charlie, Marco, Pax, and a select handful of the tribe's elders and best warriors directly down the line, creating a crescent moon shaped semi-circle around the fire.

Tiger Lily and Tinker Bell exchanged spiteful, jealous glances over Peter's shoulder while Charlie and Nibs stared each other down… when it came to lost boys and tribal braves… very little had changed in the last hundred years…

The chief stood and spoke in a booming voice —

"Sons and daughters of Neverland… peacekeepers and great warriors… I have seen a darkness in the stars…"

Curly turned to Slightly. "Darkness?" He whispered. "What's he mean?"

"Shh!" Slightly said, nodding towards the chief.

"Eternity calls forth tonight, the Great White Father, the Son of Neverland, to mediate on our behalf," the chief continued. "He will enter the void, and he will tell us what he sees."

At the chief's words, Peter had become very serious. He took a breath and centered himself. As Neverland's ultimate guardian, he had entered the void many times over the last century, and although he mostly found it enjoyable he was never sure what he'd find there. Usually, he'd just stumble across myths and riddles in the mysterious dream-like state, often coming up against infinite paradoxes or unsolvable mind problems that seemed to go on forever. Other times, he'd just laugh for a while, or talk to the different dream characters that seemed to know all sorts of interesting things about him. When he'd come back, he'd always tell the chief whatever he thought it was that he wanted to hear —

usually something serious, but that ultimately everything was going to be all right — this kept everyone calm, but tonight, he did not feel so sure, for he remembered what he felt at the top of Hangman's Tree earlier in the evening, and how it troubled him, and something inside him told him that his journey into the void tonight may not be so easy.

At the very moment Tiger Lily looked across her father at Peter, feeling his concern. Tinker Bell picked up on it as well and gave his arm a reassuring squeeze. Her eyes narrowed at the sight of Tink's hand on Peter's arm, but then she blew it off, choosing to believe it to be friendly. No matter how much of a threat she personally saw Tinker Bell as being, Peter always insisted it was platonic, and in certain cases — such as this one — she had no other choice but to believe him. Besides, they had just kissed passionately in her bedroom, and she knew how much Peter wanted her. Then she felt bad, for tonight was really about supporting Peter, not about petty jealousies, and she knew the weight he held on his shoulders was greater than anything herself or Tinker Bell or even her father for that matter could ever imagine.

All eyes stared intensely at Peter as Chief Great Big Little Panther passed him the smoking peace pipe — the ancient tool that the Great Chiefs of the Piccaninny Tribe used to enter the void millenniums before they ever set foot on Neverland — with great reverence, Peter took it, and held it aloft in the air.

"For Neverland," he said with great faith, then he raised the pipe to his lips, and inhaled…

***

There was nothing for a little while… for all of eternity was in a moment… and all of life was in eternity. This went on for an indefinite amount of time, and his mind was at peace at last… for no thought was the end of all suffering… and the end of all suffering the beginning of peace…

***

After what was either a few seconds, or a thousand years, Peter breathed the mystical contents out of his lungs, and his mind returned to him, bright and renewed. His eyes opened upon an endless sea of stars as he floated inside of eternity, for he had become pure ether — no height, no depth — planets and stars floated by him, in him, and through him… it was all perfect and unlimited…

"Surely, this must be heaven…" Peter thought. "Surely, this is the perfection of all things."

Then, suddenly, Peter was pulled forward through space and time at light speed! Planets, stars, and eternity flew by him as he was pulled helplessly through the ether, for the experience had turned on him, and there was no power he possessed that could stop it.

After the progressive pull through space and time, Peter was brought to an abrupt stop directly above Neverland. It was engulfed in flames! He watched in horror as his world burned. He heard the screams of agony from all those he loved toiling in the endless fire. He reached out to them with his very soul, but he could not move. His mind screamed for the force to take him instead, but he had no voice left in which to speak, for it had been stripped from him. He could do nothing but watch, for all he had left was an awareness now, and his body was no more.

Then, he was surrounded in flames — what it was that he knew to be himself — Peter Pan, the flying boy, the beacon of all things good and bright. His reality was burning now. He screamed in agony but no voice came forth, for there was nothing left in which to project. The flames continued to build until that was all there was left. Then, a dark sinister voice pierced the silent agony —

"You are nothing, Son of Neverland… the judgement of your world is upon you…"

Peter screamed as he fell further into the endless darkness…

***

Deep in the Southern Sea, on the shores of Eternity Island, a savage battle raged. Captain Vincent Brubaker's ruthless fleet stormed the tropical island that served as the fairy dust mining colony, laying waste to the unsuspecting and poorly armed fairy inhabitants. In truth, it was a bloodbath, and the sudden ambush was so swift that the miners were not able to get organized in time to fight back.

The pirates had nearly reached the island's summit as the last remaining miners fought valiantly to hold off the horde with a few well-placed fairy bombs — a type of anti-personnel weapon invented by Tinker Bell that was powered by fairy dust and exploded into hot, incinerating light — perhaps the most advantageous part about these bombs was that, because fairy dust was alive and conscious, they would activate only for their owners or for those their owners allowed. They were loyal in this way, and should someone try to use one that wasn't its true owner — say an enemy — they would not activate, but rather self-destruct and destroy the imposter. This was, of course, superior technology, and another endowment to the entire fairy population springing from Tinker Bell's brilliant mind.

Still, even with Tink's fairy bombs, the miners did not have enough firepower to stop the horde that descended upon them… and certain death was near

"Fall back!" A miner screamed as he threw his last fairy bomb, which exploded and incinerated two oncoming pirates below in a flash of hot light. "Fall back to the keep!"

The remaining miners turned in unison and ran back up the embankment towards the summit, where the Eternity Island Mining Bank was positioned. Tommen, a young fairy miner reached the top first and barged inside the ethereal keep, seeking a moment of sanctuary from the onslaught. The bank walls were lined with glittering, golden bars of pure fairy dust mined from the island.

At the back of the room behind his desk, Mr. Theodore Goldwater sat going over the day's numbers by lamp light. His aura was so calm and peaceful, that upon looking one would not know the island was under siege at all, or that deadly pirates were just moments away. In truth, it appeared that he couldn't care less, and Tommen felt relieved by his presence.

"Mr. Theodore, Sir," Tommen said, breathing heavily. "They are closing in. We must evacuate the island."

Mr. Theodore took a moment, then he set down his pen and looked up through his glasses with wise eyes. "Go, Tommen." He spoke in a soft, delicate tone that was both experienced and surprisingly youthful for a fairy of his years, for he was an ancient being, one of the first of the fairies, and well over tens of thousands of years old. "Warn the mainland of what has happened here."

"You're coming, Sir?" Tommen asked, concerned for his life.

Mr. Theodore smiled at the boyish fairy in front of him, and saw that he was overcome with fear. If only he knew the truth — that there was no death — then he would not be afraid, for every end was just the start of a new beginning, in which limitless possibility could be born.

"My place is here with the mine," Mr. Theodore said with a smile, and his eyes twinkled brightly.

Tommen nodded, accepting the wise being's decision. "It's been a pleasure working for you, Sir," he said with a valiant salutation, then he lifted into the air, and flew out the back doorway. Mr. Theodore watched him disappear into the air as if he already knew the young man's fate…

Outside, the pirates slaughtered the last of the fairy miner's defenses. In the wake of the destruction and lifeless bodies, Captain Vincent Brubaker stormed menacingly up the battlefield in victory towards the entrance of the now defenseless mining bank, for his men had fought well, and it was now time to claim his prize… what he had been searching the worlds for… and for so long…

"Captain." A pirate pointed up to the sky where Tommen was fleeing by air, across the South Channel, back towards the mainland. Brubaker's eyes narrowed — who was this fool to think that he could escape the all-powerful Captain Vincent Brubaker? The current terror of the seven seas, and the chosen vindicator of Neverland? The captain held out an authoritative hand, and the pirate handed him his rifle…

In the air, Tommen flew for dear life… he was almost out of range now… he was almost home free… back to the mainland… back into the arms of his loving wife and children… just a little bit further… just a little bit further and the nightmare would be over…

back into the light… back into the warm joy of the Fairy Quarters…

On the ground, the captain aimed true… he lined up a shot… and fired…

“CRACK!” — A single gunshot streaked through the air…

Tommen flew with much vigor… he could see the shores of the mainland not far away… he was so close… almost back to his home… back to the place where all things were good and bright…

Suddenly, Tommen felt something hot enter his heart. It did not hurt, but it was rather warm, but the light of life was leaving him… and the shores of Neverland faded from his vision…

“I’ll see you all again, someday, my loves… someday,” he spoke into the air, then his strength left him, and he fell from the sky…

On the embankment, the pirates watched as the fleeing fairy fell from the air and plummeted into the waters of the South Channel. Some laughed and chuckled maliciously, but from the captain, there was not a sound, not a twitch, not a single movement that would indicate that taking life was anything more to him than breathing, and the others fell silent at his disposition.

The captain handed the rifle back to the pirate and continued his ascent up the mining bank…

Mr. Theodore sat calmly behind his desk. A group of pirates trained their guns and swords upon the elder fairy as others raided the mine's keep, savoring the loot.

"Look at all this gold!" One pirate screamed in ecstasy. "We're rich!"

"Take it all, we will!" A nasty pirate with one eye and a mouth full of missing teeth exclaimed, then he leaned over Mr. Theodore. "How do you like that, old man?" He breathed into his face with rotten breath. "We're taking what's yours and there's nothing you can do to stop us — bet you never saw this coming, did cha'?"

Mr. Theodore didn't react. In fact, it looked as if he didn't have a care in the world.

Then, Captain Vincent Brubaker appeared as a shadow in the doorway. The other pirates fell silent, and moved to the sides of the golden hall, making room for him.

"He was only a boy," Mr. Theodore said softly, but his words rang sharply across the silent space, and for the first time there was a hint of pain in his voice.

"Like your god?" Brubaker responded coldly. "Is he not a boy?"

The question hung in the air, then a pirate approached. "The keep is yours, Captain. All the miners are dead."

"Bring the contents to my ship," Brubaker commanded.

"What about the old man?"

Captain Vincent Brubaker looked over at the elder fairy in disdain. “Kill him. I have what I came for here.”

The toothless, one-eyed pirate smiled greedily at the command. He moved in on Mr. Theodore with one of his bloodthirsty comrades, swords drawn, ready to kill for sport.

“You’re mine, old man,” the toothless pirate whispered as he moved in to kill. “I’m going to saw your head off your body.”

The pirates slashed down with deadly death blows, in unison, cleaving the chair Mr. Theodore was bound to in half, but there was no body to be found in the splinters of broken wood, for Mr. Theodore was floating gracefully in the air above them.

“Argh!” The pirates screamed as they received lightning quick kicks to the face, sending them both sprawling to the ground.

Mr. Theodore spun in the air and landed effortlessly on the floor. He exerted so little energy that it appeared as if he was almost asleep. The pirates recovered from their blows, stood, and charged the fairy with bloodthirsty screams. Mr. Theodore nimbly sidestepped their strikes, sending them colliding into each other. One pirate was knocked unconscious to the ground while the toothless, one-eyed pirate was impaled on his comrade’s blade.

For a moment, the surrounding horde of pirates stood in shock at the sudden turn of events, then their minds returned to them and they charged, screaming war cries of absolute wrath.

From the other end of the hall, Captain Vincent Brubaker calmly stared at the elder fairy, and their gazes transversed the space. The captain’s eyes narrowed as a slight smile spread across

Mr. Theodore's face, then his fairy eyes sparked, and he vanished in a sharp flash of golden, white light.

The startled pirates stood in awe, staring at the spot where the elder fairy just was.

"He's gone, Captain… vanished," one of the awe-struck pirates mumbled.

"He'll tell the boy god!" One of the pirates exclaimed in terror. "Our cover is blown! He will fly down from above and kill us all!"

"Run! Run for your lives!" Another pirate screamed as terror spread throughout the group. The other pirates began to yell as hysteria began to take hold, then—

"CRACK!" A single gunshot sang through the air. A moment, then the terrified pirate dropped dead, falling on his head straight into the ground.

The other pirates froze and looked down the hall to where Captain Vincent Brubaker stood holding a smoking pistol. They all held their breath.

"Any mention of the boy again, and you will suffer the same fate," the captain said coldly. "Now get the loot back to the ship."

Not a sound was uttered as the pirates obeyed the command of their captain, for his word was law, and they were as terrified of him as they were the legend of the Great Pan himself. They packed up the loot and shuffled by him cautiously, back out to the embankment, neither of them daring to look him in the eye as they did, for to do so would mean certain death in his current state, for he was the Great Captain Vincent Brubaker, the current terror of the seven seas, and feared by all the pirates in all the worlds.

The captain waited until his entire crew had exited — until he was left in the eerie silence of the now empty mining hall — he then began to walk across the space, his polished leather buccaneer boots clapped hard against the smooth, marbled surface of the floor, the sound of which reverberated off the golden walls. He reached the space where the broken chair that previously bound the old fairy now lay cleaved in half. He sneered, and continued…

At the end of the hall, he reached Mr. Theodore's desk that had remained untouched. He observed the spreadsheets and numbers that were laid out across it, lit by the lamplight, and jeered. With a mighty thrust he then kicked the desk, sending it toppling over to the ground and its contents scattering across the floor. It was not only for the joy of destruction that the captain took such an action, but for an impetus far, far greater, for in the floor where the desk just sat, was lodged a passage that was hidden in the marble. The captain smiled, grabbed a torch off the nearby wall, lifted the door to the floor passage, and entered…

The captain descended into the ancient passage, the light from the torch bouncing off the rough, golden wall of the mine. It became colder and darker the further he went, but his blood boiled with thrill of what he knew he would find, and it kept him warm. He pushed cobwebs out of his way with his sword as he continued to descend deeper and deeper into the mountain…

After what seemed like some time, the captain reached the base of the stairwell passage. He held up his torch and saw that he was standing on the edge of a sheer cliff in a circular-like cavern. He kicked a nearby rock off the ledge, which plummeted down into the abyss, past the firelight, until it disappeared completely into the deep. The captain waited, but there was no sound, and it appeared as if the fall went on forever, to some kind of unknown end.

He held up the torch and peered out further, and saw that there was a pillar of stone in the center of the cavern that shot up from the depths of the abyss, creating an island of stone level to the surface on which he stood. It occurred to him that one would have to figure out how to transverse the space to reach the island and whatever was hidden upon it, and he knew that it must have been designed by the flying boy and his fairy puppets, for it would keep all human beings out, as well as all other creatures that did not possess the gift of flight.

The captain shook any trace of fear from his mind and steadied himself, for he had triumphed over many perils in his time to uncover great treasures of old, but he had never come across anything like this — this was some kind of real magic — and to make a mistake would be his end.

"You know who I am, Dark One!" The captain shouted into the endless space, and his sinister voice echoed off the cavern. "And you know why I have come…"

A moment, and the captain held his breath…

"Avenge me," he whispered into the cold air, then he stepped out over the ledge…

The captain free fell through the air to what appeared to be certain death, but he did not scream, he did not make a sound, he fell with absolute certainty — or absolute madness — plummeting into the dark…

He fell, and fell, and fell into the depths of the abyss… and it felt as if he was falling forever… then… suddenly… he felt the inertia of the fall subside… was he still falling? Or was he suspended in the dark infinity of some endless deep? He could not tell, for there were no longer any objects for reference…

Then, his body began to glow with translucent, blue and black shaded flames, and he was rocketed back up through the endless abyss towards the top of the cavern by some kind of infinitely powerful, outside force. The captain's eyes were wide with the thrill of near-death as he was pulled through the air, and he smiled joyfully, for the Dark One had heard his call, and even fairy magic was powerless against it.

When the captain cleared the top of the plateau, the force released him and threw him upon the stone island, onto which he rolled like a rag doll… then… the presence of the force was gone.

The impact from the fall jarred the captain, momentarily taking his breath from him. When he finally recovered, he stood, brushing the cavernous dust from his jacket as he centered himself.

He then looked forward to where a small structure was laid in the center of the island… and it was then that he knew… he knew what it was…

The captain's eyes widened as he crossed the space in reverence… this was the moment… the moment he had dreamed about his whole life…

He reached the center of the island where a small shrine was erected around a beautiful stone coffin… the captain dropped to his knees… tears pouring from his eyes and down his face…

On the gravestone, he read —

"Here Lies CAPTAIN JAMES HOOK, the Great and Worthy Opponent of the Great Peter Pan, Neverland's Son and Guardian. May the Captain and All Those Who Fell with Him Rest in Peace."

Captain Vincent Brubaker continued to sob upon the gravestone… he had found his Great Grandfather at last…

* CHAPTER 6 *

— The Captain's Heir —

Tiger Lily sat on her bed holding Peter's sweating head in her lap as he convulsed back and forth. She stroked his brow with a cool cloth as she whispered a sweet spirit song over him, doing her best to comfort him in his agony, for if there was anyone in all of Neverland that could affect Peter's mind through presence alone, it was her.

From the bedside, the chief sat silently in a meditative posture, mumbling prayers in an ancient tongue, his eyes trained upon Peter, watching his every move, trying to meet him in the place of the Spirit.

Tinker Bell paced back and forth at the base of the bed. She bit her nails as she anxiously awaited whatever should come next. She didn't like feeling helpless, and the fact that her most powerful fairy potions did nothing to soothe Peter made her feel both greatly concerned and greatly embarrassed. She didn't like the look of Peter laying helpless in Tiger Lily's arms like that, but if her touch could bring him back to the land of the living… at least for the night she'd be grateful.

Outside Tiger Lily's teepee, Nibs, Slightly, Tootles, Curly, and the Twins waited at one side of the entrance. At the other, Charlie, Marco, Pax, and several other of the village's finest braves stood guard. The tension between the two groups of boys rose until it reached its climax, and Nibs couldn't take it anymore. He pointed at Charlie.

"If you had something to do with this I swear I'll—"

"You'll do what? You tiny little man…" Marco jeered, stepping forward with Pax behind him. Nibs was about to attack and go to blows, when Tootles and Curly grabbed him.

"Nibs, no!" Curly yelled, restraining him with the help of Tootles, while the Twins and Slightly squared off on Pax and the other braves.

"Why not?" Nibs exclaimed, now turning on Tootles. "You heard him in the bar. He said something was coming for us."

"We don't know anything yet," Tootles counseled. "Let's all keep it together until Peter comes to light."

Hearing Tootle's wisdom, Nibs relaxed enough to reach a momentary truce. Charlie sat down haughtily as Marco continued to jeer directly towards him. Feeling momentarily powerless to take action, Nibs kicked the ground and sat down against the teepee. He didn't like that Peter had been out so long, and for all the times he entered the void, never had it had this effect on him. He was worried, but he knew that if anyone could do anything for him, it was Tiger Lily, and especially Tinker Bell.

The thought of Tinker Bell settled him. “Surely,” he thought. “Tink will know just the thing to put Peter right,” then he leaned back against the teepee and closed his eyes...

Tiger Lily continued her song, and the chief sat silent and motionless as Peter continued to burn up with fever. Tink’s pacing grew faster, and faster, and faster until she couldn’t stand it any longer

“He’s dying in there,” Tink exclaimed. “We have to do something.”

“Once you enter the void, there is no way out but through,” the chief said solemnly.

“To hell there isn’t.” Tink went to grab Peter off the bed, but the chief grabbed her arm.

“Wait,” he said calmly.

Tinker Bell relaxed and looked at Peter, and after a moment his convulsing suddenly stopped. There was silence, then he opened his eyes and slowly sat up on the bed. He sat wearily as Tiger Lily finished her song, weaving her soft and soothing hands through his hair down to his scalp. No one spoke until the song was finished, and until Peter fully opened his eyes.

“What did you see?” The chief finally asked.

Peter took a moment to find his voice, and he found it quite difficult to speak. “Neverland…” he said as his voice reclaimed its position in his throat. “It was… it was burning.”

The silence in the room became so thick they could have heard a thimble hit the floor. The chief did not answer, but rather got up and walked to the other side of the teepee. Then, a foreign voice broke through the silence—

"Good evening."

The group turned and saw that Mr. Theodore had appeared at the entrance, undetected by those outside.

"Mr. Theodore!" Tinker Bell ran over and gave him a hug, grateful for the light of his presence at such a dark time.

Mr. Theodore laughed as if all was well with the world. "Hello, Tinker Bell, Peter… it's good to see you both."

"Speak, Mr. Theodore," The chief demanded, bringing them all back to the situation at hand. "What brings you here tonight?"

"I wish I'd come to you under better circumstances," Mr. Theodore admitted, "but pirates have returned to the shores of Neverland."

At the word *pirate* Tinker Bell fell back from him in fear. The others stared at him in disbelief.

"They just sacked the mines of eternity island," Mr. Theodore continued.

"The others?" Tiger Lily asked, her face wrought with concern.

Mr. Theodore shook his head, and the harrowing truth sent a wave of terror through the group.

"Those filthy pirate swine!" Peter screamed, enraged at the attack on his people, anguish for the loss of life pouring out of him like a geyser. "I'll slay them all!"

Tiger Lily jumped up and pulled him down. "Peace, my love, peace," she said, holding him in her arms. "You must rest. We know not yet what we face."

"How is this possible?" Tinker Bell asked the group, for she had been watching them converse deep in thought, and she could not get her mind around it. "The only way into Neverland is by flight. *'Second star to the right, and straight on till morning.'* — right, Peter?"

Peter did not answer, but rather chewed his lip — which he often did when he didn't know something right away — for he had heard stories of other ways into Neverland, but they were never proven, nor did he care, because flying — in his opinion — was the ideal way to travel. It had occurred to him before that pirates and other land bound creatures would have had to have found a way into Neverland somehow, but he could never concentrate long enough to uncover the secret, simply because it didn't interest him. Peter was really only fascinated with all the secrets of the air, in which he spent most of his time, but still, there would have had to be a way.

"The ancients used to speak of a series of portals that connected the worlds," the chief said when after Peter did not answer.

"I know the legend of these portals," Mr. Theodore confirmed. "In the southern waters of the Eternity Isles. It was mostly an old fairy tale when I was a boy."

"Yeah," Tink confirmed. "I've heard the legend too — but it's just that, a *fairy tale.*"

"Well," Mr. Theodore chuckled. "If it means anything, it's that exact *fairy tale* that's the reason why our mining ships don't venture south past Eternity Bay."

Everyone turned to stare at Mr. Theodore.

"They landed on our island first," he shrugged easily. "Just saying."

Tink then turned to Peter for the answer. "What do you think?" She asked.

Peter's mind was really pondering deeply now. He once heard it said through his channels that Hook never knew how he ended up in Neverland. Peter heard it from Curly, who said he heard it from a Piccaninny brave, who said he overheard it first hand from Hook's drunk boatswain when tribal scouts were spying on a pirate encampment. According to the scout, Hook's boatswain said they were just sailing the seas of earth one day. There was a storm, and then there was a flash, and then they ended up in what turned out to be Neverland. Hook's boatswain said that Hook tried to act like it was his intention all along, and yet, he could never find his way out of Neverland when he wanted to leave, making his crew believe that he never knew how he got them all there to begin with. They'd sail in circles around the Eternity Isles for days on end, with Hook swearing that's how they entered, and when that didn't work, he'd make them sail back across the Southern Sea, with Hook swearing they entered somewhere near the South East Inlet, and when that didn't work, they'd go back across the Southern Sea again. On and on this went, back and forth, and around and around, for centuries on end. Since Hook clearly had no idea how he entered Neverland, there were many plausibly deniable problems with this story — and this was several hundred Neverland years ago now — but still, could the legend of the portal be true? How else could it have happened?

"They are clearly not just fairy tales," Tiger Lily proclaimed, losing her patience when Peter didn't answer. "Or if they were, they are no longer. We should alert the cities at once."

"No," Tinker Bell interjected. "Warning the cities that pirates are back in Neverland will only cause terror. We need to be strategic. Pirates are selfish. They don't attack aimlessly. They attack because they want something." Tink took a moment as the question dawned upon her, then she turned — "Mr. Theodore… what did they want?"

"I know what they wanted," Peter said with a cold acceptance in his voice, and all eyes turned to face him.

Peter looked to Mr. Theodore. They locked knowing eyes for a moment, then Mr. Theodore nodded.

"They wanted the body of Captain James Hook." Peter said, and the name hung in the air like the stench of cold soup, weighing on the minds of all who heard it.

"But his body was taken by the crocodile," Tiger Lily corrected. "You told me—" Tiger Lily's voice fell as she looked at Peter, for his eyes betrayed him. "You lied."

Peter felt no need to defend himself, nor was he quick to answer, but rather, his eyes narrowed in cold remembrance as his mind was pulled into the past. "That would have been no way to send off the captain…"

Lighting cracked and lit up the sky, and rain poured down in sheets as Peter — back in his boyhood form — pursued the great crocodile through the hurricane winds as it raced towards Soothsayer's Channel, which ran from Cannibal Cove underneath the Unspoken Lands of Southern Neverland, into the open, endless waters of the South East Inlet. The crocodile moved swiftly through the water, jetting between the massive, breaking waves, which Peter nimbly dodged, staying hot on his tail. The crocodile looked back with vicious eyes and grimaced — the boy would not let up, for he had just consumed the body of his great, worthy, and delicious opponent, Captain Hook, and the boy knew it — with a howl, the great crocodile dove beneath the sea, hoping to shake him. If he could just make it through the channel into the disorienting waters of the South East Inlet, then he could lose the boy there for good…

"Through lightning," Peter narrated to the group, "and thunder, I pursued my enemy…"

Peter saw the crocodile dive beneath the waves when it reached the other side of Wayfarer Island in Soothsayer's Channel, right where the channel met the incoming breakers of the Southern Sea. It was getting close to Marauder's Rock, and if it made it past there, Peter would not be able to track it through the South East Inlet. The waters were strange there — and unpredictable.

Peter hit the jets and went straight up in the air to get some range, and then shot straight down at the sea as fast as he could, rocketing like a torpedo beneath the waves. He was so swift the arrogant crocodile did not see the boy come upon him. Peter swam beneath the fleeing beast, took his dagger, and plunged it into the bottom of the crocodile's neck, filleting the gator from the belly to the tail as the momentum of its mass carried it over the blade. The crocodile screamed a final scream as the contents of its guts spilled out and turned the sea red…

"I pursued my enemy until I slayed his corpse in the depths of the Southern Sea," Peter continued, "and I took what was *mine* to claim…"

Moments later, there was an explosion of water as Peter rocketed back out of the sea into the air towards the mainland… this time… with the body of Captain James Hook slung over his shoulder…

There was silence in the teepee as all eyes revered Peter…

“He was my greatest opponent,” Peter said with remembrance. “His body will remain in Neverland as long as I’m alive.”

“But why didn’t you just tell me the truth?” Tiger Lily asked after a moment, her eyes filling with tears.

“I had to protect you,” Peter said, standing by his decision.

“Protect me?!” Tiger Lily exclaimed. “From what? A dead pirate?!”

“Daughter, be still,” the chief interjected. “It was knowledge you did not need to know. There are few who do.”

At that moment, Tiger Lily turned coldly to Tinker Bell — “Did you know about this?”

Tinker Bell didn’t respond, for in truth, she was one of the few who knew about the magical underground cavern hiding the deceased body of the late Captain James Hook, along with Peter, Mr. Theodore, Chief Great Big Little Panther, and a select group of the elder fairies. It was classified top secret information in Neverland, and they all thought it best that the fewer that knew about the body the better in case of capture. This included all of the lost boys, the braves, and even Tiger Lily. Tinker Bell’s eyes betrayed her as well, for despite her distaste for Tiger Lily she would not lie to her, not now, not while so much was at stake.

Tiger Lily looked into Tinker Bell’s eyes, and she had her answer, then her blood boiled hot at the betrayal. How could Peter do this to her? Choose to trust his fairy with this top-secret information, over her?! His betrothed lover?! Unsure of where to put her eyes, she looked down at the floor, for she did not want the others to see her tears of rage.

"Then our worst fears have been realized," Mr. Theodore said with an unnerving ease. "The heir of Captain Hook has returned to Neverland."

"There was something else," Peter spoke up with further concern, and curiosity. "In the void… there was a voice… it said… 'the judgement of your world is upon you.'"

"Have you ever experienced this voice in the void before?" The chief asked.

"No…" Peter said honestly. "It's always been… just heavenly."

Chief Great Big Little Panther continued to ponder the flying boy's words. He moved a few paces from the group and sat down in a meditative posture, closed his eyes, and took a breath… this was something greater than them all… greater than the tyranny of Captain Hook and perhaps even as powerful as the Pan himself.

"What the Great White Father saw in the void is an ancient force," he said after a moment. "It is beyond my ability to fathom."

Peter, Tinker Bell, and Tiger Lily all then looked to Mr. Theodore.

"Don't look at me," he said, guarding himself. "I'm just a miner."

"In the Windy Mountains above Crocodile Crack," the chief continued. "There lives an ancient enchantress."

"The mountain witch?" Tinker Bell asked with a terror that took her voice.

The chief nodded his confirmation. "Her knowledge of dark magic is great. She will tell you what you need to know."

A great fear took over Tinker Bell, and suddenly she was overcome with absolute terror for the boy she loved, for even though his power was beyond them all, he still always made it a point to stay away from the Windy Mountains above Crocodile Crack, for there were ancient forces there that were beyond physical power — beyond flesh and blood, and even magic.

"No, Peter," Tinker Bell said, pleading with him. "You've heard the legends. She's dangerous. Pure evil."

"Neverland needs me," Peter said without wavering. "Pirates are on our shores. I will not stand by to watch her burn."

"But the vision," Tink continued. "Maybe that's all it was."

"It was real!" Peter snapped, and then there was silence as a shudder washed over him. "It was as real as I am… there's no doubt about it."

Tinker Bell looked into his big eyes, and nodded, for there was no fear in them, only truth, and she knew that if Peter believed that this was the way — then it was the way.

"You must not fly near Crocodile Crack," the chief warned. "Nor in the Windy Mountains. There are evil spirits there… if they catch you… you could fall to your death."

Peter didn't like the idea of not flying, for it would add a considerable amount of time to the journey, but he knew the chief was right. “I’ll go on foot,” Peter agreed. “I’ll take Solomon. He hasn’t been climbing in a while, and he’ll welcome the journey.”

“I’m coming with you,” Tinker Bell proclaimed.

“Me too,” Tiger Lily said, standing upright as she shook off any remnants of tears.

“No, Daughter. I won’t allow it,” the chief commanded. “The chasm is treacherous.”

“I’m a skilled warrior, Father, and the greatest marksman in the tribe… he will need me.”

There was truth in Tiger Lily’s words, and all knew it. She turned towards Peter. “No more secrets,” she whispered to him.

Peter looked at her and agreed silently, and he nodded his gratitude.

“Very well,” the chief said, accepting the course of action. “Tiger Lily, Charlie, and his finest braves will accompany the Great White Father to the entrance of the enchantress’ lair. It shall be a quest.”

“The quest of the Guardians of Neverland,” Mr. Theodore chuckled thoughtfully. “That has a nice ring to it.”

“Hmm, yes,” The chief muttered as he eyed Mr. Theodore, not appreciating his particular spin on his speech. “Once the entrance to the lair is reached, only the chosen can pass through her magic… The Great White Father will be on his own from there.”

“We leave at dawn,” Peter said with authority.

"There is one more thing…" The chief announced from his meditative seat, and Peter looked curiously back at him. "The Great White Father must not touch the enchantress — no matter the temptation — her magic is dark, seductive, and powerful. To do so will mean certain death."

"I understand," Peter reiterated, not fully comprehending what he was agreeing to.

"Do you?" The chief questioned.

"Yes," Peter confirmed. "I do not fear the darkness."

In that moment the chief leaned forward, and a dark, sinister shadow appeared to wash over his face. "You will, Son of Neverland… you *will…*"

Peter stared at the chief, for as quickly as the shadowed face appeared to come upon him, it was gone, and once again it was the chief staring back at him. Whether it was a trick of the mind, or perhaps his own concern becoming visible, he did not know, but it would do him no good to continue to think about it now, for tomorrow, the journey to the mountain would begin, and he had to lead them all into the unknown. For the task at hand, it would not matter if he was afraid or not, so he chose to be unafraid, for he knew that fear would not serve him.

Tiger Lily walked over and placed her hand on his shoulder, and Peter reached to touch it…

***

The melodic sound of classical music filled the candle-lit cabin as Captain Vincent Brubaker lit his pipe. He took a savory puff of pipe smoke and began to dance through his quarters, enjoying the peace of the melody — one small pleasure to savor his recent victory… one small pleasure to relax his mind…

Another puff and he dropped into the rhythm… another puff and his mind was at perfect ease…

Against the back wall of the cabin, the deceased body of the late Captain James Hook rested in a polished black coffin. By the same dark power that Brubaker had accessed to cross the chasm, he was able to use it for the return journey to his ship, and bring the bones of his ancestor with him.

Through a puff of pipe smoke, Brubaker danced over to the remains of his elder, and kneeled before the coffin, rubbing his hands over the one-hundred-year-old varnish.

"Soon, we will rule Neverland once again," he whispered to the coffin as if he was trying to pierce it. "Soon, we will have our revenge… soon… *Grandfather…*"

Then, there was a knock on the door, breaking the silence and jarring the captain's concentration. The captain scowled as he got up, for there was never any rest with his lot. They were as needy as a pack of starved dogs. He walked over to the door and opened it. There was a pirate in the doorway, holding a sack of some substance in his hand.

"We ground some gold into dust, Captain, as requested." The pirate stuttered as he handed the satchel to the captain, who began weighing it in his hand.

"Alert the crew to ready their weapons," the captain ordered upon inspection. "Then await my orders."

"Ay, ay, Captain," the pirate said with a sloppy, drunken salute, then the captain scowled and slammed the door in his face — what a relief it was to be rid of that moron, now to see if the annoyance would pay off.

The captain turned his attention to the satchel in his hand. He pulled the string at the top, and it opened. Golden light poured out, illuminating the sudden grin that spread across his dark and grizzled face. He placed his hand inside, and greedily ran his fingers through the fine golden dust — this was it — this was just what he had needed for so long…

With another victorious puff of his pipe, he walked across the hall of his cabin to the fireplace, where a small cauldron boiled with a dark, tar-like liquid inside. The captain sat down on a stool next to it, and checked it with a stirring spoon. The substance moved like it was alive… like it had some kind of strange feeling…

The captain took a final, steadying puff of his pipe, then cautiously sprinkled a handful of fairy dust into the boiling liquid. Upon contact, the fairy dust dissolved into the black stew and became a kind of dark, swirling ether.

Thrilled by the change, the captain stared wide-eyed at the contents for a moment, then, suddenly, the walls of the chamber began to shake. The light from the candles and the music was extinguished as a cold front wafted through the room, filling the once warm, melodic cabin with the silent feeling of death. The captain stood upright, for he knew that he was no longer alone…

"It is I, my Lord," the captain uttered into the air. "Captain Vincent Brubaker… I have come at last to Neverland."

There was a moment as the cabin seemed to swell and shrink at the same time, as if whatever was in the room with him was peering into his very soul. The boards continued to creak from the pressure as if they would splinter and crack at any moment, then the captain was hurled across the room, and pinned against the wall by some invisible force that was far beyond himself.

Despite the pressure, the captain showed no signs of pain, but rather, smiled in his helplessness, excited by the experience — invigorated to feel what he had longed for so long to feel.

"Yes…" the captain said with real satisfaction. "It is just as I have dreamed… immeasurable, timeless power."

Again, the captain was hurled across the room by the mysterious force and pinned to the adjacent wall.

"Take me as your vessel, My Lord," the captain continued, taking care to show no signs of weakness. "Let me give you the body that you seek."

There was a moment, followed by a deep, sinister groaning. The room once again swelled and shrunk, as if the force was burrowing into the very fabric of the captain's anatomy, then he was pulled by the mysterious power over the cauldron so that his face was held directly above it.

In the swirling, dark ether, the captain saw a vision of the Great Indian Chief handing the peace pipe to the flying boy god. The boy then took the pipe, and after he uttered a few words the captain could not hear, inhaled it, then a moment later fell back into the arms of two women — one, an Indian maiden, and another, a human sized fairy with golden hair, who must be none other than the famous Tinker Bell… the flying boy's fairy that he had heard so many legends about while sailing the high seas…

"Yes," the captain uttered, discovering the Dark One's desire for this relic. "The ancient pipe… you need it to enter this world…"

The captain was then forcefully pulled from the cauldron and held aloft in the air, powerless, like a straw man surrounded by flame. Once again, the room swelled and shrank as the force looked into him, and the captain knew his assumption was right.

"The Indian encampment is heavily guarded, my Lord," the captain stated practically, accepting the physical reality of his small fleet and armament. "It is much more formidable than that pathetic, helpless island — how can we expect to get through their defenses?"

There was a moment, then a dark voice surrounded him, and it appeared to come from all places at once. "*Leave... that... to... me...*"

Then there was a flash, and the dark ether in the cauldron vanished completely, taking with it the dark spirit's presence. The captain fell to the wooden deck, and once again he was alone in the cabin…

***

It was the middle of the night, and all was quiet in the Indian Camp, say for the occasional croak of a toad over the faint melody of crickets chirping on the fringes of Big Sky Beach, Spirit Cove, and the Princess Isles, all three of which bordered the encampment. The once blazing fire had burned down to hushed little coals that glowed a deep orange in the night, and the lost boys slept soundly by its warmth.

In the middle of the camp, there was the sacred teepee. In it, was a silent and open chamber where the tribal leaders taught from their ancient texts. Here, the villagers came to pray by day and make their peace offerings to the spirits and the gods, asking for good harvests and a continual age of peace for their children and loved ones… but tonight, it was lit only by moonlight.

In the back of the room, the peace pipe sat aloft on its stand, looking majestic in the radiant moonbeams. This was its home, and where it belonged, and none of the villagers dared touch it without the blessing of the elders or the chief, less a great pain and suffering would surely come upon them, and keep them from ever entering the happy hunting ground, in this life, or the next.

Suddenly, a single hand appeared from the shadows, silhouetted by the light of the moon beams. It reached for the pipe, then it held itself aloft above it for a moment, as if contemplating the decision. Then, all at once, the hand swiped the pipe, and pulled it into the darkness…

* CHAPTER 7 *

— The Guardians of Neverland —

The camp was alive once again at dawn's light as the guardians of Neverland prepared themselves to embark on the journey ahead. The braves and the lost boys saddled up their horses. Tiger Lily fastened her bow and quiver to Fleur, who whinnied at her touch, for she loved going on adventures.

Across the way, Peter rubbed Solomon's horns as he often did when he was warming him up for an adventure. He wore only reins, and no saddle, for Peter was so light due to his gift of flight, and his balance was so perfected, that a saddle wasn't necessary.

"You ready boy?" Peter whispered into one of Solomon's long ears, and he nodded and bucked his head in anticipation.

Peter looked down, and in his hand he held the Dagger of Truth — this was the same dagger that he used to slay Captain Hook over one hundred years ago, and to the pirates throughout the worlds it was known as Captain Hook's Bane — Peter flipped it easily around in his hand, for it was an extension of him, an old friend.

“I haven’t seen that for a while,” Tiger Lily said as she came up behind him, rubbing Solomon’s ears.

Peter locked eyes with her, and a knowingness passed between them, for during this age of peace, it had been some time since he had needed to arm himself. Fleur then whinnied in Solomon’s direction, and Solomon bucked his head in return. Peter and Tiger Lily shared a smile… their animals liked each other.

“Peter, you seen Tink?” Curly said, running up to him. “I need her help with rewiring this fairy bomb.”

Peter looked around — where was Tink?

Tinker Bell sat on the edge of her cot in the morning light, dressed for her next adventure in a style true to her fashion, except her traditional outfit was made of magic-infused, green fairy cloth, offering her extra protection from the elements. On her feet she wore brown leather fairy boots, and her golden hair was spun up on her head to keep it out of the way. Her hiking pack and provisions for the journey lay next to her, and in her hand she held a little vial of her golden neverbrew potion. She sat staring at it, contemplating.

“Hey, Tink,” Peter said, announcing himself, and Tink hid the vial behind her back as he peered through the entrance. “You ready?”

“Yes,” Tinker Bell confirmed. “Just one minute.”

Peter considered leaving for a moment, then slipped inside. "Hey, I wanted to say thanks again for coming on this adventure with me… it means a lot… I wouldn't feel safe without you."

"Yes, Peter, of course," Tink said, appeasing him, for she was not used to this level of vulnerability from him, and although she liked it, she wasn't quite sure of what to do — which was a rare occurrence for a fairy that valued being in control — their eyes met, and a moment passed between them…

"All right, well, hurry," Peter said sternly in an attempt to recover, for he felt softened by the interaction, and he didn't consider it to be a beneficial frame of mind to embark on an adventure in. "You know how Solomon gets if he has to stand still for too long."

They shared a forced laugh. "I'll be right out," Tink said, then Peter darted back out into the camp.

Tink took a moment, then pulled her hand from behind her back, and once again looked down at the little vial of neverbrew in her hand. Her beautiful smile fell from her face as she looked down at what she had done — how could something so miraculous, cause so much pain? — she didn't like counting on her own potion to be happy, but right now this was the only way… she put the vial to her lips, and took a full dose…

The small party were saddled up and preparing for embarkment. Tinker Bell had joined them, and mounted Ruby, her beautiful, white, unicorn pony. Ruby was an eternal creature, and she had journeyed through the many worlds long before the fairies came to the shores of Neverland. She was currently the only unicorn residing in this world, and she was attracted to Tinker Bell because of her purity of heart, grace, and natural love for all things living, to which Ruby represented in its highest form — they made ideal companions.

Mr. Theodore approached and stroked Ruby's mane. "I haven't seen this beauty for a while…" Ruby nodded and nuzzled him. "It's good to see you too, Ruby," he laughed.

"You sure you won't come with us, Mr. Theodore?" Tinker Bell asked.

"Pirates and mountain witches are a young fairy's game," Mr. Theodore admitted. "My place is with the mine."

"But they killed all those innocent fairies," Tinker Bell argued. "Your friends…"

"They did," he agreed without resistance.

"Doesn't that make you… you know… *angry*?" Tinker Bell said, trying to make logic of it.

"Death is a natural part of life, Tinker Bell," Mr. Theodore said, speaking of what he knew to be true. "Anger — or worse, revenge — won't serve me at this age. Acceptance is the true soil in which new life grows."

Tink nodded, trying and wanting to understand, but she could not reason how such a powerful and wise fairy could allow such events to go unjustified. Mr. Theodore chuckled, for he saw a bit of himself in the young, talented fairy, and knew that she would understand in her own time.

"Watch over him," he said, nodding towards Peter. "He needs you now more than you could ever know."

Tink nodded at the words, and although she liked the idea of Peter needing her, she felt as if a great weight was suddenly thrust upon her shoulders. Mr. Theodore conjured an apple out of thin air, fed it to Ruby, then turned to go.

"Mr. Theodore," Tinker Bell said, stopping him. "How did you escape the mine?"

Mr. Theodore turned around, locked eyes with the young fairy, and after a moment, a slight smile spread across his countenance. "You're not the only one that knows a thing or two about fairy dust," he said, then he winked at Tinker Bell and disappeared into the crowd.

***

The chief and the other villagers watched as the small party left for the mountains. Peter led the group on Solomon, followed by Tiger Lily on Fleur and Tinker Bell on Ruby on either side of him. Nibs, Curly, Slightly, Tootles, and the Twins fell behind Tinker Bell on horseback, and Charlie, Marco, and Pax fell behind Tiger Lily in similar fashion. The distinction between the two groups was tangible, and it was clear to which side each of their allegiances was on.

As the group disappeared down the cape in the growing morning sunlight, the chief held his breath. “Blessings, Great White Father,” he spoke into the air, for the anguish he felt could be hidden no longer. “Please… look after my daughter.” Then the chief fell silent, and looked up at the sky, and the entire village followed his movement… and it was there… at the end of his village… on the shores of the Great Western Ocean… that he knew the world would never be the same…

The villagers then began to sing a song in unison…

“Fair winds, dear Princess, fair winds, unto thee. May the winds be forever at your back, and the sun shine upon thee... may the Great White Father protect you, both above, and below... may the cool waters guide you, forever, in its flow... fair winds, dear Princess... fair winds unto thee...”

Then the chief smiled with joy at the sun, and tears poured down his face, and he knew that no matter what darkness was to come, his daughter, the jewel of his very life, would be protected.

He then bid them a final farewell, and turned back towards his village.

***

The brilliant sun was just breaking through the cool mist that sat upon the sands of Big Sky Beach as the party rode easily down the majestic shoreline of the Western Cape on the first leg of their adventure, for they had just embarked, and were in good spirits, and had not crossed anything that could be considered challenging yet.

The lost boys cracked jokes to entertain themselves — as they often did to pass the time — and the braves scowled at their lack of restraint, opting for silence as the way of the warrior. Peter paid them no attention, for his mind was fixed ahead, and very much focused on what was to come.

Unlike Peter, the lost boys and the braves had no deadly mountain witches waiting for them — at least none that they were destined to face — so they had the luxury of relaxing. On a lesser adventure, Peter might have joined in their fun, but not this adventure, not this time. Both Tinker Bell and Tiger Lily's intuition picked up on Peter's seriousness, and they mimicked his pointed focus, and their animal companions — Solomon, Fleur, and Ruby — seemed to as well.

By late morning, when the sun was overhead, they came to the edge of the beautiful Honeycomb Forest — a heavily wooded patch of land that lay between the Piccaninny territories of the Western Cape and the waters of Cannibal Cove — where the base of the ravine going up into the mountains of Crocodile Crack was located. It got its name because its geographical location in Neverland made it ideal for beehives, and the sweet smell of honeycomb attracted bears from around the island to feast on the delicacy. It was an enchanted place, and full of magic.

Solomon bucked as they approached the woods, sensing the change of smell, energy, and light.

"Steady boy… this is the way," Peter said, reassuring him as he rubbed his ears, and Solomon moved forward strongly into the forest…

The party rode through the realm, following a rocky but clear-cut path. The trees stood large and majestic, and were so thick at their top that they fashioned a canopy for those below, creating a feeling of eternity between them, for indeed, they were eternal, and had stood for much longer than any of its inhabitants who had lived among them.

Peter played his pan pipes, which he often liked to do on adventures, for the melody serenaded Solomon and the other nearby animals. It was the sound of good fortune, and a tune picked up from the fairy parties he used to attend during his first years in Neverland. It reminded them all of the Fairy Quarters, of Pixie's Landing and Hangman's Tree, and all that they held dear… it reminded them of what it was that they were fighting for…

"Say, what's that?" Curly asked the lost boys as he heard Peter's melody reverberate through the trees, only to be echoed back by foreign, hidden instruments that sounded just as sweet.

"It's the fairies," Tootles answered with a serenaded smile on his face. "We've entered the Wood Fairy Realm."

"Fairies?" Curly asked, confused. "In the Forest?"

"Not all fairies are domesticated, Curly," Tootles scoffed. "Surely you don't think that all fairies live in Pixie's Landing."

"No," Curly backtracked clumsily. "I know fairies live in Pixie Hollow as well."

"If Curly had it his way," Nibs teased. "All the fairies would look like Violet and walk around wearing corsets."

"She didn't seem to mind wearing one last night, mate," Curly retaliated.

"Oy! Those are fighting words!" Nibs screamed, ready to tackle Curly off his horse.

"Shh! Keep it down you two," Tootles commanded. "You'll disturb the fairies…"

The boys fell silent as the melody continued. Nibs scowled as Curly bit into an apple, pleased with himself. Tiger Lily and Tinker Bell continued to show signs of annoyance at each other's presence, and likewise, Fleur and Ruby didn't care much for each other either, picking up on their owner's energies. However, it wasn't just Ruby and Fleur that picked up on the strong wafts of dislike coming off the two women, for the tension was palpable, and it could be felt all the way down the line — even Peter felt it from the front — he looked back and saw the growing agitation between the two girls, and shook his head.

"Women," he whispered into Solomon's ear, and the great billy goat bucked his head up and down in agreement, having similar feelings towards Fleur and Ruby as Peter had towards Tinker Bell and Tiger Lily…

As they reached the south eastern end of the Wood Fairy Realm, the spacious and roomy shrubbery of the forest floor became increasingly dense as they entered the borders of the Lonely Jungle, and their path was no longer so clear cut. The jungle got its name because it was so dense that few ever dared to venture through it — hence it was lonely — but it was the only way by foot to Finder's Bluff, and the beginning of the trail that went along the shoreline of Cannibal Cove that would eventually take them to Crocodile Crack.

The jungle was a slow crawl. They were working twice as hard, and moving forward at half the pace, fighting for every inch of ground they gained. At the lead, Solomon was becoming increasingly agitated as the jungle underbrush and vines wrapped around his hooves, slowing his movement, and he stabbed at them with his horns.

"Easy boy," Peter said as he floated above him, slashing at vines with his dagger to clear a path for the others. "Let's keep it moving... slow and steady." Although Peter's words were intended to soothe Solomon and the others, he never appreciated his gift of flight more than he did then, for what would now take them days he could have done in hours, and avoided the perils and toils of the jungle completely. He knew of no clear path through the jungle, for he never had any reason to take one, and no sane person would enter the Lonely Jungle willingly. Nonetheless, he needed the others to face whatever challenges lay ahead.

Peter had done much planning all night, and he came to the conclusion that this was the best route for them to get to the mouth of Crocodile Crack by land under the current circumstances. Typically, they'd launch several canoes from Spirit Cove and hug the shoreline of the Western Cape until they reached Arrow Point. Then, they'd take the South Channel down the Southern Neverland shoreline until they reached the Southern Point, which opened into the mouth of Cannibal Cove, and skip the toils of the Lonely Jungle all together — this was the ideal method — but with pirate ships in the water, and their firing power, this was much too risky, for one well-placed cannon could end their party all together, and that was not an option.

There were no better-known routes by land either. The Windy Mountains were impenetrable from the western, northern, and eastern sides, and it wasn't favorable to transverse the northern side of the Wood Fairy Realm to the Blackwater Cliffs, as the jagged mountain terrain in that area combined with the dense shrubbery made it treacherous for climbing, and they were better off faring the dense vines of the jungle floor to keep their ankles on even ground.

The only other way to reach Crocodile Crack by foot would be to take the party all the way back up the Western Trail, east across the vast expanse of the Great Plains, and back down the Eastern Trail through Neverland City — which alone would take days — then brave the infinite dangers of the Neverending Jungle, and then, if they made it through that alive, they'd have to come up the eastern shore of Cannibal Cove, and brave the Wiley Quicksands of Pirate Eater Beach, which made even less sense than the rest of it. No, the route Peter was taking them was the only way. He was sure of it.

Towards the back, the lost boys and the braves trod through the thick brush in misery, cursing the ferns and vines, surveying the shadows and slashing at anything that moved. Suddenly, a big spider the size of a glove dropped out of the tree on Marco's head. Marco jumped and screamed, sending all the lost boys into a fit of uproarious laughter. The spider then fell to the floor, and scurried into the underbrush.

Frazzled and embarrassed, Marco jeered at all of them, for he truly hated the lost boys — every single one of them — and if he had it his way he would kill them all now, for it was truly the perfect spot, here, deep in the jungle where nobody could hear them scream. If it wasn't for the Great White Father and his fairy puppet he would surely act now, but he wasn't a fool — deadly and cunning, yes, but no fool — and although he believed he could take the other lost boys by himself if given the chance, he knew that the flying boy was his superior, especially with the aid of his fairy, who's magic gave her mysterious skills in battle that he could not begin to calculate. Indeed, now was not the time to strike… not yet… but soon… soon they'd all get what was coming for them…

Biting his tongue, Marco pointed his machete at Nibs, staring him down. Nibs returned the gesture by opening up his shirt and exposing his chest where the blade might strike true, showing no fear.

“Anytime.” Nibs mouthed silently, and Marco jeered at him in hatred.

As the sun began to set on the horizon, the party finally arrived at Finder’s Bluff — a sheer cliff overlooking the powerful white caps of Cannibal Cove that crested and broke in the evening sunlight — deep out in its shimmering waters they saw three ships… and black flags…

They all sat still, speechless for a moment at the sight, for it had been over one hundred years since any of them had seen a black flag in Neverland, and the day had come too soon.

“I thought I’d never live to see the day,” Tootles said after some time, awed by the sight, and Tinker Bell felt a shiver run through the core of her body.

Sensing her fear, Charlie rode up behind Tinker Bell on his horse. “It’s never too late to go back to your bar, little fairy,” he said, antagonizing her. “Yah!” He then yanked his reins and rode forward up the bluff.

Tiger Lily then filled Charlie’s place on Fleur, and smiled at Tink, taunting her before following Charlie up the bluff, for in her mind Charlie was right — now was not the time for fear — and if the fairy was going to let a few black flags defeat her spirit, then she should have stayed in the bar where she belonged, and let her look after Peter herself. As far as Tiger Lily was concerned the group didn't need Tinker Bell, or her magic, and to Tiger Lily even the thought of her around was dead weight.

Tinker Bell squinted her eyes in dislike as Tiger Lily followed Charlie up the cliff. "Don't listen to them, Ruby… they're stupid," Tinker Bell whispered in her unicorn's ear, and Ruby huffed in agreement.

"Come on, girl… we'll show 'em." Then Tinker Bell flicked Ruby's reins and followed the others up the steep terrain, doing her best to banish the black sails from her mind… but she couldn't… for she had seen them now… and she had a feeling they were here to stay…

***

The party continued around the ridge of Cannibal Cove, traversing the jagged walls of the Blackwater Cliffs in the evening light as Neverland's sun dipped into the ocean. The cliffs were steep and difficult, carved out by centuries of the sea beating against it, and the walls had become strong to contain such power. Other than Peter and Tinker Bell, the riders had to watch their step as they traversed the wall, for one small slip would mean certain death for them and their steeds. Being a billy goat, Solomon had the least trouble with the terrain, and leapt up the jagged rocks with little effort. Ruby, being naturally light and experienced as well, also found little trouble. The horses, however, including Fleur, found it more difficult as their hooves slipped and slid on the weather hardened rocks, but they managed, and thankfully for their riders they were the best stock in Neverland.

It was night by the time they finally reached the welcoming sands of Big Swell Beach, and they all breathed easier for having finally gotten through the cliffs before dark. They walked along the beach for some time until they reached the western shores of the Great River Basin, a large body of water that flowed down from the mountains into the northern inlet of Cannibal Cove. The river was about a quarter of a mile wide, and they would have to get across its powerful current in order to reach the ravine that would take them up into the mountains. Although Peter didn't like the idea of making camp with pirates around, it would not be safe for the others to cross the treacherous river at night, especially since one false move could send them head over heels down Breakneck Falls. With that in mind, he figured waiting until sunrise posed less risk. Pirates tended to stay clear of the river because they couldn't hear over the sound of the roaring waters, and it was too open.

Although Peter didn't fully realize the extent to which the knowledge of his existence kept pirates awake in the night, he was not entirely unaware of the psychological effect he had upon their lot. He was aware — to some extent — that they greatly feared him. One of their worst terrors was that he would fly down in the middle of the night with the fairies and kill them all in their sleep, and because of this they tended to choose encampments that were quiet and well covered. What Peter didn't know is that pirates even did their best to camp like this on earth and other worlds beyond

Neverland, as the terrifying tales of him traveled that far. This was, of course, exaggerated, and to attack a pirate encampment randomly without scouting beforehand posed a great danger to himself or any other physical, flying beings, for it only took one well-placed or randomly scattered bullet to strike true and end a life, and that had to be avoided at all costs.

The pirates didn't need to know that, of course. The more they feared him and the fairies the better as far as Peter was concerned, and tonight of all nights it was particularly working in their favor. They had come far, and traversed the entire western arm of Southern Neverland in a single day — not bad for a group of land bound beings — and although none claimed to be tired, Peter knew this to be only their adrenaline talking, and a decent night's rest would be essential for what was to come.

"We'll make camp here in the basin," Peter told the group. "Nibs, you and I have first watch. The others, try to sleep. No fires tonight. We break camp at dawn."

As the lost boys gratefully threw down their mats, Tiger Lily made Marco and Pax set up her teepee, for whether they were on an adventure or not, she was still a princess, and she had certain standards that had to be met. Marco scowled at the order, but Pax was surprisingly cheerful about it, for he felt a great pride in serving his tribe's royalty.

Pax always liked Tiger Lily, for she was nice to him, perhaps simply because she didn't go out of her way to mean to him like the other maidens did, for he was not blessed with the gift of words, and because of this impediment and his larger physique they often took him for a simpleton, but Pax was smarter than he looked or let on, and Tiger Lily of all people knew it. She knew that he would not be Charlie's number two if he was slow in the mind — even if he looked it — and if anything it gave him the ability to remain unnoticed to those that did not believe he had the intellect to follow their conversations, but he did, and he was always watching and listening.

While Marco and Pax toiled to set up Tiger Lily's tent in the dark, Tinker Bell came over so that she was near enough to be seen. She reached into her satchel, pulled out a little, golden ball, and inspected it in front of her. Once she knew Tiger Lily's eyes were on her, she threw the ball on the ground in front of her, which blossomed into a perfectly-formed fairy tent before their eyes. Marco scowled and Pax stared in awe at the sight, while Tiger Lily's eyes narrowed with agitation, for she knew exactly what the fairy was doing. Satisfied, Tinker Bell smiled and lifted her head, sticking up her nose a bit at all three of them, and disappeared inside.

As Peter and Nibs went to take their watch positions around the encampment, Charlie shot off into the dark.

"Oy!" Nibs yelled after him. "Peter said to make camp!"

"Let him go," Peter said, accepting Charlie's disobedience. "He will not sleep tonight."

"What do you mean?" Nibs asked, confused.

"He's the lead brave," Peter continued with understanding. "He will not sleep any more than I will." Peter meant what he said, for it was the first night of their adventure and pirates were already on their shores. As the leader of the group — not to mention Neverland's first guardian — he could not justify shutting a single eyelid with all his friends' lives on his shoulders… and without knowing exactly how he was aware of it… he knew that Charlie felt the same as him…

"Why are you doing that?" Nibs snapped, challenging Peter's decision.

Peter didn't answer, just turned his head towards Nibs, and squinted his eyes, as if admitting that he knew Nibs was on to something, but wasn't yet convinced and needed to hear more.

Nibs then got the familiar feeling that Peter was burrowing into his soul to see if he'd back down. It was quite unnerving to those being looked at this way, for when Peter stared at a person, but didn't speak, there was a fierceness in his countenance that could strike fear into the observed like a Lion staring down its prey, and whether Peter was aware of it or not, he often and subconsciously used this ability to his advantage. Nibs didn't judge him too much for this, for he realized that Peter's fierceness was the flip side of his greatness — the dark side that came with the territory of being who he was — and considering what he had to go through to attain his power, Nibs thought Peter managed it well. The alternative was too horrible to fathom, and the lost boys all knew that if Peter ever gave in completely to his darker nature, that would be the end of them all, and worse, the end of all things good in Neverland, so they never saw any reason to speak of it, simply because there was little they could do about it either way.

Ultimately, Nibs and the others rationalized that the Great Spirit had brought Peter to Neverland to liberate and protect it, and his reign would continue on forever, or that would be the end of life as they knew it. Nibs was a friend to Peter, and friend he would be for all time, and although he knew the ins and outs of all Peter's tricks better than just about anyone — say for maybe Tinker Bell — it didn't necessarily make it any easier to be looked at by Peter in the way that he was looking at him now, and he knew for a fact that the only way to gain Peter's respect was to challenge the lion back like few ever dared to do.

"Why are you doing that?" Nibs repeated boldly. "Letting him off the hook like that?"

"You don't like him," Peter stated, looking for the catalyst of the disagreement.

"No!" Nibs exclaimed in a harsh whisper directed only at Peter. "They're wicked. You give them an inch, you might as well let them strangle us in our sleep."

"I don't know about the other two," Peter admitted, "but Charlie I find myself trusting."

"There's no reason to trust him," Nibs disagreed. "He's their leader. The other two wouldn't be as rotten as they are if he wasn't bad as well."

Peter thought about Nibs' statement for a moment, and although he saw no reason to panic, there was truth to it. "You're right, Nibs," Peter agreed. "I'll keep a better eye on Charlie and the others — you continue to do so as well — but tonight, my decision is final. We'll see how tomorrow goes."

Nibs nodded in agreement, grateful that Peter heard him, and he felt proud that he helped Peter see what he considered to be extremely important information.

"It's good to have you out here with me," Peter said, placing a hand on his shoulder. "At night's darkest, go wake Slightly and have him take your place. If you need me, you know the whistle."

Before Nibs could say "Ay, ay, Captain," Peter leapt into the air and disappeared into the dark above, leaving Nibs feeling quite pleased with himself on the ground. Empowered, he leaned against a nearby boulder, and let his mind relax to the rushing currents of the Great River…

Peter flew up high in the sky and flew back and forth as fast as he could a few times, for being with the others he had not flown much all day — in fact, it was the least he had flown in a single day since as far back as he could remember — and he needed to stretch his flying muscles.

When he was finished, he flew back down towards their camp at the west end of the Great River Basin, and perched in a tree like some great falcon of the night, watching over all things moving below. Like the fairies, Peter had incredibly acute night vision, and his already impressive senses were heightened even further once the sun went down. He could feel Tiger Lily and Tinker Bell asleep in their tents, and he could see the lost boys and Marco and Pax lying on their mats, attempting to get rest. He saw Nibs leaned up against the boulder, slipping in and out of sleep, and Peter thought it all right if Nibs dozed off a bit, for the others had him to count on, and he would stay vigilant for their peace.

Then, some movement caught his eye. He peered down, and on the edge of the camp, next to a thicket of river bushes, there was the shape of a man. He peered further still into the dark and saw that it was Charlie. He was sitting in a meditative posture and silently chanting a spirit song over the sleeping party. Peter knew that song, for it was one Tiger Lily used to sing to him on nights when he was having bad dreams, and it was visceral to him.

"Surely, Charlie couldn't be so bad," Peter thought to himself. "To stay up all night, singing such a song..."

Then Peter thought of Tiger Lily, and how much he missed her touch. He thought that he might go to her now, while she was sleeping, and they could make up. They could say all the things they wanted to say to each other with their bodies that they were not able to say with their words during that day… yes, that would be great… to fly down now… and tell her how much he loved her…

But no, he then thought better of it, for now was not the time for weakness, and surely they could abstain from their passions until the end of this adventure… that was, if they ever came back… victory… victory was the only option to be with her again… and it was forward unto victory that he would lead them…

Peter made his final decision, and tonight, he would rest only in his imagination… so he leaned back against the tree and looked up at the sky until his thoughts floated away…

* CHAPTER 8 *

— Crocodile Crack —

True to his word, Peter flew down at dawn's first light and woke the others to break camp. The lost boys grumbled as they always did upon waking, and roused themselves from their slumber as Slightly walked back, somewhat sleep deprived, from his nightly watch. Marco and Pax awoke silently without a word as Charlie joined them, for they did not believe in speaking in the morning, as it was time for silence and for the steady waking up of the mind. Such was the way of the brave.

Tinker Bell and Tiger Lily came out of their tents dressed and ready to go. Tinker Bell's tent condensed back into a golden orb even faster than it expanded, floated up to her, and landed easily in her satchel. Marco scowled at the fairy's technology, then he and Pax began the arduous task of breaking down Tiger Lily's lavish tent.

"It makes no sense to have such a large tent on a journey like this," Marco grumbled to Pax. "It's dead weight for the rest of us to carry."

"You were saying something?"

Marco spun around to see Tiger Lily, bright, armed, and ready for the day, staring back at him.

"Uh, Princess," Marco stuttered. "I was just saying you have quite the tent here, that's all."

"Mmhmm, I do," Tiger Lily agreed. "And seeing how you care so much about it, you'll pack the whole thing on your horse today."

Marco stared at her in shock, taking great care to hide his distaste.

"Is there a problem, Marco?" Tiger Lily said sweetly.

"Nah, no problem, Princess," Marco conceded. "It will go on my horse, per your orders."

"Thank you," Tiger Lily said, then she walked off to see Fleur, and Marco's fake smile fell into a scowl as he continued to break down the tent.

Once the camp was packed up and all were back on their steeds, they approached the edge of the Great River for the inevitable crossing. Peter turned to face the group. He was not concerned about himself, Tinker Bell, or, Tiger Lily, for they could all fly over, and their animals were all gifted with great or magical strength. The lost boys had also crossed the river many times before and would manage all right… it was the braves that he saw as having the real challenge here with the sheer amount of weight they were carrying.

"The current is strong!" Peter yelled back at the group as loud as he could, barely audible over the roaring waters. "Be sure to lean into it!"

"Don't worry about us, fairy boy!" Marco yelled excitedly from the back. "Have fun flying over!" Then Marco waved at Peter enthusiastically like a little girl. Pax grunted in laughter.

"Fool," Charlie said under his breath. "Don't antagonize him." At the command of his leader, Marco fell silent.

Peter wasn't sure what all the commotion in the back was about, or why Marco was jumping up and down like a gitty fairy, so he shrugged it off. He then swooped up Tiger Lily in his arms, and began to cross, pulling Solomon behind him who handled the waters quite easily, in fact, he seemed to relish in it. Fleur also followed along in Solomon's wake quite proficiently, and although it wasn't as easy for her as it was for him, she didn't find it too challenging, especially with Peter carrying Tiger Lily for her.

Tiger Lily leaned silently against Peter as he carried her in his arms, and she also liked that she knew Tinker Bell was watching, but that wasn't all too important now. For a moment, she felt like saying something lovely in his ear, for they were alone, and nobody would be able to hear them over the roaring sounds of the river, but she didn't need to, for a knowledge passed between their bodies that was beyond words — a knowledge that came with over a century of kisses, passion, drama, fighting, making up, and romance — and whether they liked it or not, they were both completely in tune with each other. For better or for worse, there was no hiding their true feelings, and she had to give Peter the mental space he needed to focus and lead them into the unknown. She kissed his neck, then she leaned her head against his shoulder and closed her eyes, enjoying the serenity of the sounds of rushing water in her lover's strong arms… she didn't need to remind him what he was missing… she could feel from the heat in his body that he knew already…

As Peter and Tiger Lily easily crossed the river, Tink and the lost boys relaxed on the shore of the basin, relishing the moment they knew was to come…

"Aren't you going to go!" Marco jeered, for the tension of crossing was getting to him, and he couldn't stand it anymore.

"After you," Nibs said coolly, and the other boys smiled knowingly.

The six boyish smiles of the lost boys staring at him in the face of such impending danger pushed Marco over the edge. "You're all mad!" Marco screamed. "To hell with you all!"

"YAH!" Charlie yelled as he pulled tightly on his reins.

"YAH!" Marco and Pax yelled behind him, and together all three of them rushed towards the Great River…

Their horses entered with a powerful splash and were immediately met with the powerful force of the current. Charlie surged ahead with a warrior's furiosity, and Pax's natural strength aided him in holding steadfast against the pounding water. Marco, being skinny and suffering from malnutrition — mainly from his excessive tobacco use, which even the chief told him he needed to cut back on — was knocked off his horse immediately, to which he had to grab a fistful of mane in order to hold on. The lost boys all laughed hysterically from the shore.

"Curse you! All of you!" Marco screamed as he managed to flail back on to his horse. "You're all gonna pay!" Marco then continued forward against the current, but the lost boys couldn't stop laughing.

Tinker Bell and the lost boys waited for another few minutes until the braves were halfway across, then Tinker Bell yawned and stood up. "You ready, boys?"

"Ready when you are, Tink," Curly said from his lounged position on the shore, and the others nodded.

"Let's get to it, then," Tinker Bell said, and with that she jumped on Ruby and trotted her down the sands of the basin towards the river, and the lost boys followed on their steeds.

Without the slightest hesitation, Ruby approached the Great River and set out upon it, but she didn't sink down into the water, but rather, she hovered above it, walking across it as if it was solid. The lost boys followed on their steeds behind Ruby, and their horses were given the same privileges, safely protected from the roaring waters below.

Charlie, Pax, and Marco continued to struggle against the current, cursing and sputtering as they barely avoided being swallowed up altogether, then suddenly, shadows passed them, blocking the sun from their faces. They all looked up to see Tinker Bell on Ruby, walking on water, followed by the others who were all doing the same. The braves stared in awe of the group as they easily floated past them.

"Fairy dust, mate." Curly winked at Charlie, who scowled and plunged forward with even greater ferocity.

"Curse you! All of you!" Marco screamed from the back as he took on loads of water to his mouth and eyes. "I'll string you all up like wild dogs!"

Up ahead, Peter and Tiger Lily were nearly to the other side, taking their time as Peter gently led their animals from the air. Suddenly, Tiger Lily felt a shadow pass by the sun, she turned around to see Tinker Bell easily floating across the water on Ruby, followed by the lost boys on their horses. Tiger Lily's eyes narrowed as Tink and the boys quickly pulled ahead, reaching the other side before them, for she knew that Tinker Bell purposely chose not to share her magic with her, and Fleur also neighed as the other horses passed, feeling similar to her master about the situation.

Up ahead, Tink smiled, satisfied, then stroked Ruby's mane. "Good job, girl," she whispered in her ear, and Ruby whinnied in agreement.

Peter and Solomon didn't seem to mind, and remained more or less unaware of the girl's petty competition. Peter kept leading Solomon and Fleur until they reached the shoreline to join the others.

Charlie, Pax, and Marco were about three-quarters across, when suddenly, from the back, Marco shrieked for dear life! The strength of the current had overpowered him at last, knocking him off his horse, and he was headed right towards Breakneck Falls! For a moment, Charlie and Pax considered going after him, but they knew to do so would be certain death. They were helpless.

From the shore on the east side of the basin, Peter, Tinker Bell, and the lost boys showed little concern, and seemed to revel at Marco's momentary helplessness.

"All right, boys, you've had your fun," Tiger Lily scolded. "Peter, let's go."

Peter turned to Tinker Bell. "You want this one?" He asked, hopefully.

"I'm not touching him," Tink said with distaste, putting her hands in the air.

"Fine," Peter groaned, and with that, he leapt up in the air and rocketed towards Marco. Within moments, he reached the helpless brave flailing in the water. Peter easily floated above him as he held out his hand. "Take my hand," Peter said, impartial as the brave floated nearer and nearer towards certain death.

"Never!" Marco screamed through mouthfuls of water.

"Come on," Peter said, urging him to be practical. "You're no use to anyone at the bottom of Cannibal Cove."

"Screw you!" Marco screamed.

"Suit yourself," Peter said easily, and with that he flew back up into the sky.

When Marco saw the Great White Father flying away from him, he panicked. "Wait!" Marco screamed as he neared the edge of the deadly waterfall. “Come back!” He screamed again, and with that, he plummeted over the edge. “Save me!”

Peter waited from above, watching the screaming brave plummet to his death in a free fall. He didn’t want to let him off the hook easily, and he felt if there was a lesson that could be learned here, then he should learn it, for Marco’s loud mouth and current attitude were detrimental to the group’s goals and morale…

When Marco was about halfway down the falls, Peter rocketed back towards him, and held out an arm, to which Marco gratefully took this time. Marco latched on moments from the jagged rocks of Cannibal Cove below, and Peter shot back up into the air, saving him from his death. Shocked and breathless, Marco hung from Peter in the air until he dropped him on the shoreline with the others.

“Nobody say anything,” Peter commanded the group, for he knew Marco’s pride had already been wounded enough, and they needed to get refocused on what was to come. “Let’s keep it moving.”

Upon landing, Marco didn’t speak, for his pride was greatly wounded, and he burned inside with resentment. He hated the lost boys, and their jokes, and their smiling faces. He hated Tinker Bell, and her tricks, and her magical white pony, but most of all, he hated Peter Pan.

“Shake it off,” Charlie said, smacking him on the back. “You’re lucky to be alive. It will do you good to remember it.”

Marco hated that Charlie was right. The Great White Father should have just let him die on the rocks, then he wouldn't have to feel the humiliation he felt right now, for it was worse than death to him.

"They'll all pay," Marco mumbled to himself. "Every single one of them will know an agony worse than the greatest suffering… soon… they'll all pay." Then the resentful brave bit his tongue, and carried on behind the others…

***

The base of Crocodile Crack was just a few miles past the Great River, and the party reached it well before mid-day. Legend had it that a giant crocodile used to live within the canyon during the early days of Neverland — hence its name — a crocodile so enormous that it made the one that relentlessly hunted Captain Hook during his years in Neverland that Peter eventually slayed in the Southern Sea look like a guppy fish, but it was only legend, and whatever became of that ancient crocodile was still unknown.

As they all stood below, gaping up at what was literally a giant crack in the face of a sheer mountainside, they searched the sky for its peak as it loomed dark and ominous above them, and everyone — even Peter to an extent — found themselves unnerved by it. In truth, there was a reason Peter preferred to fly around it and stay clear, for he rarely did anything without purpose. He knew that along with great light, there was a dark side to Neverland that few liked to speak about — a dark side that lay dormant — but it was there, ingrained into the foundations of their world, shadowed and waiting for the guardians to turn a blind eye, and only a fool would deny its existence…

He knew the legends, and he knew the stories of what the fairies went through to claim the world, and he believed all of it. This knowledge he carried so that others didn't have to, so that others could live free, but he made it a point to not seek out Neverland's darkest secrets willingly, as to not be tempted by them, for he had lived long enough to know that whatever he saw and experienced in his mind he could not easily forget, and he took great care to fill his thoughts with as much light as possible, for that is how he preferred to rule… alive and unrestrained… completely free and devoid of fear…

Peter looked up at the crack, and for the first time in a long while he felt it — fear — just a hint of it, and it had been well over a hundred years now since he had felt even the slightest sliver of it. To his previous delight he almost forgot that it was even a feeling all together, but it was back now, and it rose up in him like an old enemy that had been lying and waiting in the shadows to take him when he passed by. Peter gazed even higher up at Crocodile Crack looming above them, and he knew that this crack was the entrance to many unknowns, many mysteries of Neverland, and it was not a place he would lead his friends willingly if given the choice. He also felt, strangely, as if he was being watched by it.

He turned around to face the group, and they all looked at him, knowing and supportive, for although they could never truly know what he was going through as a spirit, they felt all the empathy there was to feel in the present moment, and their imaginations could relate to him.

Peter looked at Tiger Lily, as beautiful as the morning sun, and she looked back at him with big brown eyes of pure trust. Tinker Bell smiled at him, and he knew she loved him, for her heart was akin to his own. The boys were all there as well, armed and at the ready. Even the braves stood silently, and for the first time, Peter felt as if he had their support.

"We're with you to the end, mate," Nibs said after a moment.

Peter nodded his gratitude towards his friends, then he turned once more to face the path through the mountain. He knew in his mind that the fear would do him no good now, for he had learned over the last century the importance of getting ahead of these things — of seeing and acknowledging these imbalances and plucking them out by the root — so he filled his mind with happy thoughts — with thoughts of the Fairy Quarters, Pixie's Landing, Hangman's Tree, Tiger Lily, Tinker Bell, and all things good and bright — then he took a deep breath and gritted down on Solomon's reins, and plunged forward into the dark…

* CHAPTER 9 *

— The Battle at Gator Gorge —

As the sun began to make its decline on the horizon, the group slowly made their way up the treacherous ravine towards Gator Gorge. They would need to traverse it — along with the perilous No Man's Pass — to reach the Windy Mountains and the entrance to the Enchantress' Lair.

The thick, eerie fog made it difficult to see, but there was no mention of it ever being easy from onset, so they all took extra care to tread lightly. As they surveyed the outskirts for signs of movement, they were all armed and at the ready. Tiger Lily had an arrow knocked in her bow, which rested on her thigh as she rode Fleur, ready to be pulled and loosed at a moment's notice. Nibs, Curly, and Sightly all had old pirate swords they had plundered from the pirate battles of old, each one seized from a defeated enemy. The Twins both wielded customized sling-shots which they were quite efficient with, for they were both nimble and slight of stature, and they had proven to be quite deadly at short and long ranges alike. Tootles, however, preferred a war hammer to match his broader size, for he was not as swift as the others, and utilized strength over speed.

Charlie, Marco, and Pax all had tomahawks, each one custom for the fighter, with Charlie's being sharp and right sized, made from cherry wood, strong and efficient, just like himself. There was no doubt to any that it was a deadly weapon, and even deadlier in the hands of the skilled warrior that wielded it. Pax's tomahawk was made out of oak. It was big and heavy, and clearly intended to smash its opponents as much as it was meant to slice. Marco, however, had a sickly-looking tomahawk, for it was knotted, and stained with the blood of animals, and when he wielded it, it was clear that he not only liked it that way, but was also good with it.

The only ones in the group that didn't have their weapons at the ready were the two leading the group — Peter and Tink — their daggers still hung on their hips, for they were used to adventuring, and they both trusted their impulses completely. They would draw if needed, and not a moment sooner.

"I have a bad feeling about this," Curly said as the silence and fog continued to press in on them as they entered the gorge.

"Silence," Charlie whispered vehemently. "Do you want to die, boy?"

Peter lifted off the ground and floated out front, trying to get a vantage point through the fog, but it was no use, for it was too thick and his knowledge of the area too limited.

Suddenly, there was a snap through the haze. Peter's ears pricked up, and he held up his fist, motioning them all to stop behind him. The group froze as Peter listened to the air intently…

"You guys…" Curly whined after a moment.

"Quiet, Curly," Nibs commanded.

Peter didn't hear them, for his focus was complete. He put his hand to his ear, his hearing sharpening…

"Something's out there…" Curly continued.

Peter continued to listen to the air, then his eyes lit up with the thrill of what was coming...

Then — THWAP — there was a sound in the distance.

Peter reached out his hand, and with lightning quick reflexes he skillfully plucked something out of the air. He looked down through the fog at his hand… he was holding a dark and callous arrow!

"Wood goblins!" Peter announced, looking back at the group. "Down!"

Suddenly, the air was lit up by arrows that blanketed the sky and rained down on them like the waters of a flash flood. The group hit the deck, diving behind rocks as arrows ricocheted and sparked all around them. The arrows bounced easily off Solomon's thick billy goat skin and Ruby's magic shield like toothpicks, but the other horses whined and neighed, as they were caught helpless in the middle of the fray. Tink reached into her satchel and pulled out a small handful of fairy dust, then she threw it in the air above the other horses and it solidified, creating a temporary shelter that the arrows couldn't penetrate.

Out front, Peter stood on top of a boulder in the middle of the fray, paying no mind to the arrows that exploded all around him.

"Where are they?" Nibs screamed, his head spinning all around as if on a swivel.

"Wait for it…" Peter said calmly.

Tiger Lily approached behind Peter, an arrow nocked in her bow. Tink crouched behind them both and reached into her satchel, when she pulled out her hands, they glowed with golden energy that she used to shield herself from incoming fire.

"I can't see anything!" Tootles screamed.

"They're everywhere!' Yelled Curly.

"Wait for it…" Peter urged them, for he was totally calm — totally confident.

Charlie, Marco, and Pax crouched down in a fighting stance behind the rocks, tomahawks at the ready as they waited out the enemy fire.

Then, the goblin arrows stopped falling from above, and as quickly as it left there was silence again. Then…

THWAP — Tiger Lily loosed an arrow just as a sinister goblin jumped out of the fog from the ridge above. The arrow caught the goblin in midair, ending his actuality and sending his lifeless corpse to the ravine floor.

There was silence, then a growl that resounded from the fog all around them and above them. Then, the sound of bodies falling through the air as goblins began to jump out of the fog in a full-on attack!

"NOW!" Peter screamed as he threw his dagger with expert precision, sending it right into an oncoming goblin's chest. He then flew to meet the goblin in mid-air, pulled his dagger out, and sent the goblin plummeting to his death.

On the ground, Tiger Lily loosed arrows, shooting goblins out of the sky before they could even touch the ground. Tink fired charged, white-hot blasts of fairy magic from her hands, blasting goblins out of the air with ease. The Twins spun back-to-back, using each other's momentum to wind up their sling-shots in perfect unison, the stones from their weapons taking down goblins with perfect headshots.

Peter darted through the thick fog of the gorge with unprecedented ability. He caught goblin after goblin in mid-air as they rained down from the ridge above, quickly dispatching them with his dagger, and sending them plummeting to their deaths below — it was too easy — and he longed for a challenge, for it had been many years since he tasted a real battle, and now that it had been thrust upon him, he would find a way to enjoy it, and per usual, he would dominate.

The braves and the lost boys stood ready in the bottom of the gorge with their tomahawks and swords, for with the combined long-range skill of Peter, Tinker Bell, and Tiger Lily no enemies had been able to breach their party for hand-to-hand combat, but the fight was closing in upon them, and they knew it.

"We won't be able to hold them off for much longer," Tink yelled back at the boys.

"Let them come!" Charlie screamed, his eyes filling with the thrill of real blood lust, and together Charlie, Marco, and Pax let out a fierce war cry!

Roused by the braves, Nibs looked at his comrades with a real thrill in his eyes. "You ready boys?!" Nibs screamed, for with Peter in the air, he was their leader on the ground, and he would be the first to enter the fray.

"AYE!" The boys screamed in unison, and there was not an ounce of fear in any of them.

"Let's take 'em down!" Nibs screamed, and the boys all yelled a battle cry, then—

Steel clashed on steel as the goblins reached the bottom of the ravine, and the Battle of Gator Gorge had officially begun.

There was a guttural sound of grunting as Nibs and the others ran goblins through with their blades. Charlie ran through the battle with his tomahawk, fiercely and skillfully cutting down all foes in his path. Tootles destroyed enemies with his battle hammer using surprising agility. Slightly expertly parried and cut down an oncoming goblin with his sword, and nobody could have done it smoother.

"Say, how did you make that look so effortless, Slightly," Curly asked as he pushed a gutted goblin off his blade.

"Beats me," Slightly said as he expertly parried an incoming goblin and slashed him in the back. "I'm used to killing pirates."

"Good answer," Curly said, still a bit awe-struck at Slightly's finesse.

A small horde of ten goblins quickly attacked Slightly and Curly from all sides. Slightly parried two of them but was quickly overwhelmed by a third. Curly stabbed one through the gut as he was tackled from the side by another. Just as they were about to be overtaken, the Twins appeared out of the fog and nimbly glided through the battle. They spun around the goblins, sending headshots with their slingshots at a rapid pace, mowing down the other seven surrounding goblins. After they saved Slightly and Curly, they continued onward into the battle, disappearing back into the fog without a word.

"Long John's Leg! It's nice to have those guys around!" Curly exclaimed, shocked at their unbelievable skill.

"Do you still think they cheated you at cards?" Slightly teased.

Curly's smile fell flat. "Absolutely."

Across the gorge, Tinker Bell blasted two pursuing goblins down at close range, which fell at her feet as another goblin snuck up behind her. She didn't have time to spin around and fire another blast as the goblin leapt through the air right towards her. Using her intuition, she pulled out her dagger and ducked as the goblin struck, filleting the beast on its underbelly.

Tink looked up and another goblin was flying through the air right at her, sword raised, about to land a devastating blow. This time it was so close she didn't have time to react. She closed her eyes… this was it…

Suddenly, Ruby jumped over Tink. She caught the goblin in mid-air and impaled it on her horn, spilling its guts and effectively saving her.

"That's my girl," Tink said, smiling her gratitude.

Elsewhere in the battle, Tiger Lily was backed up against a large rock. She rapidly mowed down goblins faster than they could approach her with expert skill. From a distant vantage point, the goblin captain saw this. His bulbous and swollen eyes narrowed with hatred.

Peter flew through the battle, slashing, slicing, and dispatching enemies with ease and precision. Solomon ran alongside him, landing devastating blows with his horns to any goblins that were unfortunate enough to cross his path.

"Get 'em, boy," Peter encouraged. "I'll give you a carrot for every one you get past thirty."

Solomon bleated in joy, accepting the challenge, and continued to smash down the gorge, destroying everything in his path as Peter made a sharp veer up into the air.

Up above the battle, Peter floated surveying the carnage. First, he looked to find Tiger Lily, and spotted her up against a rock, mowing down enemies faster than they could approach her. He couldn't help but smile.

"That's my girl," he thought, then, his eyes went wide—

He saw the goblin captain appear on the rock above her. His sword was out, and Peter knew that he was about to jump down upon her while she wasn't looking and land a blow she wouldn't see coming. He looked back at Tiger Lily, and with her focus on the oncoming enemy, there was no way she had any idea she was about to be attacked from above. Peter rocketed through the air as fast as he could towards her…

At the rock, Tiger Lily loosed arrows faster than ever, cutting down the helpless foes like fodder. She smiled — this might as well be target practice — little did she know the peril lurking above her…

Up above, the goblin captain was ready to strike. He looked down at the oblivious princess below as one by one she cut down his soldiers. She thought she was so smart, so clever, so skillful, but soon, she would pay like the rest of them. He smiled, and raised his sword…

In the air, Peter flew as fast as he could, pushing his speed to the limit as he closed the gap between himself and Tiger Lily's assassin. He heard the goblin unleash a blood-thirsty war cry as he dropped through the air…

Tiger Lily looked up and saw her assassin falling towards her. She spun around and quickly knocked an arrow, pulling it back as fast as she could, but the goblin was too close — she wasn't going to have time to fire — he was already in the air, just fractions of a second from landing a death blow… this was it…

BAM! — Peter caught the assailant at mach speed just a foot before he would have crushed Tiger Lily. Her eyes went wide with shock and gratitude as Peter spun away from her with the attacker. Breath returned to her lungs as she watched them hurtle through the air…

Peter flew with intense speed, attempting to rid himself of the menacing goblin, but the captain had latched onto him with both arms. His grip was strong, and Peter could not yet find a way to shake him. The goblin pulled himself up so that he was face to face with his enemy.

"So this is the Great Pan," the goblin stated as blood and grime shot from his mouth.

"Nice to meet you." Peter cringed, recoiling from the stink.

As the goblin released an arm to take a swing, Peter used the wiggle room to do an aerial spin just as the captain threw a devastating punch, barely missing him. Peter kept spinning and the goblin kept swinging as they hurled through the air.

"Is that all you got?!" Peter said, posing a challenge.

Angered, the captain clenched down hard, pulled himself up Peter's body, and bit him on the neck. Peter let out a scream of pain! He couldn't move. The captain dug in and then put his mouth next to his ear.

"You and your friends will make a tasty meal for my soldiers," he gargled. "Especially the little princess and the fairy."

Peter's eyes lit up with rage as he suddenly got a burst of ethereal strength. He turned on the jets, and began flying low along the canyon wall, literally trying to scrape the goblin off of him against the cliff face. Sparks, rock, and debris flew everywhere from the goblins armor as they catapulted through the ravine.

Down below, Tiger Lily and Tink continued to mow down enemies as fast as they appeared, but they just kept coming. The braves and the lost boys fought for their lives as they were literally being surrounded on all sides.

"There's too many of them!" Curly screamed.

"Keep fighting, Curly!" Nibs encouraged as he ran another goblin through.

"Come on, you dunce!" Slightly said as he coolly parried three goblins at once. "Use the fairy bombs."

"The fairy bombs! Right!" Curly reached into his satchel and pulled out a couple of little golden orbs that Tinker Bell gifted to him. He threw them both back-to-back into the horde of goblins, then ducked for cover. "Everybody down!" He screamed.

All the braves and the lost boys hit the deck. A moment went by, and there was nothing.

"Ay pygmy!" Marco jeered. "What are we ducking for?!"

As Marco stood up, two huge explosions of white-hot fairy dust incinerated a pack of goblins and sent those on the outside of the blast flying through the air like rag dolls. Marco caught the tail end of the blast. His hair was singed as he was thrown face down into the mud.

"I gotta get me some of those," he mumbled into the muck, nearly unconscious.

In the air, Peter tried to shake the captain off, but it was no use — the captain was latched on too tight — the goblin let out a sinister laugh as he foiled every attempt Peter made to be rid of him.

"So this is how the Great Pan dies," The captain jeered in premature victory. "I'm disappointed boy… I was hoping to face something more powerful." The captain reached behind his back, pulled out a dagger from his belt, and put it against Peter's throat. "Any last words?"

"Be careful what you wish for," Peter said, then he turned on the jets and rocketed straight up the ravine. The force of the sudden change of direction caused the captain to lose his dagger. Peter flew so fast that the captain was forced to hang on for dear life.

"What are you doing?!" The goblin captain screamed. "The spirits! They'll kill us both!" "They most certainly will try," he admitted as he kept flying, his eyes set on the fog line above, and within moments they blasted into it...

Instantly, it was like they were in a parallel world, for there was nothing but crystal-clear sky and silence as they left the battle below, but now there was only one problem — they were surrounded by ghoulish evil spirits! — Time seemed to slow way down to a stopping point. Everything hung in the balance as they floated, suspended in mid-air, surrounded by death.

Peter looked the goblin captain directly in his terrified eyes. "Your main problem here is… you can't fly."

Like lightning, the evil spirits bared down on them. The captain took in a deep breath of fear, then Peter used his momentary hesitation to slip his grasp, and rocketed further up into the clear sky as the captain screamed and plummeted back through the fog line into the gorge.

Peter took a moment, breathing heavy, thankful to be rid of that menacing goblin that was giving him hell for much longer than most ever could, but now there was only one more problem to deal with — all the evil spirits were looking directly at him! — Their long, sullen faces sunk back into their hoods as they reached towards him with their skeleton like hands.

"Uh, oh," Peter said, then he turned on a dime and began flying as fast as he could, and the spirits tailed him…

Down below the fog, Tiger Lily, Fleur, Ruby, Solomon, the lost boys, the braves, and their steeds were all back-to-back in the gorge, barely holding off the growing hoard. From above, Tinker Bell offered air support, incinerating goblins right and left with white-hot light, but at this point it did little to keep the onslaught at bay — there were just too many of them.

"I don't know how much longer we're gonna last!" Curly yelled.

"We need help!" Tootles exclaimed. "Where's Peter?!"

Tinker Bell looked over and saw the body of the goblin captain falling through the air. She watched in horror as he landed in a large pool of water, then looked back at the sky — whatever Peter was doing up there, he better hurry.

Way up above the battle that raged below, Peter raced through the air at record levels as the evil spirits continued to get closer. Never in his life had he ever flown against anything that could even begin to keep up with him, but now he had met his match. He veered right — they followed — he veered left — they followed — he looked back, the spirits were closing in. How was this possible? The chief told him not to fly near the mountains of Crocodile Crack for this very reason — was he a fool? He then felt hot anger shoot through his body at his own irresponsibility, for this lack of judgement could very well cost him his life.

Peter gritted his teeth and shot straight up towards the sun, giving it all he had as the life-sucking ghouls trailed him. "Maybe if I could just make it higher up in the atmosphere," Peter thought. "The air is thinner up there... maybe they'll drop off." He continued to fly up so high that all of Neverland could be seen like a continent below him. "Surely, I must have lost them," he thought. "Surely."

He looked down, but the ghouls were still there! In fact, they were just feet away from him, tailing him like a wounded never bird up in the thin atmosphere. They typically would never venture this far from the mountain, but they had tasted his spirit, and they wanted it all. They began reaching out for him with their deadly, wispy hands... this was it...

Then, just as the ghouls were about to touch him and suck the life force from his body, Peter gracefully pulled a big, arching back-dive. The spirits reached out for him, missing his feet by an inch as he rocketed back towards Neverland in a complete one-eighty maneuver initiated by absolute and infinite skill.

Peter raced back towards the ground even faster than he went up towards the sky. He knew that he had to make it to the fog line before these foul ghouls touched him if he wanted to keep any hope of retaining the light of life. He looked back, and the spirits were just inches from him — on him — they reached out for him again, closer now — they were literally touching his toes — Peter could feel his life force leaving him… this was it… and what a good life it was… but like a foolish youth he didn't listen to the wise words of the chief… and now certain death was upon him… if only he could learn to listen better… but it was not in his nature… and now it would cost him everything...

"But the others," he thought. "What would happen to the others?" It was not for his own life, but for the life of his friends that Peter dug down deep and found one last burst of energy… one more ounce of will to stay alive…

"AHHH!" Peter screamed as he rocketed through the air past mach speed, pushing the fabric of his very being to the absolute limit! His sudden burst of energy created a momentary distance between him and the spirits, but within a split second they were right back on him. How was this possible? He was giving it everything he had? And these things — these abominations — were keeping up with him? If he himself could not shake them, then surely these creatures would be the end of them all… this was it…

Then, down below as Peter raced towards the fog, he saw something tiny and golden break through the fog line. It was Tinker Bell, and she was flying right towards them! Whatever she was doing, she was either crazy, or she was the only hope they all had now. Tink reached into her satchel and grabbed a handful of fairy dust as Peter rocketed right towards her. She pulled her hands back, and gave it everything she had — every ounce of magic, every learned skill she had acquired in the last hundred years — she charged a fairy blast as white and as hot as the sun — Peter screamed as he gave it one last burst…

BOOM! — Tink unleashed a blinding flash of white-hot light energy just as Peter passed her and plunged back through the fog line! The powerful blast caught the evil spirits at full force and sent them scattering and screaming back into the atmosphere!

As the spirits scattered, Tinker Bell took a breath and sighed with relief — that was close, too close — then she smiled subtly to herself, impressed with her own skill, for she rarely got to express the full extent of her powers like that, and powerful she was indeed…

Down below, the whole gang fought for their lives as the hoard was practically on top of them in the gorge.

"We're being overrun!" Curly screamed as he pulled his pirate sword out of the split head of a goblin, just barely in time to block another attack.

"Keep fighting!" Tiger Lily screamed as she slashed and slayed multiple goblins with dual tomahawks, opening them up like melons and spilling their black guts on the ravine floor.

Charlie was on a rampage, he slayed goblin after goblin, and was covered in thick, black goblin blood, but no matter how many he ended, they just kept coming to replace their fallen.

Solomon and Ruby stabbed goblins with their horns, Fleur kicked at them with her hooves. Nibs, Slightly, and Tootles fought back-to-back. Tootles crushed goblin after goblin with his war hammer, splitting their heads open like cantaloupes. Nibs and slightly slayed enemies left and right, filleting them like guppy fish with their pirate swords, but they could not put an end to them fast enough — not anymore — they just kept coming, and they were getting tired… it was only a matter of time now…

"I'll tell you boys," Tootles said from the thick of battle. "It's been a pleasure adventuring with you all."

The boys continued to parry and defend themselves from an onslaught of enemy attacks — heads together, brothers in arms — they yelled together in unison as they made their final stand… this was it… the last stand of the lost boys… the great warriors and guardians of Neverland… then… from the air… a sound of hope…

"COCK-A-DOODLE-DOO!"

All those below looked up at the sky as Peter broke through the skyline. Dread washed over the face of the enemy as Peter soared above the battlefield, his valiant crow striking fear in the hearts of all those that were evil, and imbuing courage to all those that were good.

Infused with new life, the lost boys yelled and pursued their attackers. The braves, filled with new strength, let out a fresh battle cry as they doubled down on their assault. Solomon, Fleur, and Ruby brayed gallantly as they trampled the fleeing goblins like fodder. As the attackers fled, Tiger Lily sheathed her dual tomahawks, and pulled out her bow once again, cutting down the terrified horde with deadly speed and accuracy.

It was then that Peter plunged back down into the fight, and all hope was lost for the enemy as he darted swiftly from foe to foe, dispatching them with his Dagger of Truth. They ran for their lives, but to no avail, for such a power was too much from them, and they had nothing in which to stand against it.

"COCK-A-DOODLE-DOO!"

Triumphant, the lost boys let out a victory crow in unison as Peter soared above. Yes, he was their Savior, and he spared no use of the title now, for they were alive, breathing, and full of new life, and it was by his light that the path was made clear… yes, the guardians had won the battle… but they had much further to go…

***

When all swords had been sheathed, and the last arrow loosed, the tired victors walked through the battlefield, gathering supplies from slain enemies as they recovered from the fight. Tiger

Lily pulled her arrows from the corpses of the goblins she cut down, and the lost boys took what spoils they could off the bodies — whatever wasn't corrupted by goblin blood.

The goblin captain rested against a rock near the edge of the pool. He was still alive, but barely. He choked on his own blood as it poured from his mouth. Peter and the others gathered around.

"I watched him fall from the sky," Tinker Bell told Peter. "He should be dead."

Peter turned towards the fallen captain. "You're a difficult one, aren't you?"

"You're not the only one with a thick skin, boy," the captain mocked.

"I'll show you a thick skin!" Nibs stepped forward and drew his sword, about to run the goblin through, but Peter stayed him with his arm.

"Why did you attack us?" Peter asked calmly.

"You fools," the captain chortled. "Did you really think you could have fun forever… and nobody would have to pay for it." The goblin captain laughed between a fit of bloody coughing. "No… he is coming for you."

The goblin captain beckoned to Peter with his last bit of strength. Peter walked over and leaned down to listen, but instead of speaking, the captain attempted to stab Peter in the neck with his dagger. Peter easily grabbed his wrist, stopping the blow as life left the goblin captain's eyes. Nobody spoke or moved as they watched the goblin pass away before them…

***

Tired and weary from the fierce battle, the troop rode in silence as they made their way further up the ravine. It was getting dark, and they would need to find a place to rest soon. Peter rode out in front on Solomon, leading the group forward, and Tinker Bell rode on Ruby next to him.

"What do you think he meant by that?" She started. "When he said 'Did you think you could have fun forever, and nobody would have to pay for it.' — What do you think he meant?"

Peter took a breath, for he knew exactly what the old captain meant — well, more than anyone else in the group possibly could — for he reasoned that whatever the goblin was referring to had some connection to what he saw and experienced in the void — some great darkness, the end of all things — but he knew it would do no good to give it his voice upon the air now, especially to the others, who's burden it was not, for it was his, and his alone, and their support of him on his journey was weight enough for them to carry.

"I guess that's what we're going to find out," Peter shrugged, and they kept riding for a while.

"You saved her life today," Tinker Bell nodded back to Tiger Lily, who rode on Fleur next to Charlie and the other braves. "At the rock… that goblin… he would have killed her if you weren't there… you saved her."

"I did," Peter said easily. "And you saved me…"

A moment passed between them. Peter looked at his friend Tinker Bell — so beautiful, so full of life, so intuitive — if only she could see how much light she offered the world, then she would know just how attractive she truly was. He then flicked Solomon's reins and lunged forward up the path.

Tinker Bell was left blushing on Ruby as she watched Peter move up ahead along the path, and although she knew Tiger Lily currently had Peter's heart, she couldn't deny the sheer amount of love that existed between them, and if she felt it so strongly, she had to believe that Peter did as well. She looked down in her hand at her daily dose of her neverbrew potion… another drink and her fantasy could continue for one more day… another drink… and she was one step closer to making her dream come true for good… she closed her eyes… wishing… then…

"Ay you guys!" Curly's voice suddenly shot through the dark. "Look at this!"

Up the gorge, Curly, Slightly, and the Twins stood around a fire pit — it was fresh — Peter, Nibs, Marco, and Pax rode up.

"Good eyes, Curly," Nibs said, excited by his friend's find.

Marco bent down and pulled an empty rum bottle from the ashes, and a shiver of terror coursed through the group.

"What are pirates doing way up here?" Tootles asked. "We're almost to No Man's Pass."

"I'll tell you what they're doing," Charlie said, stepping out from the shadows. "Same thing those goblins were doing… they're looking for him." Charlie pointed to Peter, and a tense, hushed silence fell upon the group — was this brave really foolish enough to call out Peter Pan? Right in front of his friends? — In normal circumstances it would be madness. He must have had a reason to be so bold…

"What do you mean?" Curly asked, curious while still defending Peter.

"Isn't it obvious," Charlie continued. "You heard the old captain. Whatever's coming — it's him they're after — there's no reason for any of us to die."

In a fraction of a second, Tiger Lily pulled an arrow from her quiver, knocked her bow, and aimed it right at Charlie's head with fury in her eyes. "May I remind you, brave," She began with an unnerving and deadly calm. "That you address the Great White Father, the Savior of Neverland… disloyalty in a time of need is punishable by death."

Charlie fearlessly moved in towards the point of Tiger Lily's arrow. "I am not afraid to die," he said, then he moved in until the point of the arrow touched his heart. "Are you?"

Tiger Lily looked Charlie in the eyes. He had always been overly serious, but she had never seen him this way before. There was an absolution to him now — some kind of hidden desperation — and she didn't like it. Peter stepped in and pushed her bow aside.

"Anyone who wants to leave is free to do so without dishonor or punishment," Peter said to the group, then he turned to Charlie and looked him dead in the eye. "But while you are under my command, you *will* follow my lead, or I will have you banished."

Charlie stared at Peter with a burning resentment, but there was no hesitation to the Great White Father's words. He meant every single thing that he said, and to be banished from Neverland was a fate worse than death, for he would then be doomed to live out his days, away from his native home on this undying world, wandering through foreign lands until the end. Peter continued to stare at him, and Charlie finally lowered his gaze.

"Set up camp," Peter commanded, turning back to the group. "Slightly, Nibs, you take first watch. We'll continue through No Man's Pass at daybreak."

Nibs and Slightly nodded as the rest of the group dispersed and began to make camp, but Charlie couldn't take his resentful eyes off Peter…

* CHAPTER 10 *

— The Traitor —

Tootles got a small fire going. Everyone was exhausted, but there was little sleep to be had by the group because of the adrenaline still pumping through their veins from the battle. While the others dozed, Curly and the Twins played cards. Tiger Lily leaned on Peter's shoulder as they sat around the fire. Peter liked having her there next to him, and her touch was comforting after such a savage day.

"What happened up there today?" Tiger Lily asked as they both looked into the dancing flames. "Up above the clouds… how did you escape the spirits?"

Peter took a breath, and began with some difficulty. "When the spirits neared me… I could feel my life leaving me… and Tinker Bell… she saved me..." Peter looked over at Tinker Bell, who sat on the other side of the fire, looking quite stunning in the dancing light.

"She really loves you," Tiger Lily said, and she meant it, for as she looked up at the boy who had her heart, the flames flickering in his bright eyes, she knew that if it wasn't for Tinker

Bell, she may not have her love next to her on this night, and for that she had her gratitude.

Peter nodded, for he knew Tiger Lily's words were true — Tinker Bell did love him, perhaps more than he could ever know — and if it wasn't for her, he may not be alive to feel Tiger Lily's touch this night… or to gaze upon Tinker Bell's beauty as she sat in the firelight. Peter smiled at her image. Yes, he did love Tink as well — more than anything — but it was a different kind of love, a kind of love he had never felt for anyone or anything else in the universe, and perhaps he did not know what that was yet. It was a deep love, a powerful love, and it gave him life, but it was too much for him to try and comprehend now, so he took a breath and rested his head on Tiger Lily's shoulder… a place that was tried and familiar.

"On skull rock that day," Tiger Lily continued after some silence. "That day Hook captured me all those years ago… you saved me right before I drowned… do you remember?"

"I'll never forget it," Peter said honestly, and he rested his head on her lap.

"I never told you this…" Tiger Lily hesitated for a moment as she ran her fingers through his hair, then continued. "I died that day — just for a moment — I was gone from this world…"

"What was it like?" Peter asked, curious now, but he could barely bring himself to say the final word — "*death?*"

"It was like *nothing…*" Tiger Lily said, and an emptiness entered her voice as she gazed into the flames. "It was like absolutely *nothing*… this darkness you're facing… I fear for you." Peter didn't answer as Tiger Lily pulled him close and kissed his forehead. How much she loved him, perhaps Peter would never fully understand, but he felt all that he could feel for the time, so he fell back into her further, and gazed into the fire, and for a moment, he felt his eyes closing…

Across the fire, Tinker Bell sleepily gazed into the flames, for it had been a long day. She didn't even mind that Peter was across the fire leaning on Tiger Lily's shoulder instead of her own, with Tiger Lily stroking his brow, comforting him with her hand instead of Tink comforting him with her own. No, none of that mattered now, for tonight, she was grateful that Peter was alive, and she was too tired to think of anything else.

Tinker Bell's eyes were about to close, when suddenly—

SNAP! — the sound of a twig breaking.

Tinker Bell perked up, and looked around her. She seemed to be the only one that noticed, for she was the only one that possessed the senses to hear such a faint sound, except for Peter, but he was too busy losing himself in Tiger Lily's touch. She knew what she heard… something was out there in the dark…

She squinted into the night and saw a faint shadow moving up the gorge. What should she do? Should she tell Peter? No, no, he had enough weight to carry, then again, perhaps it was nothing… nothing but a shadow… or her mind playing tricks on her… then again, if it wasn't, perhaps she could be the hero this time… and Peter would continue to see how valuable she was to him… much more than that simple Tiger Lily….

Tink made her choice. She rose from the fire and quietly exited, pursuing the shadow into the trees.

"Oy! Who goes there?!" Nibs announced, popping awake from his guard post, for he thought he heard the rustling of feet nearby.

Tink held her breath, for she didn't see Nibs lounging against the backside of a tree, and she nearly walked right by him. She watched as he continued to listen to the sounds of the air, but when he heard only further silence, he nestled back into his spot. Tink steadied herself and moved silently past him… journeying further and deeper into the dark…

Once she was out of Peter's ear shot — which was quite far given his ability — she quickened her pace. The shadow was nowhere to be seen, and for a moment, she considered going back down the gorge to the camp, but she knew that she had to keep going, for she had committed to it and had a feeling that whatever she saw, it was important.

It continued to get darker, even with her fairy eyes Tink could hardly see anything, but she dared not light the way with fairy dust, lest she give away her position and all hope of ever finding out who it was that was sneaking around in the woods. She shivered as she fumbled through the underbrush, continuing to push further and further into the dark, and after some time it appeared that she had lost the shadow… so much for her great idea… now she would have to find her way back…

But Tinker Bell was determined to keep going, so she did. She knew that she was stubborn, but this was past stubbornness — this was a matter of principle — she made up her mind she would find out whose shadow was sneaking around in the woods, and so she would.

Deeper up the gorge she went, and for a moment she thought she saw the shadow again, but perhaps it really was just her mind playing tricks on her now. Either way she couldn't see anything anymore. It was so dark now that she couldn't even make out her own hands in front of her face. She figured she must be all the way up near No Man's Pass by now.

Yes, perhaps she should go back, for if she didn't she would risk being lost until morning, but she could not fly above the trees, for she saw how vicious those spirits were that almost caught Peter at his top flying speed, and how much more formidable and deadly would they be at night?! — Tink dared not try and find out.

Oh, and what would Peter think when he awoke and she wasn't there? She knew that he knew that she could take care of herself, but what would he think of his number one fairy when she was getting lost in the woods… alone… at night? Would he lose faith in her? Would he think less of her? Oh, but it was Peter, he'd forget in a day — but would he? She was supposed to be there by his side in his time of need, and yet, here she was, chasing shadows in the woods like some kind of deranged fairy.

"Yes," Tink thought to herself. "Surely I am above this childish behavior. I just followed an imaginary shadow into the woods — for what? To get back at a girl that couldn't care less about me? Come on Tinker Bell, grow up, you're better than this." Tink scolded herself relentlessly, for it became clear to her in that moment that she had let her pride and jealousy get the better of her, and now instead of resting like she should be, she was out there cold and alone in the woods, burning precious energy that Peter needed to support him on his journey.

She continued to move deeper and deeper into the dark, turning this way and that, but everything was pitch black. She dared not fly or light up the path, for those ghouls — surely they would catch her — she took a breath and remained calm, for at minimum, the sun would make all things new in the morning.

Yes, that was the solution — the sun — oh, how she loved the sunshine, and the warmth it gave to the Fairy Quarters. She loved to sit out in the morning on her balcony in the Royal Hills and look out over all of Neverland as far as her eyes could see… the lively hustle and bustle of Pixie's Landing… the shimmering waters of Port Royal… yes, pretty soon the sun would make everything all right… then she'd find her way back to Peter and maybe even get back before he found out she was missing… yes… pretty soon now… she would just need to lie down and wait for it to rise, and try to get some sleep before dawn…

Suddenly, she saw a light flickering in the distance in the dark. Was it real? Or was it her hope making things up again? She had nothing to lose, so she began to crawl through the underbrush towards it. As she got closer, the light continued to expand like a foreign star being born in empty space. She continued to fight her way through the thick underbrush towards the growing light…

As Tinker Bell got closer, voices could be heard surrounding the light… she reached the forest edge and peered out upon what appeared to be a campsite…

As her eyes adjusted, she saw that it was a band of pirates! About fifteen of them. They lounged around the campfire, drinking and cleaning their weapons.

“Say, what do you think of that Tinker Bell?” One drunk, sinewy pirate said to an older one.

“She’s all right,” The older pirate responded. “For a fairy.”

“All right?!” The skinny pirate jeered. “She’s down right beautiful she is, that potion she created turned her into a real woman… if you know what I mean.”

Tinker Bell watched from the shadows with terrified, wide eyes.

“I prefer the princess,” a fat pirate said, gargling on his rum as he listened in on their conversation.

“Come off it, you fools!” The older pirate scolded. “If the Great Pan caught you with his maiden or his fairy you’d wish you’d never been born. He’d skin you alive… or worse…”

“What could be worse than that?” The skinny pirate said, dumbfounded.

“He’d think of somethin’,” the older pirate said. “Now cut it out with that talk before you curse us.”

“Curse us!” The sinewy pirate said, raising his voice. “I’d take him right now— ”

“Sit. Down.” The older pirate stood and pushed the sinewy one forcefully back into his seat, putting his sword to his throat as he did, then he leaned in in all seriousness. “If the flying boy comes now, we’re all dead… I’ll cut out your throat before I die by the foolishness of some drunk swine.”

Tink watched as the older pirate sheathed his sword, and the sinewy one fell silent. She had really got herself into a spot now — these were some mean looking pirates, and although she was powerful, she was outnumbered, and she no longer knew how far away she was from the others — she better head back to camp before the sun rose and they spotted her.

Suddenly, there was a rustle in the bushes next to her, and a shadow walked out of the clearing just feet from where she was hidden! This must be the shadow… the shadow that she was trailing… she was right all along… but who was it?

From her hiding space at the edge of the clearing, Tink watched as the shadow walked into the firelight… and it was revealed that it was Marco!

Tink held her breath to keep from screaming. The traitor! But she did not move. She continued to watch, silent, and deathly still… waiting to see what would happen…

Marco continued moving through the camp and approached a dark, crudely handsome pirate near the far end of the campfire, and Tinker Bell laid eyes on Captain Vincent Brubaker for the first time.

"Do you have what I want?" Captain Vincent Brubaker said from the shadows, the fire light and embers from his pipe illuminating his face through puffs of smoke.

"Do you have my money?" Marco snapped back viciously, using a tone of voice the captain was likely not used to hearing.

There was a moment of silence, and when the captain didn't respond, Marco's front began to melt and he gulped back his fear. Then, the captain whistled, and a sack of gold flew out of the shadows and landed at Marco's feet, shimmering in the fire light.

Marco smiled greedily at the sight of the gold, then he reached into his pack, and pulled out the peace pipe that was taken from the Indian camp in the dead of night. Tink's eyes went wide. She had no idea the pipe was stolen. She had to tell the others, but she couldn't move, not yet. The captain murmured into the shadows and a pirate briefly appeared in the fire light. He took the pipe from Marco's hands and brought it to the captain as ordered.

Tinker Bell watched from her enclave as the captain took the pipe, and held it up, examining it in the firelight. Marco's behavior was justifiable enough. It wasn't hard to believe he'd steal just about anything for a price — but who was this man? And what did he want with the chief's old pipe? Enough to pay a sack of gold for it?

"Satisfied?" Marco asked, and he took the captain's silence as a yes. "It was a pleasure doing business with ya'." Marco grabbed his gold and started walking away.

"Wait," a pirate said, walking into the fire light — it was the same older pirate that silenced the two drunken loud mouths earlier. He turned to address the captain. "How do we know he won't squawk?"

"I won't squawk," Marco snapped back hotly. "If I do, the boy kills me — or you kill me — there's nothing in it for me, you old goat, so you best back off."

The older pirate seemed to be satisfied with Marco's answer because he didn't retaliate. Marco stuck his nose up in the air at the pirate and continued towards the forest.

"He won't squawk," the captain said calmly from the shadows, and Marco froze in place. "Or he can only pray the boy gets to him before I do."

Marco looked back and gulped. "Good one, Captain," he chuckled from the nervous energy. "You clearly have a funny bone in ya'… so I've been told," he lied, stumbling over his words like a belligerent fool, completely paralyzed by his fear. "Well… you lot have a good night now."

As Marco turned to leave the camp, Tinker Bell noticed that he was heading right in her direction! At his current trajectory, if she didn't move he'd run right into her!

"Okay Tinker Bell, remain calm," she whispered to herself as she began backing away from the clearing, step by step. "Keep going… that's it… now… go!"

Tinker Bell turned to fly and ran smack into something big and round, bouncing off the belly of a very large pirate. She fell to the ground, and her vial of neverbrew dropped out of her satchel into the brush. The big pirate held up a lantern, and a sinister grin spread across his face as he beared down upon the pretty, sparkling creature below him. Tink looked up into the blinding light of the lantern, and her eyes narrowed in spite — it was time for option B — she'd incinerate this fat pirate and the whole dirty lot. Being outnumbered, it wasn't ideal, but she now had no choice, and since she didn't have a choice, she was going to enjoy it.

Tink's eyes narrowed even further in vengeance as she reached into her satchel and charged a fairy blast. She was about to turn the fat pirate into pork rinds, when—

"Gotcha!" Marco came up behind Tinker Bell, and held her wrists behind her back, effectively stopping her attack. "Now this is just too sweet, isn't it?"

"Traitor!" Tinker Bell hissed as she spat on the ground.

"Traitor you say? I'll show you a traitor," Marco jeered, then he turned to the big pirate. "Eh, biggin'. Do your worst."

The big pirate smiled at Tinker Bell, then pulled back his fist, prepared to deal a blow. Tink's eyes went wide with fear.

"Please, Peter," Tinker Bell pleaded in her mind. "Save me…"

The pirates fist came down, and everything went dark…

***

The morning light was just piercing through the ravine when the lost boys and the braves broke down camp and began to pack up their horses. Marco was right there with them, and as far as it appeared to the others, he never left camp last night.

As Peter fed Solomon a morning carrot, he looked over and saw Ruby shimmering in the morning light. She really was a beautiful unicorn, and Peter couldn't think of a more fitting creature for Tinker Bell to ride upon. They were both shiny, and pretty, and magical, and powerful. Indeed, it was a match made in the heavens…

Peter smiled as he had this thought, for he thought it was a nice way to start the morning, then he looked around the camp — where was Tink, anyway? — He began to float through the grounds, looking for her, but found no sign.

"Tiger Lily, you seen Tink?" Peter asked her as she was packing up Fleur.

"Not since yesterday," Tiger Lily said honestly. "I thought she was with you."

"No," Peter corrected, rather harshly. "I've been with you."

"Don't snap at me," Tiger Lily said, standing up to him. "She's here somewhere."

Peter continued to look through the camp. "Hey, Nibs, you seen Tink?"

"Haven't seen her, mate," Nibs said with a yawn as he saddled his horse.

Peter then floated over to Tootles, who was eating some porridge by the dwindling fire. "Hey, Tootles, you seen Tink?"

"Not since last night," Tootles said with some concern.

Peter continued to look around the campsite. She was nowhere to be seen. "Tink!" he yelled.

By now, everyone around the campsite was looking for Tinker Bell, but she was nowhere to be seen.

"Last I saw her was by the fire," Curly told Slightly.

"Well, did you see her put up her tent?" Slightly asked.

"Come to think of it, I didn't," Curly admitted.

"Maybe she took a morning flight!" Nibs yelled.

"She wouldn't," Peter said assuredly. "Not after yesterday."

They kept looking, but to no avail. By now, a slight panic coursed through the group, especially the lost boys, who were close to her. Peter had to find a way to keep everyone calm and together. Then…

"Tiger Lily! Bring the Great White Father!" Charlie's voice could be heard at the far end of camp. Peter flew over, followed by everyone else. Charlie stood at the edge of the woods where Tinker Bell followed the shadow up the gorge last night. "The tracks are fresh," he said.

"No Man's Pass…" Tootles quivered.

Peter stared up into the menacing trees, and his stomach dropped — some great evil took place last night, but what?

***

Peter and the others stood in the clearing where the pirates had their camp the night before, searching for signs of Tink.

"It's pirates, all right," Marco said, kneeling down and expecting the ground. "You can tell by the boot prints."

Peter flew around, examining the camp, but something wasn't adding up. It wasn't like Tinker Bell to just leave in the middle of the night, especially when she knew that he needed her by his side more than ever. "There must have been a reason she came down here," he said audibly so that the group heard him, but he was really speaking to himself, affirming what he knew must be true.

"Peter! Come quick!" Nibs yelled, and he stood in the spot of the clearing where Tinker Bell fell to the ground during the night. Peter flew over and saw that the bushes were smashed down all around the area, and there was obviously a fierce struggle. Nibs then handed Peter the vial of neverbrew that fell from Tinker Bell's satchel.

Looking down at the golden vial in his hand, Peter's heart rate began to increase, his rage building. This was Tink's favorite potion. What would she do without it? Whoever took her, they wouldn't even let her take her potion. The animals! The filthy animals! They dared to touch Tinker Bell, companion to the Great Pan, the Son of Neverland! He'd slaughter them all, and not before they hurt so much they'd wish they'd never been born!

Peter's rage continued to build… his heart rate beating faster, and faster, and faster… he looked down at the golden vial in his hand one more time, and was reminded of everything that was taken from him… he squeezed it… then….

BANG! — Like an explosion from a cannon, Peter launched from the ground and transversed the camp at blazing speed, smashing Charlie to the ground where they skid across the rest of the clearing!

"Where is she?!" Peter screamed as he put his dagger to Charlie's neck.

Without hesitation, Charlie pulled his tomahawk from his side and took a swing at Peter, who was forced to dodge it, momentarily freeing the brave long enough for him to get to his feet.

Peter screamed and bombarded Charlie with a flurry of lightning quick stabs, aimed to kill. Charlie moved fast, barely dodging the deadly blows as they flashed past his face.

Around the battle, the others watched patiently and no one tried to interfere, for this was a fight that had been brewing for a long time, and they all valued their own lives enough that they dared not get caught in the middle of it. The lost boys never cared much for Charlie anyway, he was haughty, and arrogant, and seemed to hate them all for no reason. If it was true that he had something to do with Tinker Bell's disappearance, then he deserved to die.

The braves felt the same way about Peter, and if Charlie could land a lucky strike and be rid of him now, then the braves would be able to roam and raid freely in Neverland without oppression from the Great White Father and his fairy subjects — that's what Marco thought, anyway — Tiger Lily also didn't try to interfere, for she had seen Peter this angry only a few times in her life, and to interfere now would be simply dangerous. She knew that he would do anything for Tinker Bell, and if anyone stood in his way it might as well be the last decision they ever made.

Peter took a fierce flying slash that Charlie ducked just in time to avoid being decapitated, and the momentum from the missed blow pulled Peter all the way to the other edge of the clearing. The lead brave and the flying boy faced each other. Charlie was in a fighting stance, eyes wide and alert, breathing calm, his tomahawk at the ready. He knew he was innocent, but the Great White Father didn't think so, and if his senses failed him now, he wouldn't live to tell the truth — he might not live anyway — but he would fight, and if by chance he were to kill the Great White Father in his rage, he would claim the crown and be the king of Neverland, and the title sounded very fitting indeed.

On the other end, Peter stood breathing heavily, dagger in his hand, his whole body shaking with rage. He took in deep breaths to keep from hyperventilating and to cool his blood. He couldn't remember ever being this angry before, not when Hook captured Tiger Lily, not even when Tinker Bell saved him from being poisoned by Hook's hand, and sacrificed herself, nearly dying in the process. No, that was a different kind of anger, that old anger was an anger driven by fear, and this was blind rage, for he was just a boy back then — a boy fighting for the freedom of his world — and now that he was its Savior, whoever was foolish enough to cross him would feel the full extent of his wrath.

"You led Tinker Bell to the pirates!" Peter screamed at Charlie, staring him down with furious, piercing eyes.

"I didn't touch your fairy," Charlie answered calmly. "But I can see you have already made your decision."

Peter screamed savagely as for his life — for Tinker Bell was his life — and in a split second closed the gap between them, raining down a flurry of blows upon the brave that were aimed to destroy. Charlie parried Peter's attacks as fast as he could throw them, spinning and twirling his tomahawk with expert skill, deflecting the blows away from his body.

Charlie saw an opening and took a fierce swing, Peter quickly jumped back as it narrowly missed him — that was as close as anyone had gotten to landing a blow on him since Captain Hook himself — the rage drove Peter forward, and within moments he was back on top of Charlie, pummeling him with everything he had. Sparks flew as dagger clashed against tomahawk, Peter on the offensive, Charlie on the defensive.

Peter's rage wouldn't subside. He took a hard, off-balance swing. Charlie saw it coming and re-enforced his tomahawk with his other arm, creating a powerful, fortified block.

CLING! — Peter's dagger clashed hard with Charlie's tomahawk, the extra fortitude reverberated through the weapon and sent Peter's dagger flying into the dirt. Charlie's move worked — Peter was now without a weapon.

Seeing his opportunity to strike at last, Charlie ran at an unarmed Peter and attacked full force, throwing deadly swings with his tomahawk as Peter dodged them with lightning agility.

WOOSH! WOOSH! — Charlie hit nothing but air, but with intense focus he continued his assault, years of anger and resentment towards the Great White Father spilling out with every swing.

WOOSH! WOOSH! — the brave gave it everything he had, but he couldn't land a blow, his frustration building to a climax as Peter remained untouchable. It was like trying to hit a piece of dust floating through the air with a blade — it was impossible! — Sweat flew off his brow as his attacks continued to get wider and more desperate.

"Why won't you die?!" Charlie screamed.

Tired and desperate, Charlie took one last swing. Peter expertly caught him by the wrist and squeezed. Charlie yelled and threw a wild punch with the other arm, which Peter caught as well, now effectively having the leverage on both of Charlie's arms. Peter then leapt into the air, flipped his legs back to gather momentum, and then pulled on Charlie's arms and flew forward with maximum inertia, sending a powerful kick right into Charlie's chest. The momentum from the blast sent Charlie smashing haggardly into the ground, and sent his tomahawk sailing into the air. Using his opponent as a springboard, Peter backflipped gracefully into the air off the kick, and caught the dislodged weapon with ease.

Beaten, Charlie panted as he managed to come to his knees, awaiting his judgement as the Great White Father dropped down from above, staring holes through him with bright, cold eyes, hovering silently before him in the air, wielding the full extent of his power.

The rest of the party gathered around. Tiger Lily put a soft hand on Peter's shoulder as he pointed Charlie's tomahawk at his chest, hoping to calm his wrath, but his anger was beyond reproach. If this man had a part in Tinker Bell's disappearance, nothing less than his blood would be required as payment.

"To die by the hand of the Great White Father, will be an honorable death indeed," Charlie said, then he ripped open his shirt, exposing his heart. "Strike true."

Peter looked deep into Charlie's eyes, assessing the brave that had blindly resented him for so long, but Peter did not see what he was expecting to see, for indeed, there was no fear in them —

he couldn't have hurt Tink — for this man was prepared to die an honorable death, and his mind was blameless.

Another moment passed, then Peter dropped the tomahawk and flew over to retrieve his dagger. Tiger Lily ran after him.

"I'm going after her," Peter said as he retrieved his dagger and made to fly onward.

"No!" Tiger Lily screamed, grabbing his arm. "You must see the enchantress!"

"And let Tink rot with those filthy pirates," Peter said, turning on her. "You'd like that wouldn't you?"

Peter's cold words cut into Tiger Lily like a knife, but she knew he was not himself, and this task was bigger than all of them — he had to finish it or there might not be a world to call home anymore at all — but she had to get Peter to see it for himself.

"No, Peter, they'll keep her alive," she urged. "As long as they have her they know you'll come for her… you have to see the enchantress… remember what you saw in the void…"

Peter looked into Tiger Lily's big, doe eyes, and his rage cooled enough for him to think… and she was right...

"What about Tinker Bell?" He asked, for no matter the demands placed upon him, he couldn't continue in his right mind knowing she was in captivity.

"I'll go," Tiger Lily consoled. "I know the waters of Cannibal Cove better than anyone… even you…"

They locked eyes, sharing a moment of trust, and Peter knew that she was right, for as gifted as Peter was in the air, Tiger

Lily was in the water, and she moved around upon the liquid world with the grace of a mermaid, being one of Neverland's top swimmers. Overall, he knew that Tiger Lily would set aside her quarrel with Tinker Bell for his sake — if only for a time — but for now that was all he needed.

"We will continue on foot to the enchantress' lair," Peter announced to the group. "Marco, Pax, Nibs, Slightly — you'll go with Tiger Lily to hunt down the pirates and rescue Tink. She's in command — the others, you're with me." Peter then turned to Charlie. "Especially you."

A moment as Peter stared him down, but Charlie's fight had left him. He nodded in compliance, accepting the order, thankful and shocked for his life, for he thought death was certain… maybe he was wrong about Peter.

"Make ready your horses!" Peter commanded.

As the lost boys and the braves began saddling up, Marco smiled to himself — he couldn't believe his luck — first, the Great White Father pinned Charlie as the culprit for the fairy's disappearance, leaving Charlie to take the brunt of the boy's wrath while he got let off the hook. The boy's rage had completely blinded him to the truth. It was perfect! Everything was going exactly as planned. Now secondly and even better yet, something he could have never expected had happened — the boy was sending him away with Pax, and now he only had the princess and two of the lost boys to deal with. Sure, the princess was undoubtedly a formidable warrior, but she trusted him, and without the Great White Father to guard her, he reasoned he could probably kill all three of them if he had to… their time was coming… all their times were coming… pretty soon they would all pay… thinking they ever had any power over ol' Marco.

Nibs approached Marco and pointed his pirate sword right at him. "I'll have my eye on you," he said with cutting absolution, and Marco jeered back — none of them had a clue what was coming.

Ruby was restless — she clearly missed Tinker Bell — Peter approached and stroked her mane, then hopped up on Solomon as Tiger Lily galloped over on Fleur. They locked eyes. In truth, this could be the last time they ever saw each other, but neither would let their minds go to such a dark place...

"Ruby will guide you," Peter said as he stroked her mane, then he looked back into Tiger Lily's eyes. "Find her."

Tiger Lily nodded as her eyes welled with tears, but she would not let them break now — "Yah!" — She pulled on Fleur's reins before her eyes spilled over, forcing herself to pull away from the person she loved most in the world, and catapulted down the ravine back towards Cannibal Cove along with Ruby, the braves, and the lost boys assigned to her.

Peter watched until Tiger Lily and her party were out of sight, knowing in his heart that she had the power to save Tinker Bell, but feeling the loss of her presence all the same. Then he put it from his mind, and looked back up the ravine of No Man's Pass into the final ascent of Crocodile Crack into the Windy Mountains, its dark and jagged edges still looming above them like some sinister foreign power, and he knew that it was time to do what he set out to do — it was time to visit the enchantress.

He then flicked Solomon's reins, and together him and the others plunged onward into the unknown…

* CHAPTER 11*

— The Enchantress —

Tink's fairy eyes fluttered open, and she awoke in a dark, damp, and dismal chamber. Her petite body was chained up in a cell, but she couldn't see her surroundings — where was she? What happened? — She struggled against the irons on her wrists, but to no avail. She caught her breath and considered screaming, but she was smarter than that. If there was help around, then she wouldn't be where she was to begin with. No, it was much better if her captors still thought she was unconscious for as long as possible, that would give her time to think. She took a deep breath, trying to calm herself, trying to concentrate… then…

SNAP — a match was struck in the dark just beyond the bars of her cell, and the flame created a silhouette of a man's face… she knew this face… but from where? Tink peered into the darkness…

The silhouetted figure lit his pipe, and the embers of the pipe continued to light his face until the match went out…

"I always dreamed that the fairies in Neverland were beautiful," the figure said from behind a puff of illuminated pipe smoke. "I just never thought I'd meet one so… *substantial.*"

Tink gulped, she could feel her body being looked at from between the bars.

"When I was a young buccaneer," the dark and gallant voice carried on. "I had a vision about a world — a beautiful world — a world where you could sail the seas forever… a world… that was ruled by flying boy."

The figure stood up and lit a nearby lantern, revealing his presence to her at last. Tinker Bell held back a gasp as she recognized him as the pirate that bought the pipe from Marco… it was all coming back to her.

"Of course, all the others thought it was nonsense," the captain continued. "But I… I always believed… and here I am…"

Through tears of rage Tinker Bell smiled a courageous smile, for she had faith in herself, and more so in Peter, and this fool of a pirate had no idea the amount of hell that he would bring down upon himself and his crew.

"You've seen it in your visions, then," Tinker Bell said with words as sharp and as calculated as a razor blade. "The Son of Neverland cannot be killed."

The captain took a moment and smiled, amused at the sudden courage of the helpless fairy in front of him. It was clear that she believed in her god and his power to save her without a shadow of a doubt… but she had no idea… how could she? She was nothing… just a small, insignificant fairy that concocted some potion just so that she could try and fit in with the rest of the worthless lot of humanity… he had spent his life among them and he knew they were all fools… and so was she…

"Such sharp words from such a pretty little thing," the captain said easily, then he turned to face her, and his eyes narrowed. "But you'll come to find that everyone can be killed, Miss Bell… even flying boys." The captain smiled one last smile, then turned to leave, leaving Tink strung up in her cell.

Tink held her head high for as long as she could, then as soon as the captain was beyond sight, her head fell to her chest. Weakened, she prayed. She had not felt the need to pray for some time, but it's what she could do now… and the only thing she could do…

"Please, Peter," she sent up to the air. "You must succeed… for us all…" Weakened, her eyes then closed, and she fell back into unconsciousness…

***

Although the mists that wrapped around the mountain tops covered the sun, it was clearly evening by the time Peter, Charlie, Tootles, Curly, and the Twins reached the top of No Man's Pass on their steeds, which could be seen by the deep orange and red hues of light that lit up the ravine. As they reached the zenith, they came upon an enclave surrounded by sheer cliff walls that jutted up into the razor-sharp caps of the Windy Mountains all around, and it appeared that they had reached the northern end of Crocodile Crack at last.

"All right, we're here," Tootles announced. "What's next?"

"This is it, I can feel it," Peter said, sensing the magic in the air, for it was full of a powerful energy. "Spread out. Look for any sign of an entrance."

The group did as they were told and spread out across the enclave's perimeter, looking for any signs of an entry point into the mountain. Peter followed the energy, and he knew he was getting close.

"You guys, look!" Curly yelled from the back of the enclave, pointing to the opening of a cave that was suspended several hundred feet up the cliff face.

"Silence, boy!" Charlie scolded as he ran up. "I'm beginning to think you have a death wish."

"Ughh," Tootles said as he ran over, holding his nose. "What is that wretched stink? It smells like dead fish."

Peter came over and easily flew up the cliff face in a second. He hovered before the entrance to the cave, peering into the dark, but he felt no magic coming from it, however, he felt something ancient and sinister dwelling deep within. Could it be? Was the legend true? Either way, it would do them no good to provoke whatever lie dormant, and would definitely not aid them in accomplishing the current task at hand.

"This isn't the entrance," Peter said, flying back down. "Stay away from this side of the mountain, no good can come from it," he commanded. "The magic leads this way."

Peter led the group away from the back of the enclave and the entrance to the mysterious cave, and they all felt a bit lighter as he did. Then…

"Boy…" Peter heard a beautiful, girlish voice.

"Do you hear that?" Peter asked the group.

"Hear what, mate?" Curly said.

"That girl…" Peter then heard a very girlish, high-pitched giggle. He continued to walk through the clearing, searching for its origin. The others looked at each other, confused, for none of them seemed to hear anything.

"I think you're having Tiger Lily withdrawals, mate," Curly teased, then Tootles punched him hard in the shoulder to shut him up. "Ouch."

Peter continued to search the air for the voice, and to the others it looked like he had gone a bit mad, searching around for some sound that no one else could hear, but they all knew that he possessed senses that they did not, and so they trusted him.

"Come to me, child," the girlish voice said to Peter, dropping into a deeper and more seductive register. "The pleasures of life await you…"

As if pulled by an outside force, Peter instinctively walked over to a certain place in the mountain wall where the stone was polished smooth. He put his ear to the wall, and listened. It sounded cavernous inside, and hollow. He then put his hand up to the stone and pushed, and it popped and flickered with energy.

"This is it," Peter said, pulling his hand away.

"Be careful, Peter," Curly said, both confident and concerned for his friend and leader.

"We'll be right here when you get back," Tootles encouraged.

Peter took one last look at his friends, and nodded his gratitude. Then he put his hand back up against the wall, and pushed. His hand and then his arm popped and flickered with energy as it went through, then he took a breath and with the rest of his body plunged forward into the beyond, completely disappearing from sight.

"It's suicide," Charlie said with a shake of his head, for he was in complete fear of the magic. "He'll never make it back alive."

"Oh, ye of little faith," Tootles chuckled as he slapped Charlie on the back. "Let's set up a camp," he said to the others. "He might be gone a while."

The lost boys all agreed in unison as they began to unload, for they were hungry from the journey and grateful for Tootles' idea. Charlie just stood at the wall, staring at the spot where Peter stood just before — So he could walk through walls now? Who was this boy? And what was the true extent of his power?

"Don't just stand there," Tootles said. "Help us unload."

Charlie smirked at Tootles' comment, then went to help the others…

***

Peter's body popped and flickered as he rematerialized on the other side of the wall, and when he fully came through he found himself standing on a plateau inside a cavern. He turned around and quickly pressed his hand against the interior of the stone entrance, but the gate was now shut.

He looked forward, peering into the space in front of him, but it was as dark as night. Then he remembered that he still had Tinker Bell's vial of neverbrew potion that he found in the clearing from where she was taken. Perhaps it was good for more than just giving size to fairies, for it had fairy dust in it, which was full of surprises. He pulled it out, and whispered to it.

"Please… give me light…" Peter then softly shook the vial and it powerfully lit up, shining brightly and illuminating the space around him. "Thank you," he said audibly, expressing his gratitude.

Peter held the shining vial up before him, revealing a narrow and treacherous stairway leading up from the plateau into the mountain, with a narrow and treacherous drop on either side. "This should be simple enough," he thought, then he hopped up, attempting to fly, but his body came back to the ground. He jumped up again, harder this time, but to the same end — his ability to fly had somehow been negated.

"Oh, come on!" Peter yelled in frustration, then he shuddered at the treacherous path, its sheer edges falling off into the dark unknown on either side — he was going to have to try and make it on foot — he took a deep breath, centering himself in his mind, for he still had great natural balance, and he would need all of it now. Then he opened his eyes, and took his first courageous step forward...

***

Ruby raced down the gorge in pursuit of her Tinker Bell, for whoever took her oldest friend in Neverland would pay by the tip of her horn. Tinker Bell was a pure being, and Ruby was sworn to protect and give aid to all pure beings, and she needed her now. Yes, Ruby would use all of the magic and power at her disposal to save her... now was the time.

Tiger Lily raced close behind on Fleur, her eyes focused, her breath calm as she steeled her nerves. Whatever resentment existed between her and Tinker Bell over the last hundred years, she had put it completely on hold in her mind, for without Tinker Bell she knew Peter would be lost to her beyond saving, and she could never endure that level of loss. No, Peter had a bond with this fairy that perhaps even she could not understand. She was romantic with Peter, sure, and as far as she knew Peter had never shared those intimacies with the fairy, but Tinker Bell had known him since he was seven years old, and she could not claim the same…

In truth, Tinker Bell had saved Peter's life. She had brought him to Neverland, which was the key moment in his childhood that resulted in who he now was. Indeed, without Tinker Bell, Tiger Lily knew she would not have met the love of her life, and it was for this exact reason that she found herself eternally indebted to her. Yes, there would be time to settle her quarrels with the fairy, for there was a way she had about her with Peter that was no longer acceptable — an ease, a flirtatiousness — yes, a time would come, and Tiger Lily would put a stop to it, but it was not this night. Tonight, she would save the fairy, and by doing so save everything that she loved about Peter — his light, his joy, his Spirit — so they could continue on as they were… young and in love… destined to be together… forever…

Nibs, Slightly, and Pax, fell behind Ruby, Fleur, and Tiger Lily, finding it difficult to keep up with the unicorn's swift speed, but the urgency of the task at hand gave them pace, which their steeds picked up on, for they knew the gift Tinker Bell was to Neverland, and who it was that shielded them in the goblin battle from the deadly arrows above, and losing her was not an option. Because of their love for her, they ran faster than they had ever run before.

At the back of the pack, Marco grinned viciously… the fools… they had no idea what was coming for them… and they had no idea what he was capable of…

***

At the base of the Windy Mountains, Curly posted with his sword near the stone entrance, standing guard. Tootles had a small fire going, and started to pull out his cooking gear.

"What are you doing, Tootles?" Curly asked. "We're supposed to stand guard for Peter."

"Does it look like anybody's getting in there?" Tootles responded with simple logic.

Curly pushed his hand against the wall where Peter went through — nothing happened — the rotund boy had a point.

"While we're waiting, we might as well eat something," Tootles continued, then he looked up. The Twins sat cross-legged, directly across from him, staring at him with those big eyes and boyish grins. They looked like a couple of neverleemers.

"What about you two?" Tootles asked. "You hungry?"

The Twins didn't speak or move, they just kept smiling, and their eyes got a little bigger. "I'll take that as a yes," Tootles said, then he began prepping some potatoes as the Twins watched eagerly.

On the outskirts of the lost boys' small camp, Charlie patrolled the peripherals of the enclave. He was a trained warrior, the greatest of his tribe, and because of this he took on little rest and food during his missions. He knew the importance of being on high-alert at all times, for his life, and more importantly, the lives of the others, depended on it.

He was grateful that the Great White Father spared his life earlier that day, for the boy could have slain him upon defeat, and based on their history, he fully expected him to, for the Great White Father held within his powers the keys to life and death, and in that moment when he held his life in his hand, Charlie concluded that he had never given him a reason to allow him to live. He had not been kind to the boy since his arrival in Neverland centuries ago, and why should he have been? This boy appeared from another world as the prophesied savior by the fairies. He was cocky and arrogant for all the years during his upbringing, lording his peculiar ability to fly over all the other humans, believing himself superior. Then worse, he slayed the Great Captain Hook just moments before he himself could with his tomahawk, liberating Neverland and taking the crown of glory for himself. Yes, those were bitter memories, and what true man could not resent a being so gifted, so destined — so powerful?

Indeed, it was an impossible task, and Charlie did resent the boy entirely until this day, for it was this day that the Great White Father spared his life, and for what reason, he did yet not know, but this night was not the night to attempt to discover the answer, for his mind was needed in the here and now, and until that answer became clear, he now owed the boy his allegiance.

Charlie made the decision to put the weighty thoughts from his mind, and looked out into the mist. His eyes narrowed as he sensed some great danger nearby, for he had felt it since they arrived, but the cover of night gave it additional power. What it was, he did not yet know, but he felt it was some ancient evil, and until the boy was done with his task, he and the others would have to endure its presence…

***

Peter carefully walked up and along the treacherous stairway, giving diligence to each step, for although his balance was great, without his ability to fly to aid him, one false move could mean his peril.

"All right, Peter," he counseled himself. "Don't look down… just take one step at a time… that's it…"

CLINK — Peter kicked a rock that cascaded down the sheer walls of the mountain. He shuddered as he looked over into the dark abyss, the eerie black appearing as it went on forever, then, he heard that same girlish high-pitched giggle fill the cavern. Peter held up the shining vial, using the light to expose whatever he could.

"What have you done to me?!" He yelled into the air. "Why can't I fly?!"

He waited for a moment, but there was no answer, just the resounding sound of that girlish giggle that reverberated through the mountain.

"Show yourself!" Peter commanded, but there was nothing.

Peter clenched his jaw as he looked out into the darkness. Whatever this thing was, it was very powerful, and it cared very little about him. Then he steeled his nerves and continued forward up the path into the mountain…

***

By sundown, Ruby reached the edge of Cannibal Cove on Pirate Eater beach, several miles east of where the Great River fell off the basin into the shimmering sea below, and shortly after Tiger Lily came up behind her on Fleur. Together, they looked out over the water, and on the horizon they saw three ships silhouetted by the setting Neverland sun, each one glowing a haunting black against the large, orange fireball that was dipping, deeper and deeper, beneath the waves.

Ruby whinnied and stomped her hooves in the sand, bucking her horn in the direction of the ships, for she could feel Tinker Bell's energy in the air, and she knew that she was on one of them.

"I know, girl, I know…" Tiger Lily said as she stroked her mane, doing her best to relax her. "We'll find her." She then turned to the others. “Eat food. Get rest. We’ll wait for the cover of nightfall.”

“Nightfall?!” Nibs exclaimed, not approving of Tiger Lily’s decision, for he knew that every moment that they held Tink captive was another moment that she wasn’t safe and at peace, back in the company of the people that loved her, and he couldn’t stand the thought of it. “Tink needs us now!”

“No,” Tiger Lily commanded, for as emotional as she could be herself, now was not the time for it — she had to be logical — and without Peter to aid them by air, she’d have to be even more strategic than ever if they were to be successful in rescuing her. “If they see us coming, they’ll kill her.”

From the shadows, came a dark and sinister snicker, and the group turned to face it.

“Those dogs probably already did the little fairy in,” Marco jeered. “After they had some fun with her.”

“I’ll cut out your heart!” Nibs screamed, pulling out his pirate sword in total rage, and Slightly did the same. Marco and Pax countered by pulling out their tomahawks.

“Nibs! Stay your sword!” Tiger Lily ordered.

Nibs didn’t move, he just breathed heavily as he stared Marco down in a state of total annihilation. That foolish brave would lose his tongue for those words, for no one in Neverland spoke of Tinker Bell in such a way, and he would avenge her for it — right here, right now — he would cut down this swine where he stood, and his blood would be his penance as he walked the lonely halls of the underworld.

"Nibs, stay your sword," Tiger Lily continued. "I command you!"

At the princess' words, Nibs' gaze left Marco — the pig swine — and slowly trailed over to Tiger Lily. He marched over to her through the sand, and looked her right in the eye.

"You command me?" He said, at a near loss for words. "Who's side are you really on?... Ours?... Or theirs?" Nibs nodded in the direction of Marco and Pax, who both jeered with contempt.

Tiger Lily took a breath as she stared at the braves. On one hand, they were her own — two of the greatest warriors in the Piccaninny Tribe — and on the other hand, they were absolute fools. Although Tiger Lily didn't personally care for Tinker Bell herself — or her arrogance, which, at times, matched that of Peter — to use such words against the fairy in a time of peril, or to suggest she was dead, or worse, was just downright stupidity. If Peter was here to hear those words, what form punishment he would inflict upon the brave as restitution in his wrath, she didn't even want to imagine. Then again, if Peter was here, Marco wouldn't have said anything in the first place, for the braves feared the Great White Father like death itself… but clearly they didn't fear her.

"That's right Princess," Marco said as Tiger Lily approached him, satisfied with how she had commanded the lost boys. "About time you put him in his place."

BAM! — Tiger Lily punched Marco right in the mouth! He hit the beach hard, completely blindsided by the blow — BAM! BAM! — Tiger Lily jumped on top of him and started beating him senseless with formidable strength, sinking her fists further and further into his face with every blow, beating his head into the sand.

Nibs and Slightly walked over and watched without much emotion as Tiger Lily ripped Marco's face apart. To them, that man was dead the moment he spoke foul words against Tinker Bell, for if Peter was there, the brave would have already been decapitated, and it was only right that Tiger Lily was extracting vengeance in his stead.

As Tiger Lily pulverized Marco's face into the sand, she was angry, and she felt all the frustrations over the last week's tribulations pour out of her — the fight with Peter, the botched anniversary, her quarrels with Tinker Bell, the responsibility of her title, and the return of the fear that she knew Peter was carrying, that she now carried inside her — it all poured out of her in a fluster of fury right into Marco's face until it was nothing but bloody mush beneath her.

When she was finally finished and her energy was spent, Tiger Lily leaned back, took a breath of relief, and looked up at the sky. It was a clear night, and she could see all the stars swimming in it… she felt lighter… relieved to get that pent up energy out of her… surely, surely now… things would be getting better…

Silent, Pax watched in fear and awe as Tiger Lily arose from the body of his fallen comrade, her face and clothes splattered and dripping with his blood.

"You have something to say?" Tiger Lily said as she looked right at him, her fury and power beaming through her like some kind of immortal goddess after a killing spree.

Shocked and in utter terror, Pax quickly shook his head to appease her, and to avoid bringing down any residual wrath upon himself.

"There's nothing you can do to save him now," Marco chortled through his broken, bloody face as Tiger Lily began to walk away down the beach.

Tiger Lily froze at the words, then doubled back. "It was you…" she said as she shoved a foot into his chest, pinning him to the sand.

"I found this in his saddle pack." Slightly ran over and handed a sack of gold to Tiger Lily — the same sack of gold that Marco traded to the captain in exchange for the peace pipe.

"What's this?" Tiger Lily said, holding it before Marco.

Marco just laughed and gargled on the ground, he seemed to really be enjoying this moment. "You have no… you have no idea…" he chortled hysterically. "You have absolutely no idea… you'll get what's coming to you… you'll all get what's coming to you…"

Marco's harrowing laugh continued to build like a maniac, cracking up in a bout of madness that was both pitiful and terrifying to behold. Tiger Lily threw the open sack of gold on Marco's face where it clinked and exploded on impact, sending gold pieces flying everywhere. The weight of it knocked his head back into the sand, hard, shutting him up. She then knocked an arrow in her bow, aiming a kill shot right at his head.

"What is coming for us?" She demanded.

Marco laughed sinisterly as he choked on his own blood, then he used his last bit of strength to lift his head from the ground, and his eyes narrowed fiercely as he looked the princess in the eye.

"Your worst nightmare," he said with words intended to terrorize.

THWAP! — Enraged, Tiger Lily let her arrow fly, and it scalped a bloody line right through Marco's head before sinking into the sand below it. Marco's eyes went huge in shock and terror, believing he was dead.

"Bind him," Tiger Lily said to Nibs and Slightly. "When this is all over, he'll be hung as a traitor."

"What about that one?" Nibs asked, nodding towards Pax who still stood completely frozen in fear.

"Run back to camp," Tiger Lily commanded Pax. "Tell my father what you've seen here. If you're not out of my range in sixty seconds, it will be your last."

Pax just stared at Tiger Lily, blinking with wide eyes, trying to process the command.

"Fifty seconds," Tiger Lily said.

The reality of what Tiger Lily intended to do finally hit Pax, and he turned on his heel and ran for dear life westward down Pirate Eater Beach — in fact, he ran faster than any brave in Neverland had ever run before.

"Are you going to shoot him?" Nibs asked as Pax ran further and further away.

"I certainly would like to," Tiger Lily said as she holstered her bow, then she turned and walked back towards Fleur.

***

Charlie continued to patrol the peripherals of the mountain camp the lost boys had set up, serious and on guard, sensing something foul in the air.

"You're gonna make me antsy being so antsy," Curly said as he prodded at the small fire he had made.

"We shouldn't have a fire going," Charlie said in disapproval. "It may attract unwanted attention."

"Relax," Tootles said. "There's nobody up here but us." Satisfied with Curly's fire, Tootles smiled and began pulling out his cooking gear and provisions. "Hungry?"

"No," Charlie answered without hesitation. "A true brave never eats until the hunt is complete… until the journey is over."

"Uh, huh," Tootles teased. "We'll see if you say that in ten minutes when you smell these sausages."

At the word sausage, Charlie stepped out of the darkness and peered over Curly's shoulder at the provisions.

"Is that rabbit sausage?" Charlie asked, unable to hide his curiosity.

"Yup," Tootles answered. "Big fat ones. Caught 'em last week."

"Hmm," Charlie considered for a moment, then realizing he was letting his stomach rule over him — which no true brave ever did — he scowled and headed back off into the fog.

"He'll be back," Tootles chuckled as he began to roast the sausage.

"You're damn right he will." Curly agreed with a lick of his lips...

***

Peter reached the top of the stairway and emerged out onto another stone plateau. He held up Tink's shining vial of neverbrew, but there was nothing but darkness beyond its rays. Suddenly —

"Who goes there?" — A deep and commanding voice filled the cavern.

The sound was full, unnerving, and struck down to the core of Peter's being. It was the complete opposite of the sweet, girlish voice that had led him on this far. Peter took a moment and held the light aloft, searching the darkness for the source of the voice, but there was nothing but pitch black all around him. Peter took a deep breath all the way down to the base of his spine, finding his courage, for he thought it important to become as large as possible to converse with whatever this presence was…

"It is I. Peter Pan." He spoke deeply into the void, answering from his belly.

A moment, then that same girlish, high-pitched giggle once again echoed all around him, filling the cavern with the delightful and seductive sound. Peter held up the shining vial, searching for the origin, but he was still shrouded by darkness from every side…

WHOOSH… suddenly, Peter was surrounded by a pink-white mist and light as the darkness began to vanish into a new energy. Ivory walls with dark red curtains began to appear all around him, and big red sofas with golden pillows began to materialize out of thin air. At the far end of the chamber, there was a bed with long, flowing red curtains. Peter stood in awe, for it dawned on him in this moment that he had finally reached the enchantress' lair.

"Peter Pan," the beautiful voice rang out all around him, but the girlish quality was gone, and it was strictly seductive now, and entirely female. To Peter, it sounded just as enticing as Tiger Lily in their intimate moments together on Tiger Island when she was really turning it on with her feminine charms, even more so…

No, he shook his head, for he had to keep his mind about him. He remembered what the chief said, that to touch this being would mean certain death, and that was not an option when the fate of Neverland was in his hands.

"Show yourself, witch," Peter commanded into the air.

"Witch?" There was a quiet woosh as a red flowing energy left the bed and glided across the space towards Peter in a cloud of ethereal power. The energy gathered together and the enchantress began to materialize before him, taking the form of a beautiful, full-bodied youth with dark hair and red, full lips. A dark red, silk two-piece draped off her body, barely concealing the vivacious curves of her voluptuous form.

"Do you still think I'm a witch?" The enchantress spoke, cocking her head to the side.

Peter was completely mesmerized. His eyes were wider than they had ever been before as he took in the site in front of him, for this was undoubtedly the most beautiful and attractive being he had ever seen — more than any of the mermaids, more than any of the fairies, more than any girls, and even more than Tiger Lily…

"If only I could kiss her," he thought. "Then surely, she would know what to do. Surely, all my troubles would be over." As if coming out of his body, Peter felt his Spirit drawing towards her… just a little bit closer… just one kiss and all would be well…

Then, Peter thought of Tinker Bell, and the peril she was in, and how much she was counting on him to succeed, and then all at once his mind came back to him. Peter snapped out of it as he was just feet from the enchantress. He pulled out his dagger, and pointed it right at her chest.

"Give me back my flying," he commanded. "Or I'll run you through."

"You wouldn't hurt a girl, would you?" The enchantress said with big, glossy eyes.

"Don't try me," Peter said, and he stared right back into them with his own, looking past the seductive veneer to the sinister magic beneath.

There was a moment as they stared at each other, and it became clear that Peter would not break so easily. The enchantress giggled and dematerialized into red, flowing energy as she plunged into Peter's dagger and moved right over him in a river of light. Peter flinched, remembering the chief's warning, but he did not choose to touch her — she touched him — and he sensed that choice was a key component of the task.

"You want to fly… like this…" The enchantress began flowing around the room, giggling playfully as she materialized and dematerialized at will.

Peter watched hopelessly from the carpeted floor as the enchantress danced circles around him in the air, and he didn't like it one bit, for he felt entirely limited and human in this moment, and reasoned this must be what pirates and other land bound creatures felt when he was flying circles around them, and it was terrifying… whoever or whatever this being was… she was extremely powerful to be able to reduce him to such limited means…

"I was told to come see you," Peter spoke boldly.

Instantly, the enchantress rematerialized in full form right in front of him. "Have you come to play with me?" She asked.

"Play, yes, play — that's it," Peter said, getting an idea. "I've come to play with you."

"Yay!" The enchantress dematerialized and began flowing around the room like an excited little girl, then she popped back into full form right in front of him. "What kind of fun would you like to have?"

The enchantress began to move towards Peter very seductively. Peter back peddled to keep his distance and fell right into one of the big, red couches, barely keeping space between himself and the enchantress's voluptuous, heaving chest that spilled out over him, tempting him to the core of his being… he could feel himself losing control…

"You'll find I can be a lot of fun to play with," the enchantress said as she looked into Peter's eyes, and then she moved in to kiss him... this was it…

Right before their lips touched, Peter thought of Neverland, and Tinker Bell, and all things good and bright, and he found some untapped power within him to pull away from the all-consuming energy that now attempted to lord over him… he would take this being on… and he would win…

"I was thinking of a different game," Peter said, slipping out from beneath her as the enchantress landed on the couch.

"Hmph," she pouted, crossing her arms over her chest.

"How about I tell you about a dream I had," Peter continued, now thinking about his vision in the void. "And you tell me what you think it means — sound like fun?"

"No." The enchantress pouted, shaking her head. "I want to play my game!"

Suddenly, the enchantress' eyes went dark. In a swirl of energy Peter was hurled across the chamber where he landed right in the middle of her bed. Peter sunk down into it, and never had he smelt such delight. His senses were overtaken in an intoxicating ecstasy… it was as if the enchantress had infiltrated every fiber of his being… every cell… it was as if she was in his very blood… and it was wonderful…

Peter opened his eyes, and the enchantress was above him in full form, looking down on him, and he felt as if he was in some kind of wonderful dream state. Peter tried to move, but some unknown force held him to the bed. Whether in actuality he couldn't move, or didn't want to move, he could no longer tell, and it was quite possible that in this moment they were the same thing. He looked up, helplessly captivated by her beauty. The enchantress stroked Peter's brow, touching his face as she looked deeply into his bright eyes, studying him.

"Close your eyes, Son of Neverland," she whispered softly. "Allow yourself to be…"

The enchantress leaned down and kissed Peter on the mouth, and this time, Peter's mind did not fight it… for there was nothing left to fight for or against… he was swallowed up in passion now… and this was truly all there was worth living for…

Peter went into her kiss… it tasted like heaven… then…

WHOOSH… the enchantress and the chamber suddenly vanished as Peter was once again engulfed in a flash of white light… once again pulled into some strange unknown…

* CHAPTER 12 *

— BORN —

For what seemed like a great long while, Peter was being destroyed. It felt like his soul was being torn apart — like the very fabric of his being was being pulled apart like thread — there was screaming, but only in his mind, for he had no voice left to scream with, and no body. Around and around his mind went in hyperactive loops of thought and infinite paradoxes that ended in nothing. He'd look forward and he'd see only flame — universes on fire and disintegrating into ash — he'd look down, and the nothingness would swallow him whole, he'd look up, and remorse would pour like rivers of water from his eyes…

Whenever Peter thought his mind was beginning to stabilize, it turned out to be some kind of infinite jest, a trick, and the cycle would begin all over again, and around and around it went. He prayed for it to end, but it would not. Surely, he was in hell — he had to be — for Peter could conceptualize no death worse than what he was experiencing. Surely, his soul was in the pit, and here he'd stay… abandoned… locked in torment forever…

Then the darkness closed in upon him and swallowed him whole, and the thought loop closed, and for a moment there was nothing — indeed, no thought — and Peter Pan as he once knew himself to be no longer existed. There was only eternal darkness and nothingness for a great long while, and his mind finally rested…

Then…

BOOM! — There was a massive explosion of infinite light, color, and sound as Peter exploded back into being above the Misty Mountains of Neverland. Rivers of unlimited energy and vivid color poured out of his eyes as he felt himself being reborn from inside the totality of all things. From his being all of Neverland poured forth and breathed from the infinite thought in his mind, the infinite thought of all creation. Peter could not move, nor could he speak, but could only bear witness to what was, and what always would be… some kind of immutable and eternal power… the Creator of all things… the source of all Light…

Peter Pan had seen the Truth…

When the moment had passed, Peter's mind fell from the sky back towards Neverland, into the infinite white blanket of energy below him…

***

Peter opened his eyes as he began to re-comprehend himself… he looked around… he was literally floating inside a sea of white light… no height… no depth… just pure light…

He looked down and saw Neverland floating inside of a glossy, ethereal orb. In Peter's current state, Neverland basically looked like a snow globe. He lifted his hands and the orb floated within them. Peter continued to stare, mesmerized with awe and curiosity as he looked down upon his world…

"Cool, huh?" — A relaxed and boyish voice filled the air all around him.

Peter instantly recoiled from the interruption, and the orb containing Neverland zoomed out of sight. He then peered into the brightness and saw a perfect, child-like being made out of pure light. Whatever it was, it sparkled with the very ether of existence itself, and Peter thought that he couldn't imagine anything more brilliant. Indeed, Peter thought it had to be the perfection of his imagination — was it himself? His conscience? Or something far greater still?

"How did you like Andromeda?" The Great Spirit chuckled. "She's got a temper on her, but she sure is convincing."

"What was that?" Peter said, still reeling from the shock of what had happened to him.

"That was some real darkness," The Great Spirit said honestly. "It was your own, but you made it through."

Peter looked at the Great Spirit curiously.

"You were just born, man," the Great Spirit said matter-of-factly. "Everything you ever went through—"

"Was to get me to here now," Peter said, finishing his sentence, his mind trying to grasp its epic scope.

"All of it," the Great Spirit confirmed.

After a few more moments, Peter looked up.

"What *am I*, exactly?" Peter asked.

"You are the god of *whatever* you just came out of," the Great Spirit answered, and Peter took a few moments to digest it.

"Welcome to the infinity club," the Great Spirit stated, and with that, he turned and started walking through the ether.

"Wait," Peter said. "There are more of us?"

The Great Spirit didn't answer Peter directly, but chuckled knowingly, and continued walking.

"You must be hungry from your journey," the Spirit said after another moment. "How about some food?"

Instantly, every kind of food one could imagine appeared all around them — foods from different lands, different countries, different worlds — the Great Spirit rubbed his hands together and began dishing up two slices of pizza.

"This stuff right here is my favorite," the Spirit said. "It comes from this little planet called earth… they call it… *pizza.*" Peter just stared as the Spirit dished up the slices on two plates. "Don't worry, this one is vegan."

The Spirit offered a slice to Peter, who looked back at him in disbelief.

"Oh, that's right, you've been to earth," the Spirit said, doubling back. "The whole Wendy thing…"

Peter continued to stare at the Spirit — what was he going on about?

"Good times," the Spirit said. "Have you ever flown by New York? That's where I got it."

Peter was at a loss for words. How could this great and powerful Spirit be talking about food and girls at a time like this?

"Yes, I've been to earth," Peter snapped. "And I don't want to eat — I want to know what I have to do to rescue Tinker Bell and save Neverland!"

"About that," the Great Spirit said, then as quickly as it all appeared the food vanished, and thousands of glossy, ethereal orbs appeared all around them like the one Peter saw Neverland in just moments ago… they were now floating in a sea of orbs…

"Are these… worlds?" Peter asked, awestruck by the size and scope of his current reality. The Great Spirit nodded in agreement. "Amazing!" Peter exclaimed. "Which one is yours? Where are you from?"

"Oh… a place… not too unlike this one…" The Great Spirit gently wafted his hand and summoned the Neverland orb to the front and center. It floated before them like some self-contained ball of infinite light, and together they looked down into the tiny world…

"Do you know what makes Neverland so special, Peter?" the Great Spirit said after a moment. "It's that people believe…"

Peter looked over at the Great Spirit, and looked into his eyes, and he felt as if he was looking into himself — some higher version, that was — some part of himself that was unbound by all of space and time, completely limitless and without measure.

“It takes faith to find it,” the Spirit continued. “It takes faith for it to find you… faith gives you wings…”

Peter and the Spirit smiled at each other for a moment, and Peter knew the words were true, for it was utter faith that had always given him his ability to fly, something true, and deep, and innate within himself, and he knew that he possessed no power greater than his ability to believe.

Another moment, then a darkness washed over the Great Spirit’s countenance. “But not for much longer…” The Great Spirit waved his hand and a vision took Peter, and once again he was pulled from the light into some unknown beyond…

***

Peter saw Neverland forming in the ether, and glimpses of the first fairies as they began to colonize the planet for the first time… then a dark shadow passed over them… all the fairies looked up at the sky…

“Before you were born,” the Spirit said as Peter watched the vision. “Long before pirates or Indians came to her shores… Neverland was ruled by an ancient force… a force as old as existence itself… *Time…*”

As Peter was consumed by the vision, he saw the dual forces of life and death, growth and decay, new life and old life, fairies living, aging, struggling, and dying… it appeared to him that Neverland was once very much like earth.

"For thousands of years," the Spirit continued. "Fairies struggled under the relentless oppression of Time… birthing, living, and dying… everyday fighting to exist."

Peter was pulled through his vision, and he saw a little boy —just a few days old— being flown across the Gulf of Neverland in a pixie cradle by a band of hooded fairies… a little mountain goat was cuddled up next to the boy…

"The ancients prophesied the coming of a great boy-child, one who would bathe their world in eternal light, defeating time, and break the cycle of life and death once and for all…"

Among the fairies that shepherded the boy across the sea, Peter saw Tinker Bell in her tiny form. She looked down on the boy fondly, and he reached up for her through the covered blanket with his tiny hand… she smiled back at him and reached down to touch him, then…

A dark shadow crossed over the little boy's face. Peter watched through the vision as Tinker Bell turned to look up into the sky, and saw a dark ghoul flying right at them and closing in fast. Tinker Bell's eyes narrowed. She covered the little boy just as the ghoul closed in on them and she met the closing darkness with a powerful blast of light!

Peter's mind was once again consumed by white light as he continued his witness to the ensuing vision…

Tinker Bell and the other hooded fairies quickly took the cradled boy through a passage lit only by torchlight…

"The fairies took the boy deep into the underground fairy mines," the Spirit continued. "Planning to hide him away until he came of age…"

The passage opened into an underground cavern where a slightly younger Mr. Theodore was eagerly waiting for them. As they emerged, he met Tinker Bell and the others and looked down on the boy as they set his cradle to rest. He then produced a beautiful, ethereal dagger from his robes — The Dagger of Truth — and as he brought it near the boy it began to glow and hum with golden energy. Mr. Theodore looked at Tinker Bell and the other fairies and nodded — the boy was the one, the prophesied Savior of Neverland.

Mr. Theodore set the dagger outside the boy's cradle… it continued to hum brighter and louder with more and more energy as Peter was pulled deeper into the vision…

Peter's mind was now hovering above a dark chamber made out of black stone and pure obsidian. On the throne, sat an unknown being made out of smoking, black and purple flames of ethereal energy… whatever it was… Peter found it both terrifying and beautiful to behold.

"But Time caught wind of this prophecy," the Spirit went on, "and became determined to find and destroy the boy before he became powerful enough to confront him..."

A servant approached. Peter watched the dark being rise from his throne in wrath as he received news about the child's escape... the dark being wafted his hand and the room dissolved in a cloud of black smoke...

Peter was pulled through the ether until he was once again floating over a vision of Northern Neverland. He watched from above as a massive war raged on fields of the Great Plains below. Thousands of fairies bathed in light battled hundreds of thousands of dark ghouls shrouded in darkness...

"A Great War ensued," the Spirit said. "The fairies fought valiantly, but they were greatly outnumbered by Time's dark armies... thousands perished..."

"Fall back!" Peter watched as a fairy captain screamed on the battlefield... the fledgling fairy army was surrounded on all sides by the closing and formidable darkness...

Peter's mind was pulled back underground into the old fairy mines beneath what appeared to be the beginnings of Pixie's Landing. There, Tinker Bell and two other fairies guarded the boy's crib. Their hands lit up with energy as they assumed a fighting stance, ready to guard the boy against the ensuing shadows and sounds of steel that moved closer and closer to their keep from outside the door.

Tinker Bell's eyes narrowed in perfect battle-focus as she trained them upon the shadows moving in. "No matter what happens, we guard him with our lives — is that understood?" She commanded.

The other fairies nodded in complete agreement, ready to give their lives for their faith. The boy, who looked to be about two years old then, stood and looked through the bars of his crib…

"For Neverland," Tinker Bell whispered as the shadows closed in, ready to fight to the death… this was it…

On the stand next to the boy's crib… the Dagger of Truth began to glow hot and vibrate on the nightstand…

Peter's mind was pulled back up above the battle of the Great Plains where the last of the fairies had courageously surrounded the entrance to Pixie's Landing on all sides, prepared to give their lives to defend the boy that rested its depths, and the hope of life that rested with him. The endless sea of Time's dark armies closed in upon the remaining fairies, preparing to swallow them up once and for all.

In all his wrath, the dark and ethereal form of Time himself had taken to the battlefield to join the fight and deal the final death blow. In their last defense, Mr. Theodore and two other elder fairies took flight to confront the dark being with the most powerful fairy magic their race possessed.

"In the final hour of that fateful day," the Spirit's voice rang out. "The Dark Father of Time himself emerged upon the battlefield in full wrath and malice…"

Mr. Theodore and the others blasted the Dark Father with everything they had, sending massive blasts of white-hot fairy light right at him… for a moment… it appeared as though it had incinerated the Dark Father, but to no avail, for moments later the darkness of Time absorbed all the light completely, and sent two blasts of ethereal, dark fire energy right back at the ancient fairies that were ten times more sinister than the ones directed at him.

Mr. Theodore barely dodged the lethal energy blasts, but the two other ancient fairies were hit head on. He watched in horror as their bodies withered and turned to ash before his eyes, and blew away in the wind. He then turned his gaze upon Time… the hope waning from his eyes… there was nothing more him or the other fairies could do to stand against such unlimited death…

"All hope…" The Great Spirit's voice echoed through Peter's mind. "Was laid waste…"

Peter watched as the Dark Father of Time hovered above the dwindling fairy army, charging a devastating dark energy attack, preparing to deliver the final death blow. The fairies on the ground looked courageously up into the darkness growing above them, prepared to die for what they believed in, for no life was better than life without their freedom… this was truly the end… or perhaps a new beginning… then…

There was a flash of all-consuming, powerful, white light that burned through the surrounding darkness, blinding the enemy…

“Then, just as all was at its end,” the Great Spirit’s voice rang forth. “A light shined in the darkness…”

As the blinding flash from the light cooled, a little boy appeared from its center, smiling as if filled with all the life-force in the entire universe. The Dagger of Truth glowed golden hot before him….

The darkness of Time roared at the sight and blasted the boy with all the darkness he could muster — indeed, enough darkness to destroy an entire planet — but the power that was in the child could not be undone…

Before Time could process the impossibility of what was happening to him, the boy moved through the air at lighting speed until he was right upon him, then plunged the Dagger of Truth right into the center of the Dark Father’s chest. Time screamed as he felt his presence being annihilated, disappearing in a blast of dark smoke as light energy literally destroyed him from within, incinerating his physical being.

“The Dark Father of Time…” the Spirit said. “Had been vanquished…”

With the passing of the Dark Father, the dark armies of Time also vanished in clouds of black smoke as light energy surged across the Great Plains, wiping out their stain from the land. The remaining fairy army shouted in triumph and joy at their liberation from the evil one.

As the presence of Time disappeared, and all the smoke from his malice cleared, the Dagger of Truth stopped glowing, and the boy fell from the sky, unconscious…

Several warrior fairies took flight and gracefully caught their Savior in the air, laying him to rest safely on the ground.

Then Peter's mind was pulled down into the boy, and he saw through the mind of the boy… and for the first time he felt as if he was the boy… moments later, Tinker Bell stood above him, looking down on him… she was so beautiful… she smiled at him… then other fairies gathered around him, and did the same… smiling at the one who saved them all…

***

Peter re-comprehended himself, and once again he was back in the all-white space. The Great Spirit stood with his back turned, looking out into the endless light…

"The boy," Peter started. "That was me…"

The Great Spirit didn't answer, and Peter took his silence as confirmation. Peter took a moment to allow the reality of it to sink in… so many unanswered questions…

"But I thought Time doesn't exist in Neverland?" Peter asked.

"Your physical birth was the turning of the tide, Peter," the Great Spirit said, now turning to face him. "You brought Neverland into eternity. You were the answer to the prayers of thousands of fairies — trust me, I remember," the Spirit chuckled, then his countenance fell dark. "But Time… is still very much alive…"

The Great Spirit waved his hand and suddenly a dozen other war-torn worlds floated before them… earth was among them…

"Every day that the light of eternity shines on Neverland," the Great Spirit continued. "The darkness of Time grows stronger in other worlds, feeding off the fear, hate, and confusion of their inhabitants… and the Dark Father… wants revenge…"

The Great Spirit waved his hand once more, and the other worlds fell back into the ether as earth was pulled to the forefront. Together, they looked down into the tiny world…

Peter saw men in a desert, all dressed in uniform, carrying weapons that fired projectiles in rapid succession. He saw bombs exploding as men screamed in pain as they lost their limbs. He saw buildings and cities on fire as more screams of pain, suffering, and dying filled his mind…

The earth continued to spin, and Peter now saw men in suits, screaming messages of war and hatred from podiums to the fearful, unconscious population below who willingly looked to these men for their truth. The masses watched the screaming mad-men with wide-eyes from television screens, brainwashed and powerless, completely trapped in their hellish and hopeless realities…

It spun faster now… Peter witnessed famine and starvation… he saw large machines as far as his eyes could see, with so much smoke in the sky that it blotted out the sun… he saw once alive and thriving forests reduced to barren wastelands… he saw a massive, treeless city with buildings stacked on top of each other a mile high, and down below, the entire population walking around outside in masks… he saw thousands of families crying over dead loved ones… it was all too horrifying… too hopeless…

"Enough," Peter said. "I can't see anymore."

The earth and the other planets then vanished, and once again it was Peter and the Great Spirit standing in the light.

"Not too pretty, huh?" The Great Spirit said.

"It's horrible," Peter admitted. "Can you stop it?"

"The universe is made of free energy, Peter," the Great Spirit explained. "Every conscious being has to make a choice — to live in light and love, or to live in darkness and fear — that choice will affect the world they live in, for better or worse…"

Peter's mind attempted to dig into the revealed knowledge as the Great Spirit paused, for he had never heard it put into words so rightly, and it seemed to him in this moment that he understood this truth inherently without any effort at all, for absolute freedom and lightness of being is all he had ever known, and all he believed there was for him. How others did not grasp the truth, however, was the real mystery, and he could not get his mind around why someone would choose a worse life, when it was so much simpler to choose a better one.

"To answer your question," the Great Spirit continued. "No, I cannot interfere with the fate of your world, but you were born with all the power you need to protect it."

Peter's mind once again pivoted at the Great Spirit's words, for so much had been thrust upon him so quickly. So, he had defeated Time when he was a boy? Before he was old enough to remember? Yes, he supposed that did make sense. That would explain why no one really aged past the pinnacle of their youth, unless they were already older to begin with. It would also explain the fairies adoration for him, and why nobody ever seemed to talk about his past, or what he did when he first came to Neverland, and why he never really liked to think of any of that himself, much preferring to live in the present or even future than in the past.

But still, it was a bit much. So now there was an immortal deity he had to fight? Some great power that had been gathering strength to come back to Neverland once again? Some cosmic force that he defeated when he was too young to remember how, and now what? He just had to figure out how to do it again? By what power? Wasn't that hellish rebirth experience he had to go through enough? What could be worse than that? — Nothing — and now what? More was being asked of him?! What for? Why him? Why now? He wasn't a god… he was just a boy… a boy that could fly and liked to have fun… and this was all too insane… too ridiculous…

"Yes… but if what you're saying is true," Peter stuttered. "When I first defeated Time… I was only a—"

"*Child,*" the Great Spirit said, finishing Peter's thought, then he smiled, and looked directly into Peter's eyes, and Peter felt as if he was reflecting back his own soul. "*Exactly.*"

With that, the Great Spirit chuckled again and completely vanished in light…

WHOOSH! — There was another bright flash, and Peter was once again pulled from the void…

***

Charlie continued to patrol the camp's perimeter under the peaks of the Windy Mountains, guarding the others. The darker it continued to get, the more tense he became, for there was something evil in the night, and the most he could hope for was that it didn't further bother them.

Tootles laid next to the fire, passed out from his rabbit sausage feast. Curly and the Twins played cards by firelight.

"Oy! Come have a bite of these sausages, Charlie!" Curly followed with a burp. "They're delicious!"

When there was no answer from the darkness beyond the camp, Curly shrugged, then he threw down a four-of-a-kind sevens on top of a pile of buttons. "I gotcha this time boys," he said to the Twins. "They don't call it lucky number seven for nothin'…"

As Curly started to rake in the buttons, the Twins just stared at him with those same Cheshire boyish grins they stared at him with in the treehouse. “Wait, don’t tell me you two cuties got somethin’ up your sleeve?” Curly said, stopping abruptly. “Nah… not possible… you had a good run, gents, but as they say, all good things must come to an end.”

Then, the Twins also threw down a four-of-a-kind — of eights.

“What the?!” Curly yelled. “Eights?! Oh come on!”

“Oy! Keep it down, Curly,” Tootles groaned as he rolled over. “You wanna wake the whole lot of Crocodile Crack.”

“These buggers are cheating me again!” Nibs exclaimed, defending his vocal tone.

“Everyone knows you don’t play the Twins in cards,” Tootles continued. “You’ve got a better chance getting a kiss from a mermaid then beatin’ those two.”

Curly looked at the mountain of buttons that now sat in front of the smiling Twins, then he looked down at his own pile of buttons — he only had one left, not even enough to play a hand — he looked back at the Twins and shrugged, hopeless. “Spare a few buttons?”

Suddenly, a hand came out of the firelight and grabbed Curly, covering his mouth. As Curly panicked, Tootles sat up, trying to catch his bearings, and the Twins loaded their slingshots with lighting speed, ready to attack the intruder.

Then, before a battle could break out, Charlie stepped into the firelight. He motioned for them all to be silent as he pointed his tomahawk into the darkness beyond. He then slowly released Curly, who held his tongue this time. The lost boys gathered their weapons, and they backed up next to the fire, on guard.

From the darkness, a deep, powerful growl filled the ravine… something evil, and sinister, and massive was closing in on them… but what?

Tootles threw a few more logs on the coals… whatever it was… hopefully it didn't like fire….

***

Through a blinding flash of white light, Peter opened his eyes and he was back under the Enchantress — or Andromeda, supposedly, at least that's what the Great Spirit had called her — she finished kissing him and pulled away from his lips.

"This is some adventure," Peter said as he looked up at her with wide eyes.

The Enchantress giggled and stroked Peter's brow. He was sweaty and spent from the vision, and he felt as if their spirits were close now, as if they had made love. In truth, he wasn't in a hurry to leave, for he had touched her now — that much was done — and he could think of nothing greater than to stay there a while with her magnificent body pressed up against his.

Yes, his mind was finally finding its vindication… this was exactly what he needed after a long journey… after all he'd been through… that old chief… he was just superstitious… for there could be nothing greater than a goddess such as this… nothing more delicious, or right, or true… she was the very gift of life itself, and he would have her… He, The Great Peter Pan, the Son of Neverland would have her, and there could be no other, for He was the Chosen One…

Peter's mind was really taking him now. He had forgotten about Neverland, he had forgotten about those pesky pirates and their mal intent, he had forgotten about the braves, the lost boys, Tiger Lily, and even Tinker Bell in her peril — none of that mattered now — for the first time since he could remember thinking his mind needed nothing else, no other stimulus, no other entertainment, no other need for relevance or importance, nothing else other than to lie there, wrapped up in the arms of this goddess in complete surrender to her touch… if he had fallen under some sort of spell, then it was a perfect spell… and if his never-ending mind was finally satisfied after an eternity of endless desire… then he had finally found the Heaven he'd been searching for…

Peter pulled back to gaze down upon her beauty once more, then suddenly, her eyes became vacant and distant. The Enchantress tore herself away from Peter and started holding her stomach like she was sick.

"What is it? What's wrong?" Peter said, feeling the pain of the separation of their bodies immediately, and a great fear came upon him, for he longed to be near her again.

The enchantress bellied over as if dying, and suddenly, her true form began to be revealed to him. Peter watched in horror as her voluptuous figure withered into a sullen skeleton with an arching back. Her full, luscious hair became stringy and grey, her smooth skin became scaly and dry, and within moments she was no longer the blossoming youth that he had kissed and fallen in passionate love with, but rather a decrepit, ancient, lifeless hag of the underworld. When she had fully transformed, her head snapped towards Peter, and she stared at him with completely black eyes.

"You touched me, boy." She cackled. "You touched me of your own free will…"

Peter watched in terror as the witch addressed him.

"You think because you can fly, you can play in our world," the witch continued, laughing as if she had been waiting for this moment for some time. "You should have listened to Theodore — that old windbag — for I knew your heart's desire before you ever stepped foot on this mountain."

"What do you want?" Peter said, finding reason through his terror.

The witch then smiled at Peter, almost childlike, and he thought it must have been the most terrifying countenance he had ever seen.

"Oh, just your soul, dear boy," the witch said, peering into him. "Just your complete and entire soul… every piece of it… all there is."

Peter stood frozen in terror now, for he knew not what to do, and it was rare for him to be perplexed to this degree.

"Better run," the witch said with a final smile, then suddenly, the Enchantress' chamber began to vanish all around him. Peter jumped off the bed as the witch evaporated into a cloud of black smoke, and once again, he stood on a stone plateau inside of the mountain.

Peter pulled out Tinker Bell's vial of neverbrew potion to light the darkness, and the interior of the mountain began to creak and groan all around him as pieces of rock and debris began to fall from above — the cavern was collapsing in on him.

Peter leapt into the air, but his ability to fly was still gone. A deep rumbling began to resound as the mountain prepared to cave in. With what strength he had left, Peter turned and began to run back the way he came as fast his legs would carry him…

***

Charlie, Curly, Tootles, and the Twins stood back-to-back around the fire as the growls got closer.

"There's somethin' nasty out there, fellas," Curly said, barely holding it together.

"You think?" Tootles snarked.

Charlie's eyes narrowed as the growls seemed to change. Whatever it was, the growls seemed lighter than before, and there were more of them now — was it possible there were multiple creatures lurking in the dark? — He reasoned it was very possible. This could either be good or bad for them, depending on if they checked one another. Nonetheless he steadied his tomahawk, preparing for the worst…

The growling continued to get louder until it was right upon them, just beyond the edge of the firelight.

THWAP! THWAP! — The Twins loosed two stones from their slingshots into the darkness, and the growling stopped abruptly.

"Oy! I think you got 'em," Curly noted.

Then, a giant paw stepped into the firelight, followed by the growling, drooling face of a giant wolf! Its coat was a thick, ash grey, and it looked to be the size of a full-grown horse, over six feet tall at its head. Thick globs of drool fell from its rows of razor-sharp teeth.

"I guess not," Curly quivered, correcting his judgment.

Before any of the boys could react, the wolf leapt right towards them, flying savagely through the air, ready to demolish them all… this was surely their end… then…

BAM! — Solomon smashed the wolf in the side with his horns as he leapt through the air, sending it yelping and flying into the darkness. He then landed on four hooves, right in front of the boys, horns at the ready, prepared to defend his friends to the death as more growls closed in all around them.

"Solomon!" Tootles exclaimed! "Boy are we glad to have you! I'll plant you a whole garden of carrots after this!"

Solomon snorted as if he was prepared to breathe fire. He stomped his hooves on the ground, eyes focused on the coming darkness — let them come, for he was Solomon, the Great Mountain Goat, friend and companion of the Great Peter Pan, and he would show these wild dogs who was the king of beasts in Neverland…

***

As the mountain fell down all around him, Peter jumped down the stone stairwell as fast as his legs could carry him, taking great care to make sure his aim was true, for with his flying still negated he was particularly vulnerable.

Just then, a giant lava cone cascaded through the air and demolished the stairwell behind him, completely obliterating the path where he just stood. Peter's eyes went wide as more lava cones started falling all around him like missiles of death from above.

WHOOSH! — Peter leapt over a giant gap in the stairwell, soaring on pure faith, barely clearing the surface area and landing clean to the edge on the other side… just a little bit further now…

just a bit further and he'd reach the entrance… he could only pray that it would be open… or his adventure would truly be at its end…

Peter leapt over another gap in the stairwell, dodging a falling lava cone in mid-air with unprecedented agility. He landed clean and ran as fast as possible as boulders and lava cones continued to rain down from above, shaking the entire cavern like a bottle of pixie dust. Peter held up Tink's vial of neverbrew, casting the light as far as it would go. He could see the entrance! There, at the far reaches of the light… just a bit further now… just a few more steps and a little bit of luck… "Great Spirit… let the door be open…"

As Peter neared the entrance, he looked up and saw a massive lava cone shaking from the top of the cavern up ahead. When it dislodged, it would cascade down and completely destroy the entrance plateau and the rest of the path, making it impossible to enter or exit ever again. Peter would have one shot at it… and he would have to time it perfectly if he was to live…

"I hope this works," Peter yelled audibly, then he leapt from that path into the air towards the magical stone wall entrance just as the lava cone cascaded down from above, creating a giant rock face as it fell, smashing through the plateau and obliterating the path and all that was surrounding it. Peter laid out flat and soared through the air towards the rock face of the falling cone as if he was flying — his timing had to be perfect — as he neared, for a moment, it appeared as if he was going to smash right into the falling rock face of the cone, and that would be that as he fell down with it into the depths below, but just as he was feet away, the summit of the giant, falling cone cleared his path, and Peter was now soaring over the vacant abyss of the now crushed plateau below him as his falling body hurled towards the sheer rock face of the cavern's entrance. He had cleared the cone, but now he was going to smash right into the wall!

"AHHHHHH!" Peter screamed as he neared, for this had to be it — the entrance had to be open, or his adventuring, his entire life, would perish into the abyss of the Windy Mountains, and that haggard witch would have the soul she had longed to possess...

As Peter tumbled through the air, closing the last few feet between himself and the wall that represented eternal freedom or bondage, he closed his eyes... this was it...

***

Solomon stood in front of Charlie and the lost boys as the pack of giant wolves closed in. He'd take them all on if he could, but there were just too many of them. Six were visible now, surrounding them on all sides in the firelight, and more growls could be heard behind them. Solomon knew he could take three, four, maybe even all six, but it was only a matter of time before they wore him down. Solomon's hide was tough, but the lost boys were not... he could handle the razor-sharp claws and jaws for a time, but the boys were not equipped for this kind of foe... he would have to protect them all for as long as he could… if he didn't, his friends would surely die.

The wolves all got ready to leap in unison, and Solomon readied his stance. He'd have to take at least two of them out in the air before the other four touched the ground if the boys were to have a fighting chance. Then he'd have to double back and take two more out before they reached their targets. It was unlikely, but not impossible. Then he thought of all Peter had taught him — how to never give up hope, and to never stop fighting, never, not until all life has left you — then Solomon smiled his gruffiest of billy goat smiles, and prepared to kill them all.

The wolves leapt into the air, a twinkle entered Solomon's eye… this was it… the last stand of Solomon the mountain goat… the Great Guardian of Neverland… and companion to the immortal Peter Pan… long may he reign…

BANG! — In a blinding flash of light Peter flew out of the mountainside entrance in all his glory. Upon breaching the magic barrier his flying had returned to him. He held the neverbrew vial before him which shone brightly in the night as he soared through the air.

The blinding rays of the fairy light sent the wolves scattering in every direction as they ran for cover. The lost boys let out a battle cry as they chased the stragglers into the darkness. Peter Pan, their fearless leader, had returned at last.

With the wolves now gone, Peter landed valiantly before them. A beaming smile graced his countenance as new light energy now radiated off him. To the others, it appeared as if he had been reborn from some new material, as if he had ascended back from the ash and darkness of that destitute mountain, and returned to them now as some kind of higher being. It was still Peter — undoubtedly, yes, it was still Peter — but he clearly possessed some kind of higher power now, some kind of greater and higher power, and it was awesome to behold.

Solomon galloped excitedly up to Peter, for his friend had no idea how critical his timing had been.

"It's good to see you too, boy," Peter laughed as he rubbed Solomon's ears.

"Took you long enough," Curly said flatly, and Peter threw him a look to match.

"You have fun with that Enchantress I reckon'," Tootles teased, and Peter looked at him apprehensively. "Don't worry, I won't tell."

Peter cracked a smile which turned into laughter, and before he knew it all the boys were laughing, for they had escaped certain death once again, safe for now against all odds… then…

Charlie walked up and the boys fell silent. There was a moment as he studied the glowing boy before him, for he was brilliant, and bright, and as glorious as the morning sun. The Great White Father had become something greater, more powerful, and higher than he could have ever imagined. Yes, it was impossible, but the boy had done it again, and unto which there was no answer. The brave had met his master — a power that he could not fathom, and a power he could never surmount — visibly shaking, Charlie dropped to one knee…

"You are the Son of Neverland," Charlie said, and truth poured from his voice. "Forgive me… forgive my unbelief."

On his knees, Charlie expected this to be the end. Surely, the Great White Father would smite him now, surely, after all he had done, after all the problems he had caused, surely, his time was at an end. For what was he now? A mere human against such a deity? A mere human against such a god?! Yes, that is what he had become — a god — the Great White Father had become a god, and he would have no use for such a weak and troublesome mortal. He was the alpha being. The apex of all things in Neverland, and it was only natural for him to destroy whatever stood in his way. Yes, surely it would come to pass, and Charlie knew that it was exactly what he would do should the roles be reversed. If perhaps he had been granted this awesome power, Peter would be the first to go, but fate made it that it was not so, for if he didn't already before, the Great White Father clearly had all the power now, and so Charlie accepted his fate… ready for his soul to embark into the winds… quiet and peaceful on the breeze… his mind praying for a clean death and safe passage to the happy hunting ground…

Then, unexpectedly — impossibly — the Great White Father did something that Charlie could never believe… Peter knelt down across from Charlie so that they were on level ground, and looked him in the eye.

Terrified, Charlie bowed his head down in terror, for certainly the Great White Father was only toying with him now… certainly… he was only enjoying his victory before sending him to his death… certainly… for how could he do anything else to one who had hated him for so long…

Peter looked at the terrified brave in front of him, and he felt only love and respect for the man. Peter put his hand below Charlie's chin. He lifted his head so that he looked him in his eyes… as an equal… as a brother…

"Believe," Peter said, and the words fell true upon the air.

At the sign of Peter's faith, energy filled Charlie's being as he felt himself believe in Peter and all he represented for the first time. He took a deep breath as he felt himself filled with goodness and new life — love, light, joy — all that Peter was, he wanted to become it, and he wanted to share it. For the first time ever, he now knew why the Great White Father was the true Son of Neverland, for forgiveness was a true power unlike any other, and one that only the righteous possessed…

He smiled boldly at Peter as they stood. "May this be the hour," Charlie said through tear-stained eyes. "Where the Son and the Brave stand side by side."

Peter smiled back at his new friend valiantly, and stepped towards him, clasping his hand. The power of their two energies came together for the first time in harmony at the top of the Windy Mountains, and the joy of such a moment shook Charlie to the core of his being.

"FOR NEVERLAND!" Charlie screamed, sticking his tomahawk in the air, and with him Peter, Tootles, Curly, and the Twins crowed with valor. Charlie then joined in, and for the first time ever let out his best crow as well, and joy and truth filled the air. Unified at last… they would finally save their world… together…

Then…

THUMP! — There was a deep growl that was more like a groaning that seemed to surround them at once, as if something was being birthed up from the ground. All the boys looked at each other, uncertainty filling their eyes as their joy and lightness was suddenly pulled from them by the deep…. A moment passed… then…

THUMP! — The groaning grew deeper, closer. The boys still all looked back and forth at each other, hoping that one of them would have an answer, but none was any wiser than the next. They all then looked to Peter, who stood looking into the dark….

THUMP! — The sound grew louder, closer, and faster still… Peter stared into the darkness… he didn't want to believe it… but this is what it had come to…

THUMP! THUMP! — THUMP! THUMP! — The resounding sound grew faster and larger, like some sinister heartbeat in the deep…

"Go," Peter commanded as he turned to face the others. "Follow Solomon to Cannibal Cove."

Charlie and the boys just stared at Peter. Was he really telling them to run? Now? In a time of need? He had never told them to run from a fight once since they had known him, but now, true concern was upon his countenance, and it was terrifying to see him this way.

Solomon, however, picked up on Peter's command as something far beyond argument. He bleated as loud as he could, signaling to the others to follow, then he dashed down the ravine away from Peter as fast as his legs could carry him.

THUMP! THUMP! — THUMP! THUMP! — The sinister sound grew closer… as if it was upon them…. as if it was about to consume them…

"*Go. Now.*" Peter commanded his friends, and he left no room in his voice for interpretation as they stood staring at him. Then, one by one, they began to process the severity of the situation. Charlie was the first to come to his senses.

"Tootles. Curly," Charlie stated as he quickly and skillfully crafted a torch from the fire to light their way. "Let us make haste."

Charlie then went around to the others, shaking them all as the continued to stare at Peter, for they could not bear the thought of leaving him in a time of need — not tonight, not like this — at Charlie's urging, they jumped on their steeds and made ready to follow Solomon back down the ravine.

"Peter!" Curly said looking back, tears staining his eyes, for he had never left Peter in a time of need — not once in his life — and he didn't mean to start now.

"Run, Curly!" Tootles yelled, urging him forward. "This power is beyond us." He then pushed Curly forward and together they followed the others down the ravine.

Once Peter saw that all his friends had disappeared from sight, he held up the vial of neverbrew, and turned to face the darkness ascending up from Crocodile Crack…

* CHAPTER 13 *

— The Fallen Angel —

Tinker Bell and Peter were flying through the warm, balmy air way up above Pixie Hollow, laughing heartily, for they had just played their afternoon tricks on the lost boys, and no matter how many times they fooled them over the last century they could never catch on, for together they had come up with many different and creative ways to exercise their mischief, and as long as they kept rotating their ideas, no one in Neverland could ever be any wiser to one of their notorious pranks… they were truly… inseparable…

Yes, Tinker Bell was there with him now — with her favorite boy, in the air — way up above all things. She loved the fact that they could both fly. It was a special skill that set them apart from the others — a skill that made them both different, and closer at the same time — and although he rarely seemed to talk about it, she knew that Peter knew it as well. He laughed as she chased him through the air, then he looked back at her, and smiled, and she thought she might just go up and do what she had wanted to do for so long — she thought she might just go up and kiss him!

She locked eyes with Peter, and his gaze did not waver, but instead he just stared back, his big, bright eyes connecting directly with hers, and she knew that this was the moment where the world would finally give her what she wanted. She flew over to him, and he put his hand around her waist and pulled her in close. He smiled at her and she closed her eyes… this was the moment she had been waiting for since she could remember… the kiss that she had been waiting her whole life to taste… then… just as he bent down towards her…

The sound of a deep horn blew on the horizon. The sound was one of a battle horn… of a ship preparing for war. Tink opened her eyes as fear and concern filled Peter's face, for pirates were clearly on their shores. He pulled away from her.

"Peter, no!" Tink urged, but it was no use, Peter left her in the air and began darting towards the sound at a speed impossible to keep up with. "Come back…"

As Peter's presence left her, Tinker Bell began falling through the air. She tried to fly, but to no avail, for without him near she had not the strength to fly anymore… she panicked as she fell, and fell, and fell through the air… the loss of Peter's presence was too much to bear… she looked down as she free-fell towards Neverland… faster and faster and faster…. closer and closer and closer to the ground… moments to impact… this was it…

Then there was blackness, and that same sound of a war horn…

Tinker Bell awoke, weakened and tired, strung up in her cell, her eyes groggy from going in and out of consciousness… she must have been dreaming…

Again, that same sound of a war horn reverberated in her mind. Tinker Bell struggled against her bonds, attempting to pull her tiny arms out, but it was of no use — not yet — she looked through one of the cracks in the ship, up at the star strewn sky, and once again she prayed to the only being she believed in.

"Hurry, Peter," she said in her mind, then her head fell, and she entered back into her dreams once more…

***

Up on the deck of the ship, the same war horn blew as pirates scurried along under the full moon, hosting giant torches into the air that reached up into the sky, lighting up the nearby sea like lighthouses in the night. At the ship's center, a massive cauldron had been propped up over the start of a large bonfire, where a host of pirates fed it logs for fuel and monitored its beginnings. Above the cauldron, a deck had been fashioned with a stairwell on either side, in preparation for some kind of ritual.

From the captain's quarters, Vincent Brubaker watched as his crew scurried below him — the pawns, soon he would have no more use for them — soon, he would have no more use for anybody...

Next to him, the peace pipe he bought from that pathetic, sniveling, hideous brave — if he could even call himself that — sat glistening in the moonlight. The captain stroked its smooth surface as a sinister smile spread across his face… it wouldn't be long now… he had to savor these final moments… the final moments of his mortality…

***

Under the full moon, Tiger Lily surveyed the pirate ships from the shoreline on Pirate Eater Beach, the torchlight from their fires sending light across the cove — whatever the pirates plans may have been before, they clearly now wanted everyone in Neverland to know that they had arrived — she had to stay focused and remember her mission, for her job was to save Tinker Bell, and nothing more. Whatever else needed to happen in terms of dealing with these scavengers could wait until Peter arrived.

"It's time," Tiger Lily announced to the group. "I'll take Ruby. She'll know where to find her fairy — Nibs, can you make Fleur rise above water?"

"Ha," Nibs laughed. "Does a siren sing in the sea?"

"Good," Tiger Lily answered. "She's swifter than the other horses, and quieter, we need to be as silent as possible as we approach."

Nibs nodded in agreement.

“Slightly,” Tiger Lily said, turning to him. “Stay here and watch Marco. If he moves, finish him.”

“Sounds like a good time to me.” Slightly grinned coolly as he put the tip of his sword to Marco’s chest. The brave, who was now bound hand and foot against a rock, gulped under his pulverized face.

Tiger Lily looked down, and saw Nibs on the ground rubbing Fleur’s hooves. She seemed to be enjoying it. “There you go, girl,” Nibs said. “Just a lil’ bit of pixie dust.” Fleur whinnied in delight.

“What are you doing, Nibs?” Tiger Lily asked.

“Fairy dust, Miss.” Nibs said as he stood. “You rub it on their hooves, that’s how we were walking on water at the river — Tink’s idea, really.”

Tiger Lily just stared at Nibs, a bit in awe, for she had always found the ways of fairies to be peculiar, and the love for their strange way of life was the one thing her and Peter did not have in common.

“Let’s go. You’ll see,” Nibs said.

Tiger Lily hopped on Fleur, and Nibs hopped on his steed, and together they approached the shoreline. Nibs walked his steed out, and he did not sink, but rather, seemed to hover right above the surface, weightless, as if he was floating upon it.

“Come on,” Nibs said as he turned to face her, and at his urging Tiger Lily flicked Fleur’s reins and forced her to step out into the sea. When they touched the water, Tiger Lily had the strangest sensation, for they did not sink, but it did not feel solid like land either, rather, it felt as if they were walking on some kind of buoyant surface, and she reasoned it would be like walking on a cloud, if there ever could be such a thing. Fleur whinnied in a mix of strange delight, for it was clearly new for her as well.

"That's it. You're getting it," Nibs said joyfully.

"Nibs, you're a genius," Tiger Lily said as she and Fleur caught up to him.

"Like I said — Tink's idea," Nibs said, quick to give credit where credit was due. "But since she's not here to accept, I'll gladly take it on her behalf."

At the mention of Tink's name, Tiger Lily's mind was pulled back to the task at hand — she was to save Tinker Bell, that was all — she then yanked on Fleur's reins and began to soar across the water at top speed.

"A compliment from Tiger Lily," Nibs said to himself, practically stunned. "I will take that… I will take that…" Satisfied, he pulled on his steed's reins and followed her towards the ships…

***

THUMP! THUMP!...

Peter faced the closing darkness in the Windy Mountains, the vial of Tinker Bell's neverbrew shining as brightly as it could before him. He held it tightly, for it was all the light left…

THUMP! THUMP!...

The sound of the dark, ancient heartbeat was upon him now. Peter pulled out his Dagger of Truth, and it glowed golden in his hand, just like it did in the vision… he was in the presence of a great evil.

THUMP!... THUMP!...

The sound stopped, and a deep, all-consuming growl surrounded Peter from the darkness, and it felt as if the night was pressing in on him from all sides at once.

"It is I! Peter Pan!" He yelled into the black. "Son of Neverland. Defender of all things good and bright— "

SCREEEECH! — Before Peter could finish, a high-pitched screech drowned out his words, attacking his senses. Peter yelled in pain and held his ears to keep from going def.

When the terrible screech ended, there was another low growl. When Peter recovered, he looked up, and there, three hundred feet above the ground, he saw the face of something as sinister and evil as the darkness of time itself… it was the face of the ancient fiend of Old Neverland… the one the legends spoke about… it was the Great Beast of Crocodile Crack…

Peter took to the air and in less than a second was floating face-to-face before the beast. Its head was that of a giant crocodile, and its breath was as putrid and as hot as a dragon's. Peter stared right into the giant, black slits the beast had for eyes as he hovered three hundred feet in the air, his body still glistening with an afterglow of golden energy.

"There is nothing for you here," Peter said sternly. "Go back to the underworld."

For the first time, the beast's breathing was calm and steady as it stared at the tiny, flying boy in front of it. Then, the sides of its jaws around the rows of razor-sharp teeth seemed to lift up a little, as if amused by the whole display. Peter then saw his dagger glow hotter, and he knew that this would not be so easy…

Suddenly, a deep, croaking, haggard laughter came from deep within the beast — almost human in form — and Peter knew that this was no simple-minded monstrosity, but one rather possessed by some kind of demonic spirit.

When the haggard croaking stopped, a decrepit voice rang forth from deep within the beast's core. "It is I who rule the Windy Mountains, boy," the voice of the mountain witch cackled, revealing herself as the true power behind this fiend. "You entered it, and you shall never leave it. Your soul is mine!"

Just then, there was another screech and the giant beast spewed a belly full of boiling mud directly at Peter that cascaded up into the air and back down towards him, forcing Peter to take higher into the air to evade the sinister muck. As he reached the fog line, an evil spirit — like the ones that Tinker Bell saved him from earlier — jumped through and swiped at him, nearly grabbing his neck. With lightning-fast reflexes, Peter back dove just in time, and was forced back down towards the beast.

"Uh, uh, uh," The haggard demon witch croaked from within her crocodile form. "No flying away, little boy."

Peter flew back in front of the beast, and it spewed another belly full of molten muck, trailing him through the air, barely missing him and incinerating everything it landed on like lava. He kept flying, his path lit only by the vial of Tink's neverbrew potion, for he knew his only option was to use what space he had to try and out maneuver the beast, but he couldn't go up past the fog, for the spirits were there and they would surely catch him, and he couldn't run back down the ravine, for to lead the demon into the mainland would surely mean the end of all he held dear — no, his quarrel with the witch would end here, at the top of Crocodile Crack, in the peaks of the Windy Mountains, the same place where it began.

Using superior agility, Peter flew in circles around the beast. Being powered by a demonic force, the creature was surprisingly nimble, but the sheer size of it made it impossible for it to track Peter completely. He continued to fly in circles around it like a fly buzzing around a horse as he tried to think of a way to attack, dodging wave after wave of incinerating hot muck, holding his breath to avoid passing out altogether from the putrid stench. Then, Peter had his idea…

When he saw that he was momentarily out of the eye sight of the black slits, he held the shining vial of neverbrew up to his mouth and whispered—

"That's all for now, thank you."

Instantly, the source of the glowing light was pulled from within the vial and the whole ravine went pitch black. Peter couldn't see for a moment as it took his other senses a second to adjust, and he reasoned the beast could not see either. The biggest difference was that Peter was ready for it, and the beast was not.

As darkness swallowed them, Peter jetted right towards the beast, trusting his pre-planned path, and within moments he landed right on what he believed was the beast's eyelid. He then pulled out Tink's vial once more, and yelled—

"Light up!"

Instantly, the vial lit up and shone with brighter light than it ever had before! Illuminating the ravine once again, Peter's intuition did not fail him, for he was right above the beast's eye!

The beast screeched in pain as the blast of the white light blinded it, and then, Peter seeing his chance, plunged down with his Dagger of Truth, the white hot edge of the blade plunging into the beast's eye!

Peter took flight, barely missing the geyser of acid that spewed from the popped eyeball. The beast screeched in bloody pain as it began spewing liquid hot muck in all directions. Peter flew and flew and flew, dodging cascades of the death syrup as it melted the ravine all around him. "Just one more eye," he thought. "One more eye and surely I'll defeat it."

Suddenly, Peter felt himself plucked out of the air by a physical force much greater than himself. He looked back, and the beast's giant, clawed, scaly hand had him by the foot. Peter tried to fly against it, but it was no use against the demon's vice-like grip. It pulled him through the air, and held him dangling upside down before its snout. It studied him from the giant, black slit in its one good eye, as bloody, black acid poured out of the other where Peter stabbed it through.

"Bet you didn't see that coming, did ya?" Peter said defiantly as he hung helplessly in the air, the vial of glowing neverbrew in one hand, and his dagger in the other.

The witch beast laughed for a moment, really enjoying the victory of her catch. "Your arrogance has given you unnaturally long life, boy," she croaked. "You better laugh now, because where you're going, you'll wish you were dead." The beast then opened its mouth and began pulling Peter towards it, and it was clear that it was going to consume him.

In a last-ditch effort, Peter flipped up and stabbed the beast with his dagger right on the finger with as much force as he could muster, but to no avail, for the hardened, magical scales of its clawed hand resisted the dagger's power, and it ricocheted off in flashes of light — there was nothing more Peter could do.

"Wait!" Peter screamed. "Do what you want with me! But leave my friends alone!"

"I will do as I wish, with whomever I wish, you insignificant child!" The giant demon witch croaked. "And after I have feasted on your soul, what's left of you will wander the underworld, cold and alone, forever — then, and only then, will I go back and make a feast of your friends, just so that you can have some company."

The crocodile demon opened its mouth wide, and Peter held his breath as he felt himself surrounded from all sides by the putrid stink. If he was going into the depths of this foul being, he was going to need a breath of fresh air — and he'd need all the air he could get if he was going to cut his way out — which he absolutely planned to, that is, if he could withstand the heat.

As Peter neared the gaping mouth of the demonic creature, he threw up one last prayer courage… and once again prepared his soul to enter some unknown dark…

BANG! — Suddenly, a flash of white-hot fairy light flew through the sky and exploded on the crocodile demon's claw, causing it to open just as its jaws nearly clenched down on Peter. As the creature howled in pain, Peter seized his chance and slipped away into the air like lightning upon a storm, darting as far away from the sinister witch and her possessed puppet as fast he could.

When he was well out of reach, he looked back, and flying through the air towards the demon was none other than Mr. Theodore! His body glowed bright gold, and he looked old no longer, for as the magical fairy energy surged through his body, his youth seemed to have returned to him.

"You shouldn't be out here, Andromeda," Mr. Theodore said as he approached the beast's head, and he looked like a spec of glowing dust against the beast's massive, dark countenance. "Go back into the mountain."

"You old fool," the witch cackled deeply from within the beast. "A darkness rises that you cannot stop. The time of the fairies, is at an end."

"It makes no difference today, Andromeda," Mr. Theodore said plainly, as if to an old acquaintance. "You will honor the pact you made to the fairies. The magic will hold you to your word."

"I'll take no more orders from you!" The demon crocodile screeched. "You're nothing but a peasant! An arrogant old wind bag! And today, I WILL FEAST ON YOUR FLESH AFTER I MELT YOUR CORPSE INTO THE MOUNTAIN!"

The witch screeched a bloodthirsty screech, and then took a deep breath…

"Mr. Theodore! Look out!" Peter screamed, for he knew what the demon was about to do — it was about to unleash hell — but Mr. Theodore did not move, nor did he look concerned, but rather, he just continued to float in the air, as if waiting for whatever may come.

"No!" Peter screamed as the crocodile demon unleashed a tidal wave of liquid hot muck from its guts, and Mr. Theodore was completely consumed by it, disappearing beneath its weight.

"No…" Peter felt the corner of his eyes sting in agony as the demon's attack consumed its target. She could have had him, but not Mr. Theodore, not something so good and bright. Then Peter felt his sorrow turn to rage against his enemy, for after all this evil being had put him through, his wrath could no longer be contained, and he would slay this demon once and for all, or die trying.

"YOU FILTHY WITCH!" Peter screamed, his eyes still hot from the tears. "I WILL CUT OFF YOUR HEAD AND TURN YOUR BODY INTO ASH!"

Without even hearing Peter, the witch cackled in victory as she destroyed Mr. Theodore. Peter yelled and prepared to fly right at the beast, for no matter how it ended, one of them was going to die next.

But then, right as Peter took flight towards the creature, he stopped in the air, for there, still floating before the creature's head, was Mr. Theodore. He appeared to be completely unharmed and uninfected from the blast.

"What?!" The witch screeched as her laugh came to a halt.

"Go back into the mountain, Andromeda," Mr. Theodore repeated calmly.

"I'LL NEVER GO BACK!" The witch screamed, then she unleashed another river of molten muck from deep within the beast. Once again, it titled over Mr. Theodore, completely consuming him and blocking him from view, and then, when it all fell from the air, Mr. Theodore was left floating there, just as untouched, and unharmed, and as glowing as before.

"It's impossible," The witch said, truly terrified now of Mr. Theodore's power.

"Go back into the mountain, Andromeda," Mr. Theodore repeated once more. "Go back into the mountain or face the consequences."

"You can't destroy me!" The witch said from a place of true fear. "The Dark Father is more powerful than either of us!"

"There is One who is greater," Mr. Theodore answered.

"The Great One will not lift a finger for this tiny, pathetic planet!" The demon witch snapped. "Do you really think He cares about a horde of helpless fairies? Do you really think He cares for the likes of you?"

"Maybe not," Mr. Theodore said, accepting her reason. "But his Son does." Mr. Theodore then nodded in Peter's direction, and Peter watched the exchange between the two great powers in awe.

"The boy?!" The witch screeched. "You think the boy can face the Dark Father?!" She then cackled with a deep laughter beyond anything she had unleashed before.

"He will face the Dark Father," Mr. Theodore said calmly. "And he *will* win… just like last time."

The witch was really laughing now, and Peter thought it absurd to watch, this giant, three-hundred-foot demon crocodile laughing in the middle of the Windy Mountains, it's giant face hovering three hundred feet in the air, lit up only by the glow of Mr. Theodore's body — Peter thought it may have been the strangest and most frightening thing he had ever seen.

"Last time was a fluke." The demon witch cackled between spewing heavy heaves of toxic breath. "I always knew you were a fool, Theodore — that was clear — but surely this level of comedy is beyond you."

"Enough!" Mr. Theodore said sternly, and a blast of fairy light left his body, penetrating the witch's magic and incinerating a portion of the beast's scales where it connected. The demon crocodile screeched in pain.

"Go back into the mountain, Andromeda," Mr. Theodore commanded. "Go back into the mountain where you will stay for all time."

"NEVER!' Then, the witch opened the beast's mouth wide, and it snapped closed around Mr. Theodore with a thunderous snap that echoed through the mountains. Peter watched with wide eyes as Mr. Theodore disappeared beneath the great beast's jaws. He wanted to help, but the situation was beyond any of his solutions at this point… he could only watch and wait…

Then, from within the belly of the beast, there was a deep gurgle, and it was clear that the foul creature had swallowed Mr. Theodore whole. A moment, and the beast smiled, satisfied, but then, a look of concern washed over its face, and its grimace fell flat.

Suddenly, the beast wretched a great wretch from deep within, and spewed a mountain of molten muck straight up into the air as it screeched in pain. At the same time, Peter saw its belly light up as if it was being incinerated from within by a growing flash of white-hot light.

As the giant crocodile continued to screech as it was being destroyed from the inside. Its own acidic gut slime began to rain down upon it, and Peter watched in horror as it melted its own face. The witch's screech turned into a gurgle as the beast's head caved in upon itself. Then, when it could take no more, the beast exploded in a blast of incinerating white-hot light, the body blasting into the air in an explosion of dazzling, golden dust that lit up the entire ravine… and it was awesome to behold…

Peter watched in awe as his view transformed from a completely horrifying landscape into a complete, beatific paradise in one big flash, and it took his mind a few moments to catch up with it…

Then, there, at the bottom of the ravine, there was the figure of the voluptuous youth sitting in the grass. She was crying as the sparkling shards of fairy dust rained down all around her. Peter stared at her in awe, and instantly, the memories of all the pleasures he had experienced with her in the cave came flooding back, immediately replacing all the fear and loss he had gone through just moments before, and it was intoxicating.

As if pulled towards her against his will, Peter flew down to her, and landed some distance from her on the grass. He studied her for a moment, and then made his decision to approach.

"Don't," a calm voice said, then Peter turned, and saw Mr. Theodore walking towards him easily across the grassy plain, for the explosion of magic had seemed to bend reality within the scope of its blast, and had opened some kind of parallel dimension directly on top of the one they were in now. "She's still trying to trick you," Mr. Theodore smiled.

"Do you know her?" Peter asked, for his curiosity was truly peaked now, and he felt that he no longer knew anything about anything.

"Andromeda," Mr. Theodore stated, as if reliving some pleasant memory. "I knew her, yes… she was once a very powerful fairy," then he eyed Peter with those wise, all-knowing blue eyes. "This is what she once looked like, if you're wondering."

"She's beautiful," Peter stated automatically.

"She was, yes," Mr. Theodore agreed. "She was the most beautiful fairy ever created… it was said that when the Great Spirit laughed his first laugh, she was born."

"What happened?" Peter asked.

"Being so superior in beauty, she eventually became a slave to her own image, and had an unquenchable thirst for power," Mr. Theodore answered in disagreement. "When Time took his first form in Neverland, she was seduced by his power, and worshipped him as her god… when he fell—" Mr. Theodore paused to correct himself. "When you destroyed him… she fell with him."

"And you put her in this mountain," Peter stated, seeing it as the only logical conclusion.

“She agreed to it,” Mr. Theodore shrugged. “It was the only way the fairies would let her stay in Neverland… bound for all eternity by a magic pact that even the Dark Father himself cannot break.”

Peter turned to the crying girl on the ground, and she looked up at him with those big, longing eyes as tears continued to fall down, and he wanted to go to her, to hold her, to tell her it would be all right — he wanted to kiss her! — but he knew that he could not, for no matter her beauty now, he knew it was just an echo of who and what she once was… and that it wasn’t so now… it wasn’t so…

“That’s very… sad,” Peter found himself saying, for even though he now knew the truth, he couldn’t help but be captivated by the angelic being before him… there… in the form of a girl… broken and alone… sitting on the ground…

“It is,” Mr. Theodore agreed, “but there is always hope for those that look for it… I’m afraid for Andromeda here… that she has lost her ability to see…”

Mr. Theodore then chuckled, patted Peter on the shoulder, and began walking towards the crying, fallen girl.

“But you knew!” Peter yelled after him. “You knew I was going to see her. You knew I was walking right into a trap!”

Mr. Theodore stopped and turned to face Peter. “I didn’t,” he said calmly. “I don’t know anything at all.” He then shrugged, and continued walking towards the girl.

"Come on, Andromeda," he said as he approached the crying girl. "Let's get you home." Mr. Theodore then stooped down to her level, and she put her hands around his neck like a child wrapping its arms around its father, then he picked her up, and began walking back up the ravine...

"Go on, boy," Mr. Theodore said as he disappeared from the light. "You've got friends to save."

Peter watched them go until they were out of sight… and no matter the peril… a part of his heart still wished he could be with her…

* CHAPTER 14 *

— The Rescue —

Ruby, Tiger Lily, and Fleur approached the three illuminated ships over the face of the moonlit water, and Ruby whinnied as they neared the central one.

"Ruby says it's this ship," Tiger Lily remarked.

Nibs reached into his pack and pulled out a grappling rope, then he tossed it over the edge of the ship and pulled — it stuck — he then held out the rope to Tiger Lily, signaling that it was ready to go.

Tiger Lily took a moment to look at Fleur, her lifetime companion that she had grown up with and rode since she was a small girl. They were more than just master and owner, for they knew everything there was to know about each other's spirits, and that made them sisters.

"Stay girl," Tiger Lily said as she stroked her mane. "I'll be back soon." She then turned to Ruby, and stroked her horn like she remembered seeing Tinker Bell do during the journey in a way that Ruby clearly liked.

"Thank you," she whispered in Ruby's ear, then Ruby bucked her horn upwards, signaling for her to get a move on. Tiger Lily smiled, then she grabbed the rope and began making her ascent up into the ship, and Nibs followed behind her.

Like the wind, Tiger Lily scaled up the side of the ship. Her bow was out and an arrow knocked by the time her feet touched down on deck, ready to kill if needed. She was as silent as a ghost — a trained assassin — and next to Peter, there was no one in Neverland more skilled in stealth operations than her.

"Clear," Tiger Lily whispered, then Nibs came up the rope behind her, landed on the deck, and pulled out his pirate sword, and covertly they made their way across the ship like two shadows in the night…

***

Now heated by the fire, the cauldron bubbled and boiled with that same alive, dark, sinister, ethereal concoction Brubaker had created in his cabin. From the deck above it, pirates dumped barrel loads of pixie dust stolen from the mines into the mixture, adding it to the twisted contents where it was quickly swallowed up, while other pirates hoisted the coffin of the late Captain James Hook up onto the platform,

After a moment, the crew gathered below as Captain Vincent Brubaker took center stage on the platform above the boiling cauldron, the stolen Indian peace pipe glistening in his hand, and his other resting on his grandfather's coffin. He smiled, for everything was going exactly as planned, and soon, Neverland and all its pathetic inhabitants would see the wrath that they had brought upon themselves, and not even the flying boy would be powerful enough to stop him… soon…

"Bring the fairy." The captain issued the order to a pirate guard next to him, who grinned a blacked-toothed grin as he headed for the dungeon.

The captain lifted his eyes up to the full moon, and saw how it shown down upon him, as if choosing him to be there on this night. He then looked out at the shoreline of Neverland, at its large mountains looming against the moonlight in surrender, ready to be taken. He then looked out at his crew, every eye revering him as if he was their god — believing in him, counting on him — indeed, he was their god, and soon, he would be the god of this entire world… soon…

"If only you could see me now, Grandfather," he whispered towards the sky, his hand still resting on the black varnish of the coffin. "You would see what it was that you created… you would see that you were destined to rule…"

He then turned his gaze down to the boiling cauldron, and his mind was pulled further towards its seductive contents…

***

Peter flew down Crocodile Crack as fast as he could, his mind still recovering from the battle and all he had gone through in the mountain. It was unprecedented — that such a beautiful, powerful being such as Andromeda could have been locked away in the mountains of Neverland his whole life, and he never knew about it — why didn't the fairies tell him about her when he was growing up? Why was the knowledge of her hidden away from him over the centuries? Did they think if he knew of her beauty that he'd want to go to her? Of course he would! That was a given. What he experienced with her in the chamber when he first laid eyes on her — that was her true form as far as he was concerned — for clearly a being so beautiful and powerful was as eternal as he was, if not more so. The whole decrepit witch thing, that was all just an act. It wasn't her true form. No, Peter knew what she really looked like, for he had experienced her touch, the feeling of her skin, the taste of her lips, and he loved everything about her — every single inch of her — it didn't even matter that her kiss sent him spinning into hell. What was hell to the Son of Neverland?! Nothing! Fire could not kill him! Torment could not destroy him! If they dared, he'd just be reborn stronger! He had trudged through the pits of darkness, and he wanted his prize — he wanted Andromeda! — That's all he wanted anymore! He wanted to be with her forever, and he was going to have what he wanted or all would pay!

Peter felt his blood boil hotter and hotter from withdrawals with every inch he flew further away from her — and why didn't

Mr. Theodore give him more information about her at the start of the journey before throwing him into the lion's den? He knew how powerful she was, and pretending not to was not an acceptable answer. Why were these key pieces of knowledge and information being kept from him? He was the Master Guardian of Neverland and the fairies called him their Savior. Well, how was he supposed to guard it and save it if he didn't know anything about it?! He should have destroyed that old fool and taken Andromeda for himself!

Infuriated, Peter shook his head and converted all his extra energy into flight speed, attempting to concentrate on the task at hand. He held up Tink's vial of neverbrew potion as his only beacon of light, scattering the darkness before him, but just beyond the reach its rays, above and behind him, a horde of evil spirits swirled in the blackness beyond, riding upon the cover of the fog which shielded them from the burning rays of the magic fairy light… ready to close in on him at the slightest lapse in vigilance.

Peter's blood continued to boil hotter and hotter. He felt betrayed by the fairies for not telling them about Andromeda. Surely, they were trying to hide her from him — surely — the selfish maggots. They knew he'd want her if he saw her… they knew and didn't tell him…

Peter then felt that he had enough of these stupid evil spirits dogging him. He thought he just might stop and slay them all right now for fun. The fools, they had no idea what they were up against. They had no idea what he had just gone through — what he had become — well, it was time they understood what true power really was.

Peter stopped in the middle of the ravine and held up the fairy light, and the ghouls surrounded him on all sides. His eyes narrowed in disgust as they clamored like beggars, reaching out at his spirit like starved animals — that's right, they were animals, and he'd slaughter them all like animals — he didn't even need Tink's magic potion to do away with this pathetic lot… might as well try and make it a fair fight…

Peter pulled out his dagger and ignited before him, ready to aid him in battle. He was about to turn out the lights, when…

"Tinker Bell!" Peter yelled into the air, and all of a sudden, his total mind came back to him when he spoke her name. How could he have forgotten about her? About what she had gone through? About how much she needed him? All this time he had been flying down the ravine, he couldn't remember why he was leaving Andromeda until just now…

Suddenly, it dawned on Peter just how powerful Andromeda's magic was as he was finally able to put two and two together in his mind — he was still under her spell, her magic had gotten into his blood — she was still trying to destroy him!

It took saying Tink's name for Peter to think clearly enough to see the enchantment for what it was, for he was so captivated by Andromeda's beauty that he almost gave up everything he valued in life most — Tinker Bell, Tiger Lily, the lost boys — indeed, even his own soul, and he was shocked at his error.

Realizing he had wasted enough of his mind on the seductress already, and by doing so had put his friends in even greater peril than he could have ever imagined, he banished her from his thoughts, and held up the vial of light. Then, with a great and renewed determination he rocketed down the ravine to give those he loved what he knew he had been holding back from them this whole time… his entire self…

***

Tinker Bell's eyes were wide with fright as she hung in her cell, listening to the muffled sounds of cheering above, for she had no idea what the pirates planned to do with her. However, it had been about a full day since last night when she was captured, and well over a day since she had her last dose of her neverbrew potion early yesterday morning, and she knew the cell would not hold her for long. A typical dose of her neverbrew would keep her human size for a day, but on longer journeys she took larger doses in case she ran short on supplies or lost any, and although she took a big dose yesterday, the most it would keep her human size for was a day and a half — two days tops — either way, when her potion wore off, she would shrink down to her tiny size, and by sheer luck she would be free — that is, if the pirates continued to stall.

Suddenly, Tinker Bell was taken with panic. What did they plan to do with her? What was this all about? What if they got to her before she had a chance to shrink and escape? Where was Peter? Was he still coming for her? Was he even alive?

"Of course he's alive, Tinker Bell," she scolded herself. "How could you even think such a thing? He *is* alive… and he *will* save you." The comfort of that thought gave her the momentary space to breathe.

"Psst. Tink." — There came a sound from the darkness. Tink squinted, thinking them at first to be the pirates coming for her or her mind playing tricks on her, but then, her first rescuer stepped into the moonlight from the shadows.

"Nibs!" Tink exclaimed with a little more pep than she would have liked.

"Shh," Nibs said quickly, for as excited as he was to see her as well, the situation at hand required silent finesse. "I'm here with Tiger Lily. We're here to rescue you."

Tiger Lily then revealed herself, stepping out of the shadows, and without looking at Tinker Bell walked directly over the lock on her cell and examined it.

"It's no use," Tinker Bell said. "They have the key — where's Peter?"

"He went to see the Enchantress," Tiger Lily answered, then for the first time their eyes met, and all that needed to be said passed between them in this moment, for they both cared deeply for the life of a boy — a boy that was their only hope — and for now, that was enough.

"Good." Tinker Bell nodded after the moment passed. "But you shouldn't have come."

"To hell with that," Nibs said as he now fiddled with the lock, for it was never a question in his mind. "When was the last time you had your neverbrew?"

"Yesterday morning," Tinker Bell stated. "It was a big dose… but this cell won't hold me much longer no matter what."

"That's a start," Nibs said gratefully as he continued to fiddle with the difficult lock.

"It was Marco," Tiger Lily said through squinted eyes of distaste. "The coward betrayed us all."

"I know!" Tink said, excited that the others knew. "I followed him in Crocodile Crack. I saw him sell your father's pipe to the pirates."

"The peace pipe?" Tiger Lily stated curiously, and Tink nodded her affirmation. "What could he possibly want with my father's pipe?"

"I don't know," Tinker Bell admitted. "But their captain — he paid a lot for it — whatever it is, it must be important."

Tiger Lily thought on Tinker Bell's discovery for a moment, for she had not heard news that the pipe was taken until just now. What could the pirates want with the ancient pipe? Enough to seduce Marco to steal it? The pipe was only good for smoking island tobacco and ancient herbs, not much else. Her father and Peter used it to enter the void, but who really knew what went on in there? Or how to make sense of it? Surely, it must have something to do with that, but what? Why did the pirates want to enter the void?

CLUNK — suddenly, the door to the chamber opened as light from above deck poured in below. Steps could then be heard descending the stairwell. Tiger Lily silently whipped out her bow and knocked an arrow as Nibs began to pull out his sword.

"No!" Tink exclaimed in a whisper. "You have to hide."

"I won't let them touch you," Nibs vowed.

"Nibs, please," Tink pleaded. "You're trapped down here."

Nibs looked longingly at Tink, and although he couldn't bear the thought of leaving her to the hands of the pirate swine once again, he knew she was right.

"I'll be fine," Tink assured him. "I promise."

Nibs finally consented, and he ducked with Tiger Lily behind some supply barrels as the footsteps neared the bottom. He noticed that his hands were shimmering with gold from where he touched the barrel, then he noticed that the glistening substance was all over the barrels around them.

"Fairy dust," he whispered to Tiger Lily. "What do you think they want with it?"

Tiger Lily quickly shook her head, for she both didn't know, and it wasn't the time. Then, the same big pirate that captured Tinker Bell stared menacingly at her through the bars.

"Ello' sweetheart," he gargled, the fat rolls on his neck making it difficult for him to speak. "The captain is about to have some fun with you…"

Tink gritted her teeth as the cell door opened, and Nibs and Tiger Lily watched from the shadows as she was taken from her chains.

***

Peter continued to race down Crocodile Crack as fast as he could towards Cannibal Cove and Tinker Bell's captors, taking care to stay as low as possible to avoid the fog line that pressed down lower and lower into the canyon, and pushing Peter closer and closer towards the ground and all the natural hazards that came with it. The darkness seemed to be powered by a supernatural force, and as it continued to push in on the fairy light that guided his path, it gave him less and less time to dodge the obstacles that filled the ravine, such as the jagged boulders and trees that he continued to narrowly miss.

Still, Peter would not slow, and he was counting almost entirely on his intuition and heightened senses to guide him, for as the wall of fog moved in towards him, so did the horde of evil spirits that waited just beyond the safety of the light, spiraling through the darkness, and the moment they were close enough to consume him they would. Peter was being pressed in upon from all sides — from above, from below, from the front, from the back, and from the left and right — and he had to reach the end of the ravine in time, for it was no longer only his life that depended on it.

"Hold on, Tinker Bell," he said with absolute focus. "I'm coming."

As the light continued to condense all around him, Peter closed his eyes and opened his mind, delving into his other senses, knowing, believing, that every flight decision would be perfect — it had to be.

***

Tiger Lily and Nibs watched in horror from the shadows below as the pirates hung Tinker Bell up over the boiling cauldron. They tied her wrists and ankles with ropes and strung her out so that her body made an 'X' shape. For the first time since she could remember, Tiger Lily didn't know what to do. She could shoot the pirates that held Tinker Bell and kill five or six, but that would give away their position and there were just too many of them. Unless Peter arrived in time, it was up to her to save Tinker Bell, and she would have to be more strategic if they were to come out alive.

"Please, Peter," she spoke into the air with all hope. "Hurry."

Up on deck, tears stained Tinker Bell's eyes as the pirates strung her up above the boiling cauldron. She didn't so much fear what they planned to do with her, but rather, was frustrated by her own actions. If only she'd taken less neverbrew the other morning, then she'd already have shrunk and she would be safely away, but now, she was putting everyone's lives in danger — Tiger Lily,

Nibs, the others, and most of all Peter because she knew he'd stop at nothing to rescue her — if only she wasn't so obsessed with being human, then none of this would have happened. She didn't care what happened to her, but if something were to happen to Peter, it would be a pain worse than death.

Captain Vincent Brubaker looked up at the helpless, human sized fairy and smiled. What a fool she was, concocting her potion, for if she wasn't so obsessed with the flying boy she would have remained tiny and capturing her would have been next to impossible, but it was too late now… her own lust would be her downfall.

With that thought, Brubaker smiled again and looked down on his eager crew below them, for they had all been fighting for this moment for decades. Through wind and hail, fire and water, they had faced down all the great terrors the high-seas threw their way at great peril to themselves, and had come out not only alive, but successful. He looked at all their stupid faces smiling back at them, and they were like dogs. Yes, they had been a loyal and valiant crew. Indeed, no captain could have asked for one better… but he would not have need for them much longer…

He then turned his gaze towards the peace pipe resting in his hand, its smooth veneer glistening in the firelight. What fools the inhabitants of Neverland were. The gateway to everything was always right under their noses, and they never knew it. Yes, they were all fools, weak and pathetic fools, to follow the hapless dreams of some whimsical child over the power and lordship of his grandfather, the Great Captain James Hook! It didn't matter now, soon they would know what true power was, and the mistake they made a century ago by denying it.

Tinker Bell watched in disgust from her chains as the captain raised the peace pipe into the air…

"*Time…*" the captain said to his crew below. "The lord of everything… can you feel him?"

Captain Vincent Brubaker took a moment. He closed his eyes and drank in a full, hearty breath of ether, savoring all there was… for this was truly it… the moment he had been waiting for since he first set sail on the high-seas…

"Immutable, cosmic order," he continued. "Eternity waning. Perfect retribution… marvelous isn't it?"

There was a moment of silence as the crew hung on his every word. They looked up at their fearless leader with tears in their eyes, for he had promised them this day would come decades ago when they first agreed to set sail with him, and against all odds, he had delivered. This was their moment, and he, Captain Vincent Brubaker, was their savior.

"This world," The captain continued. "Is a world that worships a false god. A world that prefers to entertain the foolish fantasies of a mindless child, rather than submit to the irrevocable laws of a much greater and more powerful universe… this world… believes that they are free."

The captain paused, and resentment filled his eyes. "No one is free." Then a great darkness took his countenance. "Tonight, this world will once again remember… that *Time*… is God."

The captain's final words hung in the air with some awful power, then he turned to face Tinker Bell.

"And now, my lady," he said, and flames danced in his eyes as he pulled a dagger from his jacket. "The final ingredient."

***

Peter was pushing his flight speed to the absolute limit, dodging trees and boulders at a moment's notice as he traversed the treacherous ravine while the darkness continued to push in from all sides. The evil spirits were just feet away from him now, spiraling just outside the radius of the protective light, and they had already began reaching towards him with their wispy, boney hands, testing the fairy charm's power, for they were thirsty, and there would be no soul more satisfying then than that of the Great Peter Pan, for to feast on his spirit would mean eternal and abundant life, and freedom from the torment they now faced.

"AHH!" Peter screamed as he felt the sting of a ghoul's hand touch him, and he could feel the energy being pulled from his being, but he couldn't go down now, he had to make it.

"Please, if there is any light left in you," he whispered to Tinker Bell's vial of potion as he held it to his lips. "Let it shine now…"

As the light burned down, more and more evil spirits reached out and latched on to Peter, their boney hands like syphons as they sucked the soul from his body. Peter could feel his energy draining as he dropped closer and closer to the ground, for the darkness was heavy, like a thick blanket upon his shoulders, and he could bear it no longer… this was it…

Suddenly, the light from the vial surged bright and hot one last time, and pushed the darkness back just enough for Peter to maneuver. The spirits screamed in pain as their hands were singed, and Peter felt his energy return to him immediately upon being freed from their sinister, soul-sucking grip. This was his chance. If he was going to make it out of the God forsaken ravine of Crocodile Crack, it had to be now. Peter yelled as he gave it everything he had.

Up ahead, Solomon, Charlie, Tootles, Curly, and the Twins were nearing the end of the ravine on horseback. Solomon bleated loudly as he could see the light at the end of the tunnel.

"We're almost there!" Charlie screamed up ahead as he led the way behind Solomon, the other boys following his torchlight.

"What's that noise?!" Curly screamed from the back, for it sounded like an avalanche was coming down at them from behind in the ravine.

"Keep riding, Curly!" Tootles screamed from up ahead, for whatever it was, he already knew it wouldn't be good.

The avalanche of sound continued to get closer to them until it was all-consuming. Curly looked back over his shoulder as he rode as fast as he could. He squinted his eyes, and in the darkness he saw a small speck of light coming towards them…it couldn't be… it was!

"Peter!" Curly screamed for joy as he saw him nearing them, then his smile fell flat as he saw the tidal wave of darkness and the evil spirits that trailed him. "Ride!" Curly screamed. "Ride for your life!"

"Yah!" Charlie pulled on his reins as they neared the end of the ravine up ahead — they'd make it, they had to make it…

Peter saw Charlie's torchlight, and the sparkling sight of stars that glistened over Cannibal Cove — they had made it — thank God his friends had made it, but would he? The last of the fairy light was waning, and the spirits were back upon him now. This was his final chance, if they got hands on him one more time, he would be consumed forever.

"AHHHH!" Peter screamed as he gave it one last surge of ethereal power, and he reached down inside himself to call upon something unlimited…

"BOOM!" — The sound of a mach explosion resounded over Cannibal Cove as Peter shot out of the end of Crocodile Crack just as Charlie and the lost boys exited. The condensed fog dissipated in the moonlight, sending the spirits screaming and scattering back up the ravine.

A few miles down, on the shoreline of Pirate Eater Beach, Slightly had Marco at sword point, keeping the swine at bay.

Suddenly, they both saw a spec of glorious, golden light flying rapidly across the cove. They stared at it in wonderment.

"Peter…" Slightly whispered, and hope filled his eyes.

When Marco finally realized who and what it was, he jeered in resentment. He figured that ol' mountain witch would have killed the boy by now, but once again, the flying pest had somehow survived. It was no matter, for what was coming next, even Tiger Lily's perfect little Great White Father in all his precious fairy-boy glory wouldn't stand a chance. Yes, it would make short work of him, that was for sure, then ol' Marco would get his reward… his eternal reward.

Marco giggled like a little girl on the beach, salivating in ecstasy at the thought.

The commotion on the ground drew Slightly's attention to the disgusting sight. He cringed and shook his head, then put his sword to Marco's throat, shutting him up. Marco jeered up at Slightly in utter hatred.

"You better wipe that look off your face," Slightly said, pressing his blade into Marco's neck. "Don't give me a reason to kill you, because nothing would make me happier, and nobody is gonna raise a fuss if I do."

Slightly pressed a little harder, and Marco backed off his scorn as the blade cut into his neck, but he looked at him through eyes of pure hatred.

"Well," Slightly said to himself as he lifted his blade. "Life could be worse."

As soon as the blade was lifted, Marco's signature grimace spread right back across his annihilated countenance.

At the base of Crocodile Crack, Charlie and the lost boys heaved like drowning men that had just broken back up to the surface. They breathed in full, hearty breaths of clear night air as the last remnants of fog dispersed all around them.

When they had all caught their breath, they silently watched in reverence as Peter rocketed over Cannibal Cove towards the pirate ships, holding the vial of neverbrew before him as he soared, shining like some great angel in the night, for whatever great evil he faced up in the canyon he had defeated it, and surely there was no power greater in which they could place their lives in this world.

"Go boy," Tootles spoke into the air with tears in his eyes. "Go save us all..."

***

Tinker Bell's eyes were wide with terror as the horrible captain approached her with the knife, for she hated everything about him — his smell, his haughty gaze, the lustful look in his eye — for she knew that he would not hesitate to plunge that dagger straight into her heart if it got him one step closer to whatever it was that he wanted. She could feel the potion inside her veins growing fainter, but it wasn't wearing off fast enough! How much potion did she drink for God's sake?! She needed it to wear off, and wear off now!

Down below, Tiger Lily had an arrow knocked and trained on the captain. If he dared raise that knife to Tinker Bell, he'd be dead before the blade fell — she prayed it wouldn't have to come to that.

Nibs stood by with his pirate sword drawn. When Tiger Lily loosed her first arrow, that would be his cue to throw himself headfirst into the enemy, for his life was nothing to him if it meant saving Tinker Bell's life, for he knew she would do the same for him.

On deck, the captain's eyes narrowed in pleasure as he approached the helpless fairy. Look how weak and vulnerable she was, her big eyes pleading for dear life. It was truly magnificent to him, and he relished the sweet savory flavor of her desperation. He knew that if she felt so strongly about her own life, then the flying boy must feel it as well, for if the stories were true, they had a bond that tied their life forces together. Yes, it must be true — he knew it had to be true — any moment now, and his prediction would prove correct… any moment now…

Tiger Lily pulled back a full extension on her bow as the captain raised his knife before Tinker Bell. She would kill this man, and then kill every other pirate if it meant saving Tinker Bell's life and escaping this ship, for if Tinker Bell were to perish, then Peter — the love of her life — would never be the same, and she could not let that happen. Her mind was fully prepared for battle… her fingers softened as she prepared to loose… then…

All the heads on deck turned as a ray of golden hope shot out across the water.

"Peter," Tiger Lily sighed with relief, and hope returned to her.

On deck, the captain smiled in satisfaction as he held the blade to the fairy's neck… it was just as he predicted… it was just as he had foreseen…

"Here he comes…" the captain said to Tinker Bell just as she began popping and flickering, about to shrink back to her tiny size.

With the cold steel pressed up against her neck, Tinker Bell finally realized what the captain's true intentions were when the blade did not break her skin — it wasn't about her — it was never about her! It was about Peter! She was merely bait all along. What the captain had planned exactly, she did not know, for Peter was the most powerful being in all of Neverland, and to confront him when he was enraged would mean certain destruction for nearly all beings on this ship… but this captain — he was crafty — and if he was foolish enough to draw Peter to him in his wrath, he must have a formidable plan in place if he believed he could stand a chance against Peter in all his might…

"Just a little bit closer…" the captain continued as he watched the flying boy soar across the water like a missile of light… closer… and closer to him…

"Peter! No!" Tinker Bell screamed as she struggled against her bonds, but she knew in her heart that he would stop at nothing to save her, for he loved her more than life, and she would do the exact same for him.

***

Now free of Crocodile Crack — the fog, the spirits, the obstacles, and all the limitations that came with it — Peter was finally free to hit the gas. He rocketed across the moon-lit waters of Cannibal Cove faster than he had ever flown before, flying like the wind itself, for without Andromeda's witch magic clouding his mind, his current mission and soul purpose of being had returned to him — to save Tinker Bell at all costs, and destroy whatever evil had dared take her away from him to begin with.

As Peter neared the three ships, he held up Tinker Bell's vial of neverbrew that shone across the water for all to see, a shining testament to the truth that she was never forgotten in his mind. The special potion had aided him this far, and it would not fail him now, for without the oppression of the dark spirits in Crocodile Crack, there was nothing to limit its light, and he smiled brightly at the thought of returning it to her — she would need it, and he never forgot her.

Peter's heart leapt for joy as he began to make out Tinker Bell's form, for she was both alive and well, and nothing else mattered to him anymore, for all he could see was her — Tinker

Bell, his beautiful and glorious friend, his closest companion, was alive, and he had never felt more relief in his life. It was like a great weight he had been carrying since she disappeared in the mountains was finally lifted from his shoulders, and he felt light and limitless once again…

With the happiness of that thought, and the power he gained from surviving the perils of the mountain, he flew so fast that in a matter of seconds he was already upon the ship, flying above the front of the bow. His thoughts slowed and he could feel all his enemies staring in fear as he approached Tink, but he paid them no mind, for what had pirates ever been able to do to him in the air? Absolutely nothing. They were right to be afraid. They were helpless because he was much too fast for them — completely superior — he would free Tink and take her home to safety, then he would come back to reign down so much wrath on these swine that they would wish they had never been born… but none of that mattered now — he didn't even matter — only Tinker Bell… only her life… he was so close now… so close to saving her and it would finally be over…

Captain Brubaker's eyes lit up with pure lust and joy as the flying boy neared him, for this was it — the moment he had dreamed of his whole life — he could see that the boy thought him to be powerless, for he was paying him no mind. Indeed, the boy's eyes were completely fixed on the fairy, and her alone, just as he had intended. He was a fool, this boy, for he had taken the bait without resistance, and soon, he would be dead…

“Peter, no!” Tinker Bell screamed as Peter neared her, for she was now popping and flickering rapidly as the last of her neverbrew potion left her body. The timing couldn’t be worse! She no longer needed Peter to be free, and there was no reason for him to come an inch closer and put his life in peril, for this captain was not a fool like the others — he did not fear Peter as the others did — but it was impossible to communicate that to him now, for she could see his mind was set upon her.

As Peter soared through the air, his mind slowed as he looked into Tink’s big, blue eyes, and despite the tears, and fear, and hesitation that flowed from them, he knew that if he could just touch her, all would be well. He would take her hand and together they would fly away from this terrible place, and happiness and joy would return to her beautiful countenance once again… he was so close now… so close…

“Tink!” Peter exclaimed in joy as he reached out his free hand for her own, her vial of neverbrew still shining brightly in his other…

“Peter…” Tinker Bell said, and for a moment she thought… maybe…

Peter went to grab Tinker Bell’s hand just as she popped and flicked and nearly vanished completely before his eyes, returning to her normal, tiny size. Peter’s eyes went wide as her chains fell through the air and he grabbed a handful of nothing but sky. Tinker Bell was free… but it was too late…

The captain — who Peter was hardly aware of until just now — held out the blade of his dagger and sliced Peter across the side just as Tinker Bell disappeared and Peter flew through the falling chains. The captain's aim… was true…

Peter slowed as he flew forward through the air. He was overjoyed that Tinker Bell was finally free, but he felt peculiar, funny, as if he had accomplished what he wanted, but couldn't quite remember what it was that he wanted to accomplish to begin with…

He continued to float… disoriented for a moment… hovering in the air… then he felt the light leaving his eyes… and he fell… plummeting into the sea…

* CHAPTER 15 *

— The Dark Father —

SPLASH! — There was a moment as time seemed to stand still, as all the beings on the ship and in the air, both above and below, looked on in shock and curiosity, as if some great hoax was being played upon them, and none of them knew it yet — was it possible? Had the Great Peter Pan, the Son of Neverland, truly died?

In the shadows on the deck of the ship, Tiger Lily stared in wide-eyed horror… she couldn't believe it… she wouldn't believe it…

"No," Nibs said as tears of anguish flowed from his eyes. "It's impossible."

"At last!" Captain Vincent Brubaker screamed as he held up the dripping knife. "The blood of Pan is mine!" The captain's eyes were aflame with greed as he brought the knife to his lips. He licked the blade and rolled the blood around on his tongue, savoring the sweetness of his prize. Then, he looked down at the boiling cauldron of swirling ether below… and dropped the knife in…

BOOM! — There was a huge explosion as the cauldron began bubbling with dark and stormy energy.

Tiger Lily screamed in pain and wrath as she stood up from the shadows, revealing her position, for without Peter, her life mattered to her no longer. Grief and agony poured from her being as she began furiously loosing arrows more rapidly than she ever had before, cutting down the startled pirates faster than they could turn to face her. They had taken from her something that could never be repaid — they had taken her love from her, indeed, her very soul — and now she would slaughter the entire horde like the swine they were. Blood lust filled her eyes as she cut them down, one by one, her rage being fueled, her wrath being perfected, and when she was done with the pawns, she'd take down the captain — she would make him suffer — then, and only then, would she mourn for Peter, once the captain's blood was spilled, and his corpse lay lifeless on the ground…

Nibs yelled in rage and charged the horde of pirates, sticking his sword into the stomach of the first pirate that was unfortunate enough to cross his path, spilling his guts on the blood-soaked deck. He pulled out his sword, and cut down another, and another, and another, remnants of their blood splattering across his face. In Peter's honor, he would kill them all in vengeance, or die in the process… it didn't matter now, for without Peter, Neverland was lost…

***

Under the sea, as the start of the battle raged above him, Peter sank deeper and deeper into Cannibal Cove… he looked up through fading eyes, and could see the moon reflected on the surface of the water… and the stars surrounding it… indeed, it was beautiful… he always thought that to die would be an awfully great adventure… well… he never thought he could actually die… but it looked like he was finally going to get his chance this time… it was all right… Tinker Bell was safe… and that's all that mattered…

"Goodbye, Neverland," Peter said to the tiny glowing ball of light moving towards him in his mind's eye, for surely this was it. "Thanks for all the great adventures." Then he closed his bright eyes completely, and prepared for the next journey…

Suddenly, Tinker Bell's glow appeared right next to Peter's sinking body. She was back to her regular, tiny size again, and even Peter with his slight build looked like a giant compared to her. She held her breath and had to swim hard to keep up with the pace at which Peter sank. She checked the wound in his side — the gash was really deep, and really bad — she didn't know what to do.

"Think, Tinker Bell, think," she thought as she felt herself begin to panic, for she knew she had to stay calm if she was to find the light in this nightmare — but what was she to do? Peter was sinking faster than she could keep up with him, and she was no longer big enough or strong enough to bring him to the surface. As the moonlight from above began to fade, and Peter sank deeper and deeper into the sea, she really started to panic, and this time there was no stopping it. How could it have come to this? If only she could have figured out a potion to stay human sized forever, then none of this would be happening. If only the current neverbrew didn't wear off, then she could save him—

"The neverbrew!" Tink exclaimed, suddenly finding her answer. "That's it!" Tink spun around in the dark black of the sea, and saw a glow sinking in the distance from her through the water — it was the vial! — it was pretty far away from her. She would have to leave Peter's sinking body to swim to it, but it was her only hope…

***

On the center of the deck stage, Captain Vincent Brubaker stared down greedily as the sinister mixture perfected itself into a conscious mass of etheric soup. Yes, it was just as he had foreseen, just as he planned, for he had scoured all the worlds throughout the universe, even to the depths of Neverland herself, for the key ingredients that constituted real power, and it was he, Captain Vincent Brubaker, the noblest of all pirates, the most feared buccaneer upon the seven seas and grandson to the Great Captain James Hook, that had brought these key ingredients together.

"It is done, Grandfather." He spoke to the coffin as if its contents were alive, his hand resting gently on the surface, his eyes softening. “I have the blood of your Great and Worthy Opponent… at last… Neverland is yours once again…”

A moment, then the captain’s eyes turned fierce. With a mighty shout he turned and shoved his grandfather’s coffin into the cauldron whole, where it was greedily consumed by the mixture in an explosion of dark and stormy energy. The potion was now complete. With lust in his eyes, the captain dipped the peace pipe into the cauldron and pulled it out in reverence. He held it aloft as the end of the pipe smoked with dark, etheric energy… this was it… the moment that constituted his whole life… he put the pipe to his mouth… and inhaled…

There was a moment as the captain took the smoke into his lungs… he closed his eyes… savoring the experience as the smoke infiltrated his being…

“ARGHHH!” Suddenly, the captain’s eyes snapped open. He dropped the pipe and let out a blood curdling scream! It felt like he was on fire, as if his very blood was being boiled from within. The pain was unbearable, and he began to lose consciousness. His screaming reached a climax, then he doubled over and plunged headfirst into the cauldron where his body was greedily swallowed by the mixture.

Rain, thunder, and lightning now filled the air. Tiger Lily shot down another pirate, and watched in horror as the captain plunged headfirst into the boiling cauldron. She had been trying to cut her way through the horde to get to him, for he was the symbol of all her anger — all her loss — but there were just too many bodies in the way. Suddenly, she felt even more anger that her final stroke of vengeance was taken from her, for he deserved to taste the sting of a thousand of her arrows, but it was too late now…

She yelled, and doubled down her efforts upon the terrified pirates, for they had just lost their leader, and the princess' blood lust at the loss of the Pan was unquenchable. Truly, this girl would kill them all if they did not stop her, but none could get close enough to take her down. She continued moving up the main deck towards the stage, pulling her arrows out of the bodies of the fallen as she went, and loosing them at the cowards ducking for cover — it was not over yet — it wouldn't be over until the entire deck was washed red with their blood, then, and only then, would she stay her hand as she pulled her last arrow out of the final corpse.

Nibs ran to slay another pirate, but Tiger Lily was cutting them down before he could get to them. He didn't know if he was inspired or terrified by the total scope of her blood lust, but he knew her loss, for Peter was like a brother to him — his closest brother — and these bottom feeding pig men took that joy from him, and they would all pay, if not by the hot sting of Tiger Lily's arrows, then by the cold edge of his steel blade.

Suddenly, the cauldron began to bubble and boil over. Tiger Lily pulled back another arrow and stared up at the stage as the contents rose up from the confines of the cauldron, and a dark being began to form at the center of the substance. The first thing she could make out were the eyes. They were filled with purple and black, etheric flames, some kind of pure, dark energy. Then, she saw a head form around them, followed by a torso, then the rest of the body began to form as the captain and the entire contents of the mixture began to combine, generating a metamorphosis…

"Yes…" the forming organism groaned. "INFINITE POWER!" The newly birthed dark being leaned back as purple and black, ethereal fire exploded out of him, connecting with the sky.

Although it was both terrifying and awesome to behold, Tiger Lily pulled her gaze and continued to reign down a barrage of hell on the confused and terrified pirates. She had to get to that stage, but the only way to get there was by slaying one pirate at a time, and it wasn't fast enough…

***

Solomon, Charlie, Tootles, Curly, and the Twins traversed east down the Great River Basin until they neared the shoreline of Pirate Eater Beach — the nearest place to enter the cove without having to cross back over the Great River, or brave the deadly cliffs of Breakneck Falls.

They saw a huge surge of energy shoot up into the sky from the ship just as they were coming upon the water's edge.

"That can't be good," Tootles stated.

"Clip this to your horse," Curly said, holding out a golden rabbit's foot to Charlie as they raced across the beach.

"What is it?" Charlie asked as he took it.

"You'll see." Curly smiled a cocky, knowing smile, then pulled on his reins and surged ahead. Perplexed, Charlie clipped the rabbit's foot to his horse's mane.

As they reached the waterline of Cannibal Cove, they came upon the spot on the beach where Slightly was still holding Marco at sword point.

"Slightly!" Curly exclaimed as he saw him up ahead.

"What's up, squirt," Slightly said coolly. "I never thought I'd be so happy to see you fellas."

"No time to talk!" Tootles commanded. "Hop on Solomon."

"I'm supposed to be guarding — bollocks!" Solomon ran by and flipped Slightly up on his back just as the others leapt out onto the water, but Slightly wasn't complaining, he was looking for any excuse to join the battle, besides, what could that sniveling, whipped dog Marco do to them anyway? His skills were needed elsewhere.

Charlie looked down from his horse at the sea below him, completely amazed as they rode untouched by the waves. He looked over in wide-eyed amazement and excitement at Curly, who rode next to him.

"You're walking on water, mate," Curly said coolly, then they both shared a deep, hearty laugh as they raced towards the battle across the cove.

Back at the shoreline, Marco grimaced as he watched the others ride away from him over the sea, his bonds still holding him tight.

"You're not just gonna leave me out here!" He screamed, for as much as he hated them all before, he never hated them more than now — and what was Charlie doing riding with them? That traitor — he always had a soft spot for the princess, and her flying boy, and those stupid, worthless lost boys had clearly exploited that soft part of him for their own gain. Charlie was now just as brain-washed and just as useless as they were. Oh well, he'd get what was coming to him now, a traitor shares in a traitor's penalty, that was the rule. Soon, they would all see what a horrible decision they made in crossing him… soon…

Marco continued to stew as he watched them disappear across the water until they were out of sight, then all fell silent on Pirate Eater Beach. He looked around him, and suddenly he didn't feel so confident in the quiet, surrounding darkness that felt as if was pressing in upon him from every side. He shuddered as a chill ran through his whole body…

"Help," he squeaked.

***

All was pitch black in the depths of Cannibal Cove except for a golden vial of fairy potion that lit up the deep. Tinker Bell took the risk and swam the distance to retrieve it as Peter continued to sink deeper and deeper into the depths. When she finally got to it, she realized that it was bigger than her!

At the edge of her breath, Tink swam underneath the vial as it continued to fall deeper and deeper through the water. She got underneath it and pushed up with her back, trying to force it upwards towards the surface, but it was no use, for it was too heavy and the water pressure had become too great. She then turned and swam up the side of the sinking vial until she came to the cork. She wrapped her arms around it, placed her feet on the lip of the vial, and pushed upwards as hard as she could — she felt it give a little, but the water pressure was still too great.

Tinker Bell was out of breath and felt herself starting to lose consciousness. She only had another second now — enough energy for one more try — this had to be it. With all the strength she had left, she gave another upwards heave and pushed up on the cork as hard as she could. She felt it give a little… then…

POP! — The cork popped under the water and the neverbrew shot up at Tinker Bell just as she gasped for breath, taking in a huge gulp of seawater and the potion. Immediately, her mind came back to her as the magic potion surged through her veins, giving her a second wind as she popped and flickered back to human size. She then corked the vial trapping what remained of the neverbrew, and swam towards Peter.

Without Tink needing to audibly instruct it, the remaining neverbrew in the vial lit up brightly and shone through the darkness of the sea, lighting her surroundings, for she was its creator and it was in her blood, and it had a connection to her that surpassed language. Tinker Bell turned and saw Peter sinking far away and below her. She began swimming towards him immediately, moving as fast as she could, but he was so deep now, and badly injured. Even with her neverbrew, she feared—

No, she could not think that way — not right now — for the worst was never an option. She swam and swam and swam with all her might, the neverbrew lighting her way through the depths of the dark sea, catching up to him as he continued to sink deeper and deeper in the cove, but she was still far away from him.

"Keep swimming, Tinker Bell," she said to herself. "Keep swimming and don't stop til you get to him." Although her confidence wavered, Tink made a choice to never stop swimming, so she continued deeper towards him, for she knew the fate of their entire world was dependent on Peter being alive, and if all else failed, she would will him back to life herself.

Suddenly, three shadows passed over Peter's body. Tinker Bell squinted her eyes in the dark and saw that three mermaids had snatched him up. Two of them started rapidly swimming Peter towards the surface, while the other put her mouth over his, and blew air into his lungs — to Tinker Bell it looked as if she was kissing him passionately, and she didn't like it — her eyes narrowed as she followed them to the surface…

***

The dark energy from above surged into Vincent Brubaker's body with a final zap, and it was no longer a mere captain made of flesh and blood that stood on the deck, but an ethereal, god-like being made out of pure energy. He stood for a moment, checking out his new body that flared with black and purple, ethereal flames which compounded in on themselves, burning from some infinite source like the surface of a dark sun. He was terrifyingly beautiful. The Dark Father of Time had re-incarnated once again, but not just in any body… but in one that all the inhabitants of Neverland feared… one that the flying boy would never forget…

With two perfect shots, Tiger Lily slayed the last pirates standing in her path and finally made it to the stage just as this new power finished forming with his back turned to her. She knocked another arrow as she carefully ascended, silently, step by step, ready to fire at will.

"It's good to see you, Princess," the being said, his back still turned to her. "I see you've blossomed into a real woman."

Suddenly, Tiger Lily was gripped by fear, for it wasn't this being's power that she was afraid of, but that… that voice… it had been over one hundred years since she last heard it, but she would never forget it as long as she lived.

"No," Tiger Lily trembled as the fear worked its way through her body.

"Oh yes," the being said. "Oh yes, yes, yes, yes, yes… as they like to say in Neverland… '*Hookie's back.*'"

Tiger Lily's heart dropped into her stomach as the being finally turned his countenance upon her, and all hope was lost, for Captain James Hook had returned to Neverland mixed with this great and terrible evil that his grandson had summoned from the furthest and darkest recesses of the deep, and it appeared to be the end of all things.

THWAP! — She loosed an arrow, but it went right through the Dark Father's ethereal body and disintegrated a few feet on the other side. Her eyes went wide.

"It's interesting, isn't it," the Dark Father said easily as he swirled around some etheric flames in his hand. "All this *time* since we last met, and you're still using the same, archaic weapons… it's like you haven't changed at all, princess… but sooner or later… *time* has a way of catching up with you…"

The Dark Father in the form of Captain Hook then wafted his hand, and suddenly Tiger Lily was stricken with a vision of herself old and dying, all of her youth, life, and vitality drained. Tiger Lily screamed in torment as her mind was assaulted by this evil, and the Dark Father smiled in pleasure.

***

Charlie, Tootles, Curly, the Twins, and Slightly on Solomon finally arrived at the ship. Ruby and Fleur whinnied and jumped as they saw Solomon and the other horses approach, for they had been anxious the whole time while the battle had been raging above them, and they were grateful for the reinforcements.

"It's good to see you, girl," Tootles said as he stroked Ruby's horn.

Charlie saw the grappling hook that Tiger Lily and Nibs used to ascend into the ship, and immediately began to climb. The other's petted their steeds, bidding them a short but grateful farewell, then they turned and followed silently up the rope, for whatever evil they were to face above, they knew that destroying it was the only option if they were ever to see their animal companions again…

***

The mermaids had been above water a while by the time Tinker Bell finally caught up to them and emerged to the surface of Cannibal Cove. She took a deep, grateful breath of fresh air, savoring her return to momentary safety, then turned and saw the mermaids around Peter's floating body, studying him.

"Hey!" Tinker Bell coughed, then she began swimming towards them.

The two blonde mermaids that brought Peter to the surface dove back under and disappeared faster than they had come, but the redheaded mermaid — the one that was kissing Peter — did not flee, in fact, she didn't seem to pay Tinker Bell any mind at all. She just stayed there, her back turned to her, stroking Peter's brow.

"I've heard so much about him under the sea," the mermaid spoke in a beautiful, pure, feminine voice as she felt Tinker Bell approach behind her in the water. "He's even more beautiful than they say…"

Then, the redheaded mermaid turned to look at Tinker Bell, and for the first time she saw her full on. There was a childlike wonder in her big, blue eyes beneath all that red hair and her petite, dainty features, and there was no doubt that she was extremely beautiful.

Tinker Bell paid her no more attention as she approached Peter's body, for she had serious business to attend to. She quickly and efficiently pulled out what remained in her neverbrew vial and popped the cork, dumping a portion of the contents on Peter's wounded side. To her annoyance, the mermaid did not flee, but rather, watched her tend to Peter curiously.

"You're Tinker Bell, the boy's fairy," the mermaid giggled.

"Mmhmm," Tinker Bell said, annoyed, as she checked Peter's pulse. She had been dealing with mermaids all her life, and she didn't much care for them. Probably mostly because they tended not to care much for her, but also probably because they were all extremely beautiful, and all of them — without exception — were fascinated by Peter.

As Peter's side began to magically and rapidly heal, Tink sighed in relief as she found a steady pulse. The mermaid watched in childlike glee, then put her ear down to Peter's chest, beside herself with excitement.

"He's alive!" the mermaid exclaimed with joy.

"Mmhmm," Tink murmured through tight lips, getting more annoyed by the second by this mermaid that apparently really liked to state the obvious.

"I can feel his heart beating," the mermaid continued. "It's so strong… he's going to be okay."

"Mmhmm!" Tink exclaimed louder, for the mermaid had her pretty head hovering over Peter's sinewy chest, seemingly enjoying it much more than what was appropriate given the current circumstances, and Tinker Bell could stand it no longer.

"Listen — whoever you are!" Tink exclaimed. "Thanks for the help, but I've got it from here."

"I'd like to stay until he awakes," the mermaid answered quite boldly, still fascinated by his heartbeat. "My sisters have told me so many stories about him under the sea… and now that I have him in my arms… I want to look him in the eyes…"

"I said beat it, fish legs," Tinker Bell commanded, for this had gone on for far long enough. "Or I'll turn you into shark bait."

The redheaded mermaid turned and smiled innocently one last time at Tinker Bell as she stroked Peter's brow, then she kissed Peter on the forehead, giggled, and dove back under the surface. Tinker Bell stared at the place above the water where the mermaid disappeared, a bit mesmerized by the creature, for she had met and had dealings with many mermaids in her time, but she had never met another like this one. Although she didn't know why… something told her she was going to be seeing a lot more of her in the future…

Tink scowled and quickly pushed the thought from her mind, for although she was thankful for the mermaid's help, she didn't much care for how much curiosity and interest she was showing in Peter — or for how pretty the mermaid was, if she was being honest with herself — but it didn't matter, for the mermaid was now gone, and more importantly, Peter was alive.

She then looked down on the beautiful boy she had loved for so long, his heartbeat steady as he floated somewhere in his mind far away from here. Tinker Bell hoped it was someplace happy, for he had sacrificed everything to save her — indeed, even his own life — and she loved him for it. Yes, there were no words to express how much she loved him, and perhaps he would never know, but she just wanted him to know that she was grateful — grateful for his being, grateful that he was alive — for the light in his eyes and the joy of his soul made Neverland a better place, and she could not imagine a world without him.

Then, mustering all her strength, Tinker Bell prepared to do what she did not truly desire to do so soon, for wherever Peter was in his mind, it was clear that it was peaceful, and to bring him back to the hell he just left was the last thing she wanted, for he had gone through so much, so much already for them all, and it was unfair for her or their world to ask more of him, but it had to be done, for he was the only one with the power to save Neverland, and she knew it.

Tinker Bell looked down at Peter, and stroked his brow… it was so much weight for one boy to carry… so much weight… she knew that she would never know entirely the size and scope of his burden, but she felt that she had gotten closer to understanding him than anyone else in his life ever had… and for that… she felt truly honored and grateful that she could be there for him when he needed her most…

Now it was time to bring him back. His spirit was alive but his body was deeply tired from what he had already gone through. She had to get a powerful energy shock to his system, and the only way was to get the neverbrew as deep in his lungs as possible.

"Don't pretend like you don't want it," Tinker Bell said ironically to herself as she held what remained in the vial up to the moonlight, then she dumped the last of its contents into her mouth, and kissed Peter, forcing the magical potion deep into his lungs…

"Please, Peter…" Tinker Bell said as she pulled away from his lips, stroking his brow. "Neverland needs you. We all need you… I need you…"

There was a moment… then Peter's eyelids flickered…

***

Rain pounded as Tiger Lily faced down the dark god that had taken the form of Captain Hook. Her bow — which was useless against him — was now strapped to her back, and she had her dual tomahawks out. Tears of anguish poured down her face from the mental onslaught that she had just endured, and whether the fiend had lifted the curse, or she defeated it, she knew that she could not stand another attack like that on her mind, for with the weight of it coupled with the loss of Peter — anymore and it would surely collapse — and she would descend into death forevermore… or perhaps some insanity far, far worse…

“There’s no need for violence, Princess,” the dark being said, and although it was very much the voice of the late Captain James Hook that Tiger Lily remembered, there was a power far greater within his body that the captain never possessed. Whatever it was, it may have taken the form of Hook, and sounded like Hook, but it was something far more sinister

“My fight is not with you,” he continued. “Bow down and worship me, join me as my bride, and you will not be destroyed when I conquer this planet.”

“Neverland is a free world,” Tiger Lily said, for she felt every dark emotion there ever was to feel now — fear, resentment, hate, loss, wrath, anger, vengeance — and tears poured freely from her eyes. “It is an eternal world… and its people bow to no one.”

The Dark Father smiled at the little princess’s words… her undying love for that pathetic, flying child was humorous at best… it was sad to see, really… so much self-created suffering… such naivety… she had no idea the feast of power she was missing out on by opposing him…

"Then… I'm afraid…" he said with a waft of his hand. "Your *time* is up…" the Dark Father raised his palm towards her, and it started charging with powerful, dark energy, ready to destroy…

"Tiger Lily!" Nibs screamed from below as he saw that thing charging the devastating attack. He now took on the hoard of pirates all by himself as blood, sweat, and tears of rage poured from his face.

"Hold on! I'm coming!" Nibs screamed as he ran a pirate through, for with Peter gone, he could not bear the thought of allowing Tiger Lily to perish, for he knew how much Peter loved her, and he would do anything to try and atone for his passing.

CLING! — Nibs blocked an incoming attack from a huge pirate, but he was just too tired. The powerful attack knocked away his sword, sending it clattering across the deck, and leaving him unarmed.

BAM! — A hot feeling surged through Nibs' mind as he got punched in the face hard by the big pirate, sending him to the deck. The other pirates gathered around the big one, smiling in their victory, ready to kill the little pest once and for all.

Time seemed to slow as Nibs looked up at the stars… he smiled… knowing he had just moments left until the pain was over… and when he was taken from this world… he knew he would feel joy once again… someplace up there in the sky… someplace with Peter and the rest of his friends…

Suddenly, the sound of a valiant war cry filled his ears as Charlie and the lost boys jumped over the deck into battle. They soared over Nibs, attacking the shocked pirates as they landed, taking them completely by surprise. Whether it was just in his mind now, or actually happening, Nibs did not know, and he didn't much care anymore… he just kept staring at the stars… and all he could think about was the beautiful and peaceful place that it was taking him…

BOOM! BOOM! — Tiger Lily ducked and rolled out of the way just in time as Hook fired two deadly blasts of dark, fiery energy at her, which barely missed and completely obliterated a section of the stage. Tiger Lily then ducked behind the cauldron, giving her a moment to breathe, then — BOOM! — Hook blasted it and sent it hurling over deck, where it landed with a steamy splash in the sea.

The Dark Father smiled in satisfaction as he gazed upon the poor, helpless, princess standing in front of him. It was such a shame, for they could have been so great together if she would have just worshipped him and taken her place by his side — like Andromeda — yes, the princess should have taken a few pointers from that timeless fairy, so much beauty, so much potential. They were not so unlike, the princess and her, for they were both angelically beautiful and headstrong, and they were both destined to rule.

Andromeda, sweet Andromeda, how loyal was she! As soon as he was done wiping out these pesky, pathetic children he would fly up to the Windy Mountains and free her from that wretched tomb they called a prison, and they would rule together once and for all. Yes, he would rule with Andromeda, his fairest and most loyal subject, and when they had their fill of ruling, they would destroy this planet and erase its existence from the timeline of the universe forevermore.

The Dark Father then laughed to himself… the foolish princess… they could have accomplished so much throughout the universe, but it was too late now… too late… and now… she would die… he held up his hand and began to charge a final attack…

Down below, Charlie and the lost boys fought valiantly against the pirates, quickly evening the odds. Charlie looked up and saw Tiger Lily facing the dark god-like pirate…

With nowhere left to run, Tiger Lily crossed her tomahawks over her chest and closed her eyes, accepting her fate… this was it…

BOOM! — Hook fired his deadly ball of flaming energy… it closed in on Tiger Lily…

BAM! — Charlie climbed up one of the stabilizing pillars of the stage and shoulder charged Tiger Lily out of the way, knocking her to the deck just as the flaming ball of doom sailed over their heads, incinerating the backside of the platform.

With the front and backsides of the deck now gone, they were trapped on the small section left that was still standing. Tiger Lily was shaken to the core from the near brush with death. Charlie stood and guarded his people's princess with his tomahawk, standing between her and this demon that looked like Hook, crouched in fighting stance, ready to die defending the belle of his tribe.

The Dark Father's eyes narrowed as he looked at the intruder, annoyed — it was pathetic really, this brave — his ways were primitive, laughable even. Him standing there with his little hatchet, in his warrior's stance, believing he could do anything at all to change the outcome. Did he not know that he only merely postponed the inevitable by joining the battle? Did he not know that he would now die too? Oh, well, time to incinerate them both.

The Dark Father raised his hand to kill… and Charlie didn't move a muscle in the face of this most certain death…

There was a moment… another moment… the Dark Father did not fire…

"Wait," the Dark Father thought, lowering his hand. "It's too easy. You've come all this way, back from the edges of space and time, after waiting for centuries… might as well enjoy yourself a little."

The Dark Father smiled and lowered his hand, then he floated across the chasm in the destroyed deck to the small wooden island where Charlie and Tiger Lily were trapped.

Charlie pulled Tiger Lily up to her feet, and they fell back to the far side of the wooden island as the Dark Father landed effortlessly on the side opposite them.

"Look at this," the Dark Father said, enjoying the insights of Hook's memories. "Two Piccaninnies for the price of one."

Charlie lowered his gaze and moved back in front of Tiger Lily with his tomahawk out, once again standing between her and the Dark Father.

Then, Tiger Lily put her hand on Charlie's shoulder. He looked back—

"Together," Tiger Lily stated, finally standing to her full height as she composed herself. Charlie nodded, and Tiger Lily pulled out her dual tomahawks, and took her place by Charlie's side.

"On you," the Dark Father said, and with an amused smile he put his hands behind his back, for this was much more fun.

There was a moment…Tiger Lily and Charlie looked at each other… nodded… then…

BAM! They traversed the distance between them and the Dark Father in a split second! Tiger Lily went high, Charlie went low…

SWOOSH! SWOOSH! — They both hit nothing but air as the Dark Father effortlessly dodged them both. They recovered and reversed without pause, with Charlie going high and Tiger Lily going in low in classic Piccaninny warrior fashion, for their tribe's fighting style was known for being even more lethal in pairs.

SWOOSH! SWOOSH! — Again, nothing but air. They continued to attack with expert speed, but the Dark Father appeared to be untouchable.

Again, and again, they attacked — high, low, left, right — but nothing. They eventually spun out of the attack to the other side of the deck and stopped in a defensive stance, both of them breathing heavily.

The Dark Father stood on the other side exactly where he was before. In fact, it almost looked like he hardly moved at all.

"Whenever you're ready," the Dark Father said easily, as if the duel hadn't even begun.

This fiend's arrogance was getting to Tiger Lily. Who was this foul abomination to challenge her? A princess of Neverland?! She would send this demon to its demise!

Tiger Lily screamed in wrath and charged back at the Dark Father. Imbued with the strength and courage of his princess, Charlie gave a war cry and ran after her, and together, they descended back upon this evil.

The Dark Father smiled and conjured a flaming, ethereal energy sword with one hand right as they came upon him.

CLING! CLING! CLING! CLING! CLING! CLING! — Without moving, the Dark Father blocked all attacks from all three tomahawks effortlessly with one hand. The spirit that was infused in the wood that composed Tiger Lily and Charlie's tomahawk shafts kept them from being destroyed by the etheric fire.

“Hmm,” the Dark Father observed thoughtfully when he saw that their weapons were still intact. “Maybe not as primitive as I thought.”

Tiger Lily screamed and came back at him with both her tomahawks.

CLING! CLING! — The Dark Father blocked them both, then blocked Charlie’s attack, then the princess’ again, easily taking them both on with one hand. He continued to only play the defensive, then caught both of Tiger Lily’s tomahawks and Charlie’s tomahawk in the air under his blade, then blasted them with kind of telekinetic force with his free hand, sending them both tumbling across the stage where the both barely managed to stay on the deck.

Tiger Lily and Charlie stood a final time, both breathing heavy.

“Is that all you got?” The Dark Father teased thoughtfully as he examined the etheric edge of his blade. “That old Chief… he’s sure letting his tribe go.”

Tiger Lily’s blood boiled even hotter at the taunting of her father’s competency. She was so angry now she was either going to kill this thing, or it was going to kill her, but either way she needed this to be over. She was either going to avenge Peter, or meet him in the afterlife, and either sounded just fine with her — just as long as this stupid wretch stopped talking.

Charlie ran in front of Tiger Lily, then Tiger Lily screamed and attacked behind him. They approached the Dark Father, but just before attacking, Charlie dropped down on his feet and hands in squatting position. Tiger Lily ran up his back and Charlie sprang off the ground, sending Tiger Lily soaring ten feet in the air.

The Dark Father was caught slightly off guard by the well-coordinated attack, and was forced to split his vision. He looked up at Tiger Lily who was descending upon him from the air. She came down with dual tomahawks and he blocked them both, but as he was blocking her from above, Charlie came low and plunged his tomahawk right into the back of the Dark Father's left tendon just as the Dark Father came down with his blade. Charlie had to ride the momentum of the attack to keep from being split in two, and rolled over the side of the deck where he plummeted below into the sea.

"ARGH!" The Dark Father screamed as the spirit infused blade from the tomahawk sank into the dark matter of his leg. He grabbed Tiger Lily by the neck and threw her across the deck, where she landed on the other side with a hard crash. He then pulled the tomahawk from the back of his leg, and stared at it in fury — no one could land a blow on him! no one! — In his wrath, dark fire leapt up from his hand and consumed the tomahawk.

Tiger Lily watched from the deck as Charlie's tomahawk turned to ash in the demon's hand. She smiled — at least Charlie proved it could bleed — he truly was a great warrior. Hopefully he was all right.

Then, her eyes were drawn to the Dark Father's leg where the wound was. It seemed to be moving, closing in on itself. Her eyes went wide with horror as she realized the demon was healing. If it was truly invincible — and without Peter, and without Charlie — she shuddered, for the reality was becoming too horrible to comprehend.

The Dark Father rose to his full height as his wound healed to perfection. It was just one lucky hit — one lucky hit from a surprise attack — no bother, he wasn't even trying. He may have underestimated the princess slightly. That was fine, at least she showed some spirit before accepting her fate. He liked her passion. She would have been great by his side, but she had become too formidable now. It was time for her to die.

Tiger Lily rose slowly from the deck. Her body was exhausted and the wind got knocked clean out of her from the fall. They put up a good fight, but she realized that without Peter, there was very little any of them would be able to do against such a powerful creature for long. It was only a matter of time now — literally — whenever he decided to end it. Tiger Lily was proud of herself. She had just gone toe to toe with a god, and held her own — even managed to wound it thanks to Charlie — she knew Peter would love to hear this story, and she couldn't wait to tell him about it in the next life.

"Do what you're gonna do," Tiger Lily said without fear, then she crossed her tomahawks over her chest, and closed her eyes.

The Dark Father smiled. Even in the face of death, the princess had her pride. Oh, well, it wouldn't do much for her where she was going. He held up his hand… and fired…

Suddenly, like a flash of lighting in the night, Peter flew in and swooped up Tiger Lily moments before the lethal ball of energy would have vaporized her! Down below, the lost boys looked up in joy and amazement. Nibs still laid semiconscious on the ground when he saw Peter soar past the stars.

"Peter," Nibs mumbled, still believing he was dreaming…

"Peter!" Curly announced joyfully.

"Pan," the Dark Father said whimsically from the stage. "The Great Peter Pan…" He watched, amused, as they flew away from him, and the whole timeline history of Hook and Peter's relationship flashed before the Dark Father's eyes, for all of Hook's experiences with him were recorded in the old captain's bones that now made up the Dark Father's physical body… and he smiled when he realized just how much power this form had in this world…

In the air, Tiger Lily held tightly onto Peter as they flew over the sea. She kissed him passionately, and words couldn't describe the joy she felt being in his strong arms again. She was overcome with emotion, and cried into his chest. Peter kissed her on the forehead, and he knew that the darkness they had seen would not soon be forgotten, but someday, there would be time to heal.

"Well, that was fun," Peter teased after a moment as they flew through the air, trying to enjoy this moment of peace, for he knew the battle was far from over.

"Don't say it," Tiger Lily giggled, wiping the tears from her eyes.

"What?" Peter said. "You mean the whole flying in and saving you from getting vaporized at the very last second kind of *exactly* how I saved you from drowning at Skull Rock kind of thing?"

"That's what *friends do."* Tiger Lily said, rolling her eyes. "They protect each other."

"Did you just try and put me in the friend zone?" Peter asked apprehensively.

"Friend zone the Great White Father?" Tiger Lily said ironically. "I don't think his ego could handle it."

Peter and Tiger Lily stared at each other, and a real moment passed between them.

"Maybe I am going to have to marry you," Peter said, then he pulled her towards him and kissed her passionately, for nothing was more rewarding in the entire universe then tasting the sweetness of Tiger Lily's lips again, and he imagined for a moment that they held that kiss forever…

Then after what seemed like a great long while, he pulled his head from hers, and then brushed her nose with his like he used to back when they first met, signaling to her that he would protect her forever… then he turned his gaze upon the ship… and prepared his mind to destroy all evil.

The war between the pirates and the lost boys now raged in a full-on, multi-ship battle. Hordes of pirates from the other two ships began swinging over by ropes to lend aid to their comrades.

THWAP! THWAP! — The Twins loosed stones at lightning speed as they spun through the fray, head-shooting pirates with unreal effectiveness like silent ghosts in the night, and the pirates ducked for cover as they reigned down fury upon them. Tootles gave out a battle cry as he ran the deck with his war hammer, destroying and obliterating anything that came across his path. Slightly easily parried two pirates, then slayed both of them with expert skill, making it look effortless.

"Nibs!" Slightly yelled as he spotted him on the ground, then he ran over.

"Peter… gone…" Nibs mumbled, for he was still semiconscious, and wasn't sure what was really what yet.

"Peter, gone?" Slightly repeated, confused, then it clicked. "Peter's alive you dunce! He's alive and he needs you! Come on!" Slightly then pulled Nibs back up on his feet, put his sword in his hand, and charged back into battle.

Nibs looked down at his sword, then he looked up and watched his brave friend running into the fray, and then the truth of life returned to him at last — Peter was indeed alive, and he needed him now like he had never needed him before — Nibs yelled in victorious joy and threw himself once more into the conflict.

Tinker Bell — now back to human size — flew right over them, excited to join the fight, for she had a bone to pick with a certain captain, and by the time she was done with him, he'd wish that he'd never set sail into Neverland.

"Tink! Catch!" Curly yelled from below as he tossed Tinker Bell her satchel, for he had kept it for her ever since she disappeared from the mountain.

"It's good to see you, Curly!" Tink exclaimed as she dipped low and caught it over her shoulder, then she immediately put her hands in, charged them with fairy energy, and began offering air support from above, blasting pirates with incinerating hot light, in which they ran and ducked for cover in terror.

"No, my lady," Curly said proudly as Tink's presence began turning the tide of the battle. "You have no idea how good it is to see *you.*"

Tinker Bell smiled as she continued to rain down hell upon the fleeing pirate horde. It served them right for what they did to her — and most of all to Peter — and she wouldn't rest until every one of their filthy swine bodies was incinerated into ash, but first, she'd start with the big fish.

Amused, the Dark Father watched from the stage as the boy's fairy shot her little blasts at the useless pirates that Brubaker had called his crew. She was clearly superior to them, and he admired her tenacity… still… she was a pest that would be dealt with… and when her wrathful gaze finally turned upon him… he welcomed it openly…

Tinker Bell floated in the air for a moment as she stared this dark evil down, then, very carefully, she began to float towards him… there was something familiar about this thing… something timeless… but it was more than that… then… her eyes widened in horror…

"No… it can't be…" Tinker Bell said to herself in utter shock, for what she was seeing she knew was impossible, but it was happening anyway.

"Hello, Miss Bell," The Dark Father said elegantly from his stage, knowing the full history between Hook and Tinker Bell as well. "It has been some *time…*"

"Hook?" Tink exclaimed, half amazed, half shell-shocked. "But how? You're dead."

"Yes, and you're much larger," the Dark Father teased, using Hook's old wit, and he let it hang in the air. "There… we're even now."

Tink's eyes suddenly narrowed as her mind came back to her like a flash of lightning, then she quickly launched two bright balls of white-hot light energy at Hook—

BOOM! — they impacted with two bright flashes, but when the light cleared, Hook was less than unharmed. It was one of Tink's most powerful attacks, and she might as well have been throwing bubbles at him. Hook smiled in amusement.

"My turn," he said, then he barely flicked his finger and sent an etheric ball of dark and terrible energy right at her.

Down below, Peter set Tiger Lily down on the deck just as he saw the giant ball of energy headed right towards Tink…

Tinker Bell's eyes went wide at the awful display of power and at the incoming energy ball. She managed to generate a fairy dust light shield with her hands just before impact…

BOOM! — Her shield absorbed some of the impact but it wasn't enough! The shield shattered in a spray of gold and launched Tinker Bell helplessly out towards Cannibal Cove like a rag doll!

From the air, Peter saw the whole thing happen. He flew as fast as he could and caught Tinker Bell just before she hit the water.

"You all right, Tink?" Peter said as he held her in his arms.

Tink nodded — she was jolted, but still intact.

"How do we stop that thing?" Peter asked quite seriously, for the power that being displayed by taking two of Tinker Bell's fully charged fairy blasts without so much as a scratch was no joke.

"I don't know," Tinker Bell admitted. "But I have a feeling you're the only one who can."

Peter looked down at the beautiful fairy in his arms, and he was never more grateful to have her in his life as he was right then.

"The Son of Neverland," Tinker Bell said as she brushed the stringy hair out of his big, bright eyes. "And to think… I've known you since you were seven days old…"

Peter smiled at her as they connected, then he kissed her on the forehead, and rocketed back towards the ship…

* CHAPTER 16 *

— The Great and Worthy Opponent —

The Dark Father of Time, the late Captain James Hook, and his grandson, Captain Vincent Brubaker, all stood on stage as the battle raged below them, their unified bodies burning with dark, ethereal flames, for tonight, the three of them existed in the exact same moment. The intentions of all their souls had aligned, and together, they were made perfect as three-in-one. The Dark Father sought a body, Hook had sought power, and Brubaker had sought significance, and all three sought revenge on one being in particular… a menace that had plagued their existence for centuries… a child who had banished their souls from the light… and tonight… they would have their revenge… they would have it or they would turn Neverland into ash in the process…

Peter descended from above and landed lightly on the other side, his youthful body glowing with kinetic, golden energy, for he had been reborn in the mountain for this very moment, and the life-force of all of Neverland now resided in his being, and it was in him that the hopes and prayers of its population had found its champion.

The two gods stared each other down, and Neverland held its breath once again…

"Hello, Peter," the Dark Father said in Hook's voice with his demeanor, addressing him as one old friend to another.

Peter eyed this being cautiously. It was massive compared to him, and must have been at least nine feet tall, making him once again look like a child in comparison, and although it took the form and used the voice of Hook, he knew he was facing no mere pirate captain, for beneath that body resided the evil and formidable spirit of the reincarnated Dark Father.

"So you're Time, huh?" Peter said, his bright eyes flickering over a fearless smile. "Funny… last I remember you were afraid of clocks."

"Ah, yes," the Dark Father said thoughtfully, remembering Hook's past. "After I'm done with you I'll destroy that blasted crocodile."

"Too late," Peter smirked.

The Dark Father jeered and once again conjured his energy sword out of thin air. It smoked sinisterly with black and purple etheric flames. Directly after, Peter pulled out his Dagger of Truth and flipped it around easily in his hand. It glowed a hot gold in the night.

"That's what you used to kill me," the Dark Father noted. "Twice."

"You remember," Peter stated, his stare not wavering

"Oh, I remember all things," the Dark Father said. "And all there ever was or will be," Then he slowly lifted off the ground into the air, and Peter did as well, until they were hovering fifty feet above the battle that raged below.

"So this is what it's like to be able to fly," the Dark Father stated as he felt Hook's bones experience flight for the first time.

"Great, isn't it?" Peter agreed.

"Bad form, Peter," the Dark Father scolded, fully realizing the scope of Hook's previous disadvantage. "He never stood a chance."

Then, the Dark Father held up his palm and blasted a ball of dark, sinister energy right towards Peter, who then shot up easily and higher into the air so that the energy passed right beneath him. The Dark Father then rose up higher to meet him.

"Join me, Peter," the Dark Father said, feigning peace. "Surrender Neverland to the inevitability of its dark age, and you will have a place by my side."

Peter stared at the dark fiend in front of him, and he saw right through the façade, for he would no sooner surrender Neverland than he would betray his closest friend, and he would send this foul evil back to the abyss or die trying.

"It's a tempting offer, but…" Peter said as he stared the Dark Father down into his flaming eyes… then Peter's own bright eyes sparked with light. "You hurt my fairy."

BANG! — In a microsecond, Peter transversed the space between them and came down with a powerful slash.

CRACK! — Sparks flew as the Dark Father blocked the attack, energy exploding off energy. Peter reigned down a flurry of quick jab attacks — one of his signature moves — and the Dark Father parried them all.

BOOM! — The Dark Father blasted Peter with energy from his free hand, sending Peter soaring back through the air. Peter quickly recovered, and stared down this dark god — whatever this thing was, its power was immeasurable — Peter clenched his teeth and flew right back at him.

The Dark Father rapidly sent blasts of flaming energy through the air as the flying boy advanced upon him, but Peter dodged them as quickly as he could send them with perfect agility. Peter entered back into striking distance and came down with a devastating blow just as the Dark Father unleashed a powerful blast of energy… the two opposing forces met… and…

BOOM! — The impact from the blast sent both gods flying back, but Peter, much more so. He recovered with not too much difficulty and stared his foe down, and although he hadn't been expending himself completely just yet, it felt like the Dark Father was doing little more than toying with him. How much of his innate power the Dark Father was actually using, Peter did not yet know, but it was becoming clear to him that he was going to have to figure out something else if he was to defeat him in open battle…

***

Down on the ship, Tiger Lily was back at it with her bow, mowing down pirates with absolute vengeance. Charlie had scaled back up the ship into the battle, and Tiger Lily tossed him one of her tomahawks, which he used to wreak havoc on the enemy. Nibs and Charlie slayed buccaneers left and right. Tink offered air support from above, but it wasn't enough as more pirates continued to swing over from the nearby ships. She got an idea.

"Curly!" Tinker Bell yelled as she flew down low towards the deck. "Throw me one of those fairy bombs!"

CLING! CLING! — Curly parried an incoming attack from a pirate, rolled, then tossed Tinker Bell a fairy bomb. Tink snatched it out of the air, flew over to a neighboring ship, and placed the bomb at the base of the mast.

"I hope this works," Tink said as she armed the bomb, then she flew away.

BOOM! — There was a massive explosion as the bomb blew a huge hole in the middle of the ship. The mast started falling right where Ruby, Solomon, and Fleur were waiting on the water.

"Now, girl!" Tinker Bell yelled, and Ruby leapt up on the falling mast just as it hit the water, which created a pathway up into the battle from Cannibal Cove. Solomon and Fleur followed close behind Ruby as she raced up the mast.

Once high enough, they leapt over the water and landed on the main ship. Pirates fled and dove for cover as they ran through the battle, cleaning house.

Tiger Lily hopped on Fleur just as she ran past and kept mowing down enemies. The lost boys yelled in victory as the pirates finally began to retreat at the sight of Solomon's furiosity and Ruby's magic.

***

Up in the sky, Peter dodged blast after blast as Hook gave chase. His plan was to lead the dark god out into the Southern Sea in order to keep the battle away from the mainland, and so far, it seemed to be working.

"You can't run forever, boy!" The Dark Father yelled using Hook's menacing cadence, then he launched two more balls of flaming dark energy that honed in on Peter with synergetic force.

WHOOSH! WHOOSH! — Peter dove down to sea level in order to dodge the blasts that were swallowed up by massive waves that exploded in clouds of water and steam. The Dark Father continued to give chase through the storm, and Peter attempted to shake him by weaving in and out of the huge white caps.

Peter then leapt up onto a giant tidal wave and surfed down its back, the wall of water giving him momentary relief. He then looked behind him, but the Dark Father was nowhere to be seen. Peter continued to surf down the backs of waves as they rose and fell like liquid guardians, and he gratefully took the shelter they provided from the Dark Father's direct eyeline to recover his energy and bearings. Suddenly—

SLASH! — Peter ducked the Dark Father's energy sword just in time as he appeared out of thin air so fast it was almost as if he had teleported. With the Dark Father now back on his tail, Peter leapt off the wave and rocketed back up into the sky.

"What do you want?!" Peter screamed over the pouring rain and cracking lightning as the two gods faced each other in the air once again.

The Dark Father looked Peter directly in his bright eyes. "Everything," he said, then he turned and started rocketing away from Peter right back towards the mainland.

Peter hesitated for a moment as the Dark Father flew away from him, for it was a curious move that such a powerful opponent would retreat during the heat of battle — especially since Peter felt that he had him on the run — then, it hit Peter like a ton of bricks. The Dark Father wasn't retreating, he was going to wreak havoc on the mainland! Peter turned on the jets and gave chase.

At the ship, Tinker Bell, Tiger Lily, Charlie, Solomon, Ruby, Fleur and the lost boys had the momentum and were finally beating the pirates back. It felt good, for spirits were high, and they could see their victory at hand.

Then, Nibs turned and saw a giant ball of dark, fiery energy coming down from the sky.

"Everybody down!" He screamed.

BOOM! — There was a massive explosion as the Dark Father's giant ball of energy completely destroyed one of the other three ships, sending shrapnel and debris everywhere and incinerating the pirates that still were on it. Everyone on the main ship stared at the explosion in shock and terror as the pirates were vaporized before their very eyes…

ZOOM! ZOOM! — The sound of two beings flying by as Peter gave Chase to the Dark Father at mach speed. The others looked up in the sky, but couldn't make out their forms. They could only see two bright flashes — a purple one being chased by a golden one — headed straight for the southern mainland…

In the air, the Dark Father laughed after destroying the ship, enjoying the small display of power, for he could have easily destroyed the main ship if he so chose, and wiped out the princess, the fairy, and all of those pesky lost boys in one fell swoop, but he wasn't interested in destroying the boy's spirit so quickly and easily. No, he was enjoying this game, and he wanted to make him suffer. After he defeated the flying insect they called their Savior, he would enjoy killing his friends, one, by one, by one…

Peter gave chase and did his best to block his foe's display of power from his mind, for be it Hook, or the Dark Father, or whatever this terrible evil was that just destroyed an entire pirate ship by barely lifting a finger, its power was indeed superior to any opponent Peter had ever come across or faced… at least since he was old enough to remember…

Indeed, Peter knew that the Dark Father's raw power exceeded his own, and just like when he was a two-year-old boy, he'd have to rely on strategy to send this foul beast back to the abyss, for to try and take it head on in the open air was surely a fool's game. Peter prayed that the Great Spirit within him would come forth, and with Hook and all his cunning being powered by the spirit of the Dark Father, Peter was going to need all the help from on high that he could get.

BOOM! BOOM! — the Dark Father blasted two balls of flaming hot, dark energy behind him. Peter dodged them nimbly and easily, for he had never been more agile, and the aerial skills he now possessed appeared to be unlimited.

On the shoreline of Pirate Eater Beach, the now unguarded Marco scooched across the ground and retrieved his fallen tomahawk. He began cutting his bonds, then he saw the Dark Father flying westward across the cove.

Marco jeered as he watched the ol' captain rocket into the mainland, for he knew exactly where he was going, and took great pleasure in the fact that he was the essential key piece to the dark god's successful reincarnation into Neverland.

"Yes," Marco hissed in glory from the ground, for this was the moment of his ultimate pay off. "Burn them all."

In the air, the pounding rain stung Peter's face as visibility waned. He bit down and turned on the jets as he chased the Dark Father across the Lonely Jungle, and then up the Southern Channel towards the Western Cape… Peter's worst fears were quickly becoming a reality…

Peter tailed the Dark Father until he finally slowed just above the Indian Camp, they were so high Peter could see the entire outline of the Western Cape below him.

“Your fight is with me!” Peter called from across the air.

The Dark Father looked at Peter — at the tiny child that had destroyed him centuries ago, now a fully grown young man — how was it even possible? How was it ever possible? The child was an arrogant fool, who, by some stroke of unprecedented luck, took him off guard and struck true before he ever even knew what was happening. It was a sick joke by that rascally and devious Great Spirit — it had always been a sick joke — and now, it was time to even the score.

“You don’t have to do this!” Peter screamed, but he could see in the Dark Father’s eye that he already made his decision.

The Dark Father’s eyes narrowed, and Peter felt his heart drop into the pit of his stomach…

“No…” Peter said, then his pulse quickened…

BOOM! — There was a massive explosion as the Dark Father launched a giant flaming ball of etheric death energy at the entire Indian Camp just as Peter aerial dove as fast as he could towards it!

Down below, the chief and the tribe gathered out in the rain and looked up at the sky as they heard the explosion above.

“What’s that, papa?” A young Indian boy said as he tugged on his father’s hand, pointing to the giant ball of dark energy that grew bigger and bigger like the birth of a dark sun.

“Run,” the chief ordered as he saw the ball of purple and black fire getting larger and larger. “Everybody run for the beach!”

The tribespeople ran for their lives, grabbing their children. Men yelled and women screamed as the deadly ball of destruction grew bigger and bigger in the sky.

Peter raced at near supersonic speed towards the falling ball of death. He came up alongside the energy ball and flew in front of it — he had no choice — he took his Dagger of Truth in both hands and placed it on the hurling ball of destruction, attempting to push it back or at least divert it enough so that it didn't hit the village directly.

CRACK! CRACK! — His dagger popped and flared with energy as he tried to push it back with all his might. The heat was scorching, but his spirit infused flesh was able to withstand it. Peter slowed it down, but it kept raining down closer and closer to the village. Peter screamed as he gave it all he had, but it was no use, for the energy had too much momentum and it was too close. He looked behind him, and he had just moments before it impacted the ground. No choice—

BOOOOOM! — Peter leapt and rocketed straight up into the sky just as the energy blast incinerated the entire village, the concussion from the impact sent him hurling and somersaulting into the sky like a rag doll.

On the outskirts of the camp, the villagers dove into the waters of Piccaninny Bay with their children to avoid the blistering heat from the dark fire that consumed their village. When the concussion from the initial explosion had passed, men stared speechless from the waves, and women wept on the beach as they attempted to comfort their crying children. Valiantly, the chief stood before them all, tears of grief pouring from his open eyes as collectively he and his tribe watched the only home they'd known for centuries go up in flames before them, and they were helpless to stop it.

In the air, Peter looked down as his true love's village burned. His blood boiled hot, and it was possibly the most rage he had ever felt in his life.

"Did you… care for those people?" the Dark Father said as he dropped down effortlessly from above, enjoying every moment of the flying boy's grief, for vengeance had never tasted more divine.

Peter's bright gaze turned towards Hook or the Dark Father or whatever it was he called himself, and he felt himself changing, transforming, evolving into something vindictive, for this fiend not only hurt Tinker Bell, but he now attacked the home of his one true love. He had destroyed the homes and livelihoods of hundreds of innocent residents and he would answer to every single one of them. As Neverland's Son, Peter felt the spirit of vengeance come upon him strongly, and now he was driven, pushed forward, by something dark and powerful, something reckless and unquenchable, and although he didn't enjoy the feeling, he would use it to burn this evil to the ground. He would send this foul beast back to the underworld, where it would remain in torment forevermore, for what he had awakened in Peter now, could not be undone.

"THOSE WERE MY FRIENDS!" Peter screamed as he rocketed towards Hook with unlimited speed, rushing him with a new found strength in the face of pure darkness.

The Dark Father waited calmly as Peter flew towards him, closing the gap, ready to strike. He had finally gotten to the boy, and now he would use the child's own darkness as fuel to twist his mind.

As Peter neared at super-sonic levels, he sliced with his dagger. The Dark Father easily slipped the jab and blasted Peter in the back as his momentum from the missed attack sent him hurling through the sky. Peter recovered, and squared once again, breathing heavier.

"You have some skill, child," The Dark Father admitted. "You have some skill… but tell me… what do you know about the power of life and death?"

The Dark Father wafted his hand, and suddenly — like Tiger Lily — Peter was stricken with a vision. He saw all the damage that was just done to the village being reversed and undone. Death to life. Peter was mesmerized, then it reversed again and he had to relive all the pain and suffering once more. It was too much… too much… Peter screamed and rocketed back towards Hook, effectively breaking the trance.

CLASH! CLASH! CLASH! — Peter rained down a barrage of lightning quick dagger attacks. He moved like the speed of light itself, throwing down dozens of strikes per second at his foe, but the Dark Father slipped them all as if they were in slow motion. Peter kept striking, faster, and faster, and faster, raining down slashes, each strike aimed to destroy.

The Dark Father then conjured his energy sword and sparks flew as he blocked Peter's attacks with ease. He then stopped one of Peter's downward slices, and the blades connected in an energy lock, effectively stopping Peter's onslaught. The Dark Father grabbed Peter's wrist and pulled him in close so that they were face to face, staring down the boy's bright eyes with his own fiery ones. He wanted the boy to see every detail of his countenance — at the face of his demise — so that he would never forget it as he walked through the depravity of his next life.

"Why?" Peter asked simply, as tears of wrath and anguish poured from his eyes. It was a simple question, and he wanted to know how something could live with so much hatred.

"Ah," the Dark Father said thoughtfully as he still stared the tiny boy down with his fiery eyes of pure death. Their faces were so close at this point that their noses were inches from touching. "The exact question I asked the nothingness when you destroyed me all those centuries ago and sent me back to the deep… it is not our place to ask, child… only obey… only obey that which masters you."

BOOM! — The Dark Father blasted Peter hard in the chest with a punch fueled by dark fire, sending him straight towards the burning village. He then launched a chasing fireball of ethereal flames towards Peter's falling body, intended to blast him into the crater and incinerate him.

The force from the Dark Father's punch was so powerful Peter felt like a helpless puppet as he hurled back towards the fiery shore of the Western Cape. Seconds before impact, he managed to regain control of his body and ricocheted his momentum off the burning ground, launching back into the air just as the fiery ball of death impacted, incinerating the soil where Peter was just fractions of a second before. The concussion from the blast sent Peter helplessly somersaulting through the sky once again until eventually he managed to regain control of his body and center himself.

"There is no reason to suffer further," the Dark Father said as he floated like some untouchable deity in the sky. "Surrender Neverland… and I will quicken your passing."

"Never," Peter said as blood and tears of rage poured from his face.

"Then your people will suffer for you," the Dark Father said, then once again he turned and began rocketing north east across the Gulf of Neverland.

Peter then felt a sting course through his body in the air, for he had thought he had reached the limits of his fear, but he was wrong, for the Dark Father was now headed right towards the Fairy Quarters.

As the remnants of his true love's village burned below him, there was nothing left in Peter's mind anymore — nothing left in which to anchor it, nothing left in which to identify his former self — there was only the wrath of the Son, and there was only one way in which that wrath could be quenched…

Peter hit the jets, and once again found himself chasing the darkness towards some unknown end…

***

Upon the return of Tiger Lily and Charlie, the lost boys were able to achieve victory. They rounded up the last remaining pirates and put them in the keep below the main ship.

"That's the last of them," Nibs said as he closed and locked the door. "It's all up to Peter now." The lost boys stood, solemn and uneasy, waiting on the return of their leader.

"Something has happened," Tiger Lily said as she looked gravely up into the sky, sensing the sorrow in the air. "Something terrible."

Tinker Bell looked up to the sky, feeling it as well. Although she was terrified of that dark and terrible captain that presumably died, then rose again as a much more evil and more powerful version of Hook, she knew what Peter had gone through to save her, and that he would need her now just as he always did, for all things were at stake now — all things good, all things bright — and if she could make a difference, even at the cost of her own life, then she would do it… so she steeled her nerves, and prepared to take flight.

“This is not your fight,” Tiger Lily said, grabbing Tinker Bell’s arm and keeping her from the air. “That thing… it is not of this world.” Remembering how her arrow did nothing to hurt the demon, Tiger Lily looked Tinker Bell directly in her eyes, and there was no doubt that she was genuinely concerned for her former rival.

“I can help him,” Tinker Bell said honestly, then she broke free of Tiger Lily’s grip and darted into the sky.

Tiger Lily’s eyes narrowed as she watched Tinker Bell fly away. She wasn’t flying towards the mainland, but rather, what appeared to be the direction of the Eternity Isles. Where was she going, anyway? If Peter needed help, it was she that was going to be the one to give it to him.

Tiger Lily whistled and Fleur ran up. She hopped on as Charlie approached.

“This is not your fight, either,” Charlie stated practically as he stepped forward, but he could already see that the princess had made her decision.

“His fight is our fight, Charlie,” Tiger Lily answered, and for once, she found herself siding with Tinker Bell’s rationale. “And our fight, is his.”

Charlie nodded, accepting Tiger Lily’s answer without a challenge.

“Return to the village,” Tiger Lily commanded as she held back a shudder. “I have a feeling you’re needed there.”

Tiger Lily then yanked on Fleur's reins and they raced down the mast over the sea.

***

The two glowing, ethereal beings raced across the Gulf of Neverland, with Peter hot on the Dark Father's tail. Peter could feel blind wrath fueling him, and it continued to give him more and more strength. When it came to aerial and flight speed, Peter was lighter, smaller, and more graceful overall, and therefore superior. The Dark Father seemed to sense this, for he flew as fast as he could, but Peter remained unshakable.

BOOM! BOOM! — The Dark Father launched two more blasts of dark, ethereal, flaming balls of energy behind him in order to shake Peter, but he dodged them expertly and without difficulty. Peter then countered by throwing his Dagger of Truth through the air. It flipped end over end and plunged into the Dark Father's back! He screamed as flares of energy shot out of his wound!

Peter, seeing an opening, seized the moment to catch up to him. He turned on the jets and gracefully flew until he was right above The Dark Father. He then pulled his dagger out of his back, and began stabbing him over and over. Bursts of dark energy spilled out of the dark god as Peter stabbed him savagely in absolute wrath, days of anguish pouring out of Peter's being in rapid stabbing motions that yielded immeasurable damage.

The Dark Father screamed in agony, for every time the boy's dagger punctured him, it felt as if the light energy from the magical blade was burning out his dark soul — and he remembered the feeling, for it was the same feeling he felt all those centuries ago, when the young boy destroyed him the first time, plunging that very same dagger into his chest, sending him back to the abyss — with every devastating stab, the Dark Father fell lower and lower towards the Gulf until they were right above the cresting waves…

In a shout of fury, Peter plunged the dagger into the Dark Father's shoulder, then hopped up on his back. He then jumped up and smashed down with both feet, sending the Dark Father hurling towards the ocean.

BOOM! — The Dark Father smashed into the raging waters of the gulf in a huge explosion of water, fire, and steam! Massive waves shot into the air as the concussion from the impact sent them rolling across the sea.

Peter watched from the air, enjoying the beginning of his vengeance…

After a moment, there was a rumble, then the Dark Father blasted out of the gulf in another huge explosion of water, fire, and steam! He looked back at the child who had a curious look in his eye, now. How was it possible? How was this pathetic flying puppet going toe to toe with him? How was this menacing, devious child laying down waste upon him — the god of Time?! — It was madness. He must pull away from this tormenting youth and his childlike wrath, for something was giving power to this boy now that was both terrifying and unquenchable, and the Dark Father no longer knew what it was — it was an impossible power, this he knew, but the boy was using it anyway, and he hated him for it — he would have to destroy this boy, or surely the boy would destroy him without mercy.

Peter smiled as he gave chase, his parched wrath tasting the first drops of cooling water, for the Dark Father was powerful, sure, but he could bleed. Capitalizing on the moment of weakness, Peter jumped on his back once more and put the dagger underneath his neck, about to cut his throat and end the foul abomination.

Feeling the sting of Hook's Bane underneath his neck, the Dark Father elbowed Peter hard, knocking him off and freeing himself from the child's death grip once again. The Dark Father then roared in furiosity and hit the gas, for he knew the boy's biggest weakness was his love and compassion for the pathetic inhabitants of this tiny planet, and he would use the totality of that weakness against him.

Unexpectedly, however, it also seemed to give him some kind of strange, ethereal power, as if the boy drew some kind of strength from his pain, for the ruddy youth was much more formidable now than before he turned that pathetic, worthless Indian encampment into ash, and the Dark Father was not completely unaware of this energetic change. He knew it may not be in his best interest to antagonize the boy any longer, for he seemed to get more powerful the angrier he got… potentially too powerful for comfort.

The Dark Father never thought it would come to this, but he was actually going to have to put some thought into a strategy of how to best proceed with the child… and he knew the best way, as with all beings of light… was to strike at his *heart*…

* CHAPTER 17 *

— The Secret on Pan Island —

Tinker Bell raced across Cannibal Cove, back past Finder's Bluff, and before she knew it she was soaring over the southern channel towards Eternity Island. She needed to get to her lab — and quick — but she didn't have time to make the three hour flight across Neverland to Pixie's Hollow. Nothing may exist in three hours. No, this task required real magic. Thankfully, she still knew of one or two secrets in Neverland that even Peter himself did not know about, for Peter was still very young from an eternal perspective, and Tink was much older, having lived in Neverland for centuries before Peter was even physically born. Indirect access to some of Neverland's most ancient secrets was one of the perks of seniority… not to mention being a genius.

She continued to fly until she soared over Eternity Island and she could see the mining colony below — the location to Hook's long-time hidden tomb that had previously been ransacked by Brubaker — however, she did not fly down to it as one may be expecting, but rather, continued to soar over Eternity Bay, and further across the Eternity Isles, for there was only one island in all of Neverland that contained the secret she needed…

As she continued her route southwest, Tinker Bell could make out the glowing shoreline of the Western Cape off her right shoulder? Was the West Cape burning? Could it truly be? It was too terrible to imagine, but Tinker Bell could do nothing about it now. She shook any assumptions from her mind and doubled down on her quest, for she knew that it was the only way she could help anyone.

Tinker Bell continued across the isles until the eastern coast of Pan Island came into view. It was off the public map, and very few tribesmen, lost boys, or even fairies knew it existed. Other than Peter, the only other people that Tink knew for sure knew about it were Tiger Lily, her father, Tootles, Nibs, and Mr. Theodore, and of the group she could only confirm that herself and Mr. Theodore had ever physically been, as the island was not a place to access by sea, and was basically pirate-proof, which is exactly why Peter chose it for his hide-out.

The fairy tale legend went that there was powerful, unbound magic that existed in the southern region of the Eternity Isles, and there were legends that ships had disappeared without a trace from its waters, and were sent to unknown places, never to be seen in Neverland again. This was the very legend and fairy tale that the chief and Mr. Theodore were referring to back in Tiger Lily's tepee before their journey began.

Tinker Bell reached the coast and dropped down over the shoreline as she entered. The very lush, tropical island was completely uninhabited, except for Peter's foxhole hideout on the north western end of the island where he kept all his treasure. He'd never admit it, but he put it there so that he was on the closest side to Tiger Island in the Gulf of Creation — Tiger Lily's private island that they'd always disappear to together — Tink knew this because the north western end was not at all the best place for a hideout in terms of geography. Peter was a genius when it came to creating hideouts and land mapping, and Tink knew this would have been obvious to him as well, so the only real reason why he ever built his hideout on the north western end of the island was obvious to her from day one… to be as close to Tiger Lily as possible.

Then, feeling guilty, Tink shook the thought from her mind. Peter had just saved her — *again* — and she was getting jealous, now? Tink couldn't believe her own self. She needed to be focused on helping Peter, not being cross with him right now… besides, there were some secrets that even the Son of Neverland didn't know about, and in that she felt her sense of worth return.

Tink recentered her focus and flew low over Pan Island in the opposite direction of Peter's hide-out. It was a very small island, and by air only took several minutes to completely traverse from end to end. She reached the south west side and dropped low over the jungle trees until she came to a little enclave just off the shore, and dropped down. Tink was officially on the south western most corner of all of Neverland… and there was not a soul in sight.

She looked up at the stars that twinkled forever in the endless sky above. It was so peaceful, so quiet, so still. From here, a person may never know that their world was under siege, and yet, just several hours north, all hell was breaking loose. Tink took one more deep, calming breath of the cool, sea air, then set out to do what she set out to do.

Tink trudged across the sand under the radiant moonbeams that came down through the palm trees along the shoreline. The moonlight was so bright that she didn't even need to use magic to light her path. She kept walking until she came to a raised section in the sand that was covered by giant palm leaves. Tink moved the palm leaves aside and two, big wooden doors covered what appeared to be a circular structure in the ground. With some effort she flipped open the doors, and it was revealed that a large well was built there in the sand.

How this well got here was still a mystery to Tinker Bell. It was likely built by one of the first fairies, or perhaps a wayward pirate that had found himself marooned on the island in ancient times, and he built it to draw water. Whatever the reason, what Tinker Bell did know is that it had been here ever since she first discovered Pan Island centuries before Peter was born, and more importantly, that its magic waters were a portal to the old fairy mines under Pixie's Landing.

It was this very ancient portal that Tinker Bell used to hide Peter back during the Dark Father's first incarnation in Neverland. She retreated with him here, to Pan Island, when the Dark Father's minions would raid the mines which were their main source for food and shelter. In fact, it was those very raids that forced her to hide in the well and discover it was a portal in the first place — when she opened the doors the next day and emerged on the sunny, deserted shores of Pan Island instead of in the dark mines of Pixie's Landing.

In truth, she really had the Dark Father to thank for that one. If he ever wondered why he could never truly find Peter for all those years, this ancient secret was it, for Neverland had a way of protecting its own in times of need, or then again, maybe the southern waters of the Eternity Isles really were magical…

Tink smiled to herself when she thought of the memory, and how she had outsmarted him that first time, and then how Peter was able to eventually destroy him because of it — a little ancient history, a little pleasant memory of light in the midst of the pressing darkness.

Doing this many times before, she hopped inside, and she vanished as she entered the water.

Little did Tink know that certain, vigilante eyes were watching her from the shadows on the shoreline…

Moments later, Tinker Bell appeared in the cool, familiar waters of the well beneath the mines in Pixie's Landing. The process of teleportation in this method Tink would describe as relatively pleasant, and it felt to her like going to sleep suddenly, and then waking up hours later with no memory of any time ever going by — it was a similar experience, just without the sleepiness.

It was dark, so Tink reached into her satchel and lit up the well with her hand. As the fairy light bounced off the old, brick walls, she saw that it seemed to be relatively untouched since she last used it — which was some time ago now — and was about exactly as she remembered it.

She climbed up the stone steps that ascended to the surface and pushed on the wooden doors. They were either locked, or too heavy for her to move, for they were always open back in the days. She had no choice. She charged a right-sized fairy blast, and fired.

BOOM! — There was a small explosion as the pressure from the blast blew the doors wide open. Tink held up her shining hand as she ascended into the old dark and dusty mines beneath Pixie's Landing. They had been mostly forgotten, with some sections of the mine caved in from rock slides.

As she walked past the abandoned, homeless fairy encampments, and the graffitied walls, Tink held back tears as she remembered the past, for many of her first and fondest memories with Peter took place in these very halls, when he was barely old enough to remember, if he even did at all.

After a while, she passed his room, where his old crib used to be. Tink entered and held up her hand to shine her light in the dark place. His crib was still there. She walked over, and it was covered in graffiti now. It looked like some young braves had snuck up through the underground passages in the Western Cape, for it had 'Great White Father' scribbled all over it in war paint. Tink smiled despite the vandalism, because the memories she had with Peter in this crib could never be tarnished, for it was in this very crib that she raised the boy that saved them all.

"You did it once," Tink spoke into the vacant air of the crib, as if little Peter was still there smiling back at her. "You can do it again."

With that, Tink turned and walked out of the room, back out of the mine, and up into the bustling streets of Pixie's Landing.

Tinker Bell flew through the Fairy Quarters so rapidly that she was able to easily dodge all the neverwood photographers that sat about waiting to get a glimpse of her, for by the time they lined up a shot, she was already gone.

She entered Hangman's Tree and flew through the lounge so fast that she effectively dodged all the social conversations aimed at her. When she made it to the jewel encrusted, golden door, she whispered "thimble", and entered… Tinker Bell had finally made it back to her lab.

"*Fairy dust, fairy dust, boil and spout,*" Spark sang over his new synthesis. "*I've got a potion that will turn you inside out…*"

Just then, Tinker Bell burst in. Spark jumped, almost knocking his potion over.

"Please, Lady Tinker Bell, slow—"

"Not right now, Spark!" Tink commanded as she flew rapidly around the room, searching frantically. "I need a potion that can bind with energy."

"Bind with energy?" Spark said thoughtfully, enjoying his eureka moment. "Lady Tinker Bell… you need this."

Spark held up the new vial of neverbrew potion he had been working on. Tink lost her breath… her eyes filled with wonderment…

"Is that…" Tinker Bell said in reverence at the glow of the golden vial.

Spark just smiled and nodded proudly.

"May I?" Tinker Bell asked. Spark nodded his consent, and Tinker Bell took it in her hands like a priceless jewel.

"You finished it," Tink noted after a moment, her whole body still taken with amazement.

"Eternal neverbrew," Spark said easily. "As requested."

Suddenly, Tink felt overjoyed. Unable to control herself, she jumped up and hugged Spark excitedly.

"Whoa…" Spark said, shrinking away from her in discomfort. "No touchy the alchemist."

Tink jumped off him, but suddenly, her smile fell flat.

"Lady Tinker Bell, is everything all right?" Spark asked, sensing the sudden change in her.

"You said this binds with energy?" Tinker Bell asked pointedly.

"Yes," Spark said excitedly. "The potion will permanently bind to the light cells in your body, creating an everlasting human sized fairy girl effect!" Spark bounced off the ground as he said it, overjoyed at the possibility and what it could mean for Tinker Bell, since it had been her heart's desire and sole mission for so long.

Tinker Bell pondered over it for a moment. On one hand, she finally had it — she finally had what she had wanted to have for so long in her hands — the possibility of being Peter's size forever. Then he would truly see her for what she was and what she could offer him. Once the physical aspect was out of the way, then their hearts would truly be free to be together. On the other hand, if Peter didn't defeat Hook and the Dark Father of Time, and if she didn't help him, then there would be no world or maybe even universe for that matter to fall in love in… her decision was becoming clear.

"Spark, what if this bonded with dark energy or dark matter?" Tinker Bell asked. "What then?"

"Then, I don't know…" Spark said, puzzled for a moment, then he shrugged. "*Kaboom*."

That was it! Tinker Bell heard all she needed to hear. She leapt up into the air with the vial and shot out of the lab like lightning out of a bottle.

"How about 'thank you, Spark… good work, Spark… I love you, Spark…'" Spark mumbled somberly, then he moped back to his nearest fairy dust project and threw himself back into his work.

***

Tiger Lily was waiting on Fleur when Tinker Bell flew out of the lounge. There was no way she could have ridden across Neverland so fast.

"But how did you—"

"Please," Tiger Lily said easily, cutting Tink off.

Tinker Bell took a good, hard look at Tiger Lily. Her long black hair and clothes were still damp with water. Tinker Bell then put two and two together.

"You found the well," Tink stated flatly, not necessarily liking that Tiger Lily now knew its secret.

Tiger Lily didn't answer, just smiled cockily, reveling in the fact that she tracked Tinker Bell all the way to her secret on Pan Island without her ever being wise to it — she was one stealthy bad ass princess if there ever was one.

"But how did you keep up?" Tink asked, embarrassed, impressed, and genuinely curious at the same time, for she was flying, and Tiger Lily couldn't fly.

"Let's just say there's some perks to having the fastest mare in all of Neverland," Tiger Lily said as she stroked Fleur's mane proudly, and Fleur whinnied as she reveled with her in this moment of triumph.

Tink studied the gloating princess before her. She could tell by her demeanor that she likely didn't see the glow coming from the Western Cape — whatever that meant — if she wasn't flying, then she wouldn't have seen it from the ground, and Tink didn't have the heart to tell her. In fact, what did it matter anymore?! What did any of it matter if they were all dead?! Talking to the needy, gloating princess right now was just a waste of time.

"Well, congratulations," Tink huffed, then she flew right by her to get on with it.

Tiger Lily's moment came and went at Tink shot by her, and then her mind was pulled right back to business.

"My arrows, they did nothing to hurt the creature," Tiger Lily called after Tink, genuinely concerned for her life, for what they were facing was beyond all physical weapons — beyond all magic, even — and if Peter couldn't find a way to take down the demon, she had little faith that Tinker Bell could.

"That's what this is for." Tink held up the vial, annoyed. She didn't mind rubbing it in Tiger Lily's face, for a lot of her ways were primitive as far as Tink was concerned, and to her own detriment she had little respect or understanding of the powers of modern magic. No, all she cared about was her bow and arrows.

"You'll need my help," Tiger Lily said, trailing her.

"I think not," Tinker Bell said, for it was comical to her that a princess that had no magic skills and couldn't fly thought that she needed her help, of all people. It was a complete and total joke, and she didn't have the time for it. Tinker Bell was about to fly away, when—

"How are you going to hit him with it?" Tiger Lily said knowingly.

Tinker Bell stopped mid-stride, and looked back at the beautiful, confident-borderline-cocky princess holding her bow in front of her, a slight smile of defiance spread across her perfectly exquisite face… and Tinker Bell knew she was right...

* CHAPTER 18 *

— The Knowledge of Good and Evil —

Tink's Lounge was alive and bustling in the social epicenter of Pixie's Landing. The Neverland sun was setting perfectly just as it always did, and the breeze was cool and balmy. Fairies mingled with fresh-faced lost boys that sought solace from the woes and sufferings of time that earth and other planets throughout the universe were enslaved to, for there had never before been a place like Neverland where one's wildest dreams could come true… forever.

Indeed, it was an eternal paradise… but little did the residents know the impending evil that was coming down upon them…

Peter and the Dark Father hurled through the air as they came in off the gulf over Port Royal and entered above Pixie's Landing. The Dark Father wasted no time and desperately began trying to wreak havoc on the population below, and Peter countered by desperately trying to stop him. Peter plunged his dagger into the Dark Father's arm just as he unleashed a ball of death energy that would have devastated the whole northern section of the landing, instead diverting it towards the North Neverland Sea.

Enraged, the Dark Father knocked Peter off him with a hard elbow to the face, but being smaller and more agile, Peter jumped back on at lightning speed, attempting to stab him like a wasp attacking a steer. The Dark Father knocked him off again, but Peter jumped back on. They were fiercely wrestling in mid-air, their light and dark energies repelling each other frantically like polarizing magnets.

BANG! — The Dark Father unleashed another ball of death energy just as Peter stabbed him in the shoulder blade.

"ARGHH!" The Dark Father screamed in pain as dark energy spilled out of his wound, but Peter didn't get to him soon enough.

BOOM! — The Dark Father's fiery ball of doom destroyed a northern section of the Fairy Quarters near the coast line, just a half mile east of Pixie Hollow, incinerating the whole area in dark fire.

Peter screamed in agony as he saw his home burning, for he felt every flame — every ounce of searing pain — for he was Neverland's Son, and what was done to Neverland was done to him. With absolute wrath, Peter stabbed his Dagger of Truth right into the Dark Father's neck where it plunged into the dark energy with white hot light.

"ARGHH!" The Dark Father screamed again, and Peter pressed it in further, taking great joy in his suffering, for every ounce of pain he inflicted on Neverland, Peter made it his mission to return it tenfold, and so he did. Peter twisted the dagger in the Dark Father's neck so that it would not come out, then he pulled back on the handle, controlling his flight trajectory, and they veered off the mainland towards the Eastern Sea...

Down below, Tinker Bell flew through the Fairy Quarters and Tiger Lily raced next to her on Fleur. Screams of pain, fear, and confusion could be heard throughout the city as fairies and lost boys ran from the devastation that was released upon the northern section of the city. They looked up in the sky, and they saw bright flashes of gold and dark purple in the east where the two gods collided.

"They're headed for Skull Rock!" Tinker Bell yelled over the commotion, and Tiger Lily's eyes narrowed, for she knew Skull Rock all too well…

Together, they plunged forward towards the verdict of all things…

The sun began to rise on the Eastern Sea as Peter and the Dark Father's battle reached a massive, skull shaped stone jutting out into the Northern Strait. Peter usually did his best to avoid Skull Rock, for legend had it that it was haunted by the ghosts of dead pirates, and Peter did not have fond memories there, for it was at that very place that the love of his life was almost taken from him over a century ago by the very person he was doing battle with now, and the irony of it was like a weapon unto itself.

At the top of Skull Rock was a level plateau, and as they came upon it Peter sliced the Dark Father in the arm just as he blasted Peter with energy! The two gods were blown away from each other in opposite directions, and came to rest on both sides of Skull Rock. Peter landed on the western side, facing east, standing between the Dark Father and all of Neverland behind him. The Dark Father landed on the eastern side, facing west, staring at the vindictive child that stood in the way between him and his vengeance on a world that took everything from him.

Peter's breathing was heavy, his eyes still sharp and alert with thrill as he stared down this evil, enjoying the site of the energy and dark matter that poured out of the Dark Father's wounds like geysers, for Peter had picked him apart in the air, and was his superior with a blade — and the Dark Father knew it — now Peter was looking forward to finishing the job.

Suddenly and impossibly, the Dark Father's wounds began to close up on their own — the dark god was healing — a flicker of doubt passed through Peter's eyes as he watched this, for he had stabbed him dozens of times in the air with the most powerful weapon he possessed — was the Dark Father truly invincible?

"You know this place," The Dark Father noted as he probed Hook's memories, then a sinister smirk spread across his dark and devious countenance. He held up his hand, and once again Peter was taken by a vision…

Peter was pulled through time and space to over a century ago, and he saw a young beautiful maiden, terrified, as she was bound hand and foot in the bowels of Skull Rock, while the dark and stormy tides rose higher and higher and higher… it was Tiger Lily.

Tiger Lily screamed as the tide levels ascended all around her, but her voice was not heard as the water level rose above her mouth… she was just seconds from drowning…

A younger, boyish, and more innocent Peter flew in at the very last second. He cut her bonds, took her in his arms, and flew away, saving her from the gates of death just as a tidal wave came in and consumed the whole cavern.

As young Peter flew away from Skull Rock with Tiger Lily in his arms, a dark and menacing figure appeared from the caves above the cavern — it was the notorious Captain James Hook in his original, human form. The grin on his face made it clear that he had enjoyed every moment of the show, and took great pride in almost drowning Tiger Lily and breaking Peter's heart.

Peter screamed in his mind, for he had spent the last century attempting to forget the horror of that moment when Tiger Lily nearly died in his arms… and the memory was too much to bear…

Peter was then pulled back through time and space to the present on top of Skull Rock. He barely had time to re-comprehend himself when he saw the Dark Father flying towards him at supersonic speed!

CRACK! CRACK! CRACK! — The Dark Father took Peter's momentary lapse in vigilance and piggybacked his devastating mental onslaught with a barrage of energy sword-based attacks! Severely disoriented, Peter barely managed to fend them off.

CRACK! — Peter blocked a powerful overhead blow with his dagger, and the two blades sizzled and cracked with energy as the Dark Father bared down upon him.

He screamed in wrath and pressed down on Peter with all his might. His patience was at an end, for this was the very boy that had vanquished him twice, and he would not give him time to do it again. No, the boy would surely die, and he would surely die *now*! He lifted his sword and began pummeling Peter with vicious, overhead blows.

Peter's mind slowly came back to him, but he was barely able to block the Dark Father's vengeance-fueled attacks that seemed to be raining down upon him with more and more strength with each passing second. Whether he was getting tired, or Hook was getting more powerful, he didn't know, but he figured it was a bit of both.

BOOM! — Peter blocked the last of his savage blows, but the impact sent Peter flying back. The Dark Father now had the upper hand, and Peter had to re-establish distance to buy him some time to think. In desperation, Peter tried to fly away, for he knew he had the advantage in the air.

"Oh no, you're not flying away this *time*, boy!" The Dark Father then reached out his hand and seized Peter out of mid-air with a telekinetic grip, then hurled Peter's helpless body towards Skull Rock.

BOOM! — there was an explosion of rock and debris as Peter's body was literally imprinted into the top of Skull Rock by the force! It was only the Spirit inside him now kept his body from blowing apart on impact. A moment of darkness took him, then light slowly came back to his eyes. His head was ringing and pounding as he barely managed to make it to his feet. Just when he began to get his bearings back, Peter looked up and saw a giant flaming ball of black and purple death flying right towards him!

BOOM! — Peter barely managed to dive into the air just before the ball of doom decimated the place where he just lay, incinerating the rock into molten lava. He flew, but he was too weak to get very far, and he landed with a thud down the rock just out of harm's way. Tired, bruised, and bloody… Peter stood to his feet once again…

"Come now, Peter," The Dark Father said in Hook's familiar cadence as he landed gracefully on the other side, and he was so at ease it appeared as if he hadn't exerted any energy at all. "Lay down your weapon. Yield, for you've clearly been bested."

"Surrender to a codfish?" Peter mocked as he wiped the blood from his mouth. "Never."

"You've always had to do it the hard way," the Dark Father said, then he held up his hand, and once again Peter was seized by a dark vision…

Peter saw the sun set on Neverland as it plunged into a darkness so thick, it felt as if it would stay night forever. He now floated in a completely black space. He ran, he flew, but no matter how hard he tried, he didn't get anywhere, and once again Peter was seized by total fear.

"So much struggle…" Peter heard the Dark Father's voice in his head. "Why? You can't outlast *time,* boy… it is an impossibility… it is before you… and will be after you… must Neverland and your loved ones continue to suffer because of your pride?"

Peter then saw those he loved — Tiger Lily, Tinker Bell, the lost boys — all imprisoned in pain and suffering. He then saw himself growing older… losing the will to live… *dying*…

Peter screamed in his mind, but no voice came forth. Tears of fear, horror, and remorse poured from his eyes like rivers as he saw himself stripped bare of all that he loved.

"Let go of life," the Dark Father hissed in his mind. "Give yourself over to the inevitability of your darkness… and you will have your peace at last…"

Peter felt himself crumbling under the weight of so much death, for so much sheer hatred against the gift of life was too much for him to bear. This darkness was the antithesis of what he believed in, and dying went against the nature of his Spirit, for the child inside only knew life, and death was a curse for the broken hearted, the defeated, and those that had lost their souls… it was coming upon him now… the dark one in the hooded cloak… trying to take from him what was given to him to protect…

Peter gritted down as it felt like his mind was being probed with a thousand hot needles, for despite the pain there were larger forces at work here, an eternal battle was raging that was far greater than the battle for Neverland, and far more powerful than himself or even the Dark Father, for it was the battle of light and dark, good and evil, and it was everything there ever was or ever would be… and he had to *win.*

Peter felt his mind imploding, and his body being crushed under the weight of these great thoughts as if in a compression chamber, and it was pushing down on him, attempting to grind his body into dust against the stone of remorse. It was only a matter of time now, for despite his desire for Truth, the Dark Father and Hook held so much immutable hatred against him — a supernatural hatred that burned hot like some unquenchable inferno — and surely it would torment him until he could take it no more, for who could stand the unbearable heat of such fire?

Then Peter felt a touch of light return to him… not much… just something deep inside… something right and true… and he felt it blossom up in him and cool his mind with peace… and it gave him a strength inside the fire… a resilience… and he knew what it called upon him to do… it was the same thing that it had always called upon him to do… for he was the Great Peter Pan, the Son of Neverland, defender of all that was good and bright, and he would rise up and send this nightmare back to the shadow realm.

With the willpower of a newborn god, Peter screamed and pushed back against the Dark Father's mental onslaught with all his might, and with his last remaining strength Peter reversed the time sequence vision with infinite ability until Neverland was pulled back out of the darkness and into the shining rays of the sun!

The sheer raw power of the exchange between Peter and the Dark Father shifted them into a state of slipstream suspension — a type of parallel dimension, an eternal moment in the void — there were two suns burning on either side of them in the eternal ether, bathing their consciousness with infinity, but there was no world below them now, no Neverland, only infinite space and infinite mind.

Peter beamed like a birthed star as infinite light and power flowed out of his being. He had become pure light energy and was completely unlimited in every way there ever was or would be. He was beyond time and space, beyond light and darkness, and beyond good and evil as the Great Spirit took over and poured out from his center… He was the Infinite Beginning… the First Day… the Life in All Things… The Alpha and the Omega… the One above All.

The veneer of Hook was stripped away as The Dark Father stared at the Great Spirit in absolute awe, for he could no longer speak, but he could only bear witness to the Light, for the boy had done something he knew was impossible, but he had done it anyway once again, and there could be no victory against whatever it was that he had become. The boy had become one with the Great Spirit before his very eyes — the God of all things — and surely there could be no power that *Time* or all the forces of darkness held that could withstand such unlimited power, and he hated him for it even more with all the eternal hatred that could ever exist, and it didn't even matter.

"ARRRRGGGGHHHHH!" The Dark Father screamed against the Light, for he was pure evil, and there was nothing left in him to redeem. He just screamed in horror, agony, and defeat as he stood before the Great Spirit's awesome power, the infinite light rays pouring out of his body, incinerating the dark innards of his evil being, and he knew that if this battle went on for eternity, he was doomed to eternally loose, for such infinite light was truly the source of all things — even the source of darkness — and he was nothing against it.

"There can be no world without light and love," the Great Spirit said in absolute Truth, and tears of compassion poured from his eyes as he looked down upon this piece of the universe that hated all life without cause or reason. "And I pity you… because you have never known either… you have never known what it is like to truly be alive."

The Dark Father could only scream in absolute hatred as he stared in reverence at the effortless power of the Great Spirit as it blew his being apart, and the battle that had gone on since the beginning once again revealed its victor… and so it would be… on and on… forever, and ever, and forever still…

Then there was a great flash, and Peter was pulled once again through the infinite ether of time and space…

* CHAPTER 19 *

— The Son of Neverland —

Tinker Bell and Tiger Lily raced across Neverland's Eastern Sea in the dawn's light, traversing the Northern Strait between Skull Rock and the mainland. Above them, they could see bright flashes of gold and purple light that painted the horizon where the two beings dueled… it was all up to Peter now… but if they could help him, they would give it their all…

WHOOSH! — Peter and the Dark Father were pulled out of the parallel dimension at the same moment, neither of them fully comprehending the full scope of what happened. The Dark Father was in shock. Where was he? Was he back in Neverland? He checked is body, believing that the boy had destroyed him, for somehow, someway, the child had found a way to flip his psycho-kinetic attack back on him — a power which the Dark Father had never seen before — no, his body was still in-tact, but the boy had somehow found a way to enter his mind, and it appeared he now had the full backing of that tyrannical Great Spirit. Then, the sound of vengeance —

"AAAAHHHH…"

The Dark Father looked up and Peter was right on him!

CRACK! CRACK! CRACK! — Peter rained down a flurry of fierce attacks, wasting no time, and capitalizing on The Dark Father's moment of confusion.

The Dark Father barely conjured his energy sword in time to block the boy's savage flurry. He fell back as the child kept up the attack, and he appeared to be unstoppable, powered by something completely unlimited, something higher, and it was unreal.

As the Dark Father continued to fall back, he had no idea what was hitting him. The void, the Great Spirit, now this boy that appeared to consist of only wrath — was he actually losing? — No, it was impossible! He would not accept it! It could not be allowed to be! Not a second time! Never again!

"ARGHHH!!!" The Dark Father roared in fatal fury as he pushed back Peter's momentum by sheer force and size. This child was not a god, he was only a boy! The Dark Father then rained down a flurry of fierce attacks, for whatever form of unlimited power the boy had evolved into in the void, he was now flesh and blood once more, and he had to be done away with immediately before this great power returned to him, and he became invincible beyond defeat. It was time to end it, now!

On the receiving end, Peter fell back as he felt the Dark Father take it up a gear, and the momentum shifted. He expertly parried and countered each one of the Dark Father's attacks, for although he was once again Peter — that was, a being with a physical body, one made of flesh and blood — he felt an energy coursing through him that he had never felt so strongly before. It was the same power that he felt surge through him and all things when he was reborn above the Windy Mountains, for he had experienced a total death there — the total death of limitation — and he had been reborn in Spirit. Now, he could truly see the kingdom that had been given to him, and the world which he was entrusted to protect.

Energy exploded as dagger clashed with sword. They began circling each other, their swordplay getting faster, and faster, and faster, as neither deity could land a blow, each pushing themselves to their complete and total limit.

In a cry of desperation, the Dark Father raised his sword over his head, and brought it down in absolute wrath. Peter barely raised his arm in time to block it with his dagger, avoiding total annihilation.

BOOM! — The force of the attack sent Peter forcefully to the ground. Dark purple and golden sparks exploded from the two weapons in an energy lock as the Dark Father bared down on Peter with all his might, the energy blade just inches from Peter's neck… he had just moments left…

"Let go," the Dark Father said, the dark sparks from the energy lighting up his blood-thirsty face. "Give into the darkness prepared for you… it is inevitable…"

The dark blade began to sear Peter's neck, cutting and burning into his skin… it was just moments now… moments and it would be over… then… astonishingly… Peter did just what the Dark Father asked for… he let go…

Peter let go just as the Dark Father's blade came down and melted into the stone where he just lay. By using the momentum from the force and exerting unlimited skills, Peter spun like a top on his back and sliced the Dark Father's ankles, cutting the etheric tendons and vital organs with white hot energy.

The Dark Father screamed in agony as Peter spun out of the entrapment with perfect agility. In absolute and dire desperation, the Dark Father let loose a massive blast of doomsday energy.

BOOM! — Molten stone and debris flew everywhere as the Dark Father's attack devastated the top of Skull Rock. Peter leapt off the edge and gracefully swan dove through the air, effectively avoiding the concussion, and pulled up just before he hit the water.

On the sea, Tinker Bell and Tiger Lily raced towards him. They locked eyes with Peter, and nodded, for they both knew what they needed to do.

Peter's eyes twinkled as he gazed upon his two favorite women in the world, for they were both so beautiful, and lovely, and smart, and he never felt more gratitude for them then he did right then, and he knew that they were both worth fighting for — that they were both worth dying for — and he would move the highest heavens, the deepest foundations of Neverland, and all the space between to protect them…

Peter cracked a smile, for he knew that soon he would be back with them in paradise, then he flew back up to face the giant…

On Skull Rock, the Dark Father's oozing ankles began to heal with that same ethereal healing ability he displayed earlier. It was no matter now, no matter how powerful the boy had become, he could always heal, so if anyone was invincible in this fight, it was him. The boy was a fool and swindler, and whatever luck he pulled out of his hat by the aid of that rascally Great Spirit, that luck was gone now, and the end of his existence was pressing.

Suddenly, Peter came racing over the face of the rock right towards him, new energy and joy surging through him knowing that Tiger Lily and Tinker Bell were close by. He could feel their love for him and their life forces supporting him, and if there was ever a time to make a last stand against this foul abomination of ancient death, and send it back to the deep, it was now.

BOOM! BOOM! BOOM! — the Dark Father launched three balls of fiery death energy across the face of the rock right towards the closing boy.

SWOOSH! SWOOSH! — Peter expertly and nimbly dodged the first two, then he held his dagger straight out before him and laid flat, rocketing through the air like a missile of light…

CRACK! — Peter shot straight through the last ball of energy like a hot knife cutting through butter, then plunged his dagger right into the unexpecting Dark Father's shoulder.

"ARGHHHHHH!" the Dark Father screamed in agony as the white-hot blade burned him from within

BOOM! BOOM! BOOM! — He began frantically launching energy blasts in every direction as desperation and fear creeped into his being. He had underestimated the boy's infinite abilities, and he had let him live for far too long. If he could no longer take him head on, he would destroy everyone and everything so that there would be no world left to fight for. If he couldn't win, then he wouldn't lose.

Peter was in the zone now — locked in — he nimbly moved around the Dark Father in his desperation, slipping his blows, and jabbing at his critical points. Peter then slashed behind both of the Dark Father's knees, opening them up grapefruits.

ARGGHHHH!" The Dark Father screamed as dark matter poured from his joints, for the boy was nipping him apart like scissors on thread — giving him hell — he conjured his energy sword in one hand, slashing at the air like a mad man as he launched energy blasts with the other. Desperation and fear had him in its clutches now. The Dark Father was finally receiving the torment which he had so freely given.

Peter closed his eyes and swiftly worked around his enemy, feeling the energy, easily evading all attacks with unprecedented ability — *Peter Pan had officially entered god mode.*

SLASH! SLASH! — Peter stabbed both of the Dark Father's sides. Dark matter and energy poured out like the Great River.

BOOM! BOOM! — In desperation, the Dark Father blasted the ground beneath him, trying to shake Peter, decimating the entire surface of Skull Rock into smithereens of liquid hot magma.

WHOOSH! — Peter back flipped in the air with infinite grace and hovered above the very edge of Skull Rock. He beamed like a child, for it was the first time since he started battling this maniacal incarnation of darkness that he was really starting to have fun.

The Dark Father's wounds began to heal once more as he faced the Son of Neverland. He looked at the defiant boy staring back at him, youthful and fearless, and as glorious as the rising sun. The Dark Father's eyes narrowed, and for the first time since he began battling this flying, menacing child, he truly feared him completely.

"What? How was it possible?" The Dark Father thought. "How was it possible that this pitiful, ridiculous child was standing against him — the Lord of *Time*?!" The flying boy continued to hover across from him, smiling in joy, as if he was actually having fun in the face of his suffering, and the question that had forever been haunting Hook's mind returned —

"What are you, Peter Pan?" The Dark Father asked as he had a flashback of Hook's memory.

Peter smiled, for he remembered the first time he was asked that question — it was over one hundred years ago, by the very same being that was asking him now — in all honesty, even after all he had gone through, Peter still didn't completely know himself what he was, or how he was, but he felt he had a slightly better idea than last time…

"I Am Truth," Peter said with a smile. "I Am Joy. I Am the little bird that has broken out of the egg."

It was all gibberish! Nonsense! A hundred years and the boy had not aged a day. The Dark Father could stand it no more. Rage took him, and all sense left him.

The Dark Father screamed as he charged Peter with all the wrath he had left in him. Peter remained calm and still at the edge of the rock as his enemy closed the gap… closer… closer… the two infinite beings looked each other in the eyes… time slowed… and Peter smiled…

SWOOSH — Peter sidestepped out of the way at lightning speed just as the Dark Father lunged with his energy sword. Peter then grabbed him by the wrist with his right hand as he passed, and followed with a powerful open hand blast to the back of the Dark Father's spine with his left.

CRACK! — The Dark Father screamed as the raw inertia from Peter's blow fractured his spine and launched him off the face of Skull Rock into the air with unequivocal force.

Down below, Tiger Lily had an arrow knocked in her bow. Tinker Bell hovered above, pouring her eternal neverbrew potion on the tip of the arrow, coating the entire point…

In the air, the Dark Father's now vulnerable body flew off the rock… it hovered for a moment as it fell… open… defenseless… then…

THWAP! — Tiger Lily let her arrow loose from her bow… as always… its aim was straight and true…

BOOM! — the arrow plunged into the Dark Father's heart and exploded with dark and gold energy.

"ARGHHHHH!" the Dark Father screamed, for the pain of the light energy burning through the dark matter of his cells was pure agony.

"Nice shot," Tinker Bell said, both pleased and impressed as the Dark Father squirmed in the air from the expert marksmanship.

"Thank you," Tiger Lily said, and she took the compliment from Tinker Bell without resistance, for it truly was an ace of a shot if there ever was one.

In the air, the Dark Father continued to scream as the arrow plunged into his body, for the light burned through him hot and fierce, and the pain was immense. He spun around, disoriented, and noticed that he wasn't healing.

"What?!" The Dark Father pulled on the arrow lodged in shoulder, but it wouldn't budge. The wound was swirling with golden light energy that was spreading through the dark matter and growing larger by the moment. What had the flying boy's evil nymphs done to him?! They would pay! They would all pay!

Peter smiled at Tinker Bell and Tiger Lily below, and nodded his thanks, for he knew not what he would do without them. Now it was time to finish it. He flipped his dagger in his hand and began to fly towards the Dark Father to deal the final blow, then —

Peter saw the Dark Father's demeanor change as he looked at Tinker Bell and Tiger Lily, then he looked back at Peter, and smiled. Dread then shot through Peter's body, for he knew what the Dark Father was going to do. He held up his hand…

Peter flew as fast as he could towards his enemy… but it was too late…

BANG! — In an act of desperation, the Dark Father launched a giant, flaming ball of dark death energy at Tink and Tiger Lily just as Peter plunged his dagger into the Dark Father's chest next to the arrow that was already destroying him. The Dark Father screamed in fatality.

The ball of flaming death came down upon Tink and Tiger Lily so fast they barely had time to react. Tinker Bell reached into her satchel and conjured a fairy dust shield in front of her, Fleur, Ruby, and Tiger Lily right upon impact!

"BOOM!" The concussion from the massive blast shattered the shield and sent their unconscious bodies scattering over the expansive waters of the Northern Strait.

"No!" Peter screamed as his friends began to sink beneath the waves.

Bellows of laughter began to break through the Dark Father's screams of pain as the light energy continued to greedily consume his body — he would not leave this world without his vengeance.

"Who do you love most, boy?!" The Dark Father said as Peter's eyes darted back and forth between Tinker Bell and Tiger Lily's sinking bodies. "Who do you love most?"

For a moment, Peter floated in the air, frozen in indecision. Time slowed down as he processed the sensory overload of information — it was an impossible choice he was given — but one that had to be made. He turned on the jets and began flying over the strait towards his friend's sinking bodies as the immutable light energy continued to consume and destroy the Dark Father.

In the air, Peter pushed from his mind the possibility that he may not have time to save them both — no! He had to! He would! If anyone could make the impossible possible, it was him, for he could not go on living without them both. No, both Tinker Bell and Tiger Lily must live, or there would be no dawn for Neverland.

Ruby and Fleur surfaced just as Peter reached them. They were disoriented from the impact, and were whinnying in fear as they tried to find their masters that were nowhere to be seen. Peter veered up, and then water exploded as Peter broke the surface and dove under at lighting speed… the impossible choice was upon him...

It was a coin toss decision, but Peter went for Tiger Lily first. She was the love of his life, and he simply could not continue to exist without his soul mate. He also subconsciously saw the impact of the blast, and knew that Tiger Lily only caught the edge of Tinker Bell's fairy shield. If anyone got hit harder by the impact it was her, and he reasoned Tinker Bell already had a higher chance of survival due to the magical neverbrew in her veins. Yes, Tiger Lily needed him most now, and it was her that he would go to first.

Peter blasted deep into the water until he came upon Tiger Lily's sinking, unconscious body. She looked like a dark angel sinking into the depths of the endless sea. Peter wrapped his strong arms around her, and skyrocketed towards the sky.

BOOM! — There was an explosion as Peter blasted through the surface. He could hear the Dark Father still screaming in agony as he was being destroyed across the strait, but he paid him no mind. Fleur and Ruby whinnied as they laid eyes on Tiger Lily.

Peter did not have time to revive her, nor did he have time to think of the best or the worst-case scenario. In a split second, he draped Tiger Lily's unconscious body over the back of Fleur who swam to support her, then he flew back up into the air to gather momentum, hit the jets, and blasted back under the waves.

"ARRGHHHH!" In the air, the Dark Father was losing his mind as the light energy from the eternal neverbrew and the Dagger of Truth joined forces and decimated his being from the inside. It was agony — absolute agony — he could no longer think, he barely knew where he was, for what was happening to him was incalculable. It was never part of his equation for victory, and here it was happening with zero regard for his grand scheme. It was going to happen — it was already happening — he was going to be destroyed by this Light, then he would be cast back into the void of shadow once again, and there was nothing left that he could do to stop it. Against all odds, the maniacal pest had done it… he had done what it was impossible for nearly all beings to do… through some kind of unlimited self-belief… through some kind of delusional self-assuredness… through some kind of insane power of will… the boy had become a god.

Deeper and deeper, through infinite black, Peter swam into the depths of the Northern Strait as he searched for Tinker Bell. He swam, and swam, and swam, but he could not find her. His mind did not falter — it could not afford to falter — Tinker Bell was alive, and he would find her.

Peter's lungs burned like fire. Deeper and deeper he swam beneath the sea, but he saw nothing. Physically, he would not be able to stay submerged much longer, but he would not surface without her. No, he would find Tinker Bell or pass with her here, under the sea, and they would leave this world together…

Suddenly, rage took Peter as helplessness set in upon him. The salt from his tears would have stung his eyes blind if it wasn't for the sea water that was doing that already.

"DARK FATHER, YOU FILTHY DEMON!" Peter screamed in his mind. "IF TINKER BELL IS DEAD, THEN I

WILL EXTRACT MY VENGEANCE UPON YOU FOREVER! I WILL STAB YOU A MILLION TIMES WITH MY DAGGER, AND WHEN YOU HEAL I'LL STAB YOU A MILLION TIMES MORE! YOU WILL PRAY FOR DEATH, BUT NO RELIEF WILL BE GIVEN TO YOU! YOU WILL PLEAD FOR YOUR EXISTENCE TO END, BUT BY MY WILL YOU SHALL LIVE FOREVER IN TORMENT! YES, YOUR SUFFERING WILL BE MY JOY EVERY MORNING, AND YOUR AGONY WILL BE MY LIFE FORCE!"

Suddenly, a great sorrow took Peter, and he sobbed beneath the waves. The sheer amount of the pain he had gone through hit him all at once, and this was the last straw. "TINKER BELL!" He screamed in his mind. Why was he created to go through such agony? Why was he born to carry such weight? Why was there such darkness, and with it, such endless hate? Even if he won, would it even matter? Why was any of it created at all? Why? Why? Why? Why? Why?! It was the question that tormented him… the question that always drove him to the end…

"Tinker Bell…" Peter felt his energy give out as the light began to leave him. He began to sink lifelessly into the depths. This was it. The end of all things. Hopefully, there would be peace on the other side… hopefully…

Then, suddenly, something came back to him. Something bright and powerful, something with a deep resolve… no, Tinker Bell had to be alive… for Peter was still alive, and breathing, and living, and as long as there was an ounce of life force in his being, he would save his best friend, or die trying.

Peter forced his dimming eyes open, and there was a moment as his consciousness came back to him. Then, before him, there was a light blinking in the endless black….

"Tinker Bell!" mustering all the energy in his being, Peter surged forward through the sea until he came upon Tink's sinking body. Her light had all but gone out. She looked peaceful, like an angel that had returned to where she came down from, somewhere far, far away from the darkness and death here, but Peter knew that it was his selfishness alone that may save her, for he simply could not continue to exist without her.

"Hold on Tink!" Peter yelled into the water as he wrapped her up in his arms, then he hit the flight plan and blasted towards the sky!

"ARGHHHH!" In the air, the Dark Father continued to scream in absolute pain as the light energy from the eternal neverbrew potion spread from Tiger Lily's arrow lodged in his shoulder across and through the rest of his body. Peter's dagger that was lodged in his chest seemed to feed off the light energy from the neverbrew as if it was alive! As if it was enjoying the Dark Father's suffering, and burning him out from the inside.

The Dark Father pulled, and pulled, and pulled on the arrow — to the detriment of his fractured spine that screamed from each yank — but it would not budge. Oh, that devious blade — his bane — that flying child of evil had done it again! He had decimated him! He had destroyed him! Wrathful remorse came upon the Dark Father, but it was to no avail, for there was no darkness that could stop his destruction now, the infinite power of the Light had bested him, and he would be erased from this world…

BOOM! — There was another explosion of water as Peter surface with Tinker Bell. Immediately, Tink began coughing as the neverbrew in her veins forced the water from her lungs. It was just as Peter anticipated, her magic had protected her, Tink was going to be all right! — but Tiger Lily…

In a flash, Peter set Tink down on Ruby who was overcome with delight upon seeing her. He then dug frantically in Tink's satchel, looking for neverbrew, but she was out — she had used the whole dose on the arrow to maximize their chances of destroying the Dark Father — he then flew back over to Tiger Lily who was still lying unconscious on Fleur's back.

"Tigerlily!" Peter yelled in desperation as he looked down upon her still corpse, and fear took him as he faced one of his worst nightmares — no, he had to keep his head, for it was not a time for fear, it was a time for right thinking… he took a deep breath and steadied his mind… blocking out the sounds of the Dark Father's screams of destruction in the background…

After a moment, a thought came to him. He had once seen humans doing something peculiar on earth when a woman had almost been lost in their oceans… it apparently saved her…

Peter leaned down, placed his mouth on hers, and blew air into Tiger Lily's lungs, then he placed his hands above her left breast and began pumping her heart…

"Come on, Tiger Lily, come on…" Peter said through tears of determination, for he could still feel her life force within her — she was alive, but barely, and she wasn't coming to light — he repeated the procedure…. and again… and again… and again…

"Tigerlily!" Peter screamed as her eyes remained closed.

Then a laugh broke across the sea… a laugh of deep retribution… a laugh of absolute hate…

"It's over, boy!" The Dark Father screamed through his agony. "You may have destroyed my body, but I will annihilate your spirit!"

Peter looked down at Tiger Lily as she lay before him, lithe and peaceful, quiet and sleeping. Her spirit was still in Neverland, but he could feel her slipping away… he was losing the love of his life… and there was only one to blame…. and one who would pay for everything…

A rage was building… a deep and unstoppable rage…

"AaaaaaaaaaAAAAAHHHHH!"

BANG! — Peter blasted across the water at mach speed! He came upon the Dark Father so fast even the Dark Father himself could not track his speed.

BOOM! — Peter shoulder charged the Dark Father as he pulled his dagger from his chest, the explosion from the blast sent the Dark Father flying across the sea…

BOOM! — The Dark Father slammed into the face of skull rock! Rock and debris exploded as he blasted through the entire structure like a cannon, where he then skidded and skipped across the water on the other side like a flattened stone!

The Dark Father was helpless now, a puppet of decimation as the light energy continued to disintegrate his being from within. Peter was back on him immediately, he snatched him as he skipped off the water and pulled him back into the air.

Up, up, and up Peter pulled the Dark Father's burning body into the atmosphere of Neverland until they were parallel to the lightning and thunder. The pounding rain washed the tears of wrath out of Peter's eyes.

"AHHHH!" — With a mighty shout Peter threw the Dark Father's body back towards Neverland with unequivocal force! Peter then threw his dagger towards his falling body where it plunged into his stomach *just as* he flew down at mach speed and stomped the dagger with both feet into the core of the Dark Father's being!

"BOOOM!" — There was a massive explosion of sea water as the Dark Father shot into the Northern Strait like a meteorite, creating a crater in the surface of the sea and sending a concussion wave in every direction. Peter's dagger shot through the Dark Father's body and came down with such power that it pinned him to the ocean floor.

"AhhhhHHHH!" — Before the Dark Father could even process what happened Peter was right back on him. He grabbed the Dark Father's disintegrating carcass off the seafloor, and threw him back towards the sky as he pulled his dagger from his belly! The Dark Father screamed his agony as dark matter poured from his gullet like a river of iniquity.

"Great Spirit of Neverland!" Peter yelled as he flew back up from the sea, and his voice resounded throughout the world. "I call upon you this day! Rid us of this plague! SEND THIS DEMON'S CORPSE BACK TO THE ETERNAL PIT OF DUST AND SHADOW!"

The Dark Father continued to scream as he rocketed once again towards the sky as the source of his life trailed out of his being. The pain was immense, for the child was extracting his vengeance upon him now, and his wrath could not be resolved — not as long as The Dark Father had a body in which to be punished in — he prayed for death now, for that would be his only escape from the endless torment.

Above, the clouds over Neverland heard their Son's call. They began to group together and build as the Dark Father flew helplessly towards them. They reached a state of critical mass... then —

"BOOM!" — A massive energetic surge exploded from above in a single rod of lightning that shot right through the core of the Dark Father's being, ending all that was left of his physical actuality!

"ARRRGGGGGGHHHHHH!" The Dark Father screamed a final scream of melancholy as his body fell from the sky! The combined light energy of Tink's neverbrew that punctured his shoulder, and the lightning surge from all the life force in Neverland that pierced his core, overwhelmed the Dark Father's physical constitution, and he began to dissolve into ash.

"NOOOOOOOOO!!!" The Dark Father screamed as he felt his presence leaving Neverland…

"AaaaaHHHHH!" Peter flew back towards the Dark Father a final time and —

"BOOM!" — Peter held his dagger in front of him and blasted through the core of the Dark Father like a rocket, opening up the hole in his being that the lighting had created. The concussion from the blast split the Dark Father's body in two. His lower torso fell from his body, and disintegrated into ash, where it began to blow into the wind as if it never existed at all.

Peter floated before him, and his eyes kindled like blue flames as the Dark Father of Time was incinerated in front of him, for he had caused him and his world immense and immeasurable pain, and he would bare witness as every fiber of the demon's being was banished from the world of the living — back to the abyss of destitution, back to the darkness where it should remain forever… and it was finished.

Suddenly, Peter's ears pricked up as his super senses heard the faint sound of a cough across the Northern Strait. Peter turned his head, and…

It was Tiger Lily! She was alive! Sea water poured from her mouth as she suddenly gasped back to life as she still lay on the back of Fleur who swam to support her. Tinker Bell — who was just getting her strength back — flew over to attend to her.

In that moment Peter was suddenly filled with joy and new life as the toxic poisons of fear, anger, and vengeance vacated his being — Tiger Lily, the love of his life, was alive, and everything was going to be all right!

With tears of joy, and a smile as bright as the sun, Peter turned to face down his enemy one last time…

"It's over," Peter said as he watched the upper half of the Dark Father's body begin to dissolve into nothingness. "Go back to the underworld…"

It was impossible, but the boy had done it! He had destroyed him once again! The flying menace! The youthful fiend! Curse him! A wrath and hatred unlike anything he had ever felt rose up with the Dark Father as the entrails of his body continued to disintegrate around him, and then, somehow, at the very edge of his physical life, at the far end of this strange, strange world, some foul evil came upon the dark one, and to him, it was wonderful.

As Peter floated in the air, watching his enemy decompose before him, he noticed the change as well, for it was not the first time that he had witnessed this curious power in his Great and Worthy Opponents eye, and he took caution.

"You might have the allegiance of the Light, Pan," the Dark Father chortled with his last bit of strength, remembering Hook's last memory of Neverland. "You might have the allegiance of the Light… but I promised you one hundred years ago that I would return and put an end to all you hold dear… and I intend to keep it."

"Be gone," Peter commanded as true concern invaded his confidence. "Your time in Neverland is over."

"HA!" The Dark Father jeered with maximum force, and his physical form bearing the likeness of Hook began to melt and morph back into the essence of the Dark Father of Time as the last remnants of his physical construction collapsed. Then, suddenly, Hook's elegant voice was gone as his image gave way completely, and the deep, intelligent, sinister voice of the Dark Father returned "You may have destroyed my body, Son of Neverland… but tell me… what good is living… without your *heart?*"

Then, suddenly, gathering the last bit of strength he had in the physical world, the Dark Father held up his hand…

* CHAPTER 20 *

— The Heart of the Son —

Tiger Lily's mind was just coming back to her as she could feel the air coming into her lungs again. She squinted through blurry eyes and could see the image of Tinker Bell above her — was she dreaming — no, she could feel the beating heart of her mare, Fleur, below her, supporting her as she floated on the surface of the sea, then it all started coming back to her — she had just done battle. Despite the fact, she felt surprisingly warm, fuzzy, and happy. Tinker Bell must be using magic to cool her wounds. She didn't like magic much, but she supposed a little might be all right… and Peter… where was Peter?...

Suddenly, Tiger Lily felt her body lifted into the air. She zoomed across the Northern Strait as Tinker Bell, Ruby, and Fleur grew smaller and smaller underneath her… maybe she was dreaming after all…

In what seemed like less than a blink of the eye, Tiger Lily was now with them in the air, completely immobile in the Dark Father's telekinetic grip as the final moment of his physical existence came to a close. It all happened so quickly and unexpectedly Peter didn't even have time to comprehend or react to what was happening as Tiger Lily's body began to decompose before him… in this final moment… he looked Tiger Lily in her big, brown eyes…

"It's okay," Tiger Lily said as she looked back into her lover's bright eyes — the same eyes she had lost herself in so many times before — she could sense his fear, but she needed to make him believe that he should not be afraid, for he was the Son of Neverland, and with or without her, he had a world to lead. She could feel her body dissolving around her, but it was not painful, rather, it felt as if she was going somewhere…

Peter watched in absolute shock and fear as Tiger Lily disintegrated in the arms of the Dark Father. Time slowed in this last moment, and even though Peter knew he was losing her, he held her gaze, and looked at her as if the moment would last forever…

"It's okay," Tiger Lily said one last time through tears of peace, and then, she was gone… the sparkling, black shards of her dissolved body flickering in the fleeting wind…

All that remained was the remnants of the Dark Father's countenance, and upon seeing how much pain he had just caused this indestructible, tyrannical, child-like deity, in his final breath, he smiled, and then was gone from the world of Neverland…

There was a moment of shock, disbelief, and nothingness… then…

"AHHHHHHHH!!!" Peter screamed from the sky as the reality of what had just impossibly happened in the last two seconds hit him all at once. His being gave out as he stared at the spot in the now vacant air where Tiger Lily was just moments before, and his mind collapsed in on itself. A darkness fell heavy upon the sky as all of Neverland bore witness to the Great Pain of the Son… and they knew… the whole world knew… for the absence of Tiger Lily's bright spirit could be felt across the their world…

All the way up north in the Fairy Quarters, the inhabitants came out of their dwellings and looked up at the sky as the echo of Peter's scream reached their ears… tears of sorrow flowed from their eyes…

At the ship, the braves and lost boys stood on the deck in silence and disbelief as the pain of their leader shot through each and every one of them… tears flowing from Tiger Lily's passing…

At the outskirts of their destroyed village, the tribespeople wept as they felt the spirit of their princess leave Neverland for the first time. The chief looked up at the sky in disbelief as he processed the realization that the worst may have come to pass. He didn't react, but rather, stared at the stars, as if he knew what was happening wasn't realistic, but here it was, apparently happening anyway. The chief tried to make sense of this jest — of this riddle, of this trick —despite his disposition to hope, for the first time since he could remember, he felt there was none left in him. Without his daughter by his side, the very reason he continued to live his life was gone. The chief continued to look at the stars, believing that if he stared long enough, Tiger Lily would be returned to him… he stayed like that for a great long while…

On Pirate Eater Beach, Marco — now free of his bonds — walked along the shore bumbling to himself through his broken face. He had his sack of gold he retrieved from the ground in his hand. When the flying boy's screams reached his ear, he jeered in ecstasy, and he smiled maliciously in absolute joy.

"I told them they would pay," he hissed. "I told them they would all pay… and ol' Marco is *always* right." He then looked down greedily into his sack of plunder, the golden coins shining brightly up at him off the moonlight, and a satisfied smile spread across his bloody, exploded face. "Good thing I made it worth my while," he said lustfully.

From the back of Ruby, Tinker Bell felt Peter's scream shoot through the core of her being, and she felt as if she was being destroyed along with him. She could not believe what she just witnessed — it was impossible — one moment, Tiger Lily was underneath her, and the next, she was hurtling through the air, and now… she was…. she was — Tinker Bell could not bear the thought…

Peter continued to scream as he felt like he was being incinerated from within. The pain was unlike anything he had ever experienced, worse than any physical torment the Dark Father had caused him, and worse than dying to be reborn. It felt as if his heart and soul had been ripped from his body… he felt empty… thin… lifeless…

Suddenly, Peter dropped into a free-fall as his last bit of strength left him, and he could support himself in the air no longer. Despite his rage, his spent body could no longer withstand the power of it, and immobilizing darkness took him… down… down… down he fell…

Tinker Bell saw Peter drop from the sky, and without hesitation she leapt into the air and hit the jets, flying as fast as her wings could carry her. She was still disoriented by what just happened, but it was not a time for mourning — it was a time for action — Peter had just saved them all… and now she had to save him…

Peter looked up at the darkening sky as he continued to fall, and for the first time in his life, he felt he knew what death was. He had felt pain before, but nothing like this — this was beyond physical, beyond visceral — for without the love of his life, there was no life at all… down… down he fell… and in his mind he fell as if he was falling forever, and forever still, drifting, into some endless deep…

Then, just as Peter was about to make critical impact with the surface of the sea…

BANG! — Tinker Bell caught Peter in her arms, the dead weight and inertia from his falling body was unlike anything she had ever experienced, and it felt as if his Spirit — that typically presence that gave him his lightness of being — had been torn from him, and all there was left was lead. Tink groaned as she pushed back with all the magical strength she had left… she was able to slow them a little… but it wasn't going to be enough…

BOOM! — Peter and Tinker Bell plunged into the water, and once again the concussion from the impact separated them and sent them scattering into the deep seas of the Northern Strait!

Tinker Bell shook her head, keeping her bearings. She had no strength left, but it didn't matter. This wasn't about her anymore — it was about Peter, Neverland, everybody but her! — She swam as hard as she could, but Peter sank further and further away from her… she cried as she couldn't stand it any longer… this was it…

Suddenly, with the last bit of light in her eyes, Tinker Bell saw something bright and white swim up underneath Peter. It was Ruby! She swam with the swiftness of an etheric being as she caught Peter's falling body on her back, and quickly moved towards the surface. Then, Tinker Bell felt herself being lifted towards the sky as well… was this it… had they died…

Moments later, Tinker Bell broke through the surface and took a big gasp of air. She looked below her and saw that Fleur had saved her. As she regained her composure, Tink stroked Fleur's mane in gratitude, trying to calm her as she felt Fleur whimpering at the loss of Tiger Lily.

Tink then flew over to Peter who lay immobile on Ruby's back, completely spent from battle and all he had gone through. He was breathing, but it felt like his life force had left him. His vitals were stable, but his mind…

"Tiger Lily…" was all that Peter could murmur. "Tiger Lily…"

Tink acted quickly, trying to keep her head cool and remain rational, and not get swept up in the overwhelming reality that the very worst may have just happened — that Tiger Lily was… that she was….

She shook her head. She couldn't think of such things — not now — she reached into her satchel, but she was out of her neverbrew potion. She could get Peter some when they got back to the Fairy Quarters, until then, he'd have to sweat it out.

Tinker Bell looked down on the boy she loved as his physical strength returned to him… what he had done for Neverland… what he had done for them all… but his mind… his beautiful mind… what would become of it now that Tiger Lily was… was…

No, she could not think of it! There was nothing that could be done about that now! Surely, surely, there must be some action she could take. Surely, there must be a way to stop the bleeding, to catch those responsible—

"Those responsible," Tink said out loud to herself, and then the right thought came to her, and her eyes narrowed…

***

Marco trudged his way along the shoreline of Pirate Eater Beach towards the Unspoken Lands in the wake of the setting sun.

He was not in a hurry, and he was tired and exhausted from the lack of sleep, for his intention was to hide out there in case word got around of his dealings and any survivors came looking for revenge. Once the Dark Father conquered Neverland, he would then re-emerge victorious and take his place by his side, and now that the Piccaninny Village was destroyed, he'd claim the Western Cape as his, and rebuild what remained of the tribe how he saw fit. He'd have plenty of fairy girl slaves — oh yes, lots of those — of the exact size and shape that he had always lusted over since he was old enough to desire them, and if any of those traitorous lost boys survived, he'd keep them as personal prisoners, to torture and ridicule as he saw fit, and to entertain him and his finest braves as jesters during their wild parties. For the rest of their lives, they'd wished they'd have never tried to get the better of ol' Marco, and he'd make them pay for every day that they decided to worship their precious Great White Father over him. Ha! Yes! It was going to be the Neverland that should have always been — a Neverland made in his image — and he salivated at the thought of his marvelous scheme.

Suddenly, Marco saw a figure galloping up behind him along the beach. He squinted and held up his hand to shield his eyes from the setting sun that glistened brightly off Cannibal Cove. It couldn't be — it was — it was that blasted fairy and that one-horned abomination she rode like a horse! How was it possible?! She should be dead! But there she was, gaining on him nonetheless, and fast.

That evil nymph! He thought for sure the ol' captain would have done away with her as planned, but she had somehow survived. Never trust a pirate! They're useless scum, the lot of them! He tightened his grip on the sack of gold in his hand, for he was not about to lose what he had worked so hard to gain over the mistake of a bunch of blundering buffoons! Never trust fools to do the work of a genius! He should have killed her in her sleep when he had the chance.

Tinker Bell's eyes narrowed as she and Ruby easily gained on the fleeing coward with Fleur carrying Peter's weakened body behind her. The traitor! It wasn't her place to destroy him, but she'd make sure he felt it. She reached into her satchel and charged a fairy blast…

BANG! — There was a bright light, then Marco felt a searing, white-hot pain shoot course through his being as the concussion from the blast sent him sprawling to the sand. All went black for a moment, and when he came to he found himself laid out flat on his back, with the contents of his gold satchel scattered all around him. His eyes went wide when he realized he had narrowly missed landing in a puddle of quicksand just several feet from him, for they had reached the southern side of Pirate Eater Beach, and the Wiley Quicksands were a known hazard at the mouth of the Unspoken Lands.

"You blasted fairy!" Marco spat out in defeat and rage from the ground. "You conniving evil nymph! Curse you!"

Tinker Bell looked down on the pathetic excuse for a warrior as she stood above him. He looked like a goon, and the topline of his hair was shaved off where Tiger Lily's arrow scalped him, making him look even more ridiculous than before, which was plenty enough to begin with. She would not speak to him — he wasn't worth a single one of her words — instead, she charged another fairy blast.

"He got the Princess too, eh?" Marco chortled. "Bet you didn't see that one coming, did cha? Ha! So much for your flying dream boy! Now you're all screwed!"

Marco cackled in ecstasy from the ground. He found such pleasure in this moment that he couldn't keep his body from rolling around in delight. "I told you I'd get you!" He projected through bouts of laughter. "I told you I'd get you all! I was always one step ahead of you… the whole time… always one step ahead… and now… now you have no one to protect you…"

He was laughing so hard he could barely speak, for the time of his victory was at hand, and he'd been waiting for decades to experience this very moment. "Just face it, sweetheart," he said with a final deep breath. "I *won.*"

Tinker Bell looked down on the scum babbling below her, and her hand glowed hot…

"Go ahead! Blast me with your insignificant, fairy magic! See what happens!" Marco barked antagonistically, then he settled into a devious smile. "What the Dark Father has given me can't be undone… better side with me now… because when the Dark Father rewards me… you'll be my main prize."

Marco puckered his haggard lips and blew a kiss at Tink as he gazed lustfully up at her in spite. Tink's eyes narrowed and her hands glowed hotter as she met his gaze — she'd like nothing more to incinerate that stupid grin right off his pulverized face — but for a traitor of this level, there were higher plans for him…

"I'm sorry to disappoint you, but…" Tinker Bell said easily as she took a deep, calming breath. "You're not my type."

She stepped aside, and there, silhouetted just beyond where Tink just stood… a shadow… then the head of the shadow lifted… and two bright eyes lit up in its center…

"No," Marco mumbled as dread shot through the bone marrow of his body, and his ecstasy turned into pure fear. "It's not possible…"

The figure did not move, just continued to stare back with eyes that burned like bright fire, and Marco's gloating turned into whimpering, for he had heard rumors about the wrath of the Great White Father when it came to those who threatened the princess, and that he became almost demon-like in his vengeance. Aside from their love for her, this was the main reason the entire tribe feared Tiger Lily so much, for she held the Great White Father's favor, and had the power to influence his actions. Because of this, no brave had ever made an advance on her, and Marco always kept his distance due to fear of invoking this legendary wrath. He hated him, sure, but he was no common fool — he was a survivor — and being found out as the key piece to Tiger Lily's destruction while the Great White Father still drew breath, was the very antithesis to Marco's own self-interest.

"You have to kill me," he pleaded, turning to Tinker Bell. "Please kill me." His words were true, for he was ready to take his chances in the after-life where the Dark Father could redeem him, then face torment of this legendary being.

Tinker Bell didn't answer, but continued to stare coldly back, and Marco's eyes nearly exploded out of his face with fear as Great White Father stepped towards him. He was bloodied and bruised from the battle, but he had a glow around him now that made him awesome to behold. Marco couldn't believe the impracticality of it. It was immutable, completely impossible… the Great White Father had become a god!

"Where is she?" Peter said coldly.

Marco was laid frozen by the sight — oh, the greatness, the greatness of this being before him — he was prostrated before a god, a true deity, for who other than the Ancient of Days Himself could face the Dark Father in battle, and live?

"I don't…" Marco stuttered. "I don't kno—"

"— *Where… is she*?" Peter repeated calmly and exactly.

"I don't know, honest." Marco said, his vile words spilling from his mouth in reverence. "No one faces the Dark Father and lives to tell the tale… you shouldn't be alive… it's not possible… it must be… it has to be… you're a god!"

Peter then flew upon Marco, and before he could even blink he was up to his neck in the pool of the Wiley Quicksands that he had narrowly missed previously.

"Everything I did, I did for Neverland!" Marco blurted out in total fear as he sank, centimeter by centimeter, into the greedy mixtures that had consumed countless bodies, for it wasn't called Pirate Eater Beach for nothing.

"It was really, Charlie," Marco babbled frantically. "Yes, he was the mastermind behind it all — and Pax, that blockhead of a fool they call a warrior! I knew from the start he should have never made brave! I was on to him from the beginning, but no one listens to poor ol' Marco — no one listens! — That old chief, he never pays any attention to me! I'm just trying to do right by my tribe. I could have saved them, but no one listens to a word I say…

Peter looked down on the sniveling excuse for a warrior sinking into the sand, then his eyes shifted to the gold scattered all around him.

"It's not mine!" Marco exclaimed as he saw Peter notice. "It was really the Princess's, she made me take it!"

"SILENCE!"

Before Marco could blurt out another lie, Peter grabbed the traitor by his half-scalped head, pulled him out of the pool of quicksand, and held him in the air with his dagger pressed against his throat, and Marco prayed for a quick death.

After a moment, Peter's wrath cooled, and he threw him once again to the dry ground. Dripping-wet with sand, Marco gasped and wheezed for breath as Peter dropped back down from above.

"Are you going to torture me?" Marco said as regained his bearing from the ground.

"That depends on how much you like the taste of quicksand," Peter stated, emotionlessly, for one way or another, he was going to get the information he needed.

Then, suddenly, in Marco's helplessness, a strange thing happened, for nothing could stop the newborn god from doing whatever he was going to do with him now, and all those memories from his childhood came flooding back, when the Great White Father would fly over the village, always doing as he pleased, and nobody could stop him.

The Great White Father was huge to him, back in those days. All the young braves told stories about him and wanted to be him, but in Marco's eyes, he had always known what he really was — the Great White Demon —coming into their tribe, taking their princess for himself. The injustice!

The demon tried to talk to him once back when he was a boy. Marco had gotten in a fight with another brave, and killed the boy's dog for revenge. It was really the other boy's fault. He made fun of his tracking skills, and he deserved it, but that old, stupid chief always thought he was a troublesome child, full of sick impulses, and that sending Tiger Lily's demon to talk to his troubled soul would help raise his spirits and correct his way, since it seemed to work on the others.

And so it did come — flying through the air, dropping out of the sky, with bright eyes of fire like a demon — Marco remembered how terrified he was when it smiled at him, trying to be nice to him, but Marco knew it was a trick. He dared not stay in his presence to let him speak, lest the demon curse him, and put him under the same spell that made all the other braves worship him mindlessly. No, not this young brave, not ol' Marco. He would not be enchanted and taken by the white demon's lies. He would not be a weak fool like the other boys. In terror and spite, he ran away from the ancient demon all those years ago, when he was young. He thought for sure it would fly upon him and kill him for this open act of rebellion, but it didn't. Marco looked back and the demon just stood there — it didn't chase him, it didn't yell at him — it just stood there without any type of response to his fear. In fact, it almost felt as if the demon was saddened by him running away, but Marco knew it was another trick, just another spell intended to seduce his mind to go back and worship him, but ol' Marco would not be tricked, for he knew that the demon fed off the praise of others, and he would never willingly be its slave. The demon let him go that day… and it never tried to speak to him as a boy again.

As Marco grew older, he saw that the demon never hurt anyone that didn't directly threaten him, his fairy, his lost boy minions, or especially Tiger Lily, but it was the fact that it could if it wanted to, and that nobody could do anything to stop it, that Marco resented beyond anything else. He felt powerless, and it was this very feeling of powerlessness that had haunted him in his dreams ever since he first saw it flying through the sky. He had always slept very little because of these night terrors.

One day, while hunting deer in the Neverland Forest, a brave told him another story about the Great White Father — a story that he had never heard before — legend had it that a dark god used to rule Neverland. An ancient, demon-like creature that used dark fire and even time itself as a weapon. This god was all powerful and enslaved the fairy race. It ruled for eons and nobody had the power to stop it. The brave also told Marco that people used to die much faster back in those days. Marco asked why, and the brave shrugged and said he didn't know.

The brave then also told him that the fairies also had an old legend. It said that a child would be born, and that it would be their Savior. It would come to Neverland to destroy the dark god, and free the fairies once and for all. Well, it was believed that the fairy legend came true… and the Great White Father… was that Savior.

Marco stopped hunting and asked the brave if it was true. He shrugged and said, "it's only a legend," and they continued their hunt, but Marco never forgot the story.

It was that very night that he first prayed to the spirit of the Dark Father to aid him — to give him power to destroy the Great White Demon and rid his village of his tyranny forever — to which the Dark Father answered him, quietly, slowly, in his prayers, growing his presence in his thoughts over years and years, twisting his mind to become his ultimate inside weapon… his ultimate means to his reincarnation into Neverland… and his ultimate revenge…

Now that the power of the Dark Father was gone from Neverland, and the Great White Demon had become a god, Marco felt once again — *was* once again — completely and totally powerless, and it was in this complete and total powerlessness, that he finally found liberation from his fear…

"Go ahead!" Marco screamed as he pushed himself up with the last of his remaining strength. "Do it! Become what I've always known you to be. They call you their Savior, but I've always seen you for exactly what you always were — a tyrant!"

Peter didn't react, and Marco found a renewed sense of valor.

"How does it feel, Great White Father?" Marco mocked. "How does it feel? Huh? To be *helpless*?"

Peter stared back, and the rage was building, but not because he was angry, or sad, or any other emotion that typically set him off, but it was because the traitor was right — he did feel helpless.

"How does it feel to have your heart ripped out?" Marco continued. "And to have absolutely no power to stop it."

"AHHHHH!" Peter could hear no more of the fiend's words, he took to the air and came down hard with his dagger.

After a moment, Marco opened his eyes in an explosion of bafflement, but the boy's dagger was not lodged through his skull like he was expecting, but precisely down the ridge where Tiger Lily's arrow had already scalped him the previous night.

"You will pay for what you have done," Peter said as he stood above him. "But not with your blood."

***

There was black, then a bright light broke the darkness as Mr. Theodore held up his hand, revealing Peter and Tinker Bell there with him at the interior entrance to Andromeda's Lair. Behind them, Marco was bound hand and foot as he was led reluctantly by a rope, whimpering through his gag.

"How is this possible?" Tink said as she looked around in awe at the large cavern. "Peter said it collapsed behind him."

"This is not a physical space, Tinker Bell." Mr. Theodore said knowingly. "It only collapsed according to Peter's mind, but to mine, it's still very much intact."

Peter and Tinker Bell exchanged glances, then Mr. Theodore turned back to them and lifted an eyebrow. "There's more to the mind than one thinks..."

Mr. Theodore then turned back and faced the empty black of the cavern. He took a deep belly full of air…

"ANDROMEDA!" He bellowed out.

There was a moment, then the whole cavern began to shake. Marco fell to the ground flat on his side, whimpering in fear.

Tinker Bell and Peter continued to stare in awe as the cavern transformed all around them, changing from the familiar dark and open cave, to a lush, tropical paradise. Suddenly, they were standing in the bottom of a wooded ravine, surrounded by majestic palms and ferns, with waterfalls cascading down on either side, and a river as bright as crystal bubbling through a brook.

"I've never seen this before," Peter said as he looked up at the blue sky above and the waterfalls cascading down all around them.

"Ah, it's just how I remember it," Mr. Theodore said as he reminisced, and suddenly he took on the persona and physicality of youth that Peter had only seen in his visions from the past of old Neverland. His tone was both pleased, but also vacantly sad, as if he had just stepped into a place long forgotten. "We're in my mind now…"

Suddenly, a group of beautiful and youthful female fairies peeked from their fern enclosures, staring at Peter. They giggled as they whispered to each other in some kind of unidentifiable, fairy language. Marco's eyes were wide from their beauty as he lay still frozen on the ground.

"Are they real?" Tinker Bell asked.

"Oh, yes," Mr. Theodore answered. "They are as real as you and I… but this was a long time ago…"

Peter and Tink continued to stare, captivated, then…

"Leave us," a beautiful female voice said from the air, and it had no point of origin, but appeared to come from everywhere.

The fairies took one last look at Peter, then scattered as they were told, giggling as they disappeared beneath the ferns.

There was a moment, and then a bright light slowly built before them as an etheric, female being began to form in the air. When the apparition was complete, Peter recognized her immediately to be Andromeda. She looked nearly identical to the being he met the first time in the cave — the same voluptuous form, the same big, dark eyes, the same full lips — but there was something different about her now… something had changed…

"Hello, Theodore," Andromeda said as she floated towards them, and although she was youthful in form she moved with the grace of an angel, and the wisdom of thousands of years. "I see you've brought friends."

"Andromeda," Mr. Theodore said in reverence as he gave a slight bow, and upon seeing it, Peter and Tink exchanged quick glances and then followed suit.

"We've met each other," Andromeda said, turning her gaze upon Peter.

They had met each other indeed — Peter's conception, that was, in form at least — he blushed, not knowing how to respond. Tinker Bell saw the exchange from the corner of her eye, and her eyes narrowed. Maybe she would never know the full truth of what happened to Peter in the mountain — maybe she didn't want to know.

After a moment, Andromeda smiled. "You must be weary from your journey. My fairies will tend to you."

Without signaling, three fairy maidens appeared rapidly from the ferns carrying goblets of golden liquid. They approached the group and held out the goblets. Mr. Theodore bowed gratefully as he accepted his goblet, then Peter and Tink followed suit. Then as quickly as they came, the fairies disappeared again behind their fern enclaves, giggling and looking back at Peter as they did. Although he couldn't understand the language, something told him they were whispering about what happened to him the first time with Andromeda in the mountain…

"Is this… *neverbrew*?" Tink asked as she looked down in fascination at her goblet's contents, for it was a spitting image of the potion that she concocted herself.

"Ah, yes…" Andromeda began knowingly. "I've heard you've rediscovered the magical properties of fairy dust."

"*Rediscovered?*" Tink said, taking offense — and she also didn't like how all of Peter's energy seemed to be directed towards her. "I invented it."

Andromeda just smiled at the young fairy's display of passion.

"Didn't I?" Tink said, having second thoughts.

"There is nothing new under the sun, Tinker Bell," Mr. Theodore said with a chuckle. "You are the first fairy to tap into the old magic long forgotten, so in that sense, you *reinvented* it."

"I'll take that," Tinker Bell said as she composed herself, but she couldn't hide her slight disappointment.

Mr. Theodore let out another chuckle, then threw back his goblet, downing his contents in one go. "Ah, just how I remember it," he exclaimed in satisfaction. "Hits of wild honey and neverfruit." Then, he turned to Peter and Tink. "Go ahead."

Peter and Tink were about to drink, when —

"Wait," Peter said, stopping Tinker Bell from drinking with his hand. "How do we know it's not a trick?"

"You don't." Mr. Theodore answered easily. "But that's the beauty, isn't it?"

Peter studied Mr. Theodore's mischievous grin. He was great at reading people, and there was no malicious way in him. If it was a trick, then he knew it would not be an evil trick. He then looked at Andromeda, and felt the beautiful and peaceful light that emanated off her being — her very existence was seductive to him — and he knew that no matter how great he felt now, there could be no way of knowing if she was trapping him again, or not — at least not by his intuition — it had already proven to be nearly useless against her charms.

"What do you think?" Peter asked, turning to Tinker Bell.

Tinker Bell glanced at Mr. Theodore, then to Andromeda, and then back to Peter. "Do we really have much of a choice?" She said honestly.

Peter looked at Tinker Bell, and he trusted her completely — she was the only person in the world he trusted anymore — and she was right. If he was going to find Tiger lily, powerful magic was likely the only way. He nodded, and together they threw back the potion.

There was a moment, and then Peter and Tink felt a warm, calming effect wash over them, soothing their anxious minds. In truth, neither of them knew how tired they were from battle, until they had this state to compare it to. They had both been completely exhausted, battling for days on very little sleep, and existing only on adrenaline and the power their spirits provided them. They both suddenly felt brightened with vitality as much of their strength and energy was restored. Peter watched in amazement as many of the wounds he suffered from his battle with the Dark Father healed before his very eyes.

"Wow," Tinker Bell admitted as she felt her spirit brighten. "That's much better than mine." Tink had many questions, and wanted to know how to make it, but there were more important matters at hand…

Mr. Theodore chuckled, then turned his gaze. "Andromeda—"

"I know why you have come to seek my counsel, Theodore," she began, and the trio stared at her in earnest.

"You want to know the whereabouts of the Dark Father," she finished her thought, and the silence seemed to shatter at the name.

Mr. Theodore nodded slightly. Andromeda then turned her gaze upon Peter, and he felt as if she was peering into his very soul. "You want to know if your lover is still alive."

Peter didn't react, just stared at Andromeda as he awaited the answer that had been gnawing at his stomach since the end of their final battle.

"It's strange," Andromeda continued as she gazed at Peter in a mix of longing, pity, and lust. "So much power, and yet, so much love for a mortal… and all she'll ever cause you is pain." Then her eyes narrowed, and true desire filled them. "You're much better suited for the higher kind, Son of Neverland… we could have been great, you and I."

Peter didn't like how he was being looked at by this sorceress — by this conjurer of smoke and mirrors.

"I'm not here to play games," Peter stated.

"And someone informed you I wasn't?" Andromeda stated back, and Peter didn't have a response to the polarizing question.

Andromeda then looked to Tinker Bell, and a knowing smile spread across her face. "It appears there is another who loves you as well."

Tinker Bell recoiled as the truth of her soul was laid bare, but Peter really couldn't hear another word — not now.

"Just tell me," Peter began after a moment, stomaching the fear that had been pushing him away from the question. "Is she alive?"

Andromeda looked back to Peter, and when she saw that his love was truly not for her, she conceded. "The Dark Father will not have taken kindly to being defeated a second time… he knew from the moment he entered this world that you'd give your life for the princess… in that sense, she will be alive… but what is your definition of *life*, Son of Neverland?"

A pain shot through Peter's body in this moment, and he could not entertain the idea that Tiger Lily would be anything other than what she always was — he simply could not bear it.

"Will I ever see her again?" Peter asked.

"You can," she began slowly, "but the path that leads to your princess's soul is filled with pain… it depends on what you are willing to sacrifice."

"Everything," Peter said without hesitation.

"*Everything*?" Andromeda asked curiously. "Are you really willing to sacrifice everything? Your world? Your friends?" Then she looked to Tinker Bell. "Even her?"

Peter looked to Tinker Bell, her big, blue eyes glossed over with tears. Was he really willing to sacrifice Tinker Bell to save Tiger Lily? Especially since there were no guarantees that saving Tiger Lily would even be possible? Could he really lose his best and closest friend — a friend he loved more than life itself — to save his true love?

Tinker Bell stared back at Peter, and her tears were not those of fear or sorrow, but those of helpless rage — she knew the sorceress had put Peter into an impossible position — but she wanted him to know that she would go with him, yes, until the very end. An unspoken knowing passed between them, and Peter nodded his gratitude.

"We'll do what we must," Peter said, turning back to Andromeda.

Andromeda smiled at their display of affection. It was cute — the young god and his fairy — it was endearing, but…

"The bond between you is strong," Andromeda admitted, "but I wonder… will it be enough?"

Peter didn't answer. He just stared at Andromeda, and his eyes narrowed at the curious statement.

"When all you know changes," Andromeda continued. "When you leave this world behind, and when the light you thought you believed in — the very light that built your soul — turns out to be *nothing*... I wonder then…. will it be enough?"

There was a moment as the unnerving words sank into Peter and Tink's marrow.

"We've beat the Dark Father twice now," Peter stated, defending their accomplishments. "I don't see why a third time isn't in order."

Andromeda couldn't help but smile at the young god's statement — he was bold, just as he had always been — and he was powerful. Despite her higher nature, she couldn't help her attraction to him.

"Cocky," Andromeda stated with a coy smile. "But where the Dark Father holds the princess' soul cannot be reached by any mortal power."

"That's why he has me," Tinker Bell said, stepping forward.

"No," Andromeda snapped. "You are talented, young fairy, but inexperienced. Your skills are currently limited outside of the physical plane… the astral and etheric realms will require knowledge of the old ways."

"I'll show you inexperienced," Tinker Bell mumbled under her breath, and it was all she could do to keep herself from blasting the mouthy conjurer right then and there.

"She's right," Mr. Theodore chuckled at Tinker Bell's offense. "I'm afraid even my knowledge is not enough to guide you… there is only one that can get you there…"

Tinker Bell looked at Mr. Theodore, and saw there was no glint of mischief in his eyes. Suddenly, the reality of what he was saying hit her all at once.

"Oh, no!" Tinker Bell exclaimed, then she turned to Peter and pointed fiercely at Andromeda. "She is not going with us!"

"If this is the only way," Peter said, keeping emotion out of it. "Then this is the only way."

Peter stepped forward, unable to shake his thoughts of Tiger Lily in chains, suffering in some cold and lonely cell in the blackness of the void. "Let's go."

"You need rest, Peter." Mr. Theodore injected, stating the obvious. "And proper training, strategy, this is not a journey to be taken lightly."

"Theodore is right," Andromeda said. "To attempt the journey now would mean certain death."

"Every moment we sit around here talking, is another moment Tiger Lily has to suffer!" Peter's energy lifted him off the ground — which it often did when his passion flared — and Tinker Bell put a calming hand on his arm.

"She will not suffer, Son of Neverland," Andromeda stated. "So ease your mind."

"How do you know?" Peter questioned, not believing her.

"Did you suffer the first time you met me?" Andromeda said with a seductive smile.

"Speak plainly," Peter demanded, for he knew that smile, and its power. "I have not gone through fire and hell to deal in your worthless riddles."

Andromeda's eyes narrowed. She saw that Peter wasn't interested, which made her desire for him increase.

"I know that the princess will not suffer," Andromeda continued, "because I was once in love with him."

Andromeda spoke the words Peter already knew to be true from their first conflict — as Mr. Theodore had informed him — but for Tinker Bell it was the first time.

"You were once in love with… that— *that— thing!?"* Tink exclaimed, for she could not bring herself to believe it.

"Oh, yes," Andromeda stated. "The Dark Father is so much more than you saw in that limited incarnation… he is wise… *powerful*… unlimited…"

Tink's confusion turned subtly to horror as she saw the lust enter Andromeda's eyes.

"He is the glory of all polarity in the universe… worthy of all worship… the darkness to the light… in truth, without him we wouldn't exist." Andromeda then turned her gaze back upon Peter. "The Dark Father is not a tormenter, if anything, the precious mortal you love so much will be enjoying herself."

There it was again — that helplessness — Peter felt that searing pain shoot through the core of his being, for the thought of Tiger Lily enjoying — or worse, desiring — being in the presence of the Dark Father, was a torment unlike any kind he had ever experienced in the physical world. In just the little time he had known her, Andromeda had him wrapped around her finger, and she could play with his heart at will.

"Are you sure you're not still in love with him?" Tink stated after witnessing her display of reverence. "You can see how that would be a problem."

"Part of me will always love him," Andromeda answered honestly. "That's why I'm the only one who can find him."

The statement landed hard. There was a moment, but nobody argued the truth of it.

"How do we know you won't turn on us?" Tinker Bell asked, really doing her diligence if they were to trust this… *this* — Tink didn't even know what to call her anymore.

"We don't," Peter answered for her, accepting the powerlessness of their current position. "But like you said, do we really have a choice?"

There was a moment as Peter and Tink stared at Andromeda. They were in a stalemate. Peter didn't like it — not one bit — he was out of patience, and he was not so quick to forget the sinister other side of her being that lay dormant beneath her sparkling veneer.

"You will take us to him," Peter commanded as true frustration turned to vengeance in his throat. "Or mark my words… I will *end* you."

Peter then turned his attention on Marco, who was still bound upon the ground. He was in awe of Andromeda's beauty, and was completely immobilized by it as he could not stop staring at her. To Marco's surprise, Peter cut the bonds on his hands, and began walking away from the group through the imaginative, lush valley. Marco could hardly believe it, without taking his eyes off Andromeda, he pulled the gag from his mouth.

Tinker Bell took one last look at Andromeda. She didn't trust her, and she didn't like that she would be their guide, but there was no other way — *currently* — her eyes narrowed, then her gaze fell upon Marco.

"You see something you like, honeybun?" Marco babbled up through his smashed face.

"Stay," Tinker Bell commanded as she pointed a charged blast right at him, and Marco shrunk back to the ground in fear. She then turned to follow Peter into the valley.

"I look forward to our journey, Son of Neverland!" Andromeda called after them in her elegant voice, and she was apparently unfazed by their small conflict. Then, when they were some ways away, her veneer broke, and a single tear rolled down her cheek.

"After all these centuries…" Mr. Theodore finally spoke, for he had been standing idly by for a while, silently witnessing…

Andromeda didn't respond to him directly, and in her countenance, he had his answer.

"The great part about being immortal, Theodore, is that you can count on feeling tomorrow exactly like you felt today." Andromeda said, finally composing herself. "Or maybe you're still too young to understand that."

Mr. Theodore chuckled at her back handed statement, then he turned to follow Peter and Tinker Bell into the valley of his mind…

When Mr. Theodore was finally out of sight, Marco couldn't believe his luck, for they had left him alone with this beautiful, magnificent creature. "Surely, she was the glory of all things," Marco thought. "And surely, this was the Dark Father's reward for his service to his plan. Yes, this was his ultimate payment for how loyal he had been for all those years!"

"That ol' Dark Father" Marco continued in his mind. "That ol' trickster — even at the end he was still pulling pranks! He sure had a way about doing things, didn't he? Making him think he was captured, when really he was leading him right into heaven! What a jester! What a clown! He sure has a funny bone in him, that ol' dark one, but boy did he know how to come through when it counted!" This was the most delicious beauty Marco had ever seen… and she was all his now…

In his lust, Marco finally found the strength to rise from the ground, which drew Andromeda's gaze to him for the first time. In fact, he was so low on the magic scale, that she hardly even knew he was there.

"Hello." Andromeda's voice fell into that girlish, high-pitched voice again that Peter first heard on the mountain. "Have you come to play with me?"

Had he come to play with her?! Oh, did he ever! Marco couldn't believe his luck! What a peach! What a gem! That ol' Dark Father, he really knew how to reward those that served him.

"Oh, yes, my lovely," Marco said, salivating as he crept towards her fleshy body. "I've come to play with you."

"What games would you like to play?" Andromeda said innocently.

"Oh, so many games," Marco drooled as a sinister look spread across his face. "So… so many games, my sweet…"

Every cell of Marco's body was on fire with passion as he neared within just feet of her. He clearly made the right choice by praying to the Dark Father all those decades ago in his mind, for he had rewarded him with eternal paradise. This was the most beautiful being he had ever witnessed. Yes, his mind could never conceive of such beauty until resting his eyes upon it, and now she would be his, forever…

"Come to daddy," Marco said in ecstasy as he reached out to touch her supple flesh, and his eyes rolled back in his head, but when his hand connected, it was not warm to the touch as he was anticipating, but rather frigid…

"What?!" The cold sobered Marco, pulling him out of his trance, and he blinked as his eyes rolled back to the front of his face. To his shock and horror, he realized that his hand was resting on the dried, cracked, withered flesh of an old witch!

"I'll be your baby," Andromeda cackled with a wicked smile, and her haggard form was revealed.

Marco recoiled from the shock. His eyes bulged from the sullen sockets of his busted face in true horror at the rotting corpse before him, terrified out of his mind with fear.

"Come to mama!" Before he could react, Andromeda opened her haggard jaws and pounced upon him, biting into his pulverized face.

"NOOOOOOOOOOOO!!!" Marco screamed as Andromeda feasted on his blackened soul… then the lush paradise disintegrated before his very eyes, and darkness sank in all around him as he fell deeper, deeper, and deeper still… yes, ever deeper… into the eternal emptiness of his forsaken mind…

* CHAPTER 21 *

— Reclaimer —

The remaining survivors of Captain Brubaker's crew all cowered in fear as Nibs unlocked the gate, for he loathed them all to the core of his being for what they had put him and his friends through, and the resentment on his face was so clear and strong they feared he would gut them one by one in the bowels of this cell.

"Come on," Nibs teased, sensing their fear, for it was so thick it could be cut with a knife. "You have a higher power to answer to."

Nibs opened the gate, then turned and walked back up towards the main deck, and slowly, one by one, the remaining survivors followed him up towards the light above…

The lost boys formed a semi-circle on the deck as the pirates cautiously stepped out into the light, shielding their eyes from the blinding morning sun. If Nibs struck fear in their hearts with a single pirate sword, the terror they felt when Peter dropped down from the sky, glowing in his god form, was unimaginable. Some fell to their knees as their strength gave out completely, for they all knew the myths and legends of the flying boy, and it was a known fact among them that he took great pleasure in torturing and destroying pirates. What he would do to them now after the loss of his Indian maiden… they could only imagine it would live up to their greatest nightmares…

"Your leader has been destroyed," Peter said as he floated above them in dominance, shining before them in the air. "The Dark Father of Time that you helped to unleash upon Neverland has been sent back to the abyss, and your captain is now lying in a pile of ashes. There is no foul beast left for you to serve… now what to do with all of you?"

"Let's destroy them!" Nibs yelled, for he was the angriest out of all of them.

"Yeah! Let's run them all through!" Curly followed, savoring the idea.

The pirates all panicked and screamed for mercy, expecting the flying boy to come down upon them and slay them all at any moment. The lost boys drew their swords, and yelled in unison, desiring to quench their blood lust and vengeance for Tiger Lily's memory, however, they dared not scream out her name, for fear that they may trigger Peter to accidentally kill them instead in his wrath.

"Silence," Peter demanded, and all fell silent on the deck awaiting his judgement. "You aided the dark one in taking something from me… something I care about very much… and because of this… death would be a proper payment… I *ought* to destroy you…"

The lost boys fell silent as they felt the pain of their leader course through them. They wanted to scream, but the treacherous behavior of their enemy was beyond words. As the pirates looked upon Peter in fear, the boys only wanted their blood.

"But…" Peter continued as the pirates hinged on his words. "Enough blood has been shed upon the night… and I will see no more under the sun today."

The pirates breathed a sigh of relief, some collapsed to their knees from the release of tension. Others broke down into tears of gratitude.

"You will leave Neverland," Peter continued after a moment. "You will go back to your world, and you will sail the seven great seas where you reside… and when you come across your kind and others like you… you *will* tell them what happened here…"

It was so quiet on the deck you could hear a pin drop. All the pirates stared at Peter with wide eyes and frozen muscles as if the commandment of God was being injected into their bones from on high.

"You will tell them that you tried to take Neverland, but she would not yield. You will tell them that you tried to bring darkness and death, but were defeated by Truth and Light. You will tell them that the Guardians of Neverland destroyed your captain and the dark god he conjured from the abyss, and sent them both back to the furthest recesses of the deep, where they will remain forevermore."

All eyes revered Peter as he floated in the air, shocked by this unexpected display of compassion, but the pirate's fear of living with the knowledge of him over their shoulder was perhaps a torment worse than death, for there could be no more hiding from what he was now to them —omniscient, all knowing — and they truly believed that he could see all things…

"And when you tell this story," Peter continued. "Your lives will speak testament to the mercy you received here, and as you continue to draw breath by Neverland's grace, you will tell them your lives were spared so that you could live to tell others to never search for the hidden shores of Neverland, for if they did come, they would receive none of your mercy, and surely they would die."

The strength of the Pan's words was so powerful, it decimated any courage they had left, and the pirates were truly defeated in every way. Yes, they would tell the others — they would tell them all — for to come here ever again would mean total annihilation for all those that dared, and there was not a sliver of doubt in any of their minds of that truth.

"That is my judgement," Peter said in finality. "I hereby banish you from the world of Neverland… *forever*."

The silence lay heavy as the Pan's judgement was passed upon them. A moment, then—

"Mr. Theodore," Peter commanded.

"Here," said a voice on the far end of the ship. The others turned to see none other than a small, elderly fairy walking towards them. He was back to his older physical self again, and that veneer of youth Peter had witnessed in the void was all but gone. He had clearly teleported or arrived by some other means of fairy magic, unto which, none of the lost boys knew.

"Did you find the portal?" Peter asked.

"We found it," Mr. Theodore confirmed easily. "Well, as much of it that can be found, that is."

"Does it lead to earth?" Peter asked from the air.

Mr. Theodore shrugged cluelessly. "It will get them out of here," he followed. "You can bet all your buttons on that."

The small group of pirate survivors shuddered at the old man's words, trembling at the unpredictably.

"Good enough," Peter stated. "Accompany the pirates to Eternity Island," he commanded. "They'll clean up their mess before returning home." Then he turned his gaze back on the pirates. "*All of it.*"

The pirates gulped, and despite their dread of the unknown, none dared question him.

"It would be my pleasure," Mr. Theodore croaked. "Come on you scurvy dogs," he teased. "It's not the first time I've dealt with the likes of you, but if you're lucky, it will be the last."

The pirates began to spread out around the ship, manning their posts as ordered. The lost boys sheathed their swords, and although they wanted blood for the loss of Tiger Lily, they trusted the wisdom of Peter, for his way was much higher than theirs when it came to the dealings of adults.

As they were left in each other's company, they stood for a while in silence, for there was rarely a time in which words were less needed. Gulls were crooning overhead, and the breakers from Cannibal Cove could be heard lapping against the wooden hull of the ship. It was quite peaceful, really, which on the surface almost made it appear as if nothing had changed… and yet everything had.

"You all fought valiantly," Peter said after some time. "I owe you my life."

The lost boys didn't respond verbally. They all just looked at Peter, holding back the tears in their eyes, for they couldn't even begin to imagine what he was going through.

"What's done is done," Peter stated after another moment. "Words of sorrow will not bring her back to us now. I have a course of action."

"We'll go to the end with you, Peter," Curly said, wiping the tears from his eyes. "As deep as the pit goes, as dark as it gets, we'll always be there by your side — all of us."

"Aye," the lost boys said in unison, nodding their heads in agreement.

Peter was moved by their loyalty.

"That's very brave of you, Curly," Peter responded. "You're my brothers, and I'm grateful to all of you, but where I am going soon… you cannot follow."

"What do you mean?" Nibs said, concerned. "Where are you going?"

Peter smiled at Nibs. He knew that of all the boys, he would be the first to follow him into the shadow without question or hesitation, but he could not tell them, for despite their willingness and courage, none of them had the magical disposition to follow him and Tinker Bell into the void, and he could not bear to burden them with more fear, for they had been through enough already.

"For a little while," Peter said lightly, choosing his words carefully. "You will not see me, but when I return you shall see me again, and we will rejoice together once more."

The lost boys knew that Peter wasn't telling them something, but they were too exhausted to push further into it. As in most cases in Neverland, it usually came down them blindly trusting that Peter knew what he was doing — this was the pinnacle of one of those cases — but in the last week, he had never given them more reason to believe in him.

"When are you going?" Curly said, who was saddened the most by the thought of Peter leaving.

"In a little while," Peter said again, gently. "But not today."

At that thought, Curly was able to smile a little, and the rest of the group eased up as well.

"Accompany Mr. Theodore to Eternity Island," Peter commanded, giving his final orders. "Make sure everything goes smoothly at the portal. I want every piece of pirate swine gone from Neverland. If any of those dogs try and escape… you know what to do."

"I hope they do," Slightly said with his signature, cocky swagger, pulling out his sword. "I haven't even got the rust off yet."

"I second that," Nibs followed, pulling out his blade.

The whole group chuckled, grateful to relieve some tension.

"Good," Peter said. "After return to the treehouse and get some sleep. I'll meet you back in Pixie's Landing. I'll need you rested up to help me restore order to the quarters."

Silence again took the group as they were faced with the reality of the destruction that had been cast upon their world.

"This is the real thing, boys," Peter said. "It's time to step up. I'll need you to look after Neverland while I'm away. I know you can do it."

All the boys looked at their fearless leader. If he could go through what he had gone through, and still believe at the end of the day, then they could do whatever he required of them.

"All right," Peter said strongly. "Let's get to it."

With renewed energy, the lost boys dispersed across the deck and began to help Mr. Theodore with his assignment in removing the pirates from Neverland.

Tootles, who was standing quietly in the back, came up to Peter as the others spread out. Peter felt his front melt a little when left alone with the most mature of the lost boys.

"I feel the worst has come to pass, Tootles," Peter said as he looked across the deck. "Sometimes I feel like I don't know what I'm doing."

"Yeah, you do," Tootles chuckled. "You know *exactly* what you're doing."

With that, Tootles put a calming hand on Peter's shoulder, then went to help the others.

Peter oversaw the movement of the ship as it sailed south west out of Cannibal Cove towards Eternity Island, but as the last of the black flags disappeared around the Southern Point at the tip of Neverland, and disappeared up the South Channel, he felt no further peace, for a great sorrow still draped over their world, and he could feel its weight on his shoulders.

Knowing the pain of what was inevitably and unavoidably to come, he turned and began flying northward towards the Western Cape… leaving the shimmering waters of Cannibal Cove behind him… still and undisturbed once more… quiet and eternal… in the setting sun….

***

Peter floated through the smoldering remains of his true love's home, the Neverland sun just bright enough now through the smoke to illuminate the disaster that was laid upon it. Literally everything was destroyed — incinerated to ash on the ground —

Peter solemnly took it in as he processed the savage reality of what had come to pass…

He continued walking through the decimated village until he came to the place where Tiger Lily's beautiful tepee once stood on the south western most tip of the cape, overlooking the Princess Isles. There was nothing left of her residence — nothing physical to claim that it ever even existed — nothing at all, just dust and echoes of what once was.

Peter fought back hot tears when he thought of all the lovely memories they had experienced there together, all the lovely times they had, and how beautiful the tepee itself actually was. It was lithe, and graceful, and exquisitely constructed in the highest of Piccaninny tradesmanship — a true piece of art — made in perfect likeness to Tiger Lily's boundless and captivating spirit… to see it destroyed for no reason was… was…

Peter felt the vengeance of Neverland rising up in him again… vengeance for Tiger Lily… vengeance for all injustice done upon their world… a vengeance that was hot and unquenchable… and it felt… terrible…

Peter took a deep breath of ocean air to cool his blood, and looked out over the isles from the shore. It was a beautiful evening, with the sun setting in just the right way, majestic and familiar, just how it always did during his and Tiger Lily's fondest evenings together. Across the way, the shores of Tiger Island glistened in the setting sun, and appeared to be — thankfully — untouched by the carnage. At least when he'd bring Tiger Lily back from the shadow, once she was safe again from the eternal darkness, she'd still have a piece of home to come back to, and for that, Peter was grateful.

In the wake of such mindless destruction, Peter let that one happy thought renew his being. He looked out over the isles, closed his eyes, and thought of Tiger Lily, and for a moment, just a moment, he thought he felt her spirit touch him in the wind…

Then he opened his bright eyes… and walked back towards the village…

The tribe's people stood in a group near the mouth of the camp, braves with their maidens and their children now without a home. Chief Great Big Little Panther stood stolidly before the group, remaining strong for his people, for now was not the time for grief. There had been grief enough already on this night as the gates of hell were opened upon his village and his daughter was taken from him, and his tears would not redeem them now.

As Peter approached the Great Chief, he remembered how much he had taught him since he first came to Neverland — how to venture into the astral realms, how to trust his spirit — yes, the wise chief had taught him much, and one day he would be his father-in-law... that was…

"Thank you for your sacrifice, Great White Father." The chief's eyes remained on his decimated village. "For without you, there would be no world left to live in."

Peter could hardly believe it. Was the chief really thanking him? After he had let the Dark Father steal Tiger Lily right out from under his nose? Peter then thought of how impossible that would be for him to take the same action, should the roles be reversed.

Then, Peter was suddenly attacked by guilt. He wanted to admit defeat. He wanted to ask forgiveness for not protecting his daughter. He wanted to cry, and weep, and break down, for the pain of Tiger Lily's loss could be felt around them all, ever present, and Peter felt the entire weight of it on his chest. Yes, it was his fault, and now a father would be going to sleep without knowing his daughter was safe this night, and the pressure of that thought upon Peter's mind felt as if it might crush him.

"I *will* find her," Peter stated with absolution, and he felt he owed it to the chief to at least appear in control.

The chief then turned to Peter, and smiled. "I know," he said. "I know."

The chief's strong faith could not be shaken despite what may rise up from the underworld, and aside from Tiger Lily's capture, every one of his tribesman, their wives, and their children were still alive — say for that traitor, Marco — and for that he found the spark of gratitude in his tribulation, for he more than most knew that flesh was flesh, susceptible to the cruelties of time and the forces of darkness, but that which was Spirit was unlimited — indeed, above all things — and the fruits of such power remained forever.

Peter could hardly believe it, was the chief really smiling, now? With his daughter gone, and his village burned to the ground? It was an impossible smile, but it seemed the chief was doing it all the same. Peter stared at the chief, perplexed, for he couldn't make sense of it.

"So much weight, Son of Neverland," the chief chuckled after a moment. He then grabbed Peter by both shoulders, and peered into him with twinkling eyes. "You will discover the child again," he smiled, mischievously. "He is hiding, but where He goes you know… and the way you know…"

Peter didn't know how to make heads or tails of the statement, but something told him the chief knew what he was talking about — he always did.

The chief smiled one last time at Peter, then turned to face his people. So many familiar faces that he had so many memories with throughout the centuries now hung downtrodden, the spark of life nearly stripped from them all, but there was still light left in them, and he had to ignite it.

"By the might of the Great White Father," The chief began. "Evil has been vanquished from this land. By the grace of the Great Spirit, none of ours fell prey to the spirit of darkness… none except one… a traitor that has been dealt with…"

Peter looked to Charlie who stood near the edge of the crowd. He had been betrayed by a man he considered for many moons to be a brother, but Marco's actions were irredeemable, and his fate was on his own head. His devious presence had been scoured from the land, and Charlie was grateful that he had lost no other true friends, and that he had made a few new ones in the process. Tiger Lily may have been taken, but he knew the Son of Neverland would find her, and he would aid him in whatever way he could.

Next to him, like an oak tree, stood Pax. Although he was a man of few words and few emotions, he was never privy to Marco's allegiance to the Dark Father, and truly loved his tribe. He too, felt mortally betrayed by a brother, and for the first time that Peter could ever remember seeing, he looked deeply burdened, truly sad. He had been brothers in arms with Neverland's greatest traitor for all these years, breaking bread with him, sleeping near him, and he never had the foresight to see it, and because of that, his village was in ashes. That was a weight even his trunk like body could hardly withstand, and a weight he'd have to live with.

"We have suffered a great loss this night," the chief admitted. "My daughter, the Princess Tiger Lily, has been captured by the Dark Father of Time."

The chief paused amidst the shrieks of panic.

"Where's the Princess?!" A tribesman called out.

"Yes!" Another screamed. "Vengeance! We want vengeance!"

The crowd began to yell in unison, raising their bows and tomahawks into the air, true bloodlust coursing through them now....

"SILENCE!" The chief yelled after a moment, and the crowd fell quiet.

"The Princess is being held in the void," he continued. "The Great White Father will venture there, and reclaim her."

"We've had enough of him!" that same mouthy tribesman yelled out. "He doesn't care about us! Look what he let happen to our village!"

"He has too much power!" Another brave screamed out. "The Princess is gone! We need to protect ourselves from him, now!"

"Yeah!" the crowd screamed in unison, turning suddenly on Peter.

Peter didn't react, just stared stolidly at the angry crowd. They had every right to be angry, especially at him. Their village was gone. Their princess was gone. It was all his fault.

Suddenly, Charlie broke through the crowd, and took the stage.

"When we were in the Windy Mountains," Charlie began, and the crowd quieted themselves. "Marco aided the pirates to capture of The Great White Father's fairy, and on the surface it appeared that it was me who planned it."

Silent outrage coursed through the tribe now.

"It is no mystery that we did not care much for each other, but I would never participate in such evil." Charlie continued. "Marco was my brave. He was under my command, and for that, I accept full responsibility."

Further silence as the people hung on Charlie's every word.

"I fought The Great White Father over this matter," Charlie continued. "We did battle, and... I *lost*."

Charlie took a moment. It was not easy for him to admit further defeat in front of his people, but it was what was necessary — Tiger Lily's life depended on it.

"For my actions that day, and the evidence that pointed to me, fair judgement was death… The Great White Father spared my life."

Charlie's words softened the hearts of his people, and regret filled their eyes.

"The Great White Father is not a tyrant," Charlie stated, then turned to look at Peter, and despite his pain, gratitude filled his eyes. "He is a leader. A god that we can follow… he *is* the Son of Neverland."

It was a title that he never wanted — a title that was thrust upon him — by the fairies, by the tribe, by the Great Spirit Himself, but if that's what they wanted him to be — what they *needed* him to be — then he could be that for them, and he would be that greatly.

"In the dark days that lie ahead," Charlie said, turning once again to the crowd. "Our battles will not be won by the sacrifice of flesh and blood, but by the Great Spirit that guides us all… He is our only hope."

With that final word, Charlie left the stage, and all eyes revered Peter as they silently agreed with their finest brave. Peter felt every eye — every hope — resting upon him now, and he knew not what to do. He felt stuck. He couldn't speak, and yet, he could not fly away… he just stood there… and he knew that he no longer had to save Tiger Lily just for himself, or for her sake, but for their entire world.

"The Great White Father will reclaim our Princess," the chief followed, once again taking center stage. "And as the early autumn brings with it a new harvest, so will we endure… we will rebuild… not only our homes… but our joy as well… and with that joy new life will arise from the ground… and the spring rains will wash away the ashes…"

The tribes people looked at their fearless chief standing before them. He was solid like stone, a rock in which to stand in the face of much peril, and although they had lost their homes and their village, they believed his and Charlie's words to be true. There was still plenty to fear. They could not control the actions of The Great White Father, for his power was beyond them, but they had seen him battle the dark demon in the sky, and without him, they would have been powerless to stop it from destroying all there is. Deep down, they believed that he loved their princess, and that he would sacrifice his life to save hers. They made their decision… and collectively they decided to follow their chief's lead into the future.

Peter looked out at the silent crowd, for their hope in all things was upon him now, and he felt it give him strength — their hope was his strength — the hope of every being in Neverland, and he would need all of it for what he knew lay ahead, for to go off-world, confront the Dark Father on his turf, and reclaim Tiger Lily would be the antithesis of an easy task, but after what he had survived and experienced over the last week, something deep down told him that he knew he could take it.

And that is why, he, The Great Pan, existed… to reclaim fair maidens when they were taken against their will by powerful, evil forces… to confront and cut through the perils of space and time so that the people of Neverland didn't have to… to go into the beyond, into the endless abyss of infinite darkness, and birth light… yes, this was his reason for being… to do just that… for it was the very definition of being a god…

* CHAPTER 22 *

— The Boy and His Fairy —

Tiger Lily's big, brown eyes fluttered open. She looked up, and above her hung dark crimson and black curtains… it was unfamiliar…

She began to move her body and noticed she was laying in the middle of a very large, pillowy bed. Her body was covered by crimson sheets, and she was surrounded by crimson and black throw pillows. It was comfortable — she was comfortable — how long had she been sleeping?

Tiger Lily yawned as she began to catch her bearings. She sat up on the edge of the bed and noticed she was wrapped in crimson garments, the cut and shape which matched her typical wardrobe. She didn't remember putting them on, and she didn't like the idea that she had been changed. Who changed her? How was she there?

She looked around the room — it was circular, and lavish — there were multiple black and crimson lounge couches set about, and in one corner, a large vanity table with a large mirror.

Not far from it was a wet bar. Suddenly, Tiger Lily realized that she was very thirsty… she thought to move towards it…

She threw the covers off her and got out of bed. She placed her bare feet on the ground, and the black fabric was soft to the touch — silk — she knew it from the gifts she had been brought by great explorers from back in the days. They said it came from a continent on earth called Asia… but who really knew?

Tiger Lily moved across the lavish space towards the drink stand, taking it in. What was this place? How was she here? There were no windows of any kind? And where was the entrance?

She reached the drink stand. There was a crimson drink that appeared to be wine, or some kind of potion, and a clear substance she assumed to be water. Tiger Lily grabbed a goblet and poured herself a full glass of the clear liquid — she was thirsty, that was for sure, extremely thirsty — she raised the goblet to her lips…

Suddenly, she stopped. What was she doing? Where did that liquid come from? Who placed it there? It could be poison. Further, where was she? And how did she get here?

In a sudden panic, Tiger Lily dropped the goblet of clear liquid that crashed the floor and soaked into the black, silk carpet. She ran to the large vanity mirror and looked at herself — it was her all right — and at first glance, she had reasoned that she had never looked more beautiful. She looked well rested and bright eyed, and the way her full-hair was done up was better than she or her servant girls could ever manage with it. The crimson garments looked good on her soft, copper skin, and complimented her complexion well. Whoever had attended to her knew what they were doing…

Then, suddenly, her mind turned… how was she there again? And Peter… what had happened to Peter?...

“I see you’re awake.” A deep and elegant voice filled the space. It was well spoken, but seemed to come from nowhere and everywhere at the same time.

Tiger Lily looked up at the black, obsidian ceilings that shined like the material of her arrowheads, and at the walls that had a similar veneer, searching for its origin…

“You can drink, Princess,” the elegant voice continued. “It is the substance you call ‘water’ I assure you… and it doesn’t only exist in Neverland.”

Tiger Lily was so overcome with thirst, that when she heard the word ‘water’, she ran to the table, poured another full goblet, and drank it down. She followed it with a second, and a third…

“I hope you are feeling better,” the voice continued. “I want you to feel comfortable here.”

When Tiger Lily’s madness of thirst was quenched, her mind really started coming back to her…

“How long was I sleeping?” Tiger Lily asked, attempting to get a grip on her place in space and time.

“You were tired, Princess,” The elegant voice continued. “Where you are now, there is no time to reference it, but if it helps, your world has revolved around its sun thirty times.”

"Thirty," Tiger Lily's breath dropped out of her lungs as she repeated it — a Neverland month — she had been asleep for a month!

Suddenly, true panic took her as she began to remember. Peter was battling the demon. She and Tinker Bell helped him. She shot the demon in the sky. Then there was an explosion — water, darkness, nothing — Peter saved her from drowning… and then that thing… that thing took her…

Tiger Lily was gripped by fear as the realization that she may have been abducted finally hit her. She ran around the room, frantically looking for an entrance, but there was nothing she could see — the room was completely enclosed — encased by the black, obsidian like substance.

"It is no use, Princess," the voice said practically. "There is no physical entrance to this room."

Tiger Lily continued her search, but to no avail. The room appeared to come from nowhere, and end in nowhere. She couldn't even think of how she got in there to begin with. It was a trick… a nightmare… a *cage*…

"Can my servants get you anything else?" The voice asked calmly. "I want you to have everything you need."

"Show yourself!" Tiger Lily demanded.

Silence filled the room as the demand hung sharply in the air.

"No." The voice responded thoughtfully after a moment. "I don't think I will."

Tiger Lily stopped. Her heartbeat increased and her anger flared. She did not like hearing that word. Not from anybody, not ever.

"What did you say?" Tiger Lily said coldly, her tone razor sharp.

"I said 'no'," the voice repeated. "I don't think I will."

"I am a princess of Neverland." Tiger Lily spoke boldly. "And you *will* show yourself immediately."

"So much spirit," the voice chuckled, finding her display of passion amusing. "And not easily broken. You are clearly denied no luxury."

"And you won't be the first to deny me," Tiger Lily said, leaning into her position, for she had gone through the process of dealing with and accepting her privilege hundreds of years ago now, and she wouldn't be belittled for it by some conjurer in the air.

The elegant voice let out a full belly laugh that filled the lavish room. "In due time, Princess, in due time… but first you must learn the beauty of submission."

"I told you before," Tiger Lily said coldly. "I submit to no one."

"Oh, yes, I remember." The voice reminisced in the memory as if speaking to a child. "But I think you'll find that infinite *time* has a way of changing the mind…"

"Peter," Tiger Lily announced, playing her final card. "He will come for me and you'll wish you never laid a hand on me."

"I find it funny," the voice said thoughtfully. "You tell me now that you submit to no one, but are you not betrothed to that flying child? — *The Great White Father,* I believe your people call him."

"When you say *child,* I assume you're referring to the one who beat you," Tiger Lily said, throwing it right back. "And yes, we're engaged to be married. We're partners. He does not rule over me."

"Does he not?" The voice asked again, and there was a level of practicality in it that made Tiger Lily uncomfortable.

"No," she answered strongly. "As I said, we're equals."

"And this *equal* of yours," the voice continued, exploring the conversation. "What rules exactly does he follow? What limitations does he have?"

"None," Tiger Lily answered, defending her true love. "He has no limitations. He is *unlimited.* And mark my words he *will* come for me, and he *will* destroy you."

"And you — being his *equal,*" the voice continued. "You're unlimited as well?"

"I never said that," Tiger Lily said, backtracking slightly.

"Did you not just say that you were his *equal*?"

Tiger Lily froze. The logic the voice was using to present its argument was picking away at her resolve, frustrating her. If the voice had a head, she'd shoot it, but she'd also need her bow for that.

"He's a god," Tiger Lily said, gathering herself. "It's different."

"Ah," the voice said, satisfied with where the conversation had led. "Now we're getting somewhere, aren't we?"

Tiger Lily was not naïve. Whatever this voice was, it was right from a factual standpoint, but how did it matter? Why did anything this thing had to say matter?

"What do you want from me?" Tiger Lily asked.

"Just the truth, dear Princess," the voice answered. "Just the truth, and you shall be free."

"Why don't we skip the mind games and you just tell me what this *truth* is," Tiger Lily snapped.

"Unfortunately, the truth is not something that can be taught by words," The voice said practically. "It has to be experienced, then true understanding can be had… you'll come to find that you are as powerless against your so-called 'god' as you are to leave this very room."

Tiger Lily's eyes glossed over in frustration. She wanted to drown out this voice of melancholy — anything to make it stop — but she knew that she couldn't, and to show any signs of weakness would likely only encourage this sinister entity towards its end goal.

"You're a coward," Tiger Lily exclaimed in utter spite.

"A coward, am I?"

There was a moment, then the ether in the room was filled by some kind of silvery substance. It took a moment for Tiger

Lily's eyes to adjust, then she looked up and there was the ethereal countenance of the Dark Father floating in the air. He revealed no body, just a face that was made up by some kind of ethereal, dark, and mysterious power, that danced with brilliant black and purple flames. The rough, physical expression of Hook he used in Neverland was completely gone now. His countenance was beautiful to behold, like that of a glorious human, youthful — like Peter's — only untethered by the limitations of flesh and blood. Tiger Lily found herself in awe of him… and drawn to him…

As if by hypnosis, Tiger Lily began to move towards him. What was the curious being? What was this strange and unlimited power? It made her feel a certain way… she had to experience it…

Suddenly, as if falling out of the sky and back into her body, her mind came back to her — what was she doing?! Why was she moving towards the very thing that captured her?! That had caused her and her friends so much suffering?!

Through great will power, Tiger Lily pulled herself from this being's strange, hypnotic field, and fell back into one of the lavish couches, shielding her eyes, for she could not think clearly if she looked at it directly.

"You will not be the first to love me," the Dark Father said through his etheric countenance that floated in the air, "but if we work together, you *can* be the last… through the eroding eons of *time* your limited memory of the boy will wither and die, and along with it, so will your love for him. You will see that it was I who freed you from the prison he held you in, and when that *time* comes… you *will* love me for it."

"I will *never* love you," Tiger Lily exclaimed with finality, and she took her arms away and forced herself to look into the being's countenance, using her entire memory and love for Peter as an anchor. "And when he comes to free me… I *will* destroy you myself."

There was a moment as the Dark Father stared back at the defiant princess before him. She was beautiful, full of spirit, and had royal blood flowing through her veins — she also had a stronger will than he ever previously imagined — she was *perfect.*

"We'll see," The Dark Father said, and although Tiger Lily couldn't make out his full countenance through the powerful and bright, etheric light, she thought she saw a smile.

Then, there was a rush, and the Dark Father's energy was pulled from the room, and with it, his entire presence.

Tiger Lily was left there, strewn out on that lavish couch, once again alone in her mind in the center of some distant place, and although she knew she wasn't… she already felt like she was forgotten.

Then she closed her eyes, and fell asleep…

***

Just as he did every day, Peter floated coolly through Pixie's Landing for his morning ritual. It had already been over a month since the attack on the northern quarters, and it seemed as if the reality of it was just now starting to sink into the population. For a while, it was impossible — unacceptable — that an attack could be made on Neverland after one hundred years of peace. It had been so long, much of the younger population didn't even know what war or death even was… but they did now.

There was an old saying that Wendy taught to him many decades ago during one of his visits — this was back when Wendy was still young, but too old to return to Neverland, and Earth was going through one of its world wars — it was spoken by one of the great leaders in Wendy's country at the time. Peter couldn't remember his name, but he was pudgy, and gruff, wore a big hat, and always seemed to be smoking a large stick of rolled Indian tobacco. Peter didn't take much stock in the sayings of men, for he found them to be mostly full of hot air, but Wendy said he was as wise as they made them, so for once, Peter listened. The saying went something like this—

"*Those who do not remember the past, are condemned to repeat it.*"

Peter didn't care much for the statement at the time, mostly because it didn't make him feel very good, but he'd be lying to himself if he said he didn't see the relevance now. Neverland had all but forgotten about the Dark Father of Time and his reign — in fact, Peter himself didn't even know the true story until his rebirth experience in the Windy Mountains — and the consequences of such mindlessness spoke for themselves. He was raised by the fairies to forget the past. Well, look what that led to…

Tiger Lily was gone, the Indian Village was destroyed, and the most tragic of all — over one hundred fairies had been slaughtered during the attack on the northern quarters — males, females, families, elders, children — good fairies. Good, noble fairies of Neverland. Many of them Peter's friends and acquaintances. The memory of it brought tears to his eyes, and he felt like a fool. All he ever wanted was to have fun, and look at what his disregard for the past had brought to him and his world.

Yes, it was gone now, that old, warm feeling of joy when he floated through the quarters… his battle with the Dark Father had left him feeling cold and savage… and without Tiger Lily, he felt vacant and empty, as if half his soul was gone… as if all the joy in life was gone…

"'Ello, Peter," the cart boy said joyfully as Peter approached to get Solomon's breakfast. "The usual, I take it?"

Peter nodded without a word.

"'Ere you go," the lad said, holding out two large carrots. "A nice, juicy one for Solomon, and one for the mare."

Peter nodded at the curious lad as he took the carrots, then he held out a full sack of buttons.

"Nah," the lad said. "On the house today, Peter."

Peter nodded, then left the sack of buttons anyway. He began to float away, then doubled back at the lad who still smiled as if he didn't have a care in the world.

“Let me ask you something,” Peter started. “Do you still hope?”

“Hope?” The lad asked, confused. “What do you mean?”

“I mean…” Peter continued. “Do you still believe that good things can happen?”

“Well of course I do, Peter,” the lad said as it was a commonplace. “What kind of question is that?”

Peter hesitated for a moment, as if he knew the boy was right, but he couldn’t quite remember what for.

“Why?” Peter asked quietly as he leaned in, as if he didn’t want anyone else to hear.

“What’s that?” The lad asked, getting a bit concerned now by Peter’s peculiar questions and demeanor.

“I mean…” Peter whispered. “Why do you still believe?”

The lad leaned back, thought about it for a moment, then leaned in, and looked at Peter with true conviction.

“Because I’m talking to Peter Pan,” the lad whispered back, then he raised his eyebrows to close his statement.

Peter continued to stare at the lad, then a second later it clicked — he got it — he was a clever lad, that was for sure. Peter’s eyes narrowed, then he chuckled at the absurdness of it all, and headed towards Solomon’s stable.

“Have a good day, Peter!” The lad called after him, then he whistled and went back to tending his cart.

Peter continued to float through the grim, overcast fog of the landing until he reached Solomon's stable. Per usual, Solomon bucked his head up and down in anticipation as Peter approached, for no matter the state of the world, he loved carrots!

"Here you go, boy," Peter said, holding out the bigger carrot. "Compliments of a clever lad."

Peter chuckled as Solomon consumed the carrot heartily, bucking his head up and down as he did — it was a great carrot, if there ever was one.

Next to Solomon, Fleur stood. Peter had been looking after her since Tiger Lily's disappearance. She was thinner now, and had lost weight. She expressed very little interest in food, but would usually eat at Peter's insistence. She clearly missed Tiger Lily dearly, and Peter thought it would be good to keep her around Solomon, for they had established a bond during the perils of their journey, and there was not an animal in Neverland better charged to protect her day and night.

"Hey, Fleur. Hey, girl…" Peter spoke softly as he approached Fleur and stroked her mane. Fleur whinnied at his touch, as if in fear, for she was still suffering some trauma from the battle in the Northern Straight. It was traumatizing enough for Peter… he couldn't imagine how traumatizing it must have been for her…

"Whoa, easy… easy," Peter said as he continued to stroke her mane. "It's just me… it's just Peter…"

Eventually, Fleur's body softened and she gave into his touch, for without Tiger Lily, Peter had the most familiar hands around, and she needed to allow herself to be loved from time to time. It was hard for her now. She wanted Tiger Lily. As Peter continued to pet her, she continued to whinny.

"I know," Peter said. "I know… I miss her too… but I'll find her."

Peter's encouraging words eased Fleur's restless heart, at least momentarily. She nodded her head up and down and gave into his touch.

As Peter continued to stroke Fleur's mane, he looked across the landing and saw Ruby through the fog in the distance, watching them. Being a unicorn, she didn't like crowded spaces, and if any of the young fairies saw her they would try to catch her for good fortune. Being as ancient as she was, she no longer had the patience for that sort of thing. Now that the journey was over, her purpose was served, for like Peter, she also needed to roam free, and have her own adventures… she would return to aid Tinker Bell should the day ever come that she needed her again.

Peter nodded his thanks, then Ruby's eyes twinkled brightly, and she turned and disappeared into the fog.

When Ruby was out of sight, Peter turned back to Fleur. He tried to feed her the carrot, but she wouldn't have it.

"All right," Peter said. "Well, I'll set it right here, okay, in case you get hungry later."

Peter set Fleur's carrot down on the edge of their water trough, and noticed that someone had their eye on it…

"Don't eat it," Peter said sternly to Solomon, and he bleated gruffly and bucked his head.

Peter stroked Fleur's mane one last time, and he could feel her quivering at his touch. He wanted nothing more than to bring her mother back — he would bring her back — for them both… the time was coming.

"Look after her," Peter said to Solomon. "If any steeds come poking around… you know what to do." Solomon bucked his head up and down in agreement, for there was nothing more he liked in the world than a good fight and protecting his friends… except maybe a bucket of carrots…

On the next leg of his morning flight, Peter approached Hangman's Tree, and the camera's blew up—

FLASH. FLASH. FLASH — FLASH. FLASH. FLASH.

"Peter, is it true that Tiger Lily was abducted — there's been rumors that she's still on the island."

"Peter, can you confirm that you are with Tinker Bell now? People have been saying that Tiger lily disappeared because you broke up?"

FLASH. FLASH. FLASH — FLASH. FLASH. FLASH. Every day, it was the same stupid questions.

"Peter, there are rumors that you were in on the attack on the Indian Village. Can you comment?"

Peter scowled. Some questions just flat out pissed him off.

FLASH. FLASH. FLASH — FLASH. FLASH. FLASH.

"Peter, tell us about the battle?"

"Peter, there's rumors that the Dark Father of Time is back — is Neverland safe? Can you confirm?"

"Peter, I'm with the *Fairy Journal,* Neverland needs a statement from you."

"Peter, is Tiger Lily alive?"

For the first time, Peter stopped and faced all the cameras, and every eye, every lens, every note pad held its breath, waiting for him to speak. He felt open, vulnerable, he didn't like it, but he wanted the world to know a few simple truths.

"Neverland is safe," Peter stated, taking care to hold back his emotions, and speak plainly. "I will find her."

With that, Peter launched into the air as the cameras exploded below him. The reporters screamed out his name for more answers, but he was already gone…

In the center of Pixie's Landing, towards the back of *Tink's Lounge*, two familiar fairies were hard at work on their next concoction. The last month had been difficult on Tinker Bell. She had done much soul searching, and although she was supposed to be resting and recovering mentally, physically, and spiritually from the traumatic events she had gone through, she found it difficult to stop moving, and welcomed all distractions.

Frankly, she was grateful that all her friends were still alive — she still blamed herself unnecessarily for Peter's close brush with death, and for the capture of Tiger Lily, and although she rarely spoke about it, she knew that it was her curiosity and carelessness that had gotten her captured, thus risking the lives of them all. She subconsciously made it a point to suppress those parts of her, throwing herself ever further into her work, for there was a massive and important task at hand, and she reasoned that how she felt about anything else wouldn't and *couldn't* matter until it was completed.

"A tad bit warmer," Tinker Bell said to Spark, for they were both bent over a boiling beaker. "That's it! The perfect temperature."

"Hi," Peter said as he appeared behind them.

"Holy mother of fairies! Peter Pan!" Spark jumped, nearly knocking over the beaker.

"Oh good, Peter, you're here," Tinker Bell said quickly, for it was clear that she was pleased to see him. She then reached up and yanked a hair off his head.

"Ouch, Tink!" Peter exclaimed. "What did you do that for?!"

"Shh!" Tink demanded. "Watch…"

Spark, Peter, and Tinker Bell all gathered around the beaker as she dropped Peter's hair into the potion… a moment… then it started bubbling… then it started boiling… and then… a golden boy popped out!

"Eureka!" Spark exclaimed, for it was the spitting image of Peter.

"Well, I'll be," Peter said, somewhat impressed. "A golden shadow."

"Do you like it?" Tinker Bell asked as Peter watched it dart around the room.

"It's nice, Tink." Peter said, quickly losing interest.

"It's a decoy," Tink explained. "For when we go on our journey. I have one as well. I thought they'd be useful in case we come across any more evil spirits that we need to distract."

Peter didn't respond, and his gaze drifted towards nowhere, and there was something hollow about him now — something vacant — Peter loved shadows, and loved chasing things that were challenging to catch. Just last year, if Tink would have given him a golden shadow he would have chased that shadow around Neverland for weeks on end without eating or sleeping, but not anymore. Tink knew why this was of course, and she felt it was her responsibility to get him through. Peter might have to carry Neverland, but she had to carry him.

"I've created all sorts of other useful potions and items," Tink continued spiritedly, attempting to engage him. "I created a new potion called 'liquid sleep', which we should be able to substitute for a good night's sleep when needed. This one was really hard to make. Spark and I had to scour Neverland for the ingredients, but I think I figured it out. I also created a bunch of short-term energy boosters — those were easy — cell regenerators, and oh — you'll love this one — I came up with a little something I like to call 'time warp' — I thought the title was fitting for where we're going — basically, it allows your mind to absorb more information and process reality faster, making everything around you appear in slow motion. I only have a few of them, but they should be very useful in key battles, especially since we'll probably be outnumbered — but when has that ever stopped the Great Peter Pan and his fairy sidekick, huh? — Like never in eternity, right? I also threw in as many invisibility potions as I could fit. They don't last very long, as you know, but will definitely be useful for key stealth operations, and— Peter!"

"Yeah," Peter said, returning his vacant gaze to her.

"Are you even listening to me?" Tink asked, both concerned and now annoyed.

"It's all great, Tink, really," Peter said, trying to appease her. "Great job."

"Thimble," Tink announced as she held an empty vial aloft. The golden shadow, hearing its call, darted out from behind a giant golden beaker and dove towards the vial head first, disappearing through the top like a genie into a bottle. Tink followed by placing a cork over the top.

"It's for you," Tink said, handing it to Peter. "You can play with it if you want, just say 'thimble' if you need him to come home."

Peter tried to express gratitude as he accepted the vial from Tink, but he had a hard time masking his somber state as he couldn't find the words. He was a great actor when they were playing make-believe — the best there was — but when dealing with real matters he was not great at hiding his true feelings, especially from Tinker Bell. In fact, hiding any feelings at all from her was impossible for him, and always had been.

Tink knew why Peter couldn't be happy — because the girl he loved was captured and being held in some unknown place — and Tink figured that if Peter was captured, or was no longer with her, then she wouldn't be able to find an ounce of joy in life either. In truth, she figured she might die, and in comparison to that, she reasoned Peter was handling it rather well. Even further, she knew that Peter wasn't being strong only for himself, but for the entire population of Neverland. By what power Peter managed to do this, Tinker Bell did not know, but she *did know* that it was for this very reason that he was their Savior.

"Everything's changed hasn't it," Tink said as she sat down next to Peter on a round, glass orb full of fairy dust.

"Yes," Peter nodded honestly. "It has."

"Do you think we'll ever have fun, again?" Tink asked. "You know, after we save Tiger Lily and all?"

Peter smiled thoughtfully. "I don't see why not."

"I'm sorry, that was selfish of me to ask," Tink blurted out, suddenly backtracking.

"It's all right."

"The love of your life has gone missing," she continued rapidly. "And here I am thinking about myself."

“Tink, it’s all—”

“That was selfish — that was a completely selfish thing for me to ask!”

“Tink,” Peter said firmly, looking into Tinker Bell’s big, blue tear-stained eyes, effectively calming her. “It’s all right, really.”

Tink looked back into the bright eyes of the smiling boy looking at her. He still had the same countenance of the Peter she had always known, but there was something different about him now — something ancient — as if his innocence had been stripped from him, and replaced with some kind of real, eternal power. He had evolved before her very eyes, and when Tink looked back at him now, she was no longer just looking just at her oldest friend, but at the very god that had saved her.

As Tinker Bell blinked back her tears, she knew that Peter did not yet fully understand this about himself yet, and as far as she was concerned, she didn’t see any reason that he ever needed to, for the greatest burden of all was that he never had a choice, and for that reason alone, she would love him until the end.

“All right,” Tinker Bell said, finally accepting his console.

Peter put his arm out and wrapped it around her. Tink nestled her head into his shoulder blade, and Peter let his head fall on hers, and they sat like that for a while, there, in that golden room full of light, finding one last bit of comfort in each other before the infinite unknowns that lay ahead, there, at the very edge of space and time…

* ABOUT THE AUTHOR *

CAL R. BARNES is an American novelist, actor, and filmmaker. He was born in Salem, OR in 1988. After studying creative writing, journalism, and drama at Portland State University in Portland, OR, Cal moved to Los Angeles in 2009 where he immediately began acting and writing screenplays. In 2011 he wrote his first novel, *True Grandeur* (published in 2017), a coming-of-age novel inspired by some of his earliest experiences as a young artist in Hollywood. At this time he began producing films as well, enjoying all aspects of the creative process. Between writing novels, acting jobs, and filmmaking, Cal runs his production company, Nineteen Films, in Los Angeles, CA. He recently wrote, directed, and starred in his feature film directorial debut, *The Astrid Experience,* which is scheduled to be released in 2022. *Son of Neverland* is his second novel. He was inspired to write it due to his love for J.M. Barrie's original novels *The Little White Bird* (1902), *Peter Pan in Kensington Gardens* (1906), and the ever-popular *Peter and Wendy* (1911), in which he discovered the seed for a great idea. His current goal in the entertainment industry is to make the feature film adaptation of *Son of Neverland,* in which he is attached to star as the titular character of Peter Pan. When Cal is not working, he is a connoisseur of film, literature, music, yoga, fruits, vegetables, coffee, tea, and sunshine.

* MORE LITERARY WORKS BY CAL R. BARNES *

True Grandeur, A Hollywood Novel (*Magic Hour Press,* 2017)

* MORE ABOUT THE AUTHOR *

www.CalBarnes.com

@CalBarnes

* MORE ABOUT THE ILLUSTRATOR *

www.AdrianDKC.com

@AdrianDKC

* WILL YOU FOLLOW THE SON? *

Sign Up for the *Son of Neverland* Official Newsletter At —

WWW.SONOFNEVERLAND.COM

www.ingramcontent.com/pod-product-compliance
Lightning Source LLC
Chambersburg PA
CBHW020324030826
48979CB00022B/1013

* 9 7 8 0 9 9 9 1 6 1 0 7 4 *